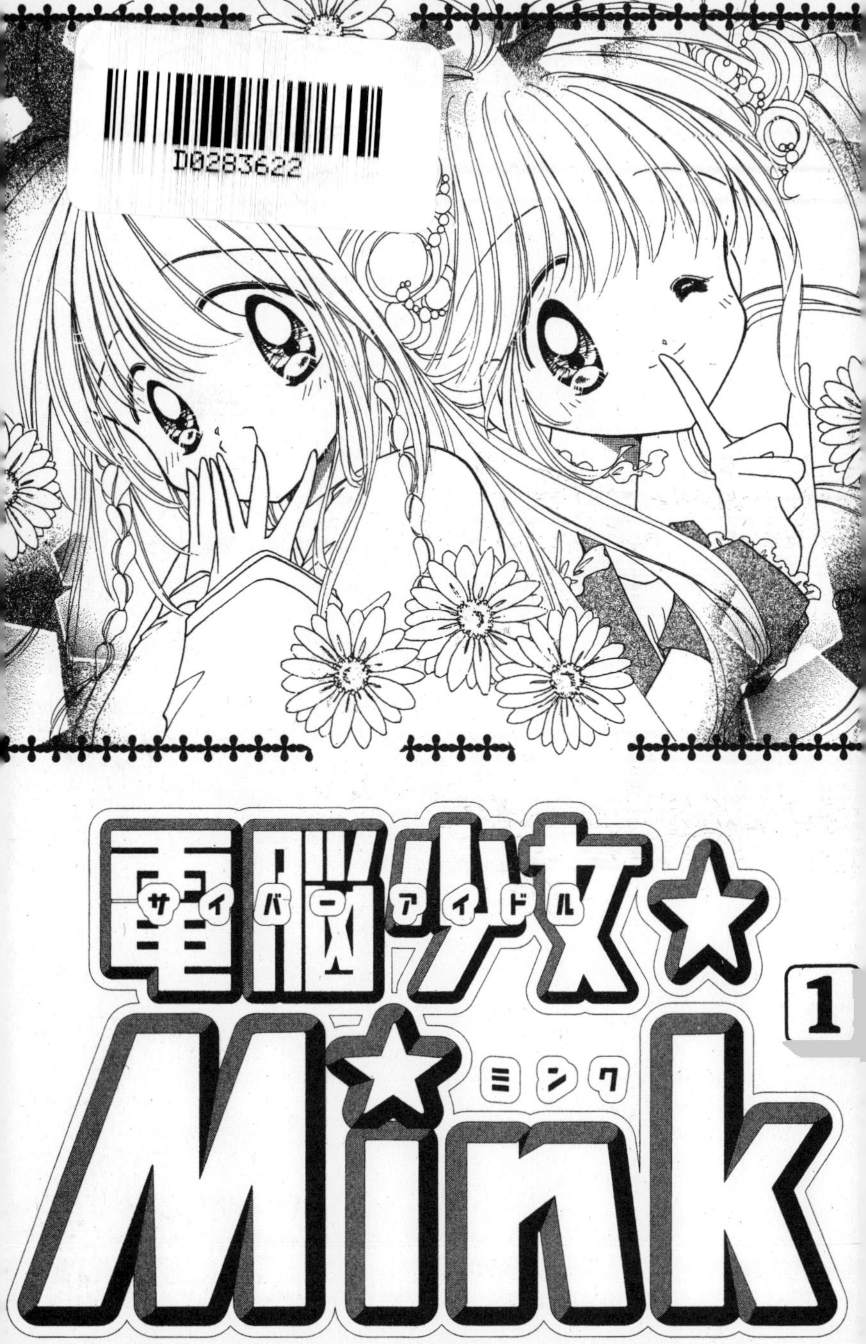

電脳少女☆Mink

サイバーアイドル

ミンク

1

ALSO AVAILABLE FROM ☁TOKYOPOP®

For more information visit www.TOKYOPOP.com

02.03.04T

Translator - Michele Kriegman
English Adaptation - Darcy Lockman
Contibuting Editor - Jodi Bryson
Copy Editor - Alexis Hirsch
Retouch and Lettering - Vicente Rivera Jr.
Cover Layout - Harlin Harris
Graphic Designer - John Lo
Interns - Katherine Schilling, Christine Schilling

Editor - Nora Wong
Digital Imaging Manager - Chris Buford
Pre-Press Manager - Antonio DePietro
Production Managers - Jennifer Miller, Mutsumi Miyazaki
Art Director - Matt Alford
Managing Editor - Jill Freshney
VP of Production - Ron Klamert
President & C.O.O. - John Parker
Publisher & C.E.O. - Stuart Levy

E-mail: info@TOKYOPOP.com
Come visit us online at www.TOKYOPOP.com

A  Manga

TOKYOPOP Inc.
5900 Wilshire Blvd. Suite 2000
Los Angeles, CA 90036

Mink Vol. 1

ISBN: 1-59182-715-9

First TOKYOPOP printing: April 2004

10 9 8 7 6 5 4 3 2 1

Printed in the USA

電脳少女☆Mink

サイバーアイドル ミンク

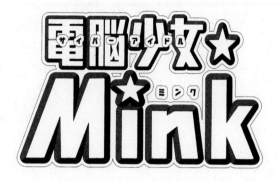

Volume 1

By
Megumi Tachikawa

TOKYOPOP®
Los Angeles • Tokyo • London

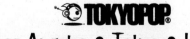

電脳少女★Mink

サイバーアイドル　ミンク

CONTENTS

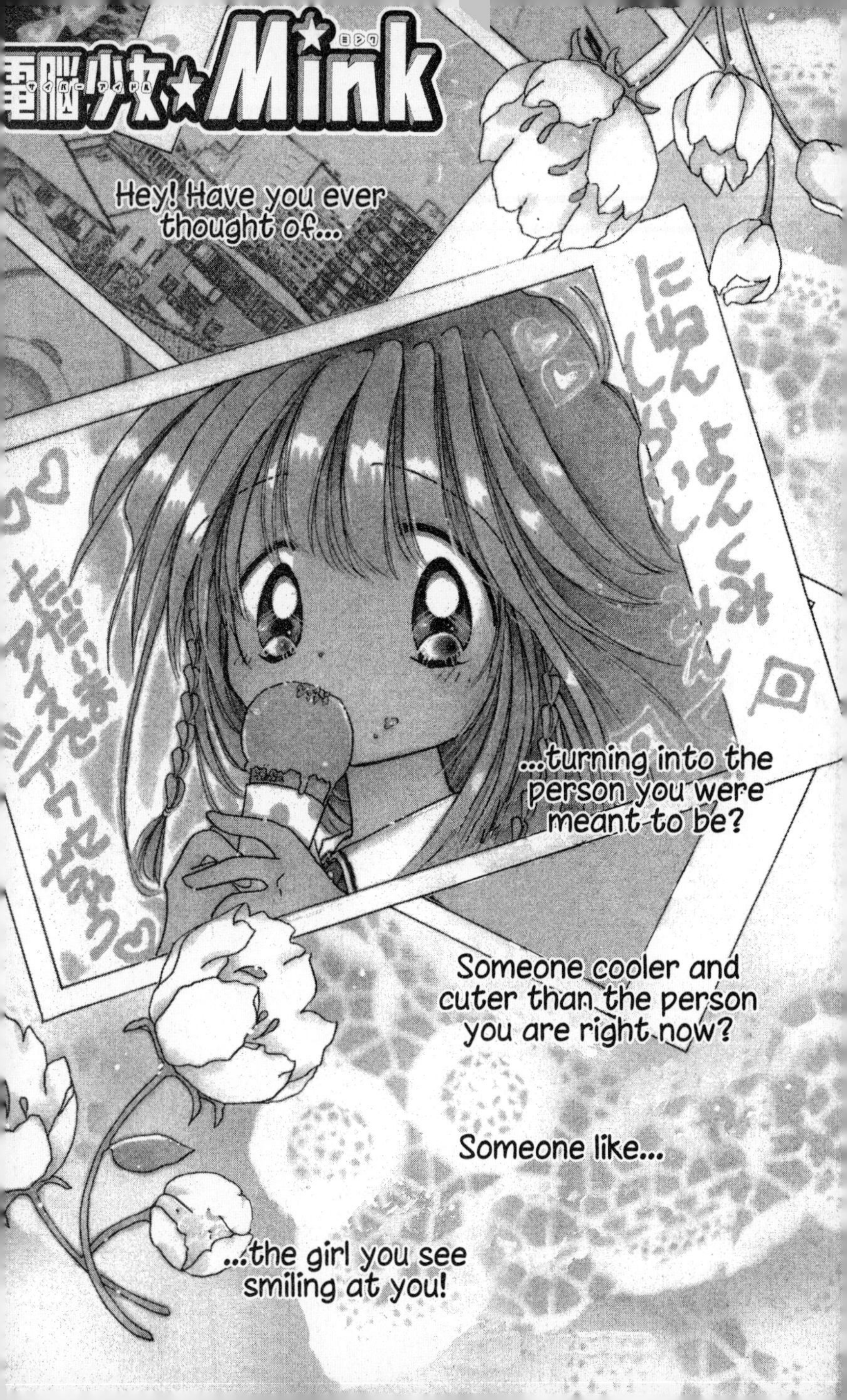
電脳少女★Mink
Hey! Have you ever thought of...
...turning into the person you were meant to be?
Someone cooler and cuter than the person you are right now?
Someone like...
...the girl you see smiling at you!

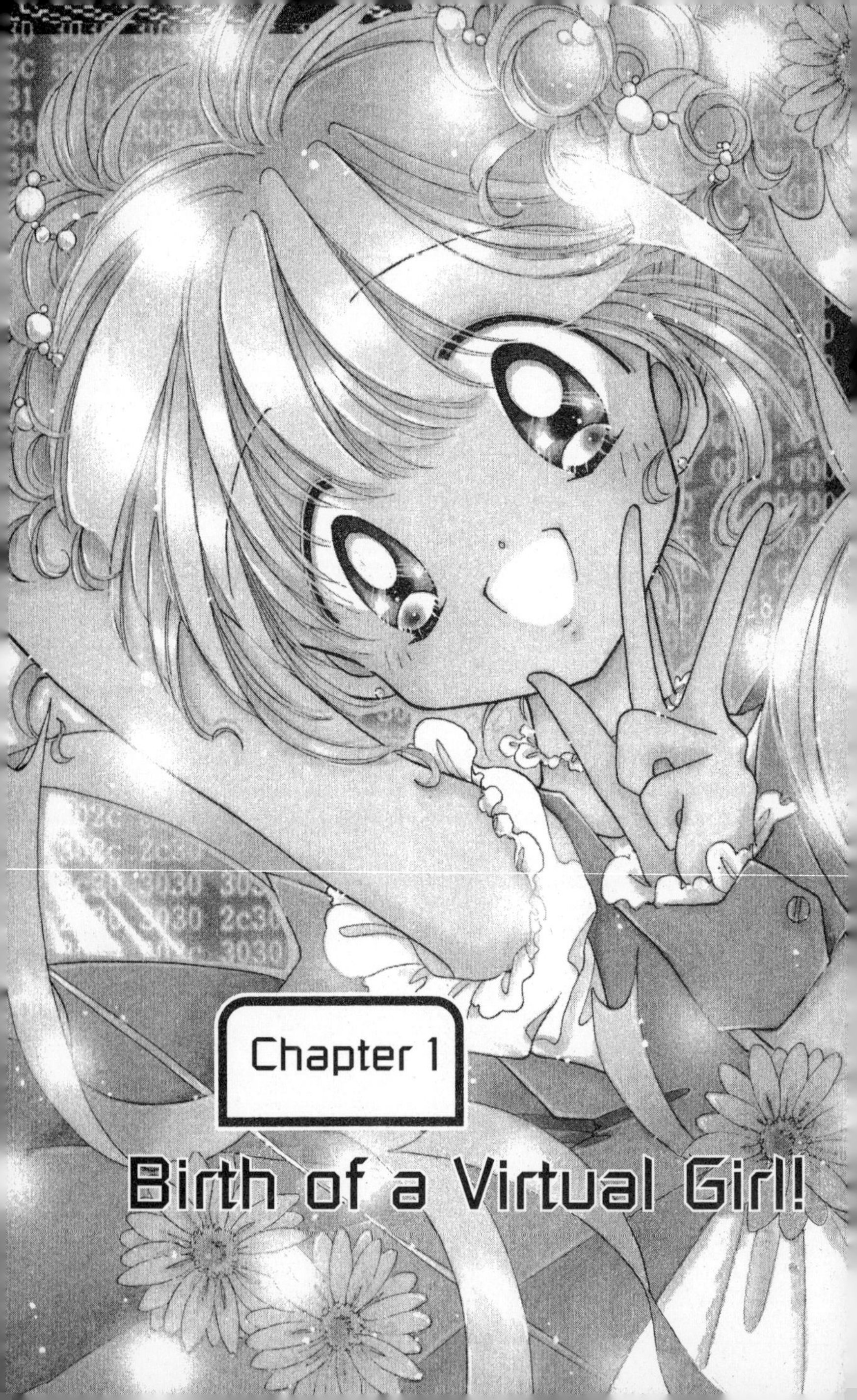
Chapter 1
Birth of a Virtual Girl!

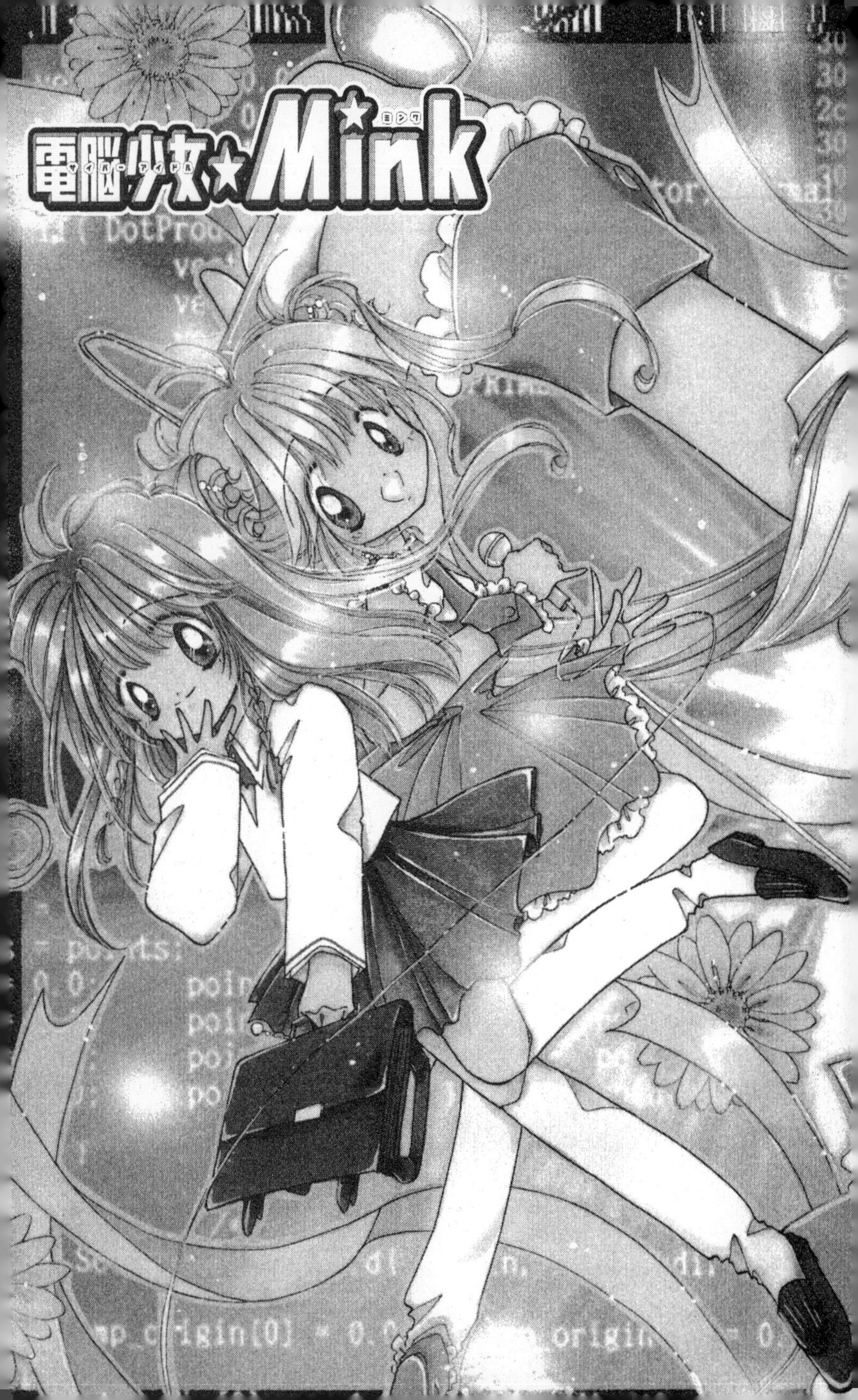
電脳少女☆Mink

Mink Rap!!

Hello, I'm Megumi Tachikawa! I'm writing this after finishing the first volume of Mink. This is the fourth series I've published and I can't believe I've drawn this many illustrations! Seriously though, 2002 marks ten years since I first made my debut and I still can't believe it's real. Please wish me luck, so I can keep drawing these for you.

Okay, let's talk about Mink. The entertainment world is one thing I don't know much about, and I've always said that I'd never draw comics about the entertainment world! Even though I'm a total space case when it comes to techie things, I somehow had this crazy idea to do a story about the cyber world...go figure! People tease me that I don't even know how to use a cell phone! Who cares?! So now I've drawn a manga about the entertainment and the cyber world! Please join me for a glimpse into both worlds with Mink!

I'd like to answer everyone's questions. There are a lot of them, especially about drawing manga, so I'll try to focus on answering those in particular, okay? Here we go...off to cyber space with Mink. That sounded lame, but you know what I mean, right?!

-Megumi

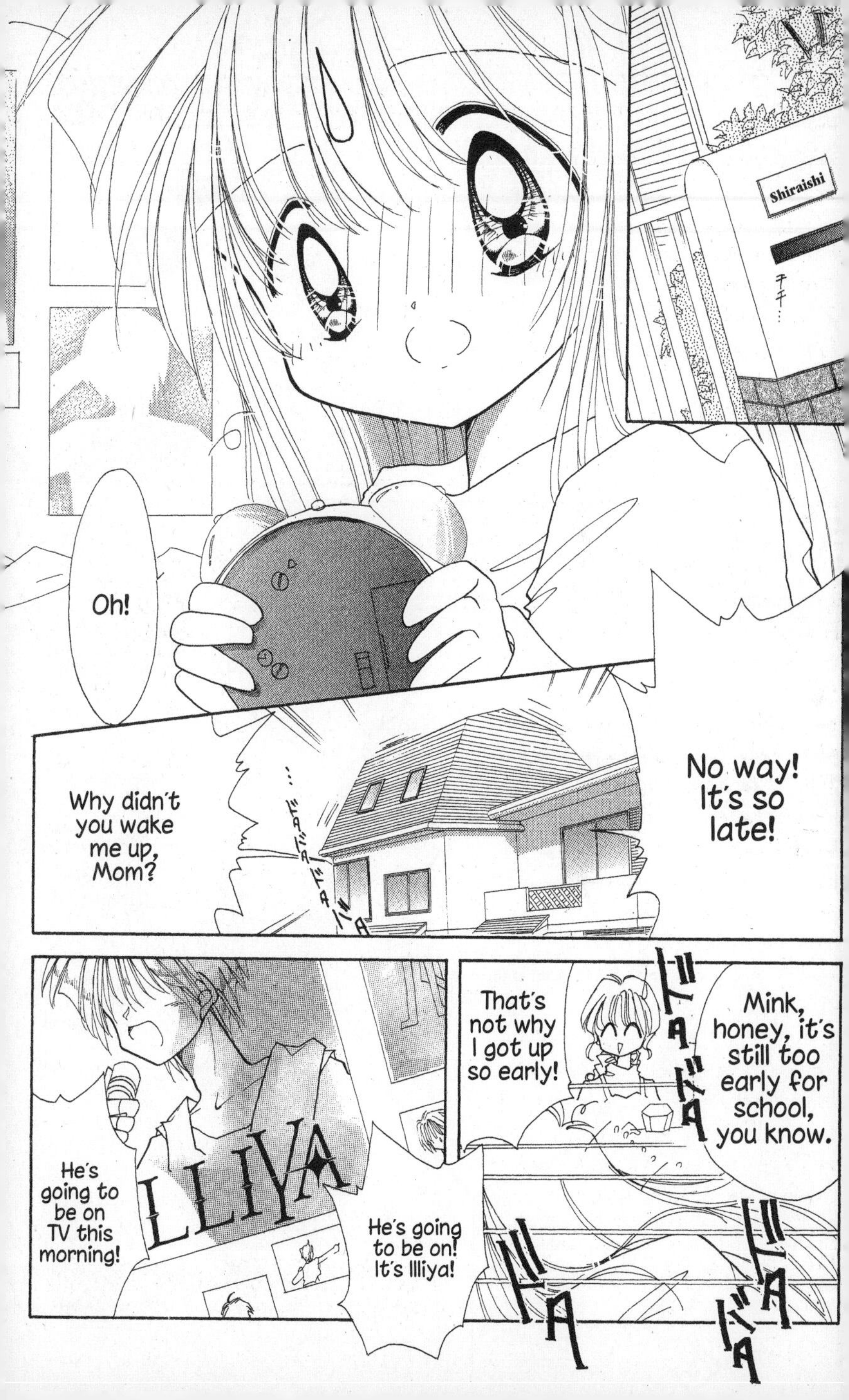
Shiraishi
チチ…
Oh!
No way! It's so late!
Why didn't you wake me up, Mom?
Mink, honey, it's still too early for school, you know.
That's not why I got up so early!
ドタバタ
ドタバタ
He's going to be on! It's Illiya!
LLIYA
He's going to be on TV this morning!
ドタバタ

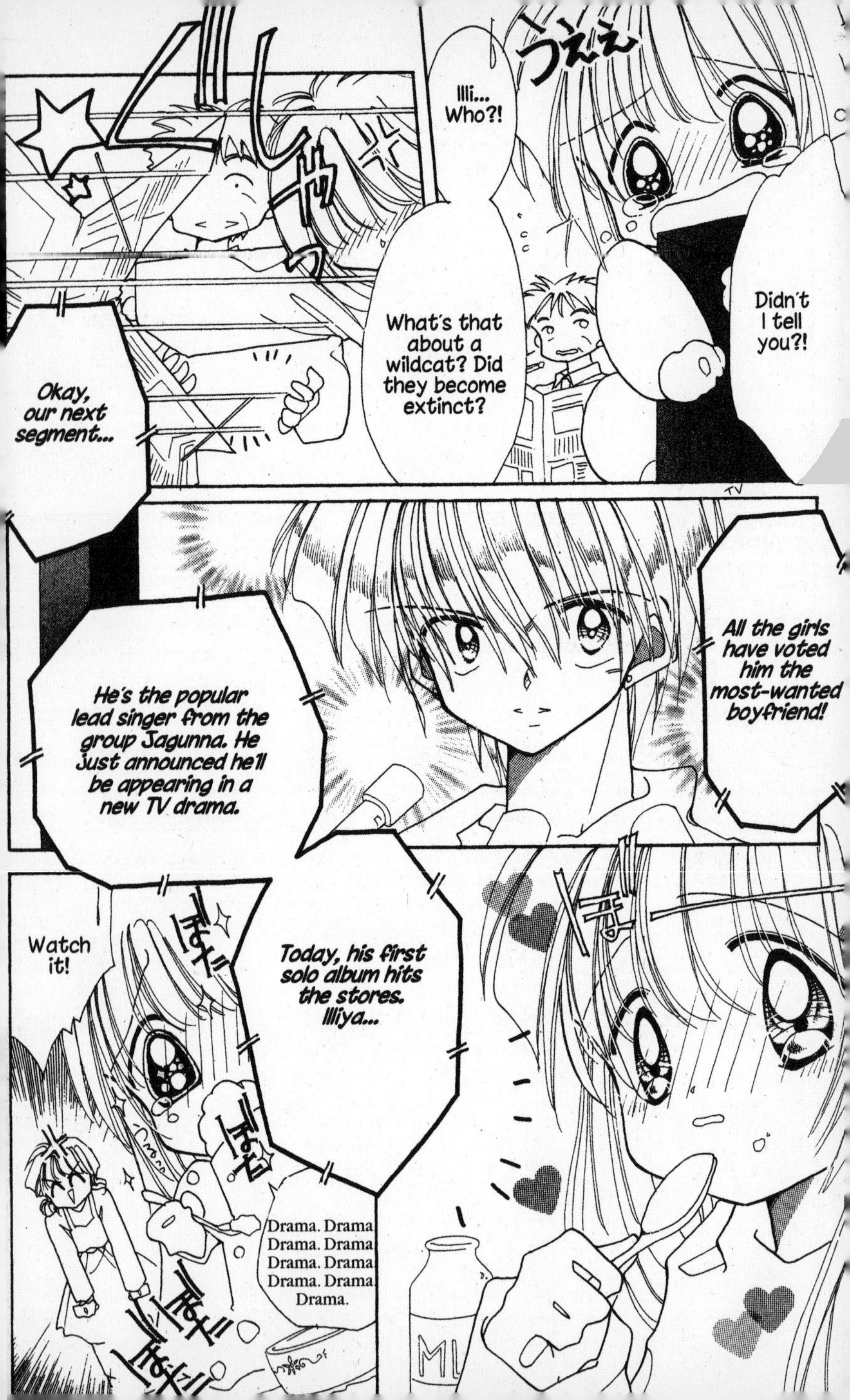

うえぇ
Illi... Who?!
Didn't I tell you?!
What's that about a wildcat? Did they become extinct?
Okay, our next segment...
TV
All the girls have voted him the most-wanted boyfriend!
He's the popular lead singer from the group Jagunna. He just announced he'll be appearing in a new TV drama.
Today, his first solo album hits the stores. Illiya...
Drama. Drama. Drama. Drama. Drama. Drama. Drama. Drama. Drama.
Watch it!

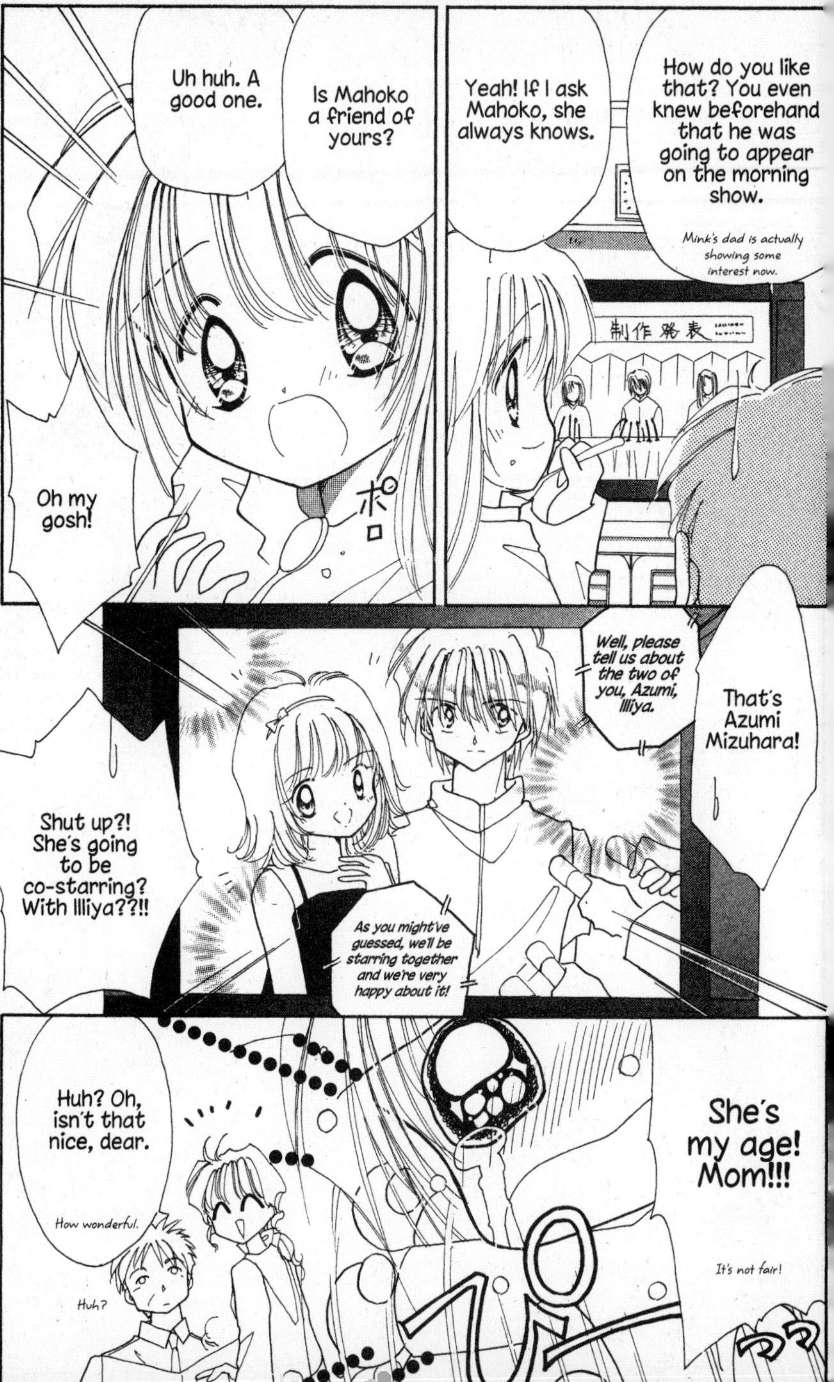
How do you like that? You even knew beforehand that he was going to appear on the morning show.
Mink's dad is actually showing some interest now.
制作発表
Yeah! If I ask Mahoko, she always knows.
Is Mahoko a friend of yours?
Uh huh. A good one.
ポロ
Oh my gosh!
That's Azumi Mizuhara!
Well, please tell us about the two of you, Azumi, Illiya.
As you might've guessed, we'll be starring together and we're very happy about it!
Shut up?! She's going to be co-starring? With Illiya??!!
She's my age! Mom!!!
It's not fair!
Huh? Oh, isn't that nice, dear.
How wonderful.
Huh?

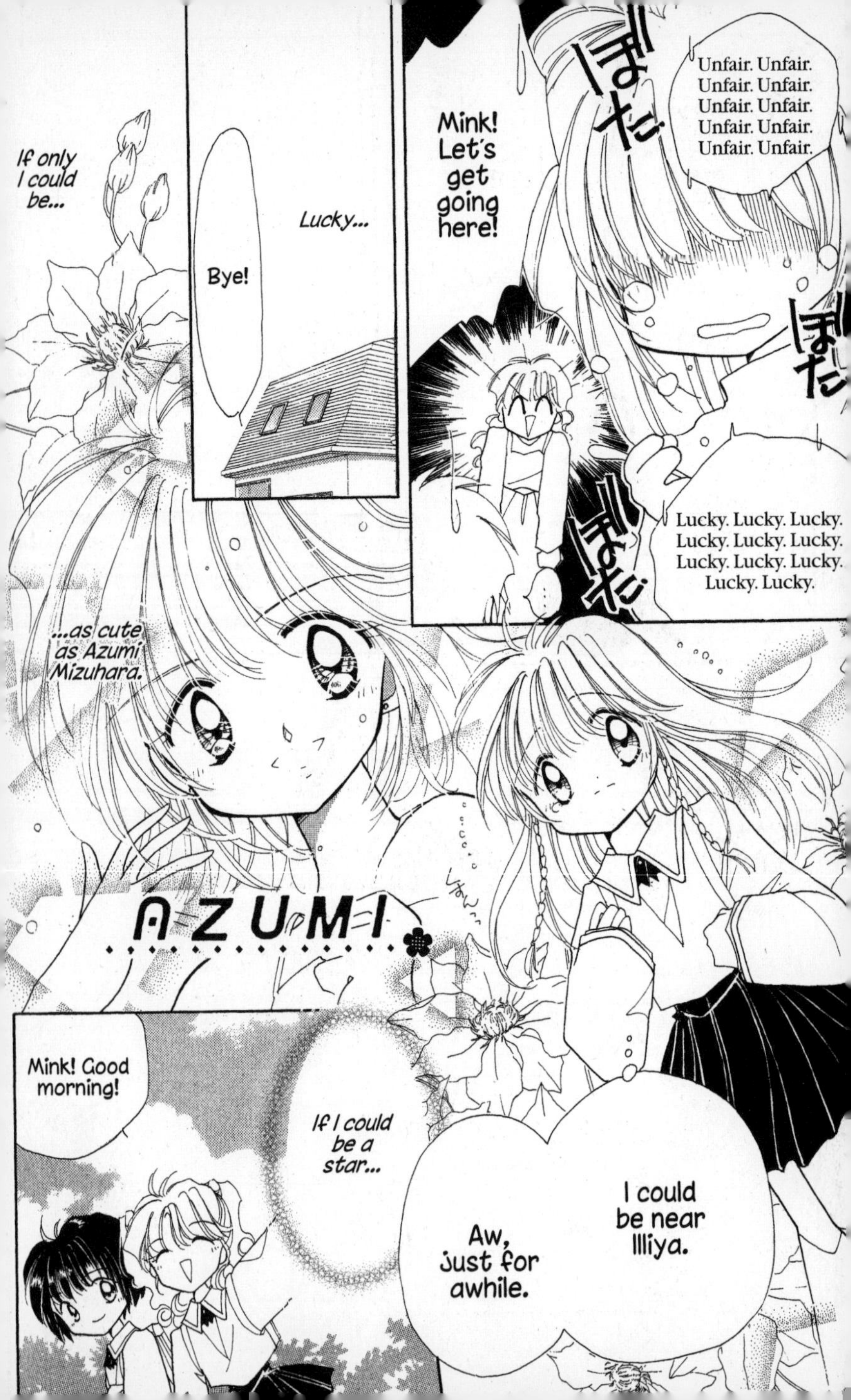

Unfair. Unfair. Unfair. Unfair. Unfair. Unfair. Unfair. Unfair. Unfair. Unfair.
ぽた
Mink! Let's get going here!
ぽた
ぽた
Lucky. Lucky. Lucky. Lucky. Lucky. Lucky. Lucky. Lucky. Lucky. Lucky. Lucky.
Lucky...
Bye!
If only I could be...
...as cute as Azumi Mizuhara.
AZUMI
If I could be a star...
I could be near Illiya.
Aw, just for awhile.
Mink! Good morning!

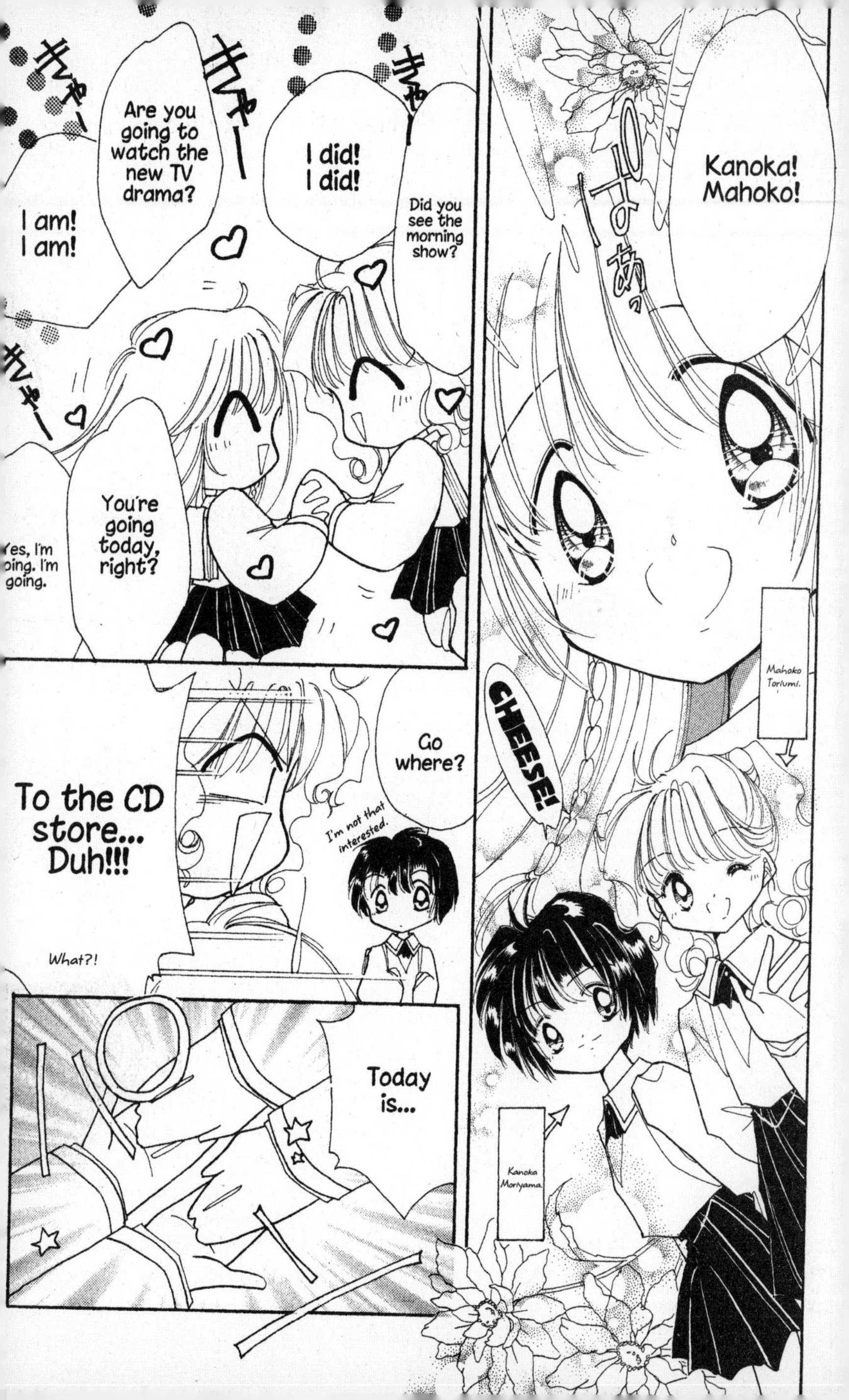
Kanoka! Mahoko!
CHEESE!
Mahoko Toriumi.
Kanoka Moriyama.
きゃー
I did! I did!
Did you see the morning show?
きゃー
Are you going to watch the new TV drama?
きゃー
I am! I am!
きゃー
You're going today, right?
es, I'm oing. I'm going.
Go where?
I'm not that interested.
To the CD store... Duh!!!
What?!
Today is...

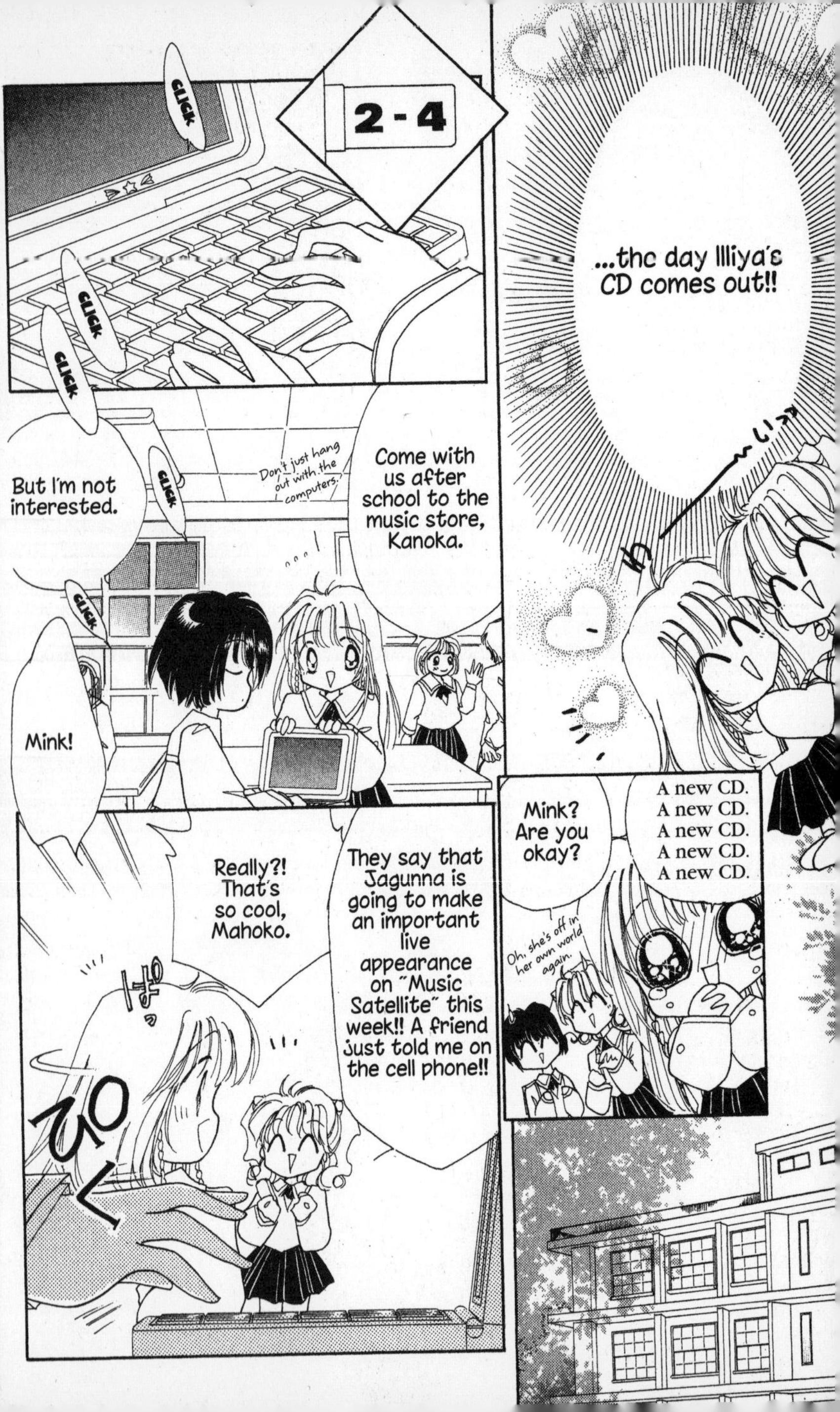
...the day Illiya's CD comes out!!
A new CD.
A new CD.
A new CD.
A new CD.
A new CD.
Mink? Are you okay?
Oh, she's off in her own world again.
2-4
CLICK
CLICK
CLICK
Come with us after school to the music store, Kanoka.
Don't just hang out with the computers.
But I'm not interested.
CLICK
CLICK
Mink!
They say that Jagunna is going to make an important live appearance on "Music Satellite" this week!! A friend just told me on the cell phone!!
Really?! That's so cool, Mahoko.

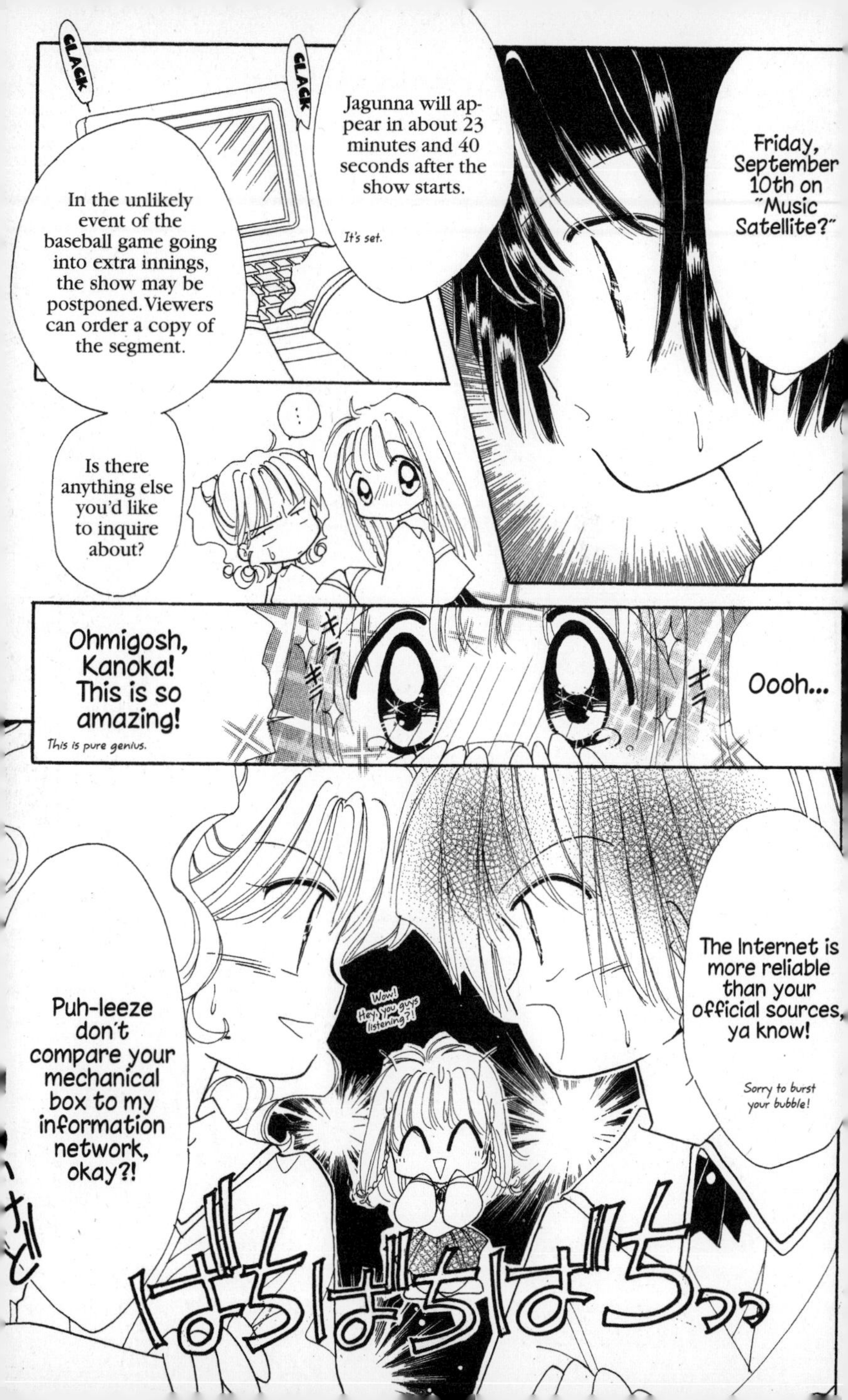

Friday, September 10th on "Music Satellite?"
CLACK
CLACK
Jagunna will appear in about 23 minutes and 40 seconds after the show starts.
It's set.
In the unlikely event of the baseball game going into extra innings, the show may be postponed. Viewers can order a copy of the segment.
...
Is there anything else you'd like to inquire about?
Oooh...
キラ
キラ
キラ
Ohmigosh, Kanoka! This is so amazing!
This is pure genius.
The Internet is more reliable than your official sources, ya know!
Sorry to burst your bubble!
Wow! Hey, you guys listening?!
Puh-leeze don't compare your mechanical box to my information network, okay?!
ばちばちばちっっ

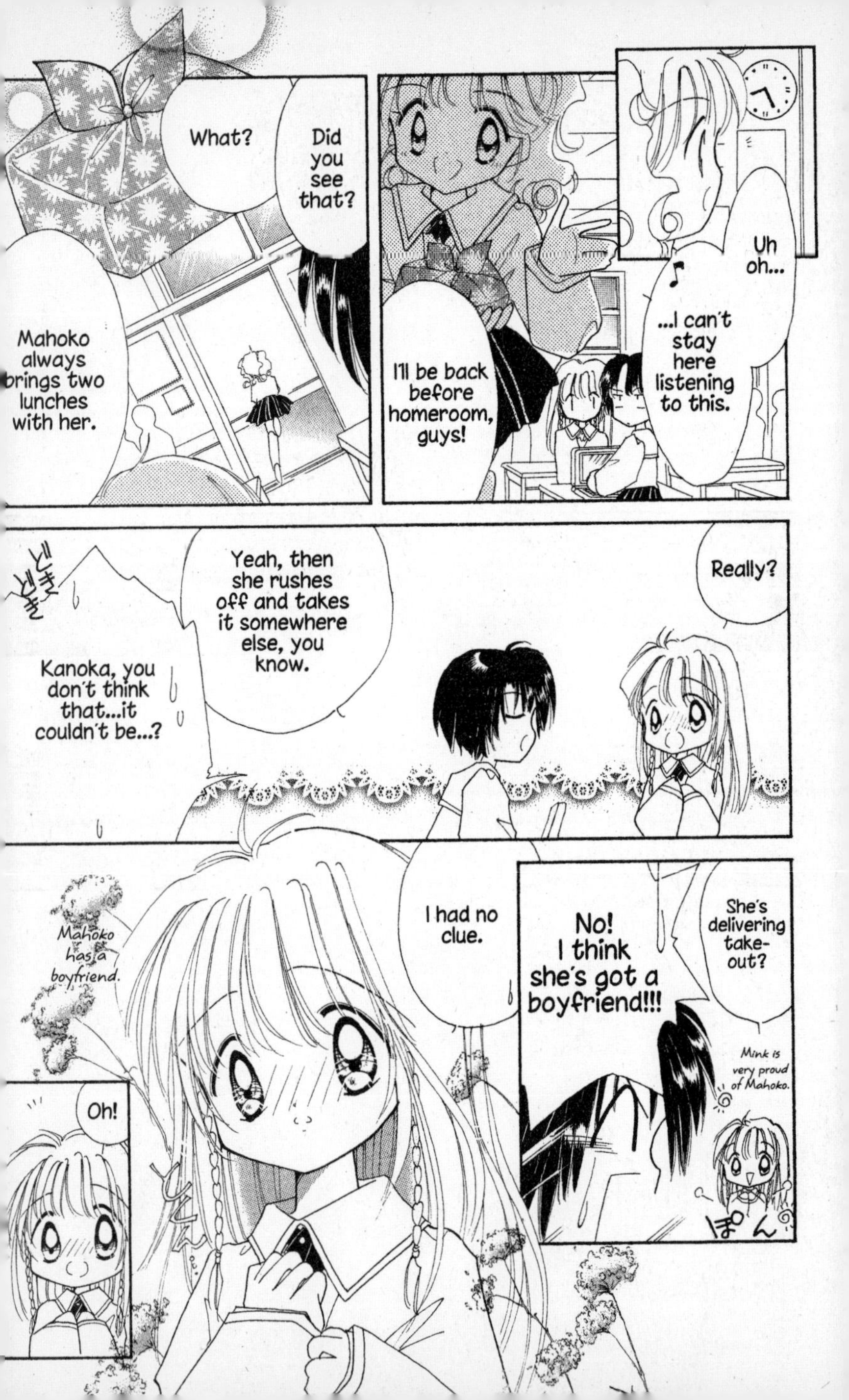
Uh oh...
...I can't stay here listening to this.
I'll be back before homeroom, guys!
Did you see that?
What?
Mahoko always brings two lunches with her.
Really?
Yeah, then she rushes off and takes it somewhere else, you know.
どきどき
Kanoka, you don't think that...it couldn't be...?
She's delivering take-out?
No! I think she's got a boyfriend!!!
Mink is very proud of Mahoko.
ぽん
I had no clue.
Mahoko has a boyfriend.
Oh!

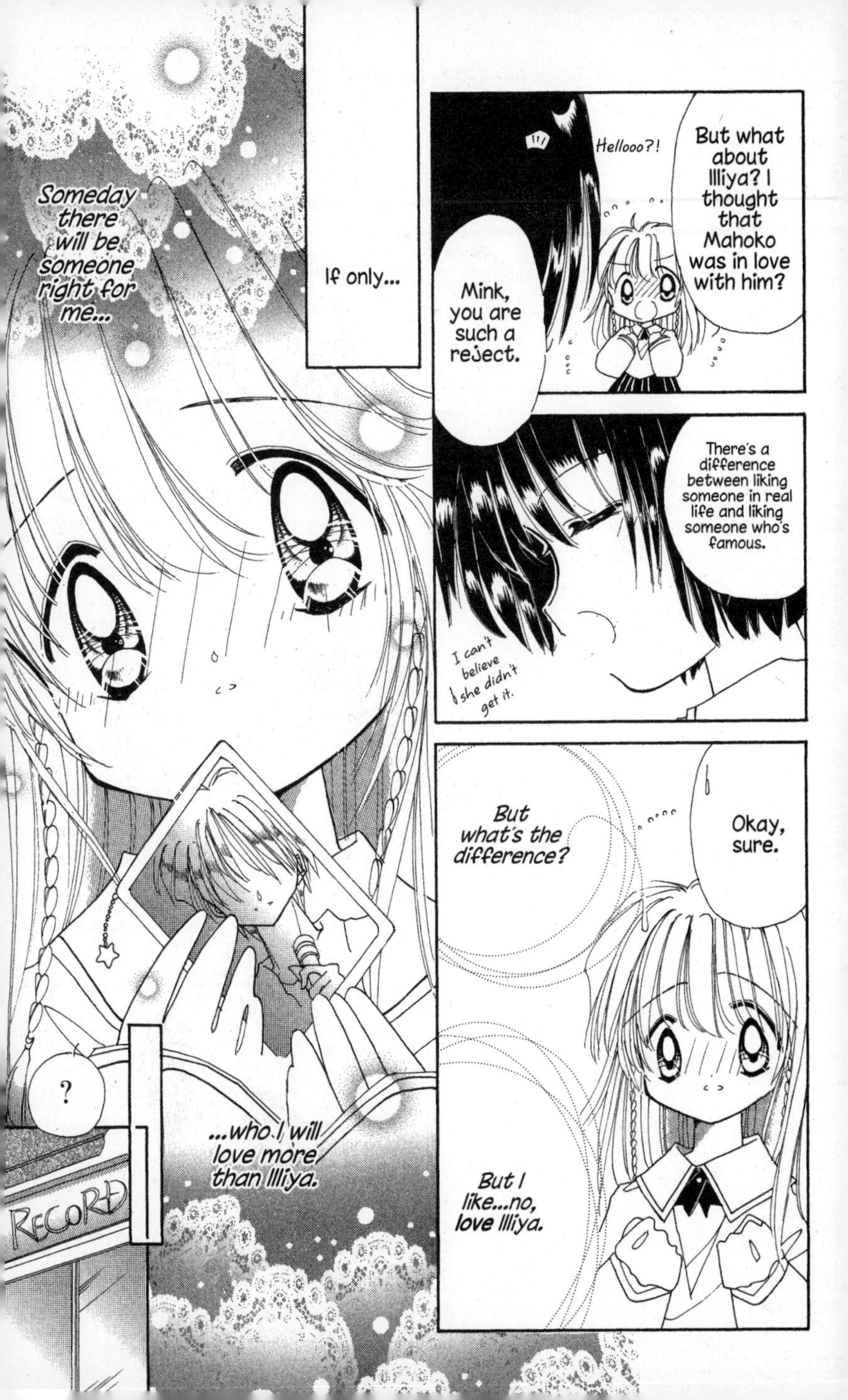
But what about Illiya? I thought that Mahoko was in love with him?
Hellooo?!
Mink, you are such a reject.
There's a difference between liking someone in real life and liking someone who's famous.
I can't believe she didn't get it.
Okay, sure.
But what's the difference?
But I like...no, love Illiya.
If only...
Someday there will be someone right for me...
?
...who I will love more than Illiya.
RECORD

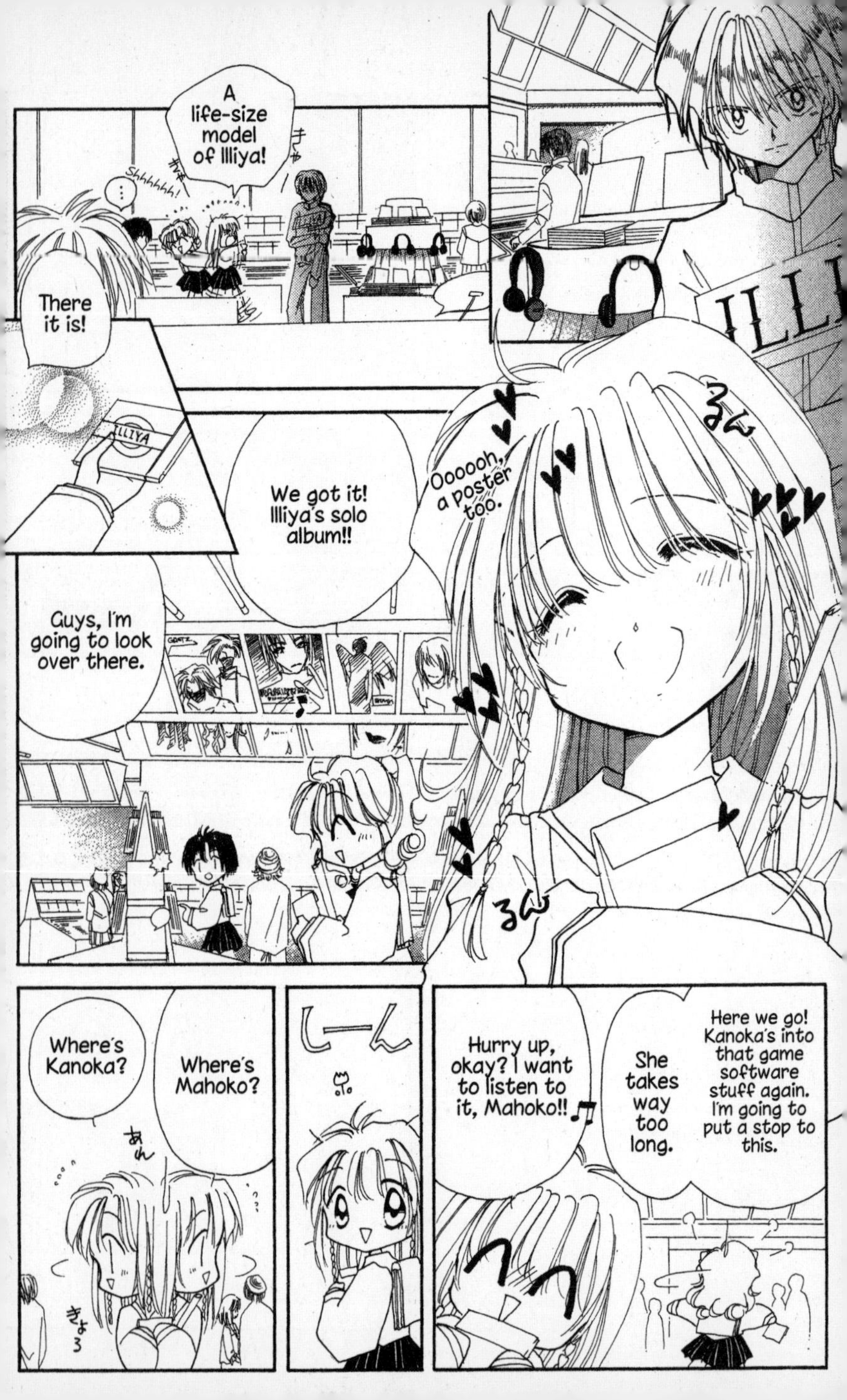
ILLI
A life-size model of Illiya!
Shhhhhh!
…
There it is!
るん
Oooooh, a poster too.
るん
ILLIYA
We got it! Illiya's solo album!!
Guys, I'm going to look over there.
Here we go! Kanoka's into that game software stuff again. I'm going to put a stop to this.
She takes way too long.
Hurry up, okay? I want to listen to it, Mahoko!!
しーん
Where's Mahoko?
Where's Kanoka?
きょろ

Mink Rap!!

Q: What does "tone number" mean and how many tones are there? If you don't memorize all the color tone numbers, can you still become a cartoon artist?

A: It's okay, guys (really, relax!). It's true that tones have numbers assigned to them but I barely memorized any of them. I only remember #61 and #30 (I use these a lot.). Other than that, we just make up names that fit like "the tears thing" or "the sparkling thing."

Q: Do you use a computer to add text in the dialogue balloons?

A: No. Someone in the editing department does that for me. I just write words in with pencil first. That's what I do when I submit rough drafts too.

-Megumi

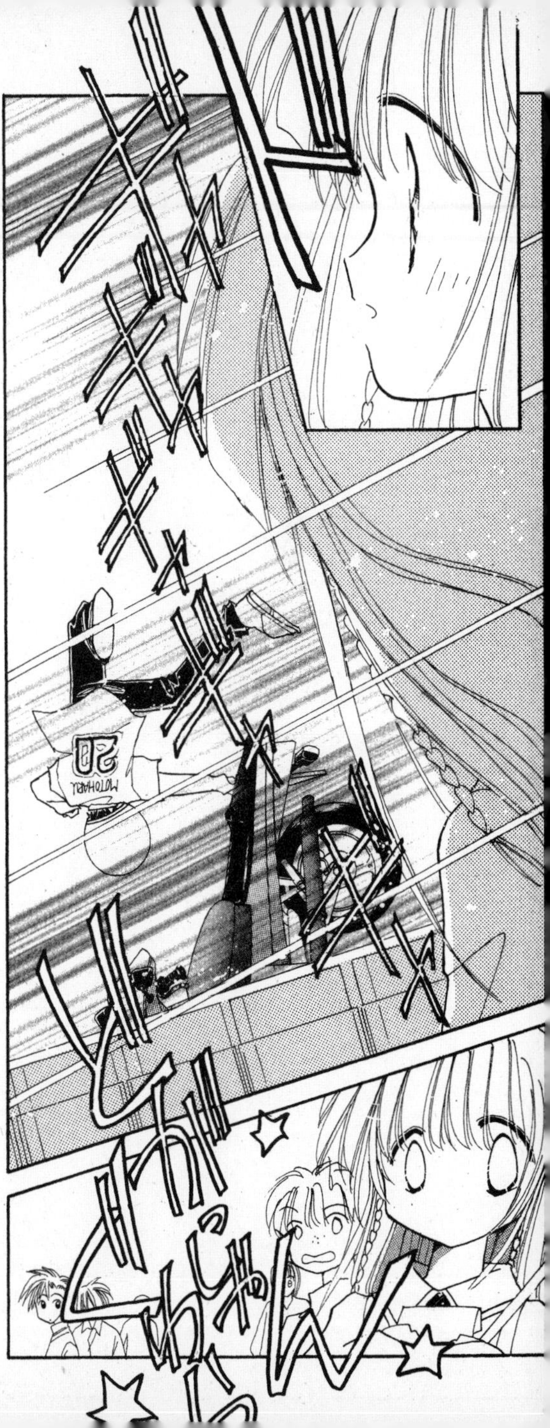

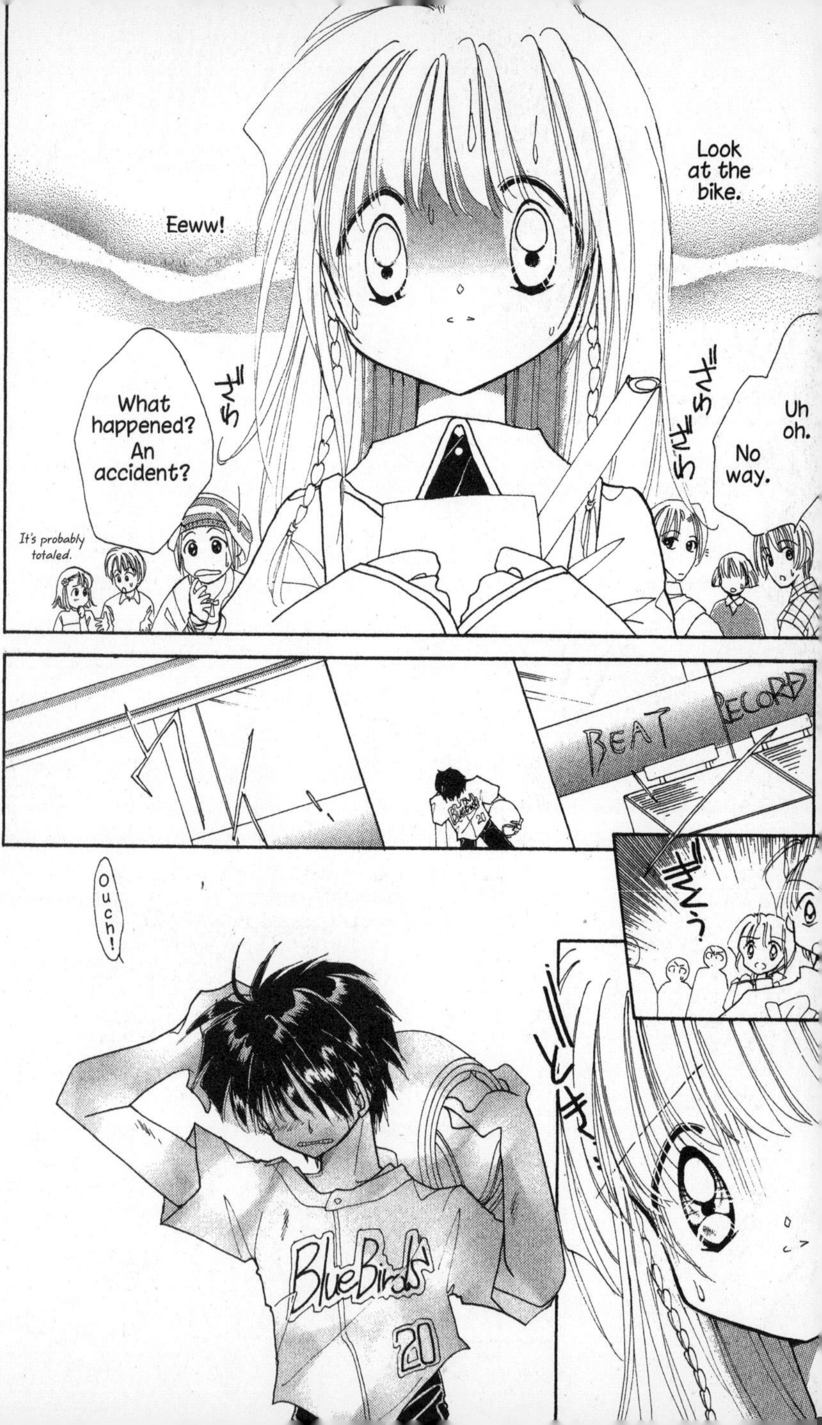
Look at the bike.
Uh oh.
No way.
Eeww!
What happened? An accident?
It's probably totaled.
BEAT RECORD
Ouch!

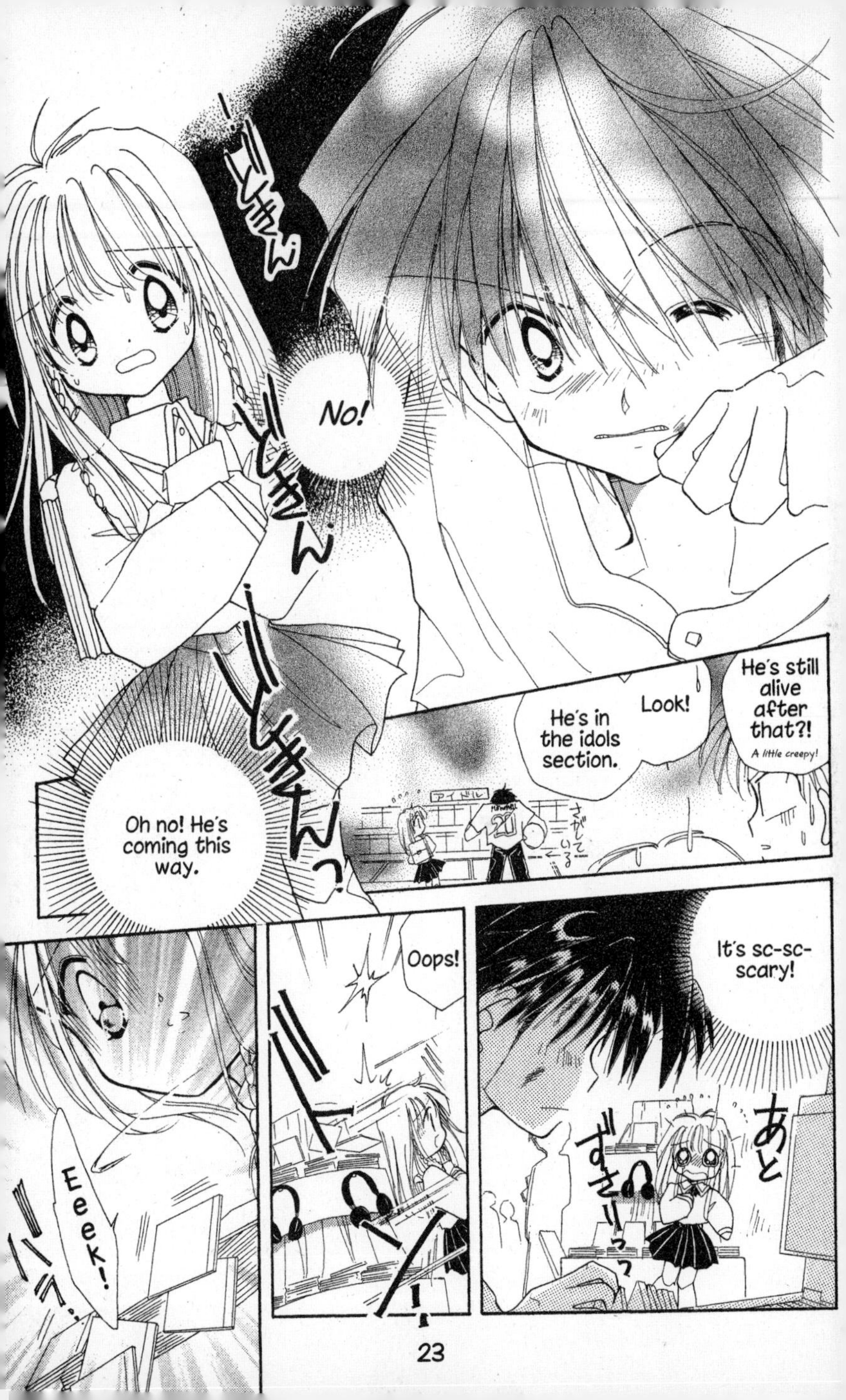
No!
He's still alive after that?!
A little creepy!
Look!
He's in the idols section.
アイドル
さがしている
Oh no! He's coming this way.
It's sc-sc-scary!
あと
ずさりっ
Oops!
Eeek!

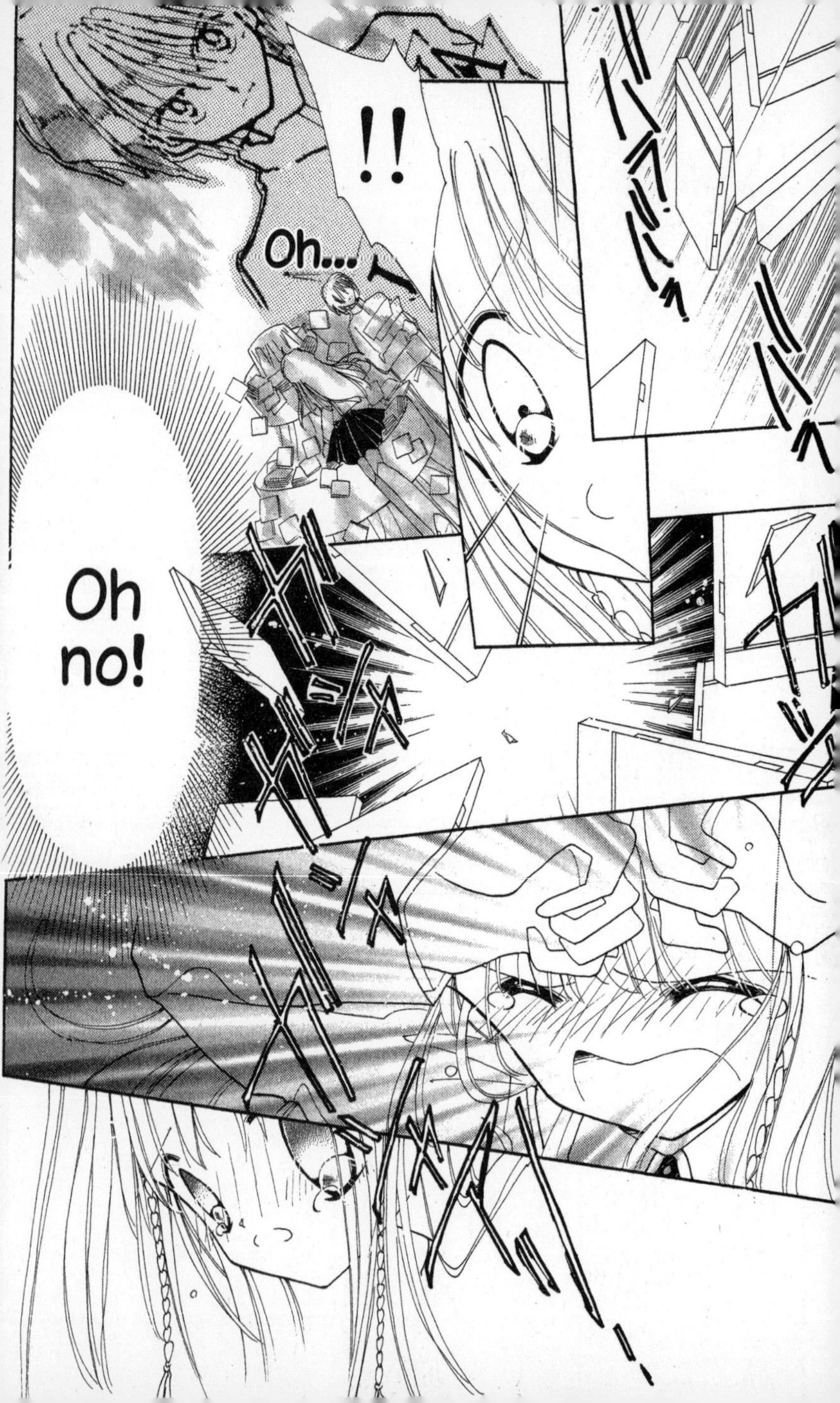
!!
Oh...
Oh no!

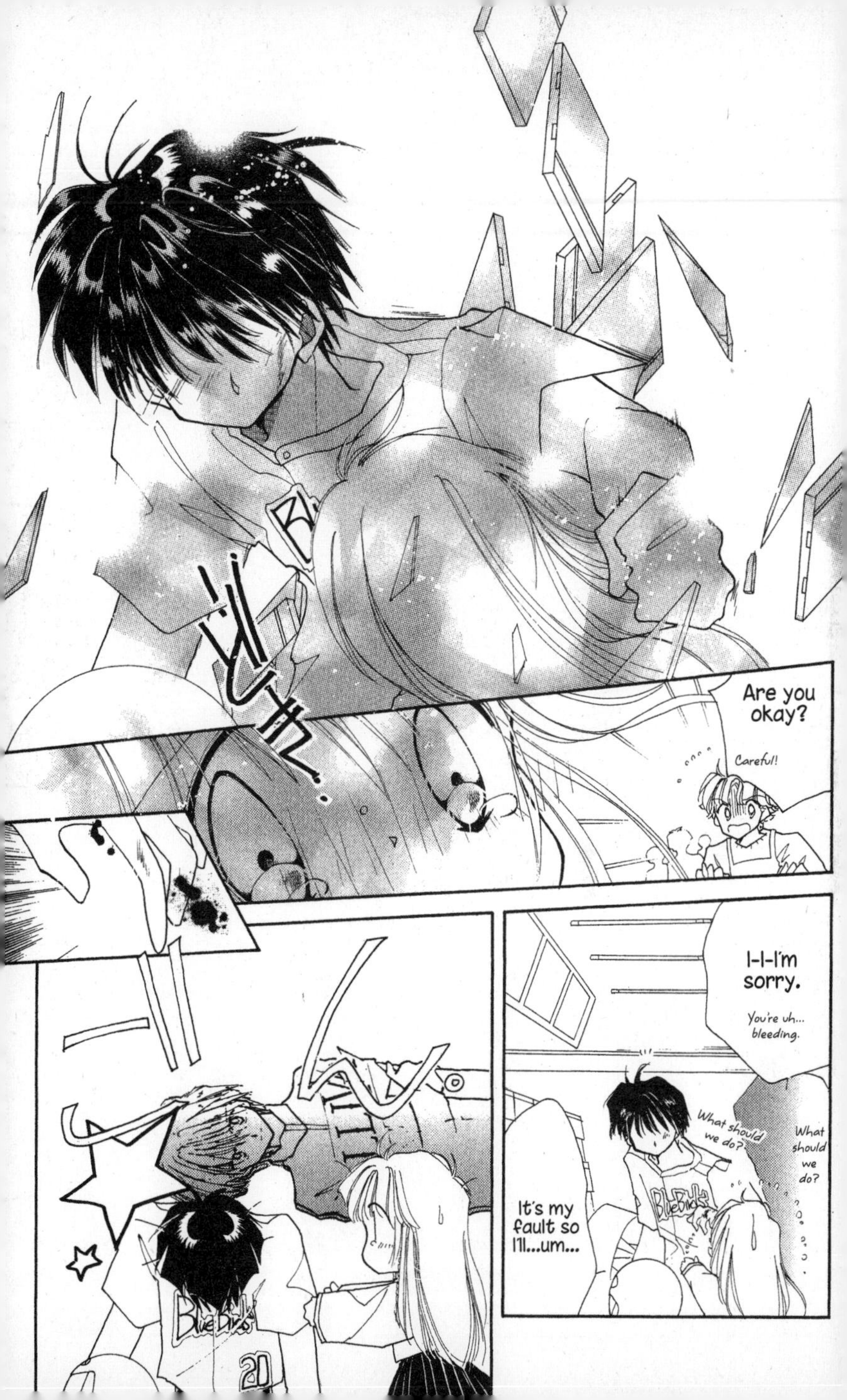
Are you okay?
Careful!
I-I-I'm sorry.
You're uh... bleeding.
What should we do?
What should we do?
It's my fault so I'll...um...

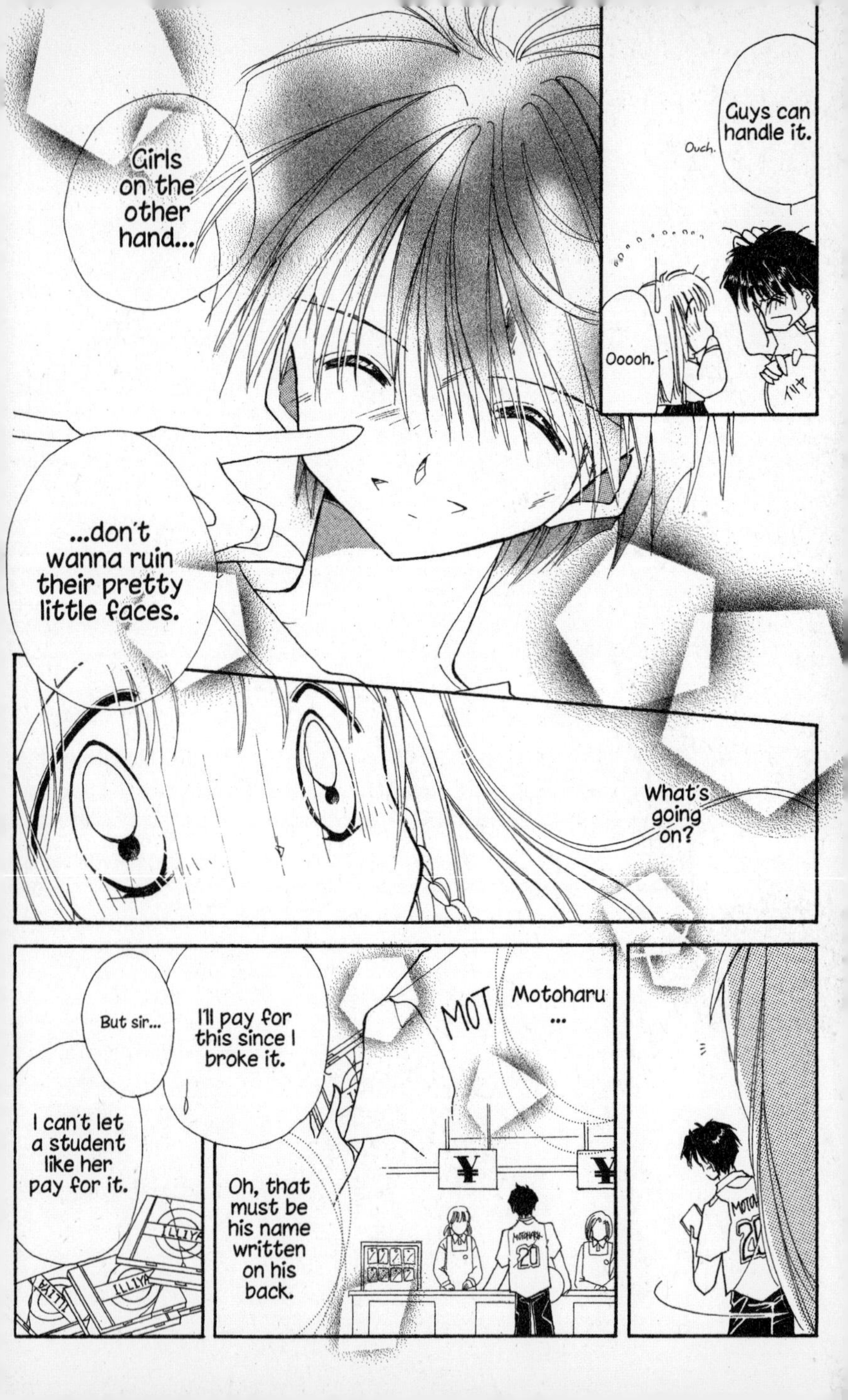
Guys can handle it.
Ouch.
Ooooh.
Girls on the other hand...
...don't wanna ruin their pretty little faces.
What's going on?
Motoharu ...
MOT
Oh, that must be his name written on his back.
I'll pay for this since I broke it.
But sir...
I can't let a student like her pay for it.
ILLIYA

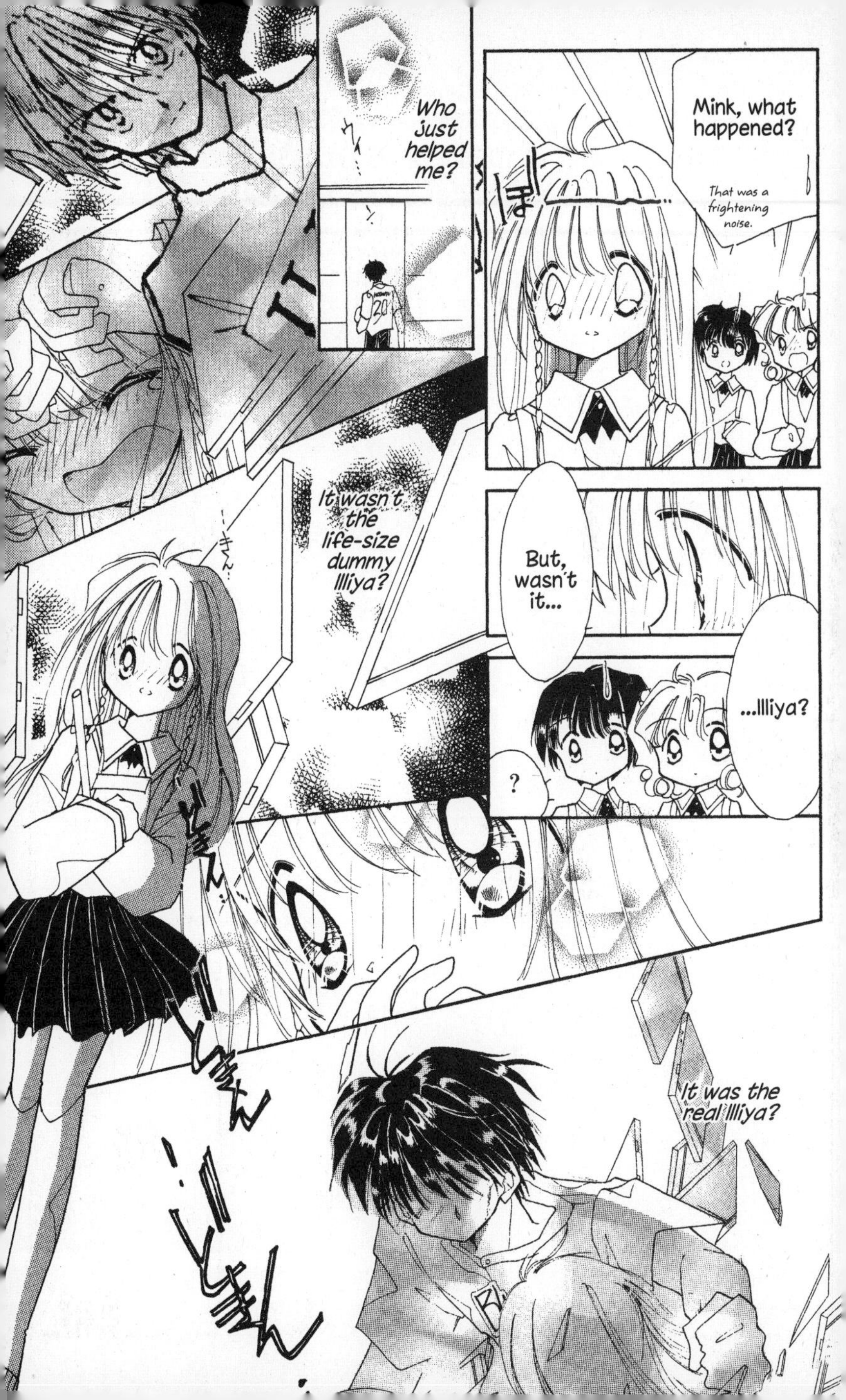
Mink, what happened?
That was a frightening noise.
Who just helped me?
But, wasn't it...
...Illiya?
?
It wasn't the life-size dummy Illiya?
It was the real Illiya?

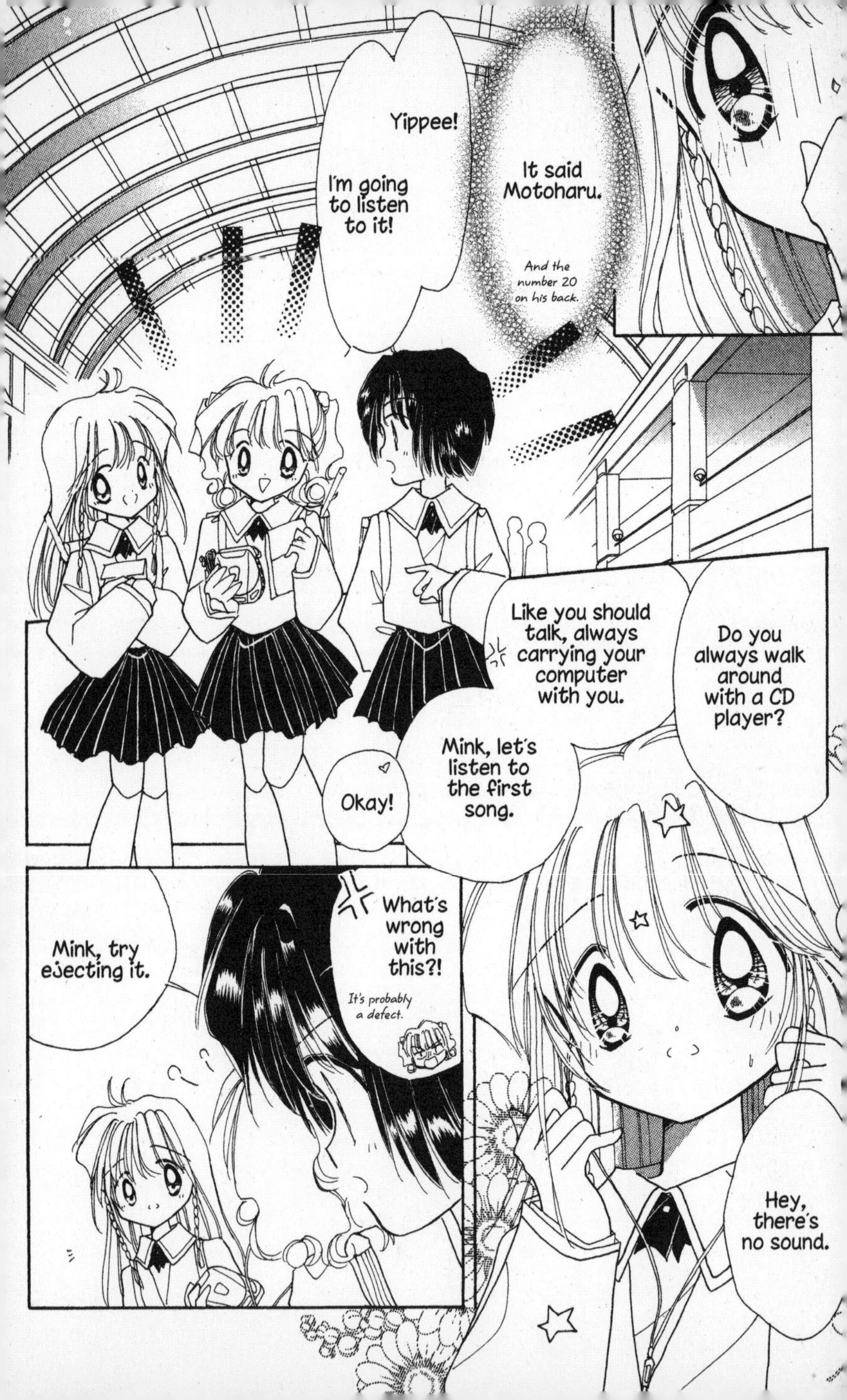
It said Motoharu.
And the number 20 on his back.
Yippee!
I'm going to listen to it!
Do you always walk around with a CD player?
Like you should talk, always carrying your computer with you.
Mink, let's listen to the first song.
Okay!
Hey, there's no sound.
What's wrong with this?!
It's probably a defect.
Mink, try ejecting it.

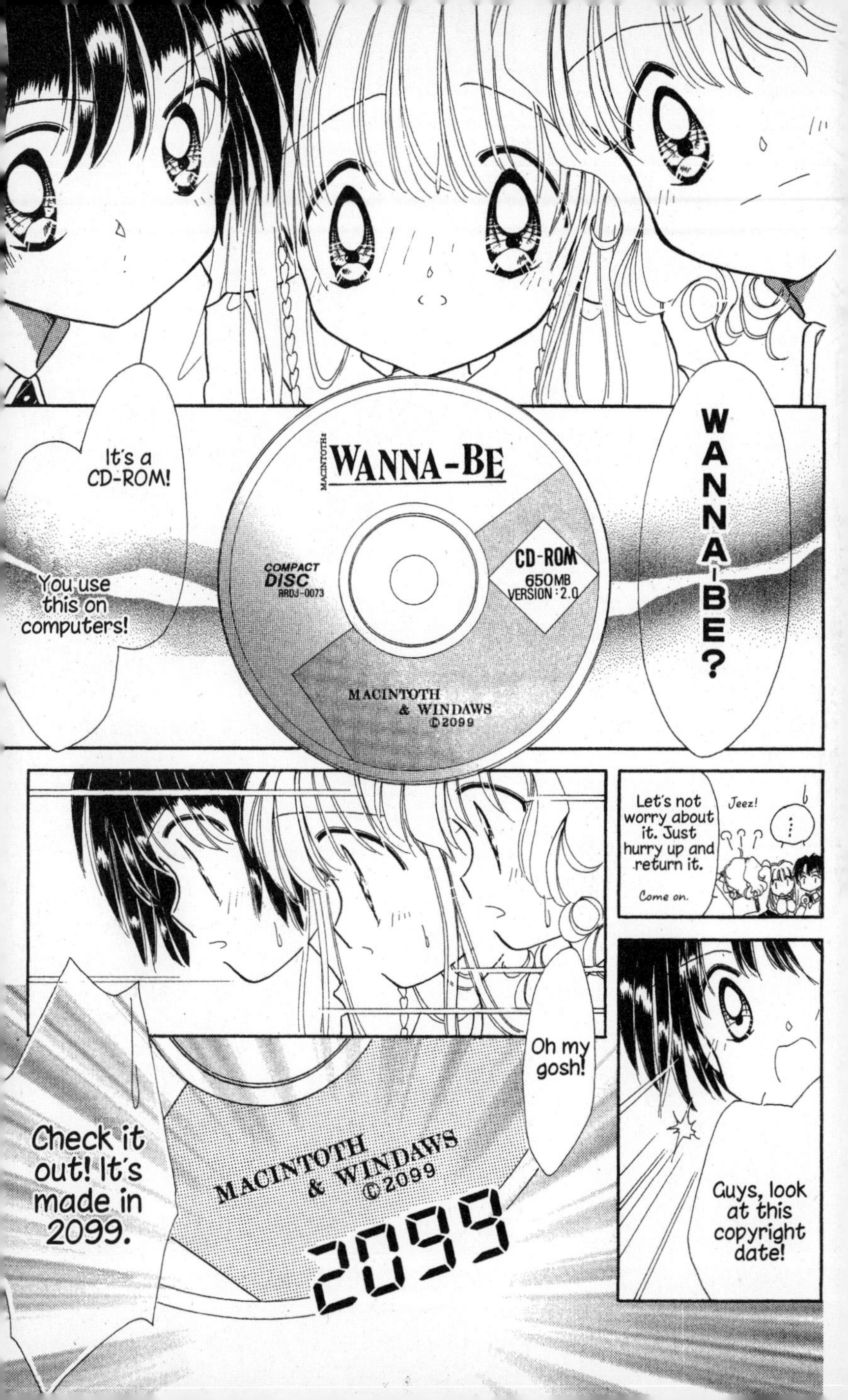
WANNA-BE?
WANNA-BE
CD-ROM
650MB
VERSION : 2.0
COMPACT
DISC
RRDJ-0073
MACINTOTH
& WINDAWS
©2099
It's a CD-ROM!
You use this on computers!
Let's not worry about it. Just hurry up and return it.
Jeez!
...
Come on.
Guys, look at this copyright date!
Oh my gosh!
MACINTOTH
& WINDAWS
©2099
2099
Check it out! It's made in 2099.

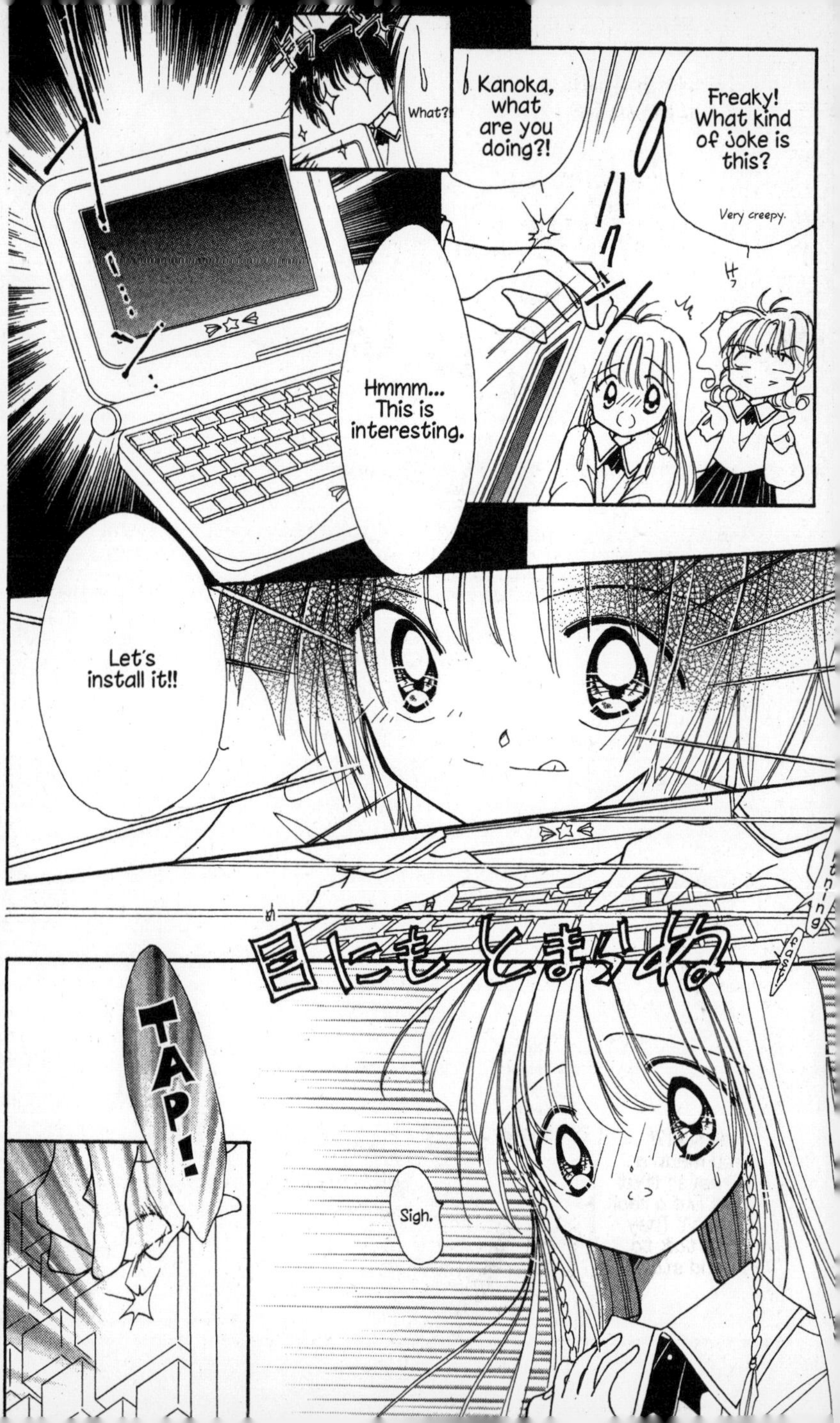
Freaky! What kind of joke is this?
Very creepy.
Kanoka, what are you doing?!
What?!
Hmmm... This is interesting.
Let's install it!!
目にも とまらぬ
TAP!
Sigh.

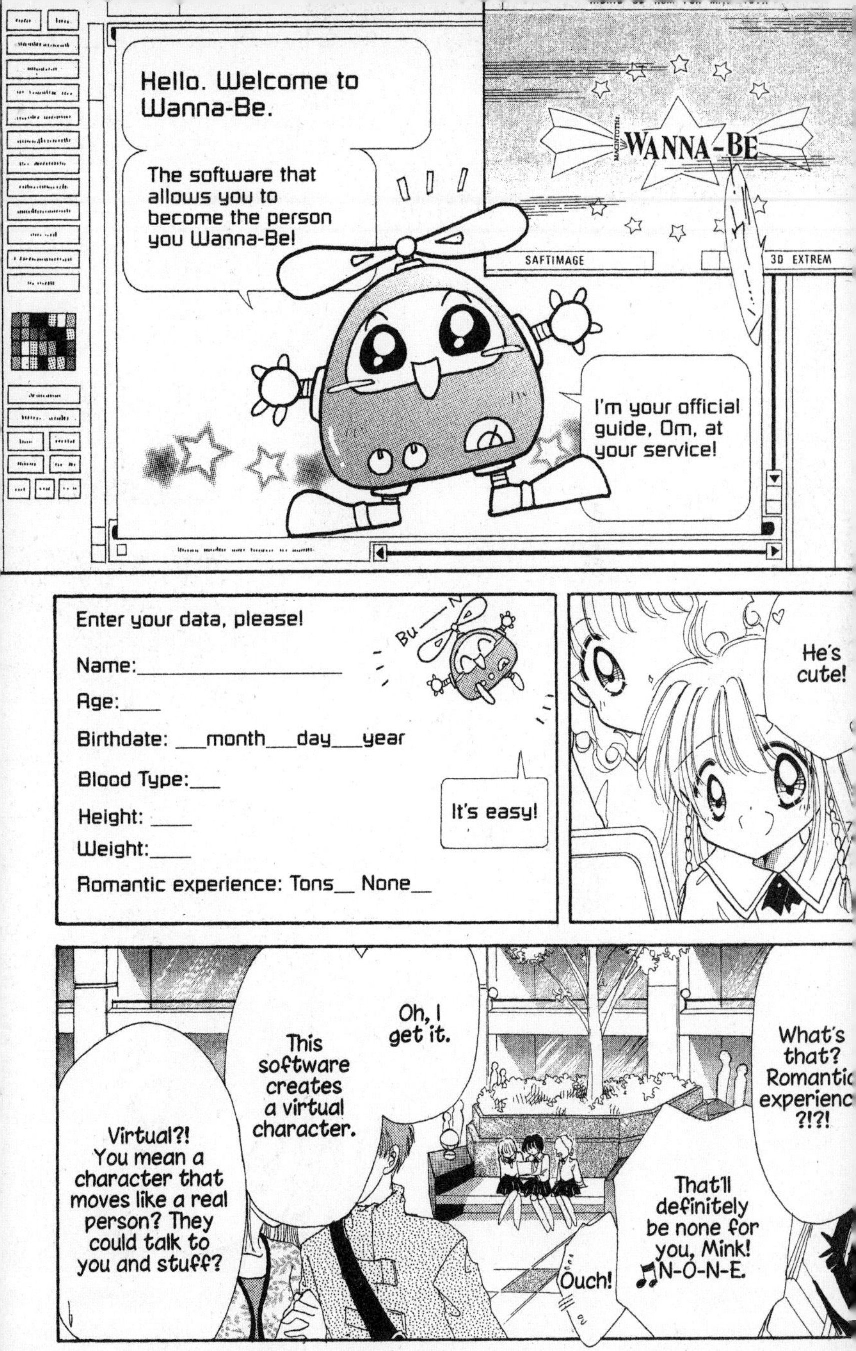

WANNA-BE
SAFTIMAGE
3D EXTREM
Hello. Welcome to Wanna-Be.
The software that allows you to become the person you Wanna-Be!
I'm your official guide, Om, at your service!
He's cute!
Enter your data, please!
Name:____________
Age:____
Birthdate: ___month___day___year
Blood Type:___
Height: ____
Weight:____
Romantic experience: Tons__ None__
BU—N
It's easy!
What's that? Romantic experienc ?!?!
That'll definitely be none for you, Mink! N-O-N-E.
Ouch!
Oh, I get it.
This software creates a virtual character.
Virtual?! You mean a character that moves like a real person? They could talk to you and stuff?

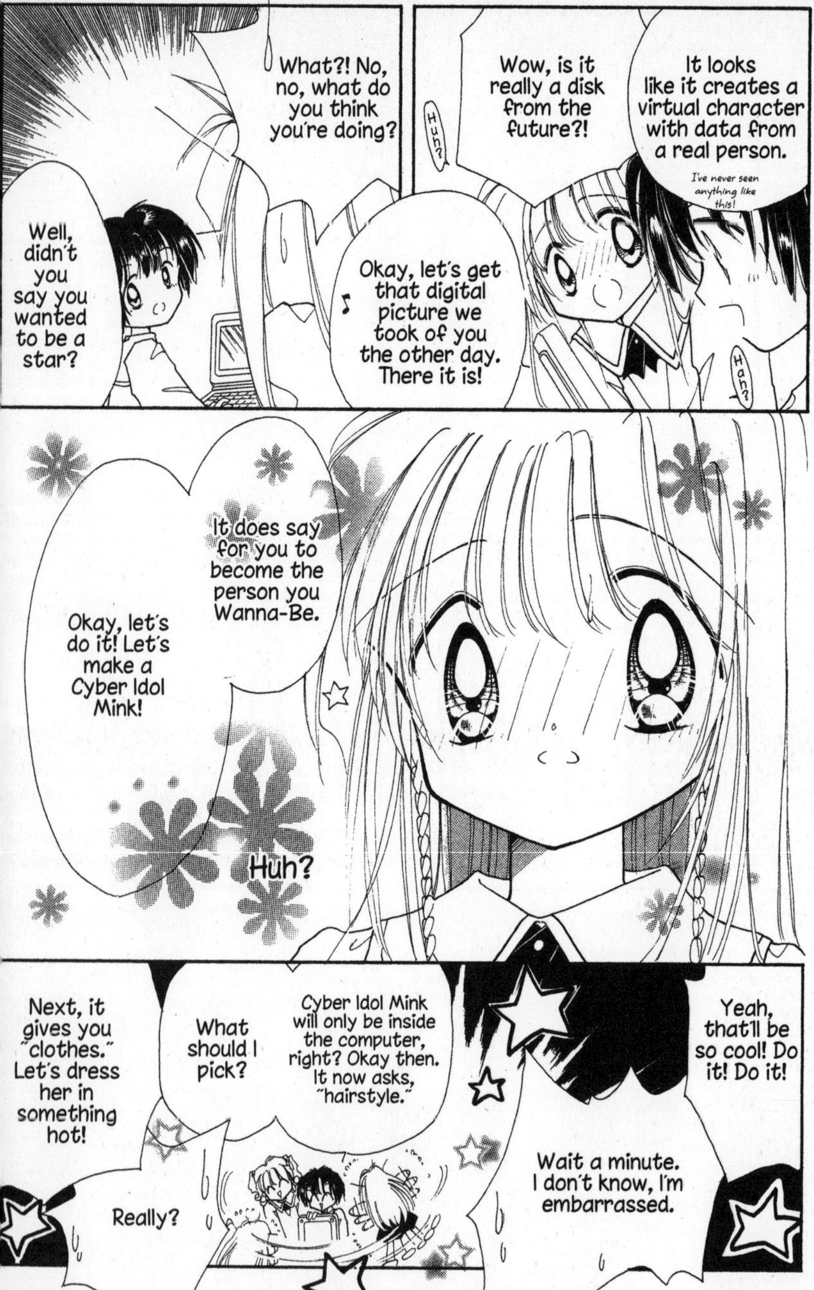
It looks like it creates a virtual character with data from a real person.
I've never seen anything like this!
Wow, is it really a disk from the future?!
Hah?
Okay, let's get that digital picture we took of you the other day. There it is!
Huh?
What?! No, no, what do you think you're doing?
Well, didn't you say you wanted to be a star?
It does say for you to become the person you Wanna-Be.
Okay, let's do it! Let's make a Cyber Idol Mink!
Huh?
Yeah, that'll be so cool! Do it! Do it!
Wait a minute. I don't know, I'm embarrassed.
Cyber Idol Mink will only be inside the computer, right? Okay then. It now asks, "hairstyle."
What should I pick?
Next, it gives you "clothes." Let's dress her in something hot!
Really?

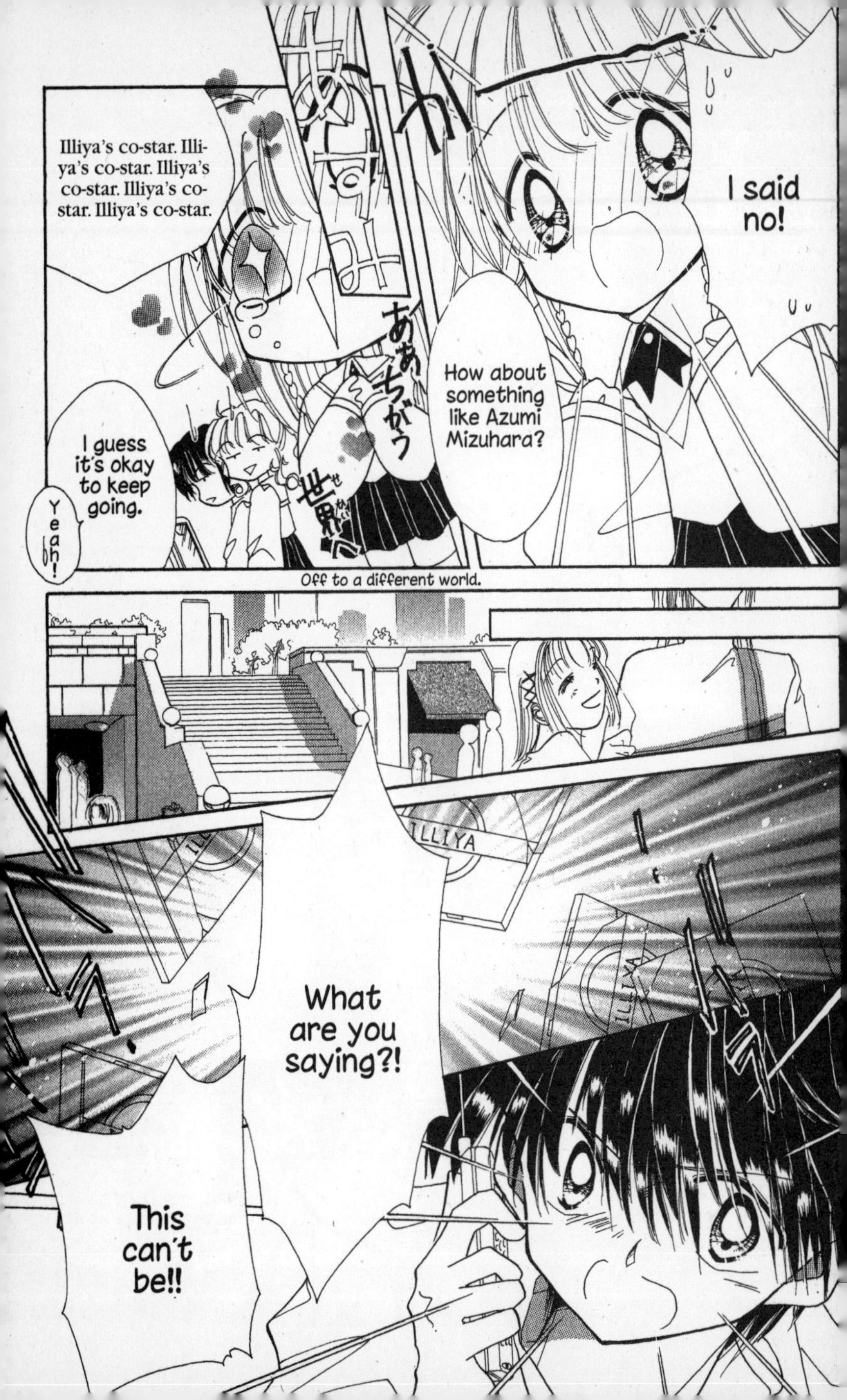

I said no!
How about something like Azumi Mizuhara?
ああ ちがう
世界へ
Illiya's co-star. Illiya's co-star. Illiya's co-star. Illiya's co-star. Illiya's co-star.
I guess it's okay to keep going.
Yeah!
Off to a different world.
ILLIYA
What are you saying?!
This can't be!!

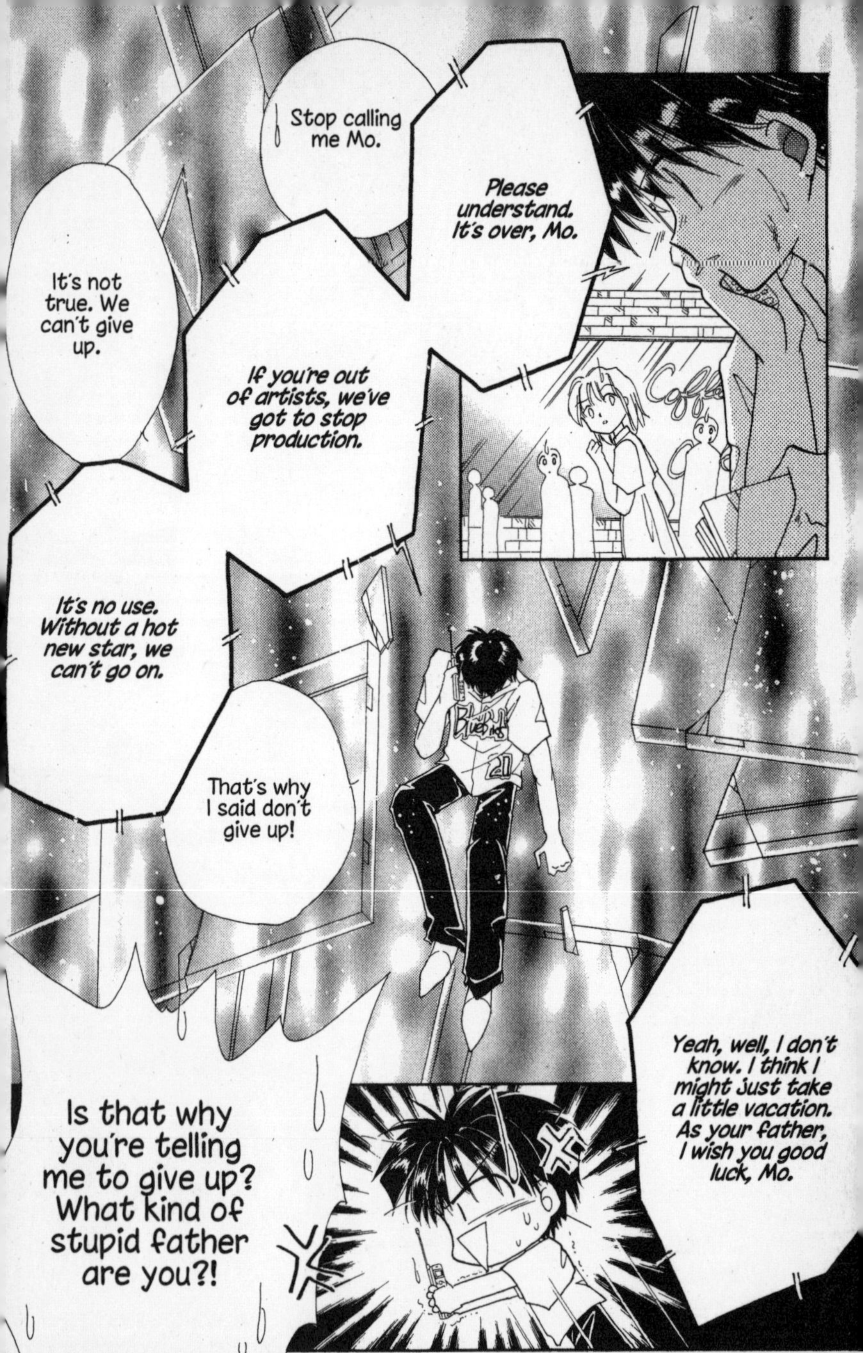
Please understand. It's over, Mo.
Stop calling me Mo.
It's not true. We can't give up.
If you're out of artists, we've got to stop production.
It's no use. Without a hot new star, we can't go on.
That's why I said don't give up!
Yeah, well, I don't know. I think I might just take a little vacation. As your father, I wish you good luck, Mo.
Is that why you're telling me to give up? What kind of stupid father are you?!

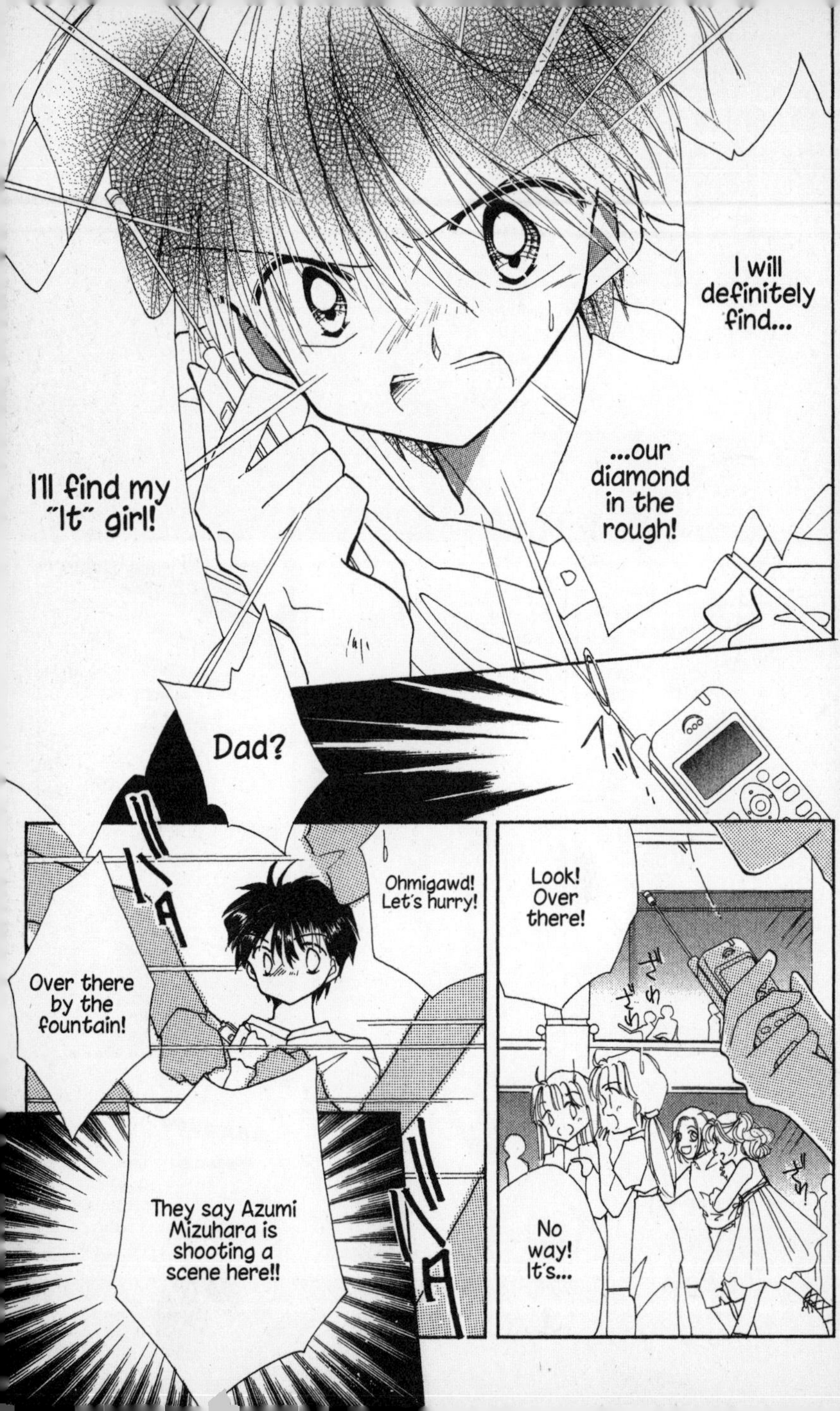
I will definitely find...
...our diamond in the rough!
I'll find my "It" girl!
Dad?
Look! Over there!
No way! It's...
Ohmigawd! Let's hurry!
Over there by the fountain!
They say Azumi Mizuhara is shooting a scene here!!

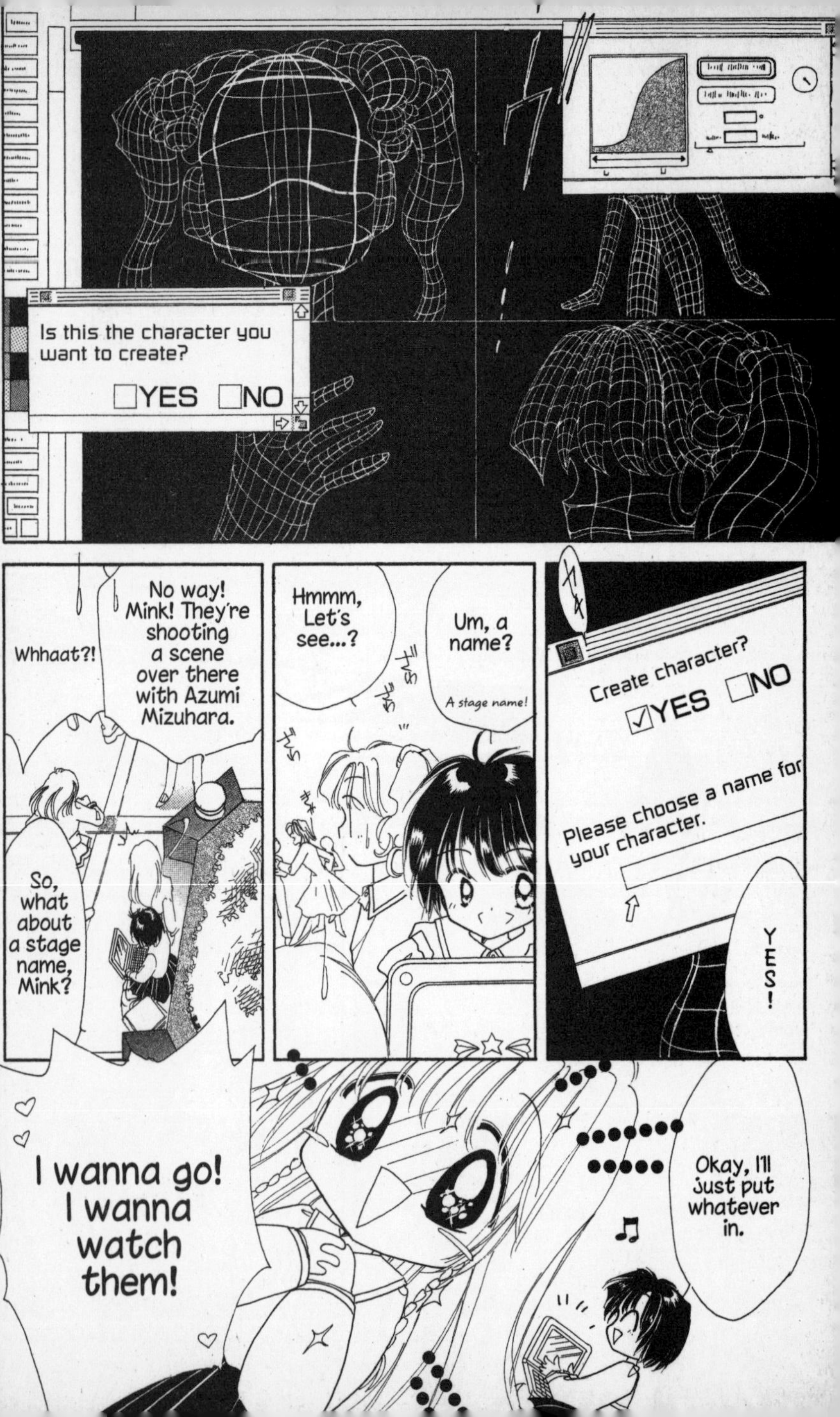

Is this the character you want to create?
YES NO
Create character?
YES NO
Please choose a name for your character.
YES!
Um, a name?
A stage name!
Hmmm, Let's see...?
No way! Mink! They're shooting a scene over there with Azumi Mizuhara.
Whhaat?!
So, what about a stage name, Mink?
Okay, I'll just put whatever in.
I wanna go! I wanna watch them!

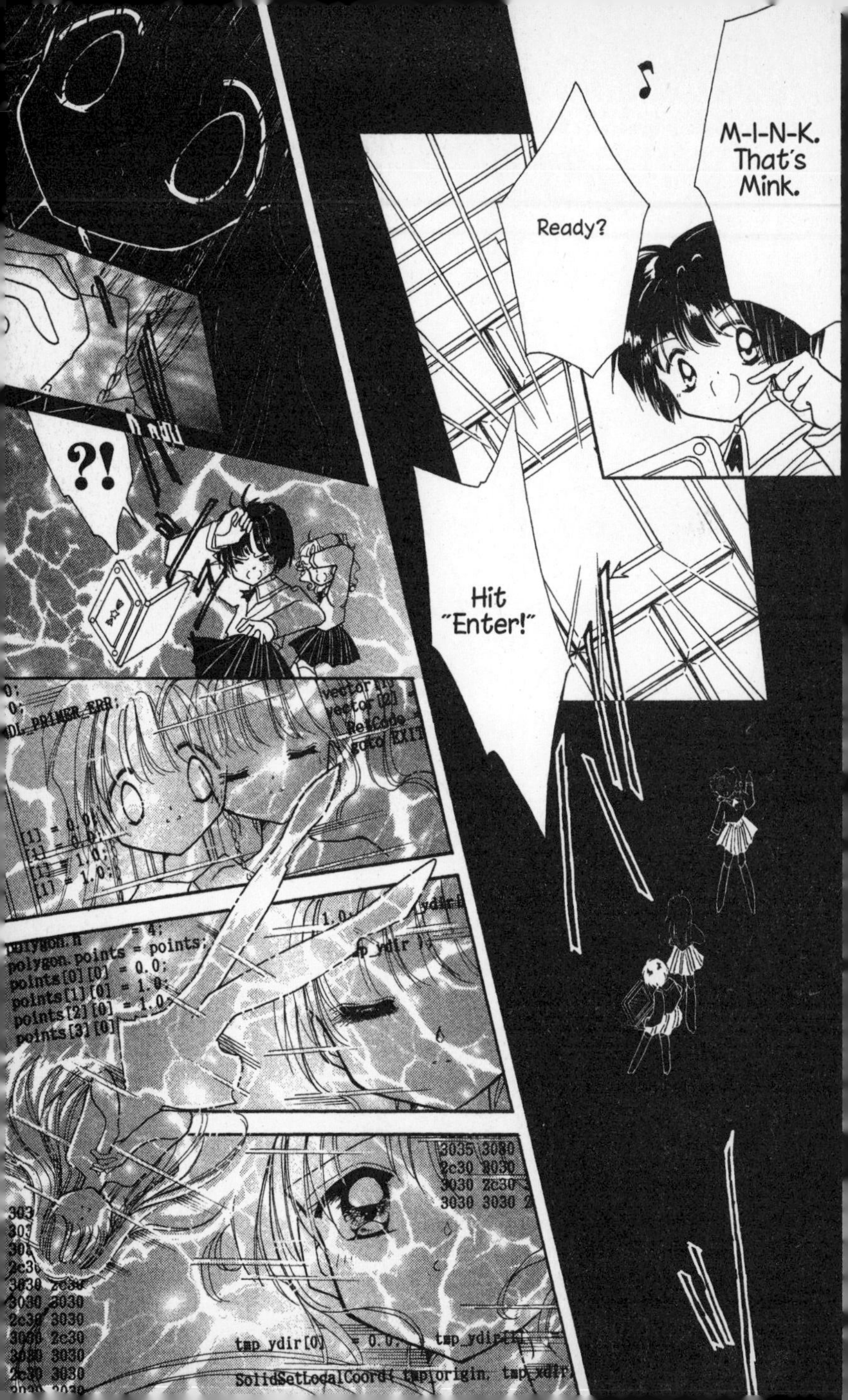
M-I-N-K. That's Mink.
Ready?
Hit "Enter!"
?!

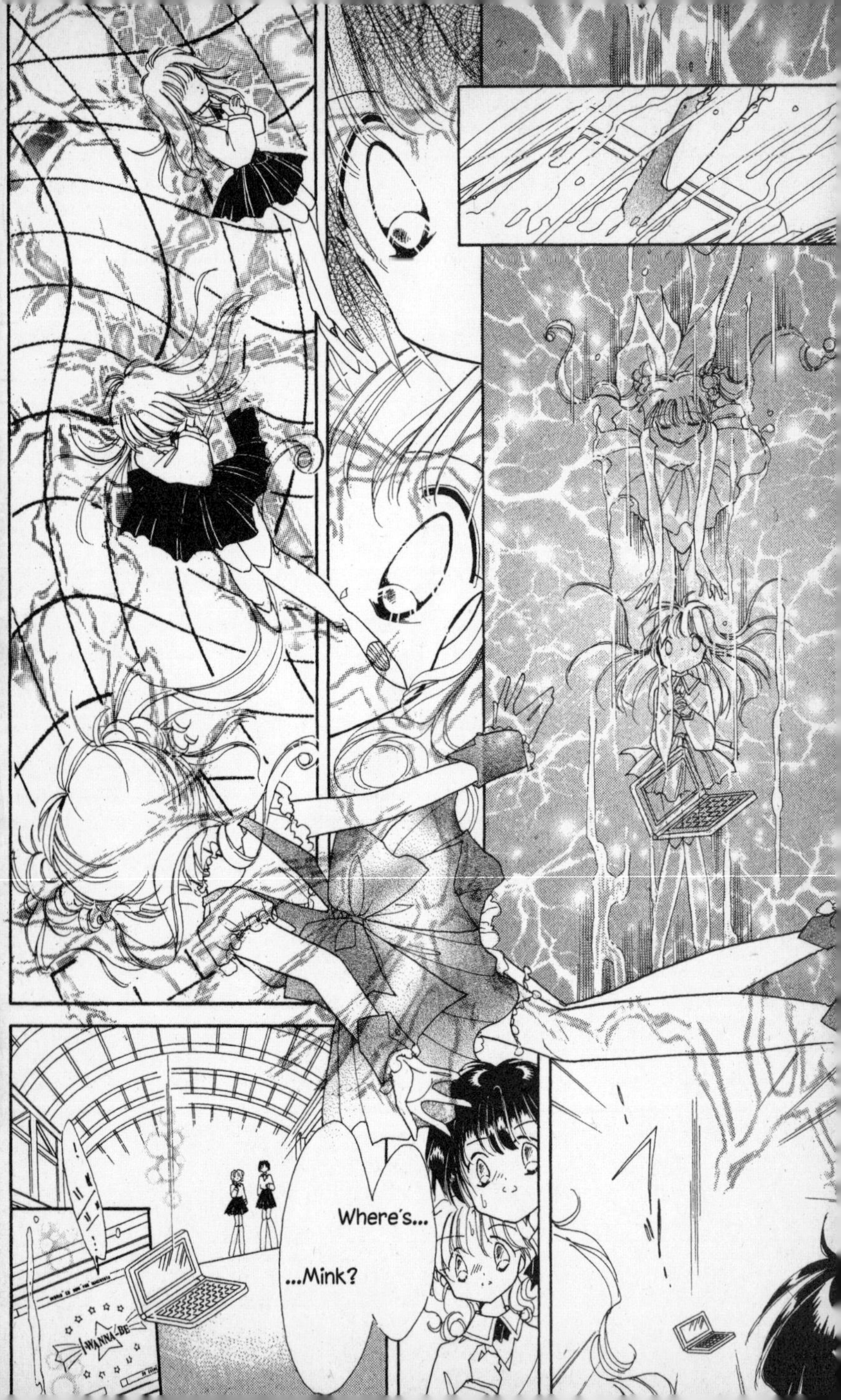
Where's...
...Mink?
I-WANNA-BE

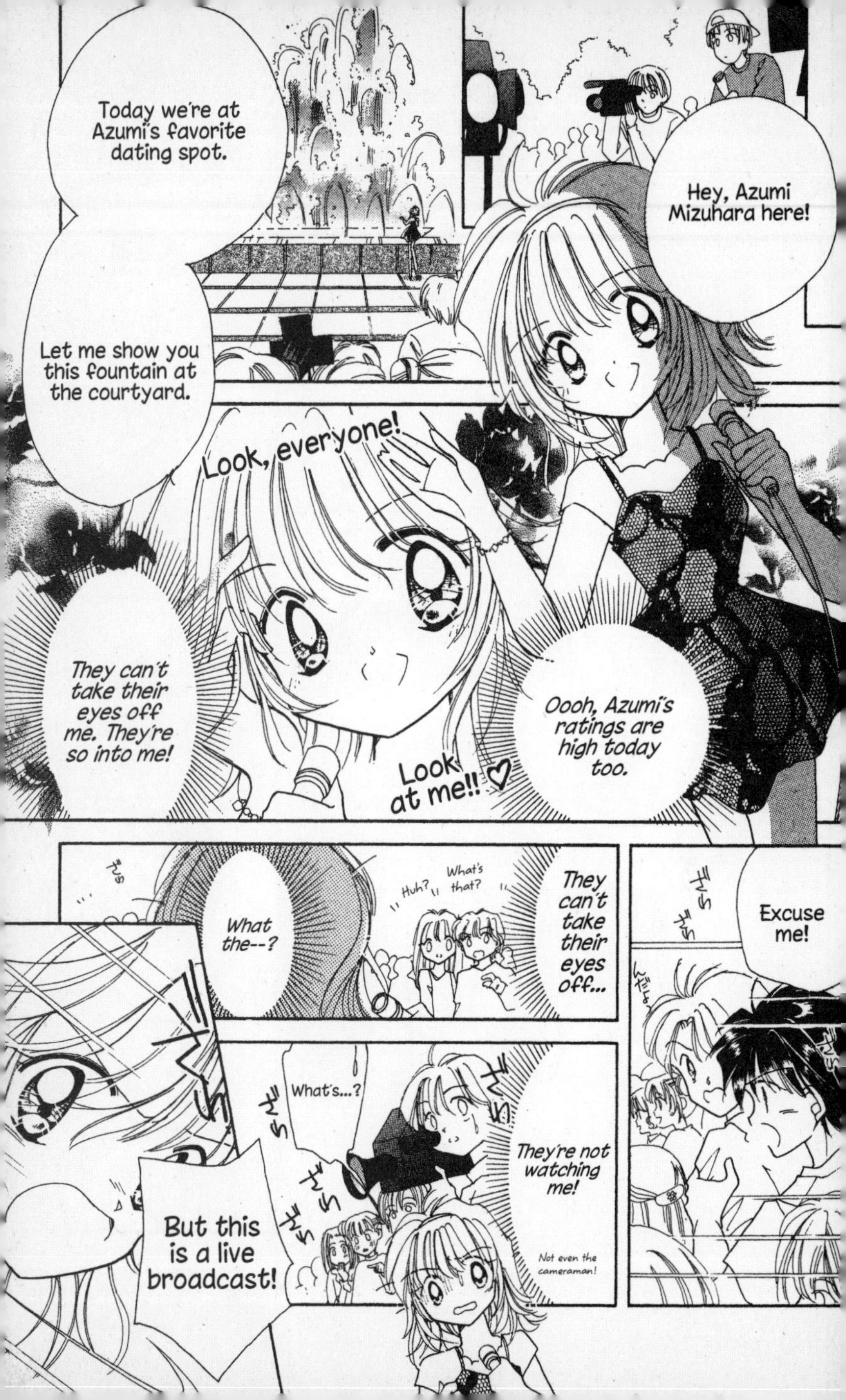
Hey, Azumi Mizuhara here!
Today we're at Azumi's favorite dating spot.
Let me show you this fountain at the courtyard.
Look, everyone!
Oooh, Azumi's ratings are high today too.
Look at me!! ♡
They can't take their eyes off me. They're so into me!
Excuse me!
They can't take their eyes off...
What's that?
Huh?
What the--?
They're not watching me!
Not even the cameraman!
What's...?
But this is a live broadcast!

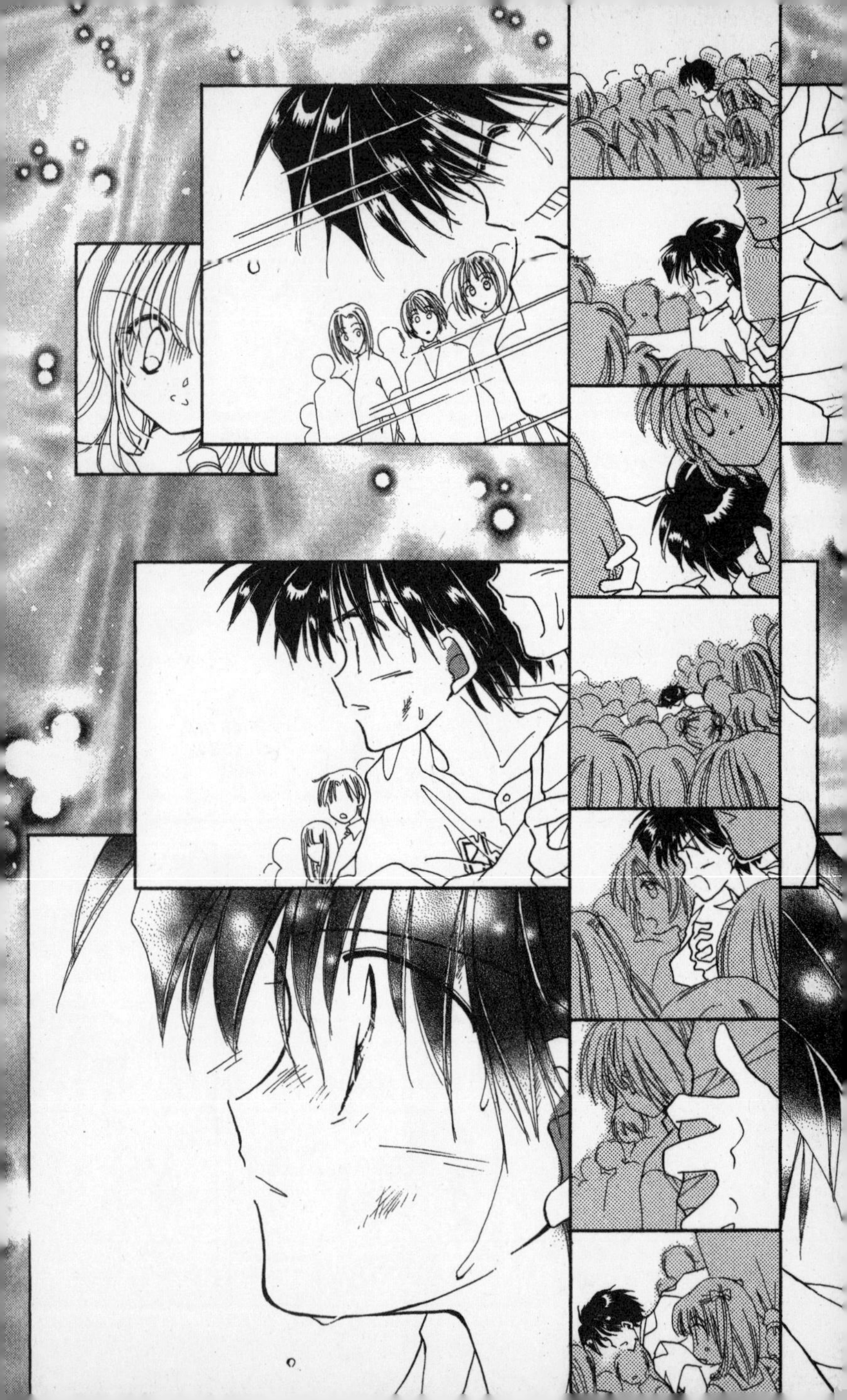

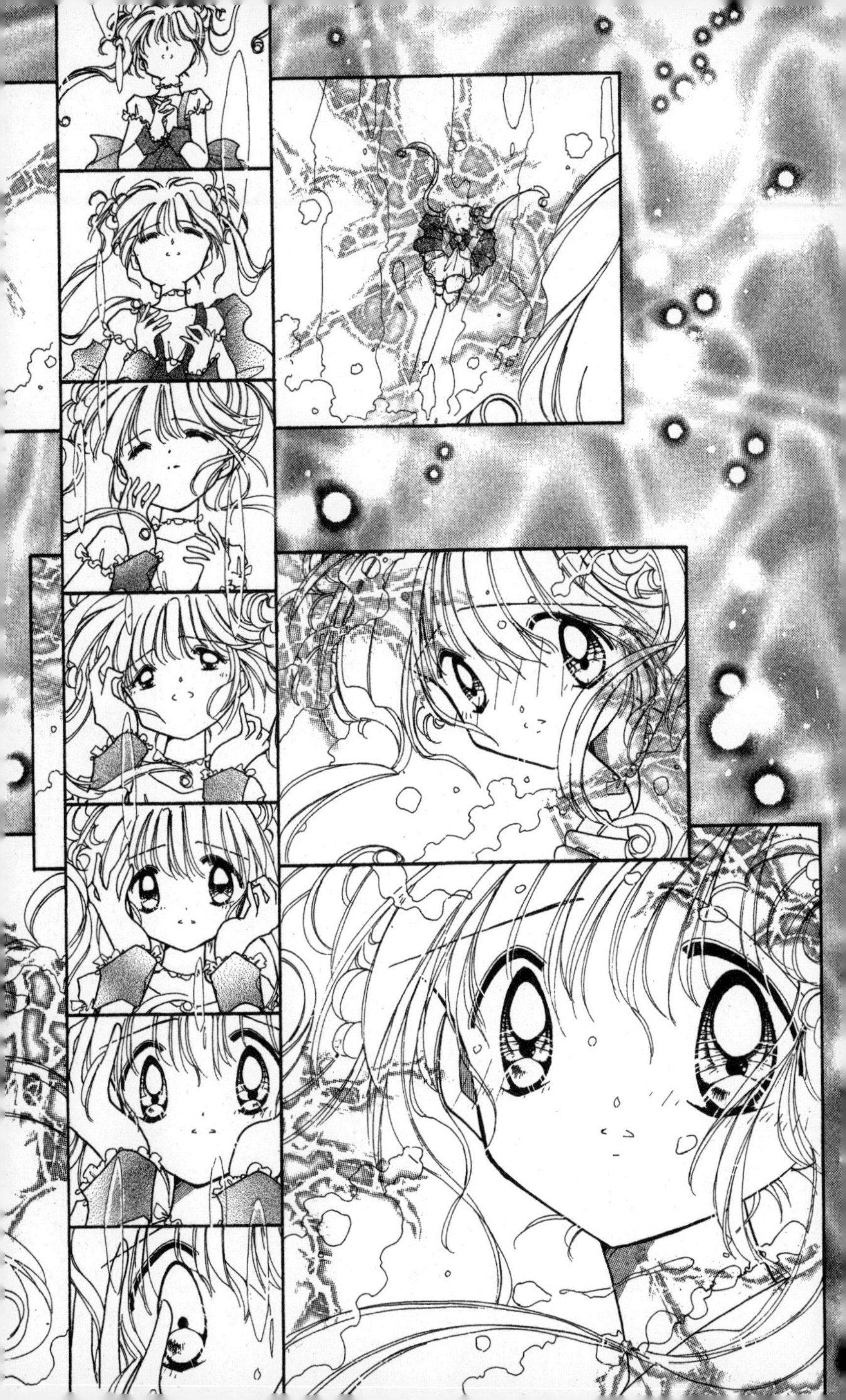

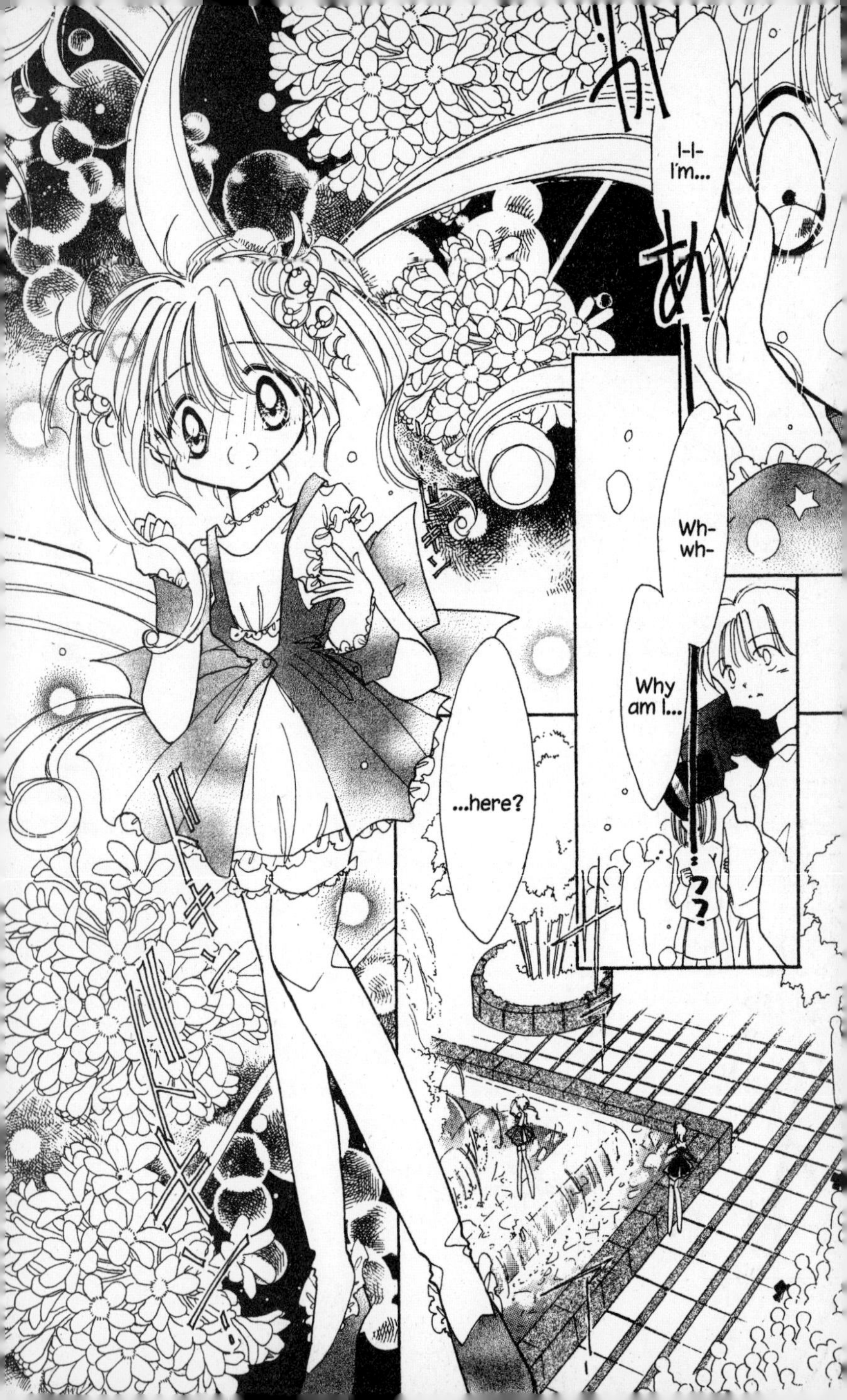
I-I-
I'm...
Wh-
wh-
Why am I...
...here?

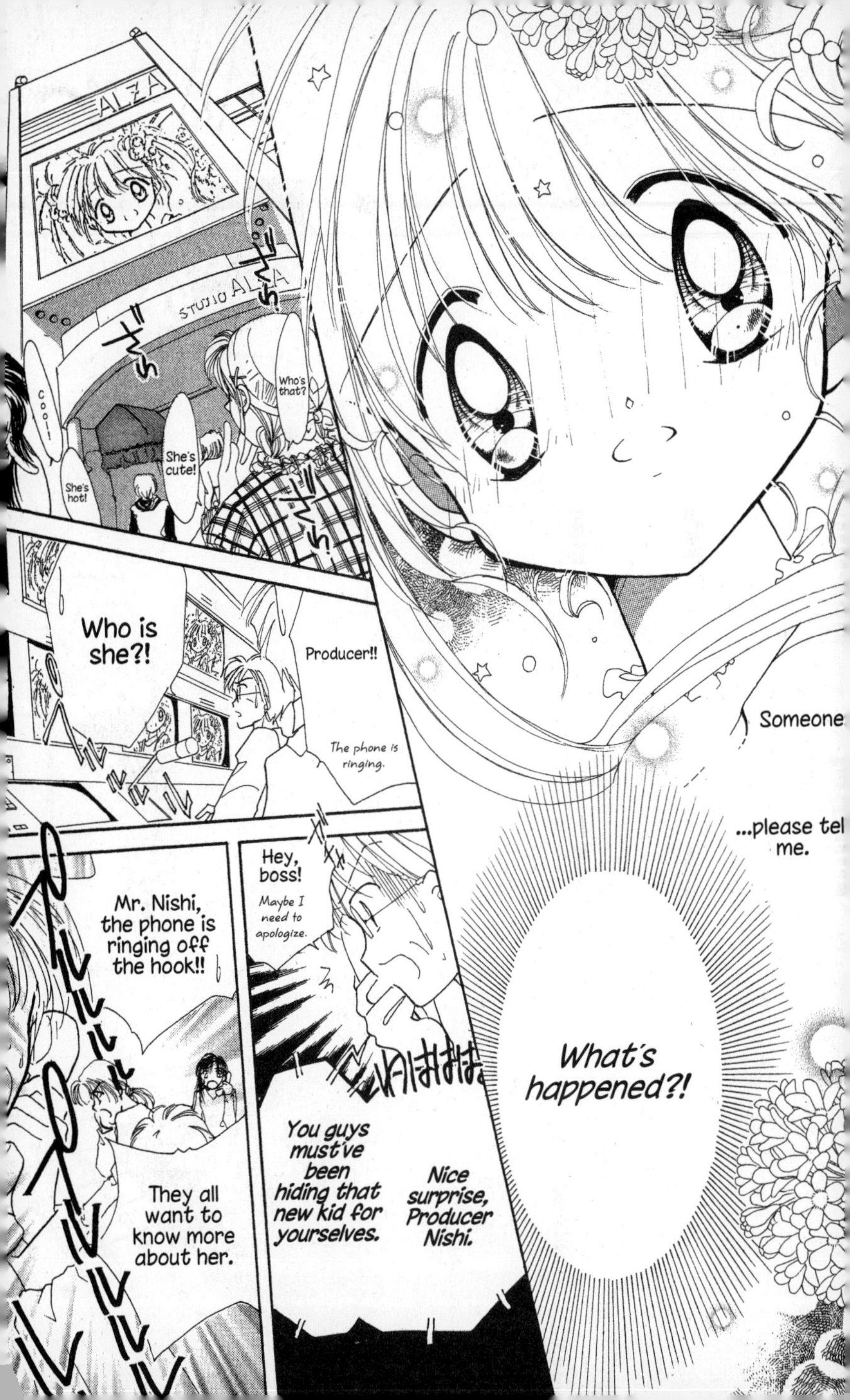
Someone
...please tell me.
What's happened?!
ALZA
STUDIO ALZA
Who's that?
She's cute!
She's hot!
Cool!
Producer!!
The phone is ringing.
Who is she?!
Hey, boss!
Maybe I need to apologize.
Nice surprise, Producer Nishi.
You guys must've been hiding that new kid for yourselves.
Mr. Nishi, the phone is ringing off the hook!!
They all want to know more about her.

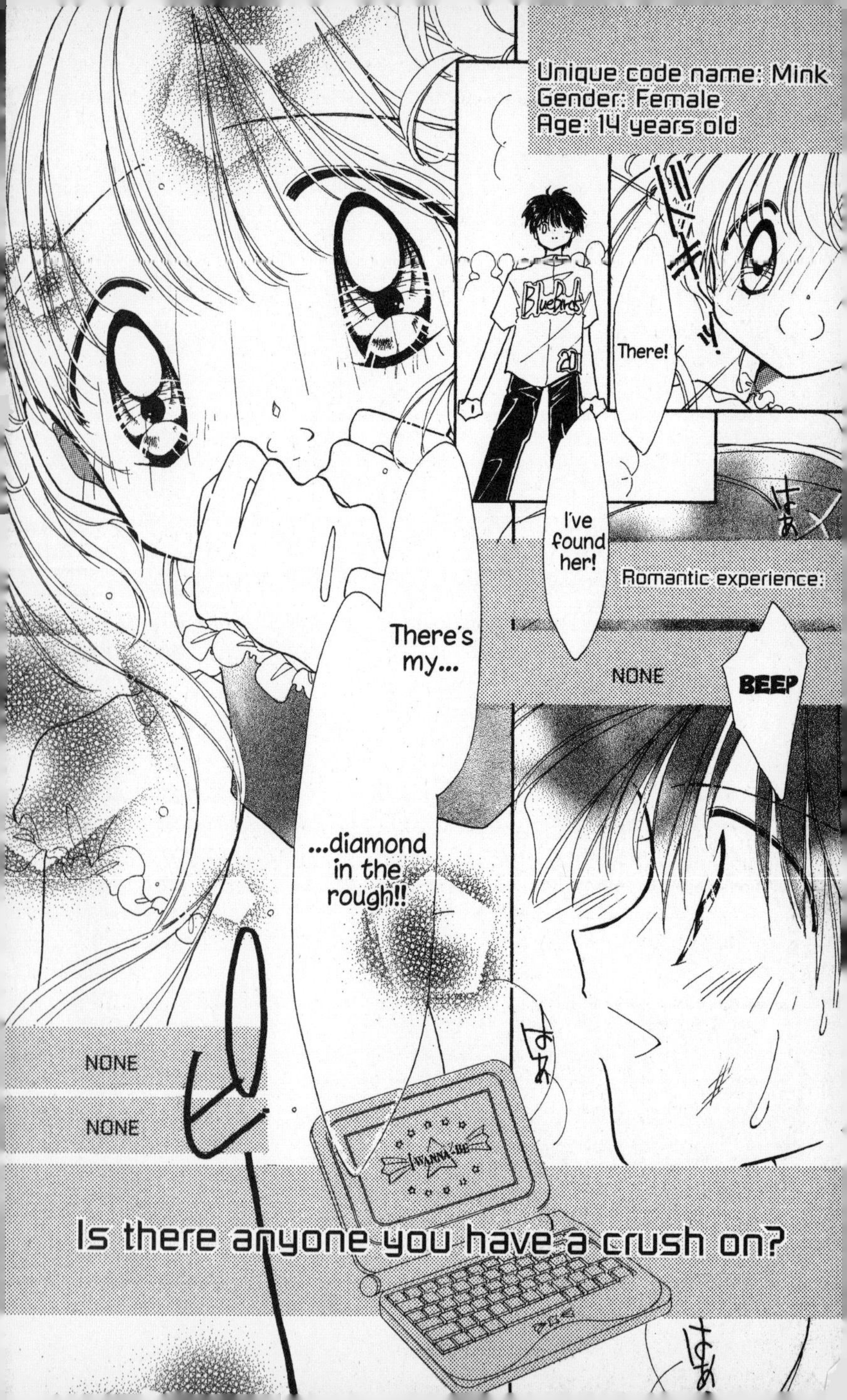
Unique code name: Mink
Gender: Female
Age: 14 years old
There!
I've found her!
Romantic experience:
NONE
BEEP
There's my...
...diamond in the rough!!
NONE
NONE
Is there anyone you have a crush on?

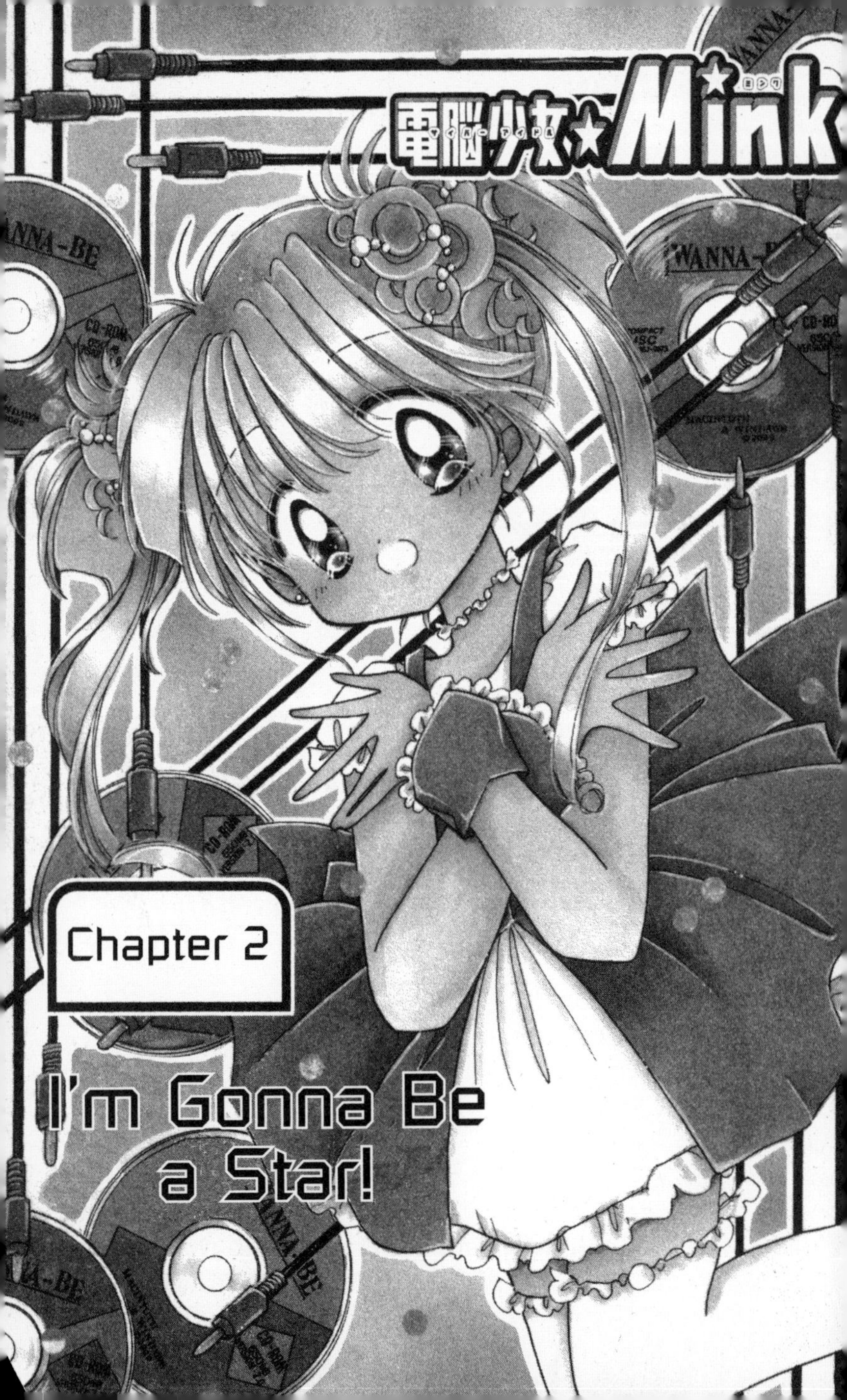
電脳少女★Mink
Chapter 2
I'm Gonna Be a Star!
WANNA-BE

Mink Rap!!

Q: Before your debut, did you master drawing with colors?

A: No, I didn't know anything about drawing with colors. I only learned after my debut. The first color sheet I did was the inside cover of *Hot Typhoon Volume 1*. I was so nervous when I was drawing it! It's all trial and error when you first dabble in color. When you mess up, it's back to the drawing board! But even now, I still find working with color pictures very painstaking.

Q: What type of pen do you use when you draw the characters' faces? What do you use for the beta or practice drawing?

A: I use a "G" pen. For the eyes, nose and mouth area, I use a round-tip pen. As for the betas, I use a fountain pen for any detailed areas and a magic marker for wide strokes.

Q: In Japan, can elementary school kids attend manga school?

A: Absolutely, you bet! Go for it!

Megumi

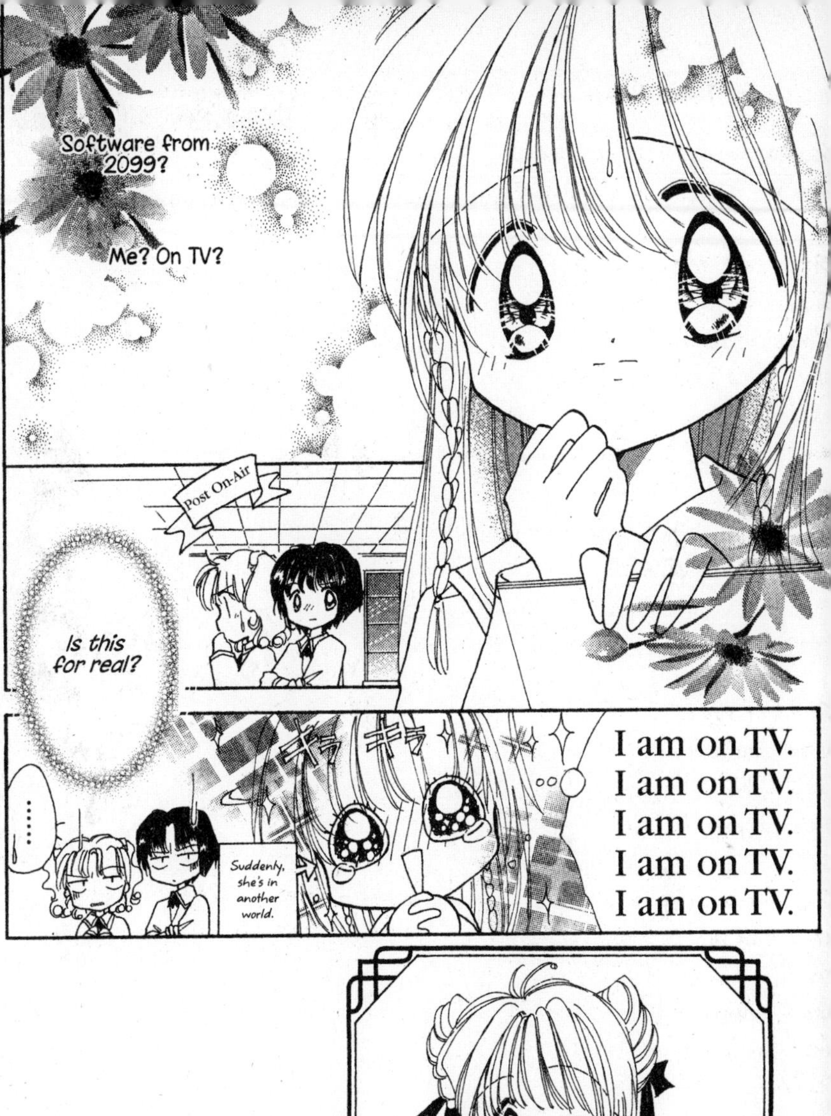
Software from 2099?
Me? On TV?
Post On-Air
Is this for real?
I am on TV.
I am on TV.
I am on TV.
I am on TV.
I am on TV.
Suddenly, she's in another world.
......

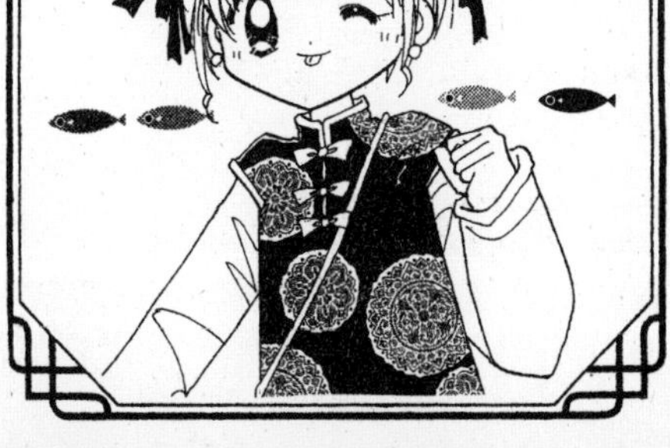

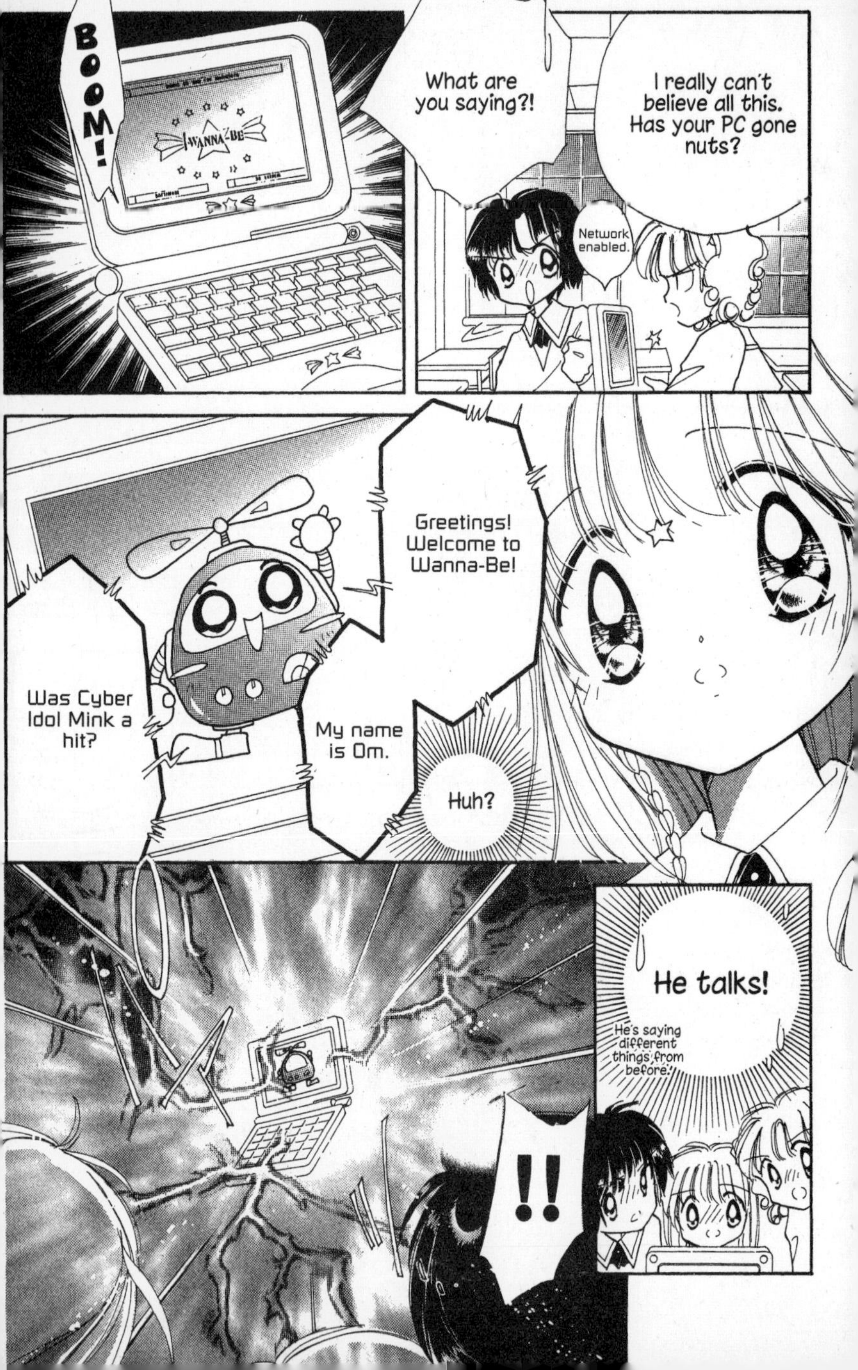
I really can't believe all this. Has your PC gone nuts?
What are you saying?!
Network enabled.
BOOM!
WANNA-BE
Greetings! Welcome to Wanna-Be!
My name is Om.
Was Cyber Idol Mink a hit?
Huh?
He talks!
He's saying different things from before.
!!

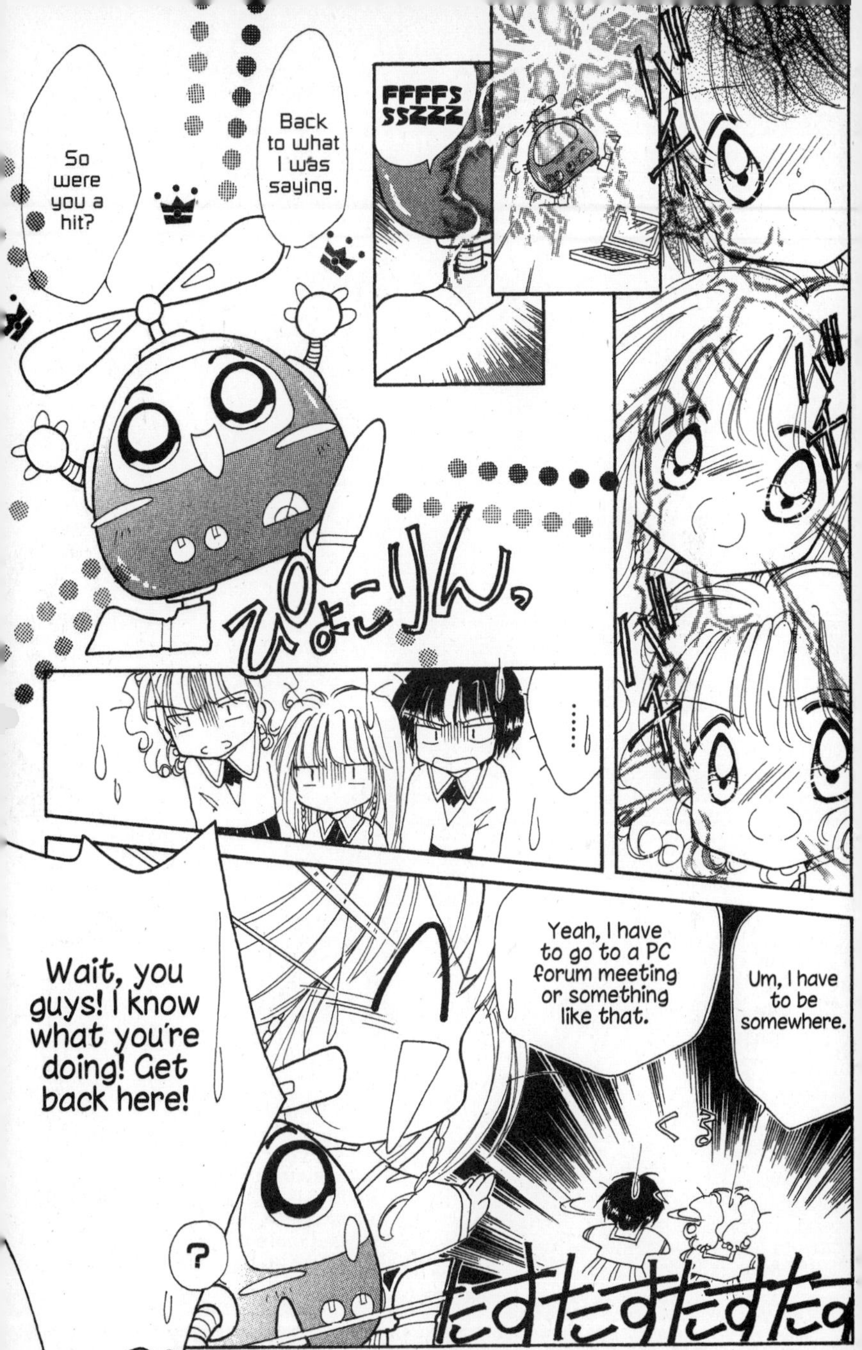
FFFFS SSZZZ
Back to what I was saying.
So were you a hit?
ぴょこりんっ
……
Um, I have to be somewhere.
Yeah, I have to go to a PC forum meeting or something like that.
くる
たすたすたすたっ
?
Wait, you guys! I know what you're doing! Get back here!

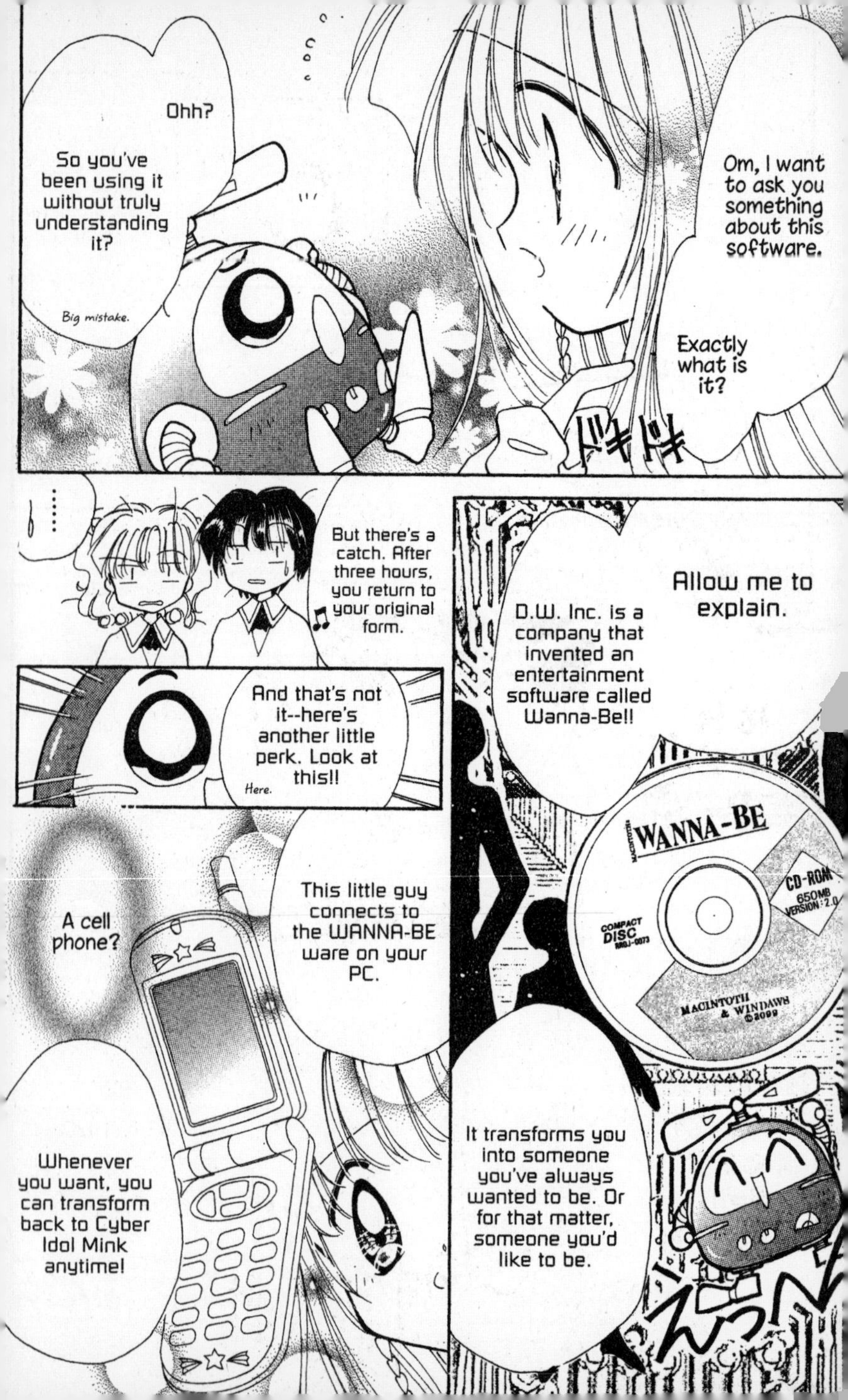
Om, I want to ask you something about this software.
Exactly what is it?
ドキドキ
Ohh?
So you've been using it without truly understanding it?
Big mistake.
Allow me to explain.
D.W. Inc. is a company that invented an entertainment software called Wanna-Be!!
WANNA-BE
MACINTOSH
CD-ROM
650MB
VERSION : 2.0
COMPACT DISC
MACINTOTH & WINDAWS
©2099
It transforms you into someone you've always wanted to be. Or for that matter, someone you'd like to be.
But there's a catch. After three hours, you return to your original form.
......
And that's not it--here's another little perk. Look at this!!
Here.
This little guy connects to the WANNA-BE ware on your PC.
A cell phone?
Whenever you want, you can transform back to Cyber Idol Mink anytime!

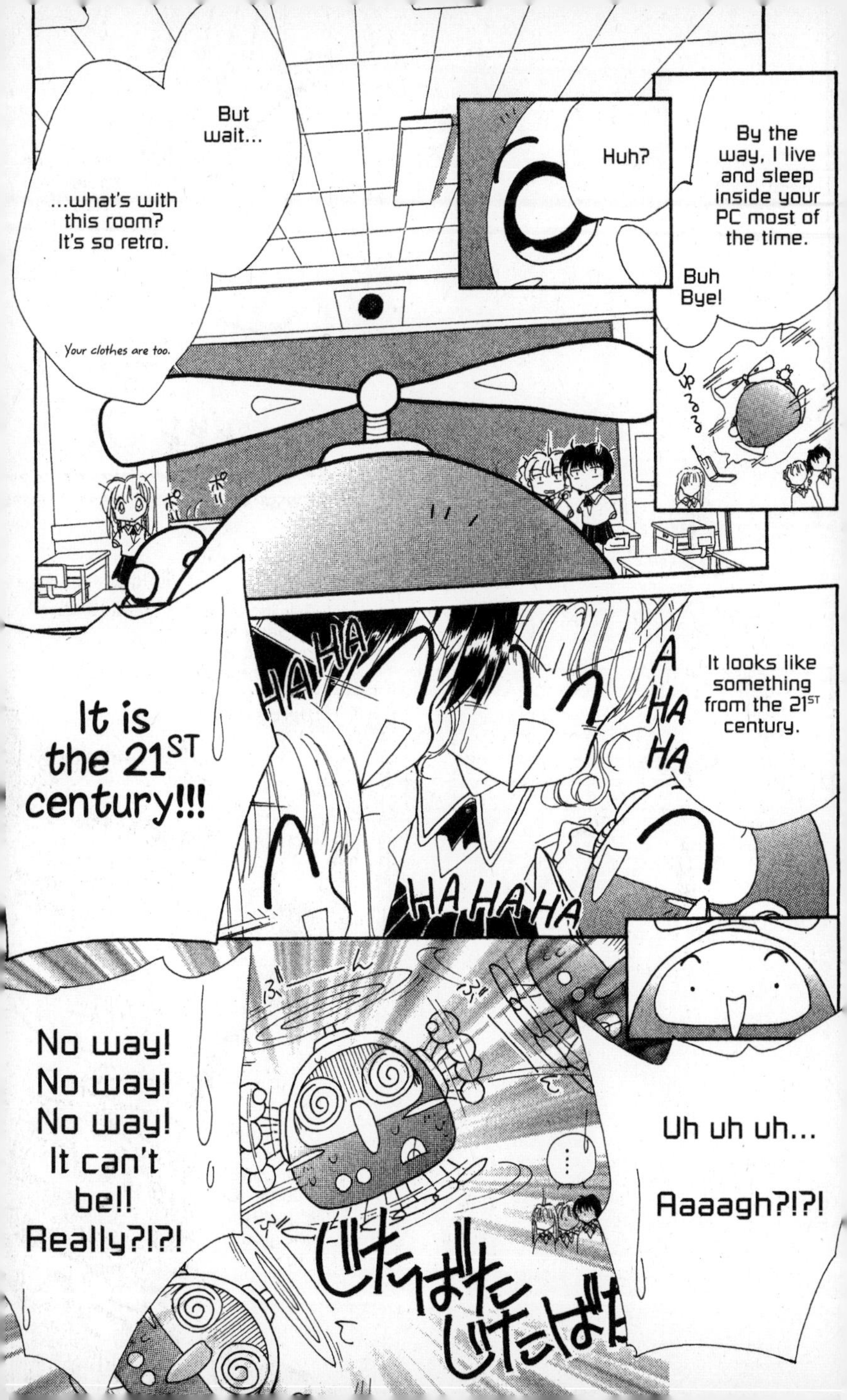
By the way, I live and sleep inside your PC most of the time.
Buh Bye!
Huh?
But wait...
...what's with this room? It's so retro.
Your clothes are too.
It looks like something from the 21ST century.
A HA HA HA
HA HA HA
HA HA HA HA
It is the 21ST century!!!
Uh uh uh...
Aaaagh?!?!
...
じたばた じたばた
No way! No way! No way! It can't be!! Really?!?!

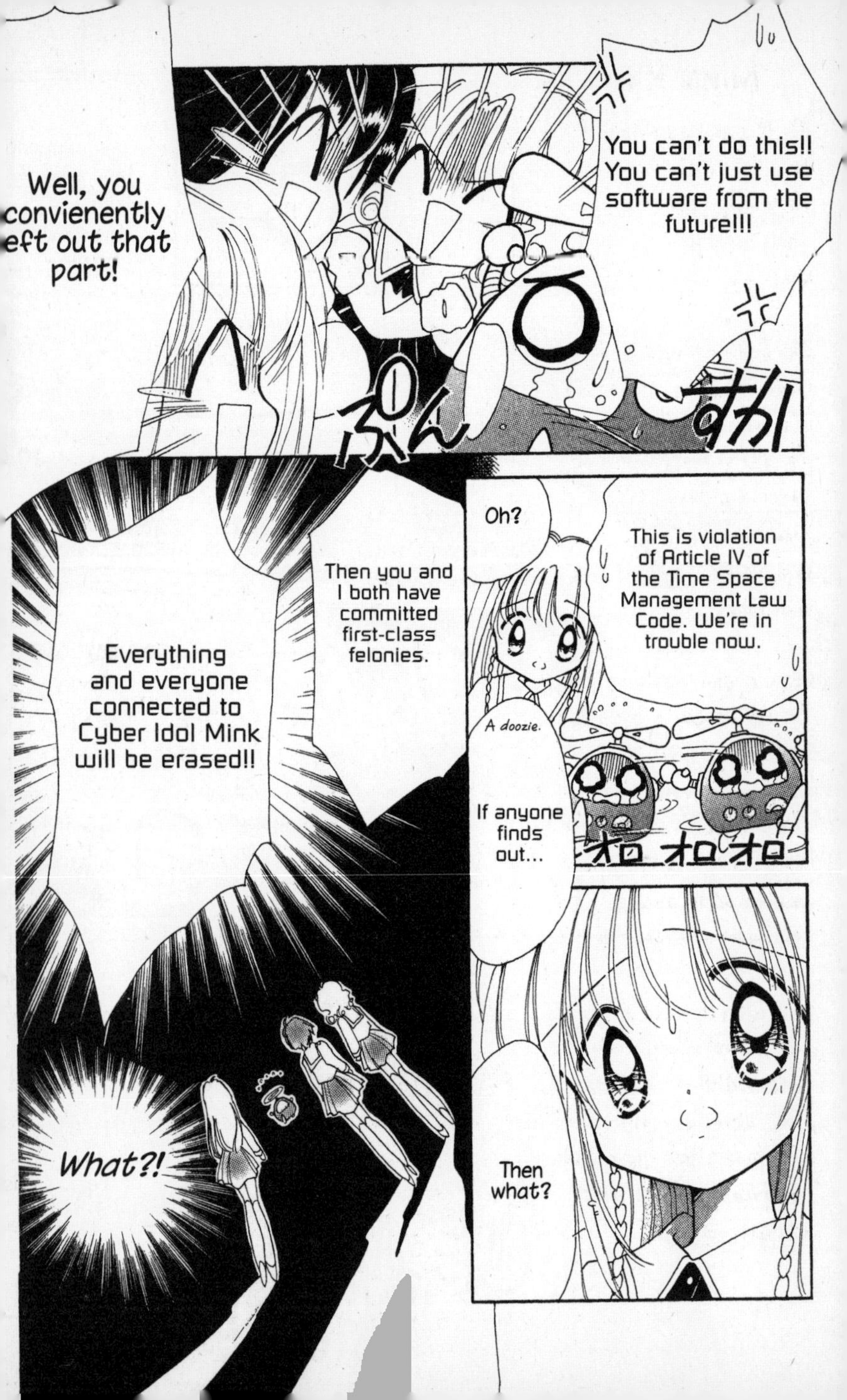
You can't do this!! You can't just use software from the future!!!
Well, you convienently eft out that part!
Oh?
This is violation of Article IV of the Time Space Management Law Code. We're in trouble now.
A doozie.
オロ オロオロ
If anyone finds out...
Then what?
Then you and I both have committed first-class felonies.
Everything and everyone connected to Cyber Idol Mink will be erased!!
What?!

Mink Rap!!

Q: Please tell me if there's another way to draw the frame lines besides using a Rotring pen?

A: I don't use that type of pen. I just use a marker. As long as it's a fine-tip pen, that's all that matters♡. Oh, I use a pigma graphic 1.0 marker.

Q: Do you have to be in Tokyo to be a manga artist?

A: No, you can work from anywhere. While you're still young though, you should be with your parents since you can always move to Tokyo when you're older. But then again, I'm from Tokyo so I'm not the right person to give you the best advice, sorry!

-Megumi

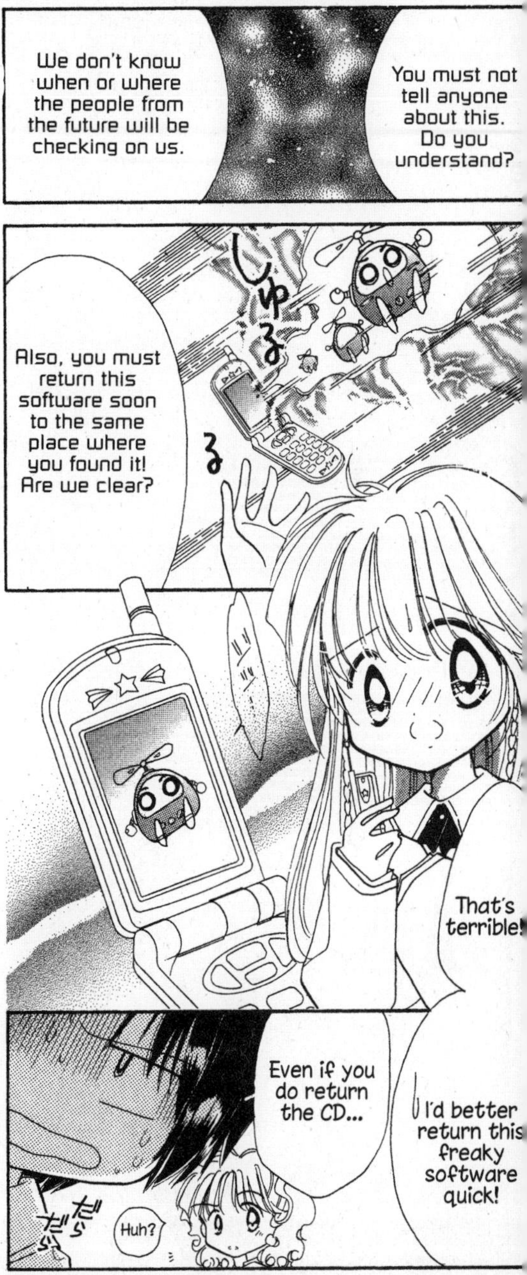
You must not tell anyone about this. Do you understand?
We don't know when or where the people from the future will be checking on us.
Also, you must return this software soon to the same place where you found it! Are we clear?
That's terrible!
I'd better return this freaky software quick!
Even if you do return the CD...
Huh?

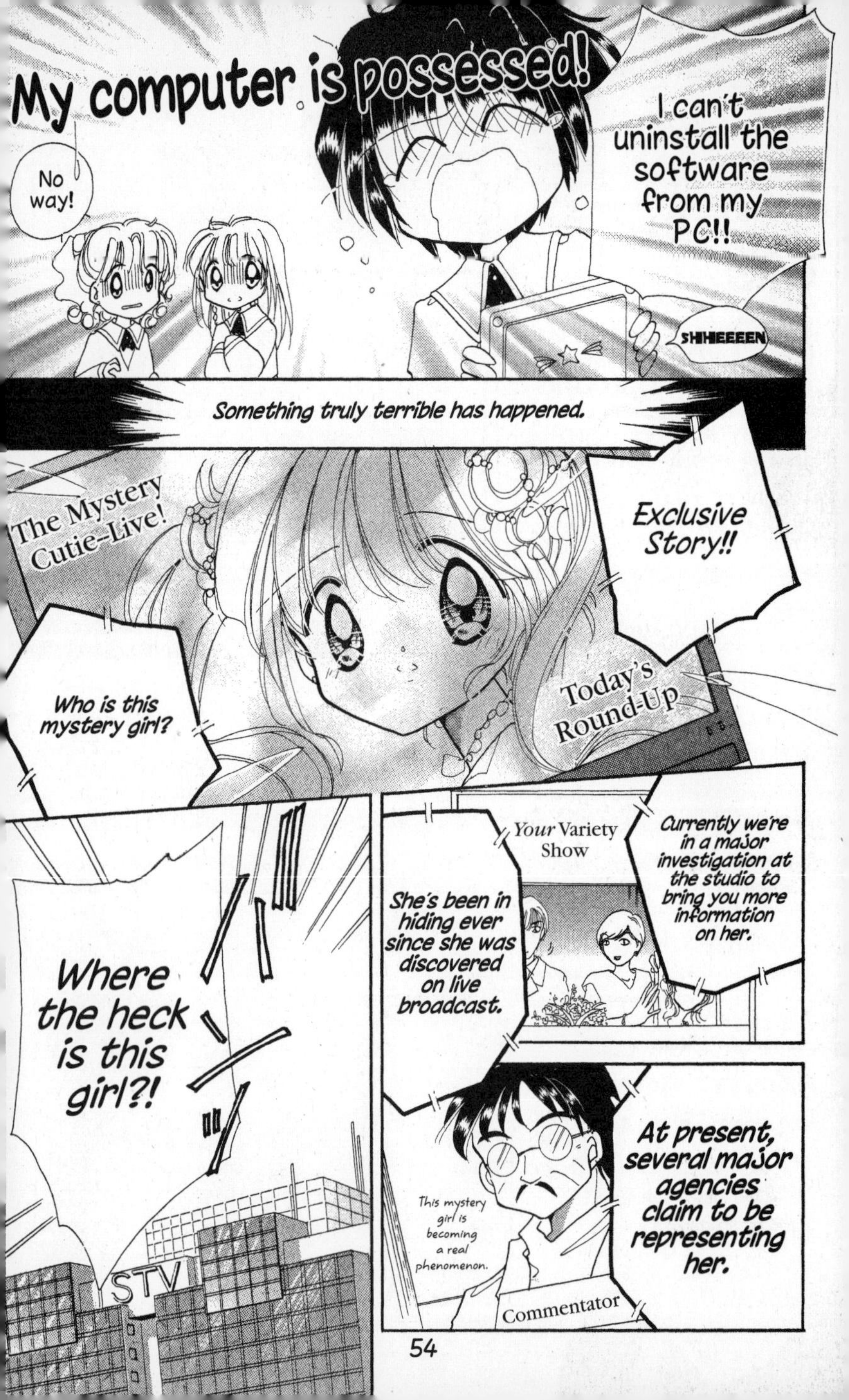
My computer is possessed!
I can't uninstall the software from my PC!!
SHIHEEEEN
No way!
Something truly terrible has happened.
Exclusive Story!!
The Mystery Cutie-Live!
Today's Round-Up
Who is this mystery girl?
Your Variety Show
Currently we're in a major investigation at the studio to bring you more information on her.
She's been in hiding ever since she was discovered on live broadcast.
At present, several major agencies claim to be representing her.
This mystery girl is becoming a real phenomenon.
Commentator
Where the heck is this girl?!
STV

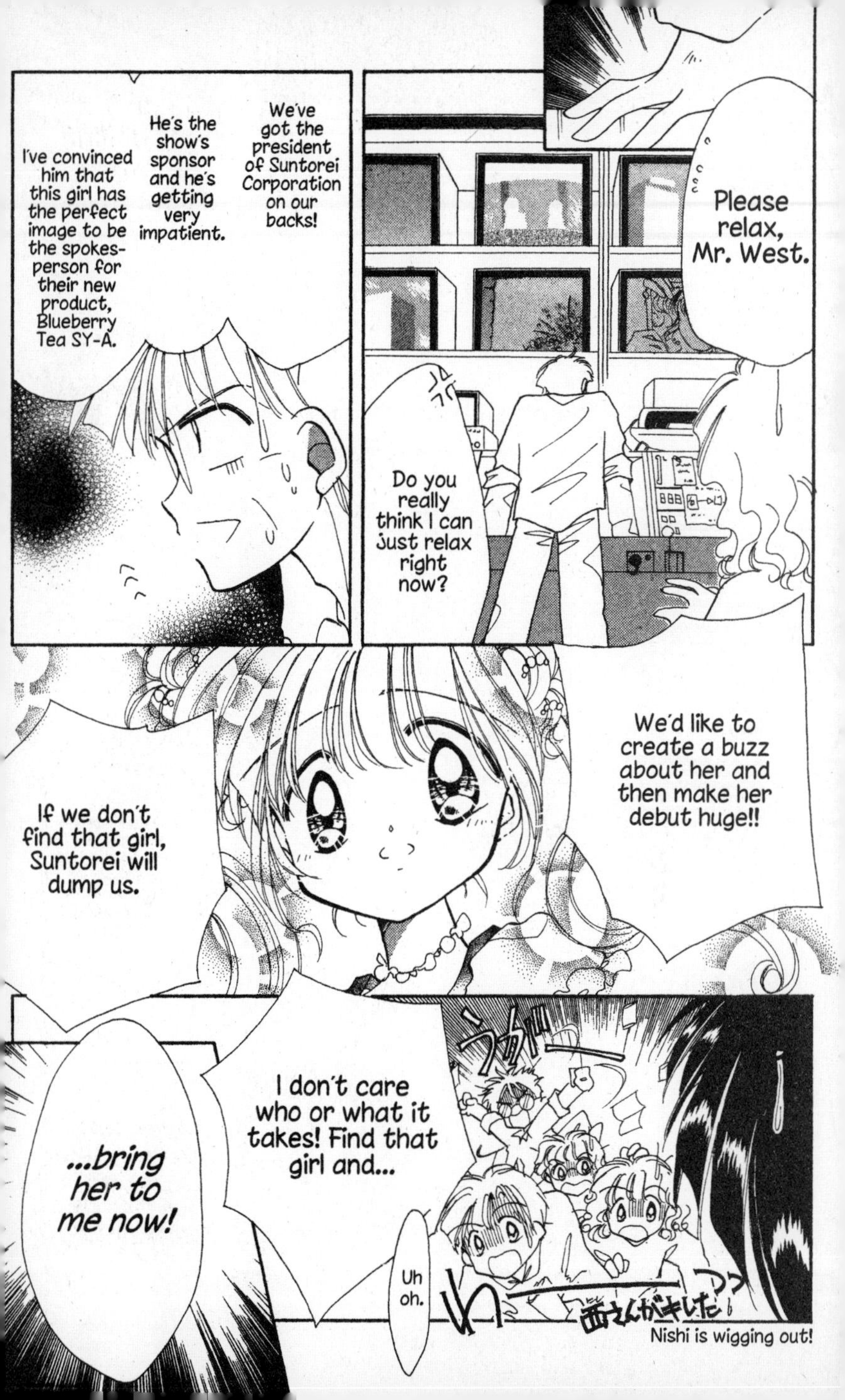
Please relax, Mr. West.
Do you really think I can just relax right now?
We've got the president of Suntorei Corporation on our backs!
He's the show's sponsor and he's getting very impatient.
I've convinced him that this girl has the perfect image to be the spokes-person for their new product, Blueberry Tea SY-A.
We'd like to create a buzz about her and then make her debut huge!!
If we don't find that girl, Suntorei will dump us.
うがー
I don't care who or what it takes! Find that girl and...
...bring her to me now!
Uh oh.
わー
西さんがキレた
Nishi is wigging out!

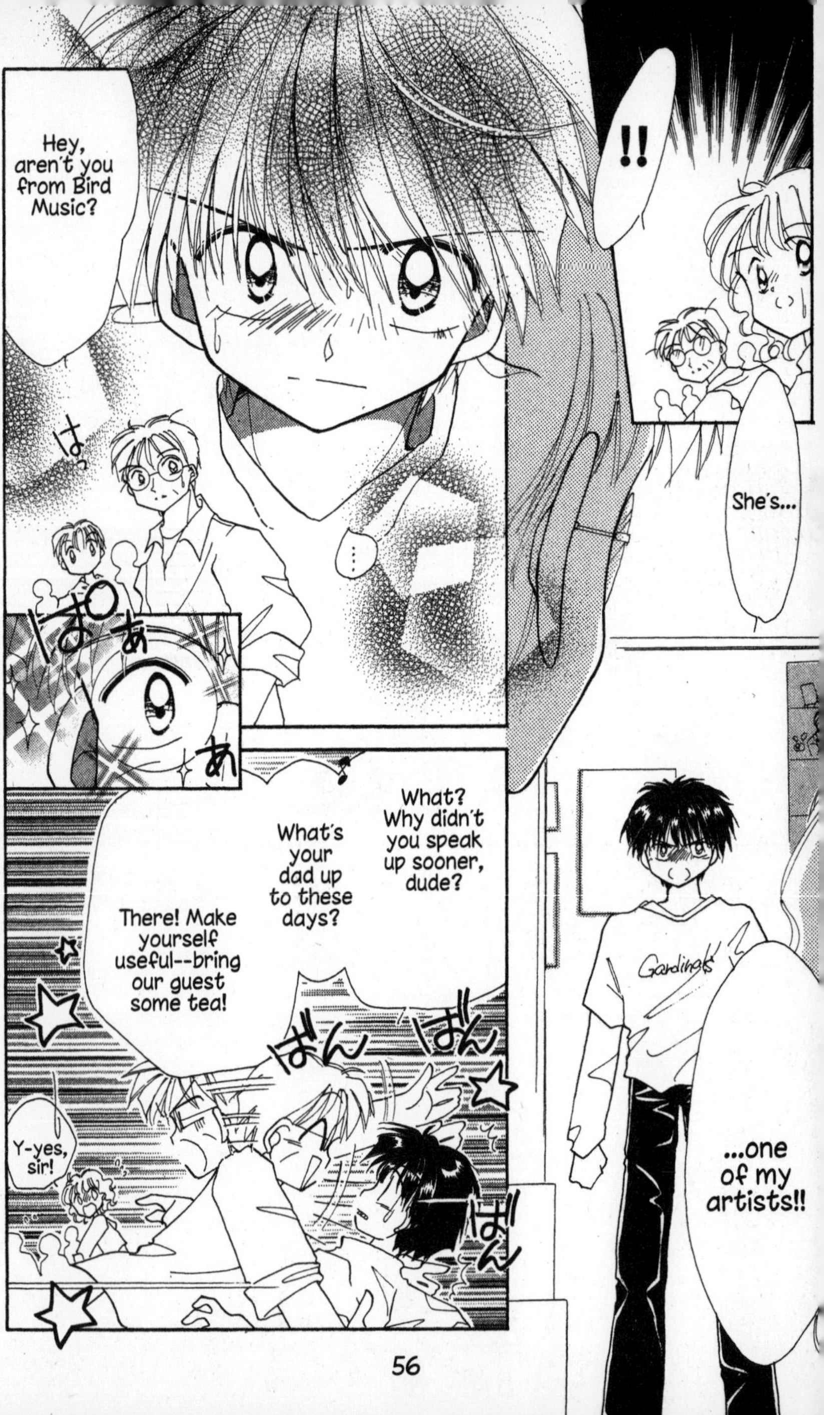

!!
She's...
...one of my artists!!
Hey, aren't you from Bird Music?
はっ
...
ぽあ
あ
What? Why didn't you speak up sooner, dude?
What's your dad up to these days?
There! Make yourself useful--bring our guest some tea!
ばん
ばん
ばん
Y-yes, sir!

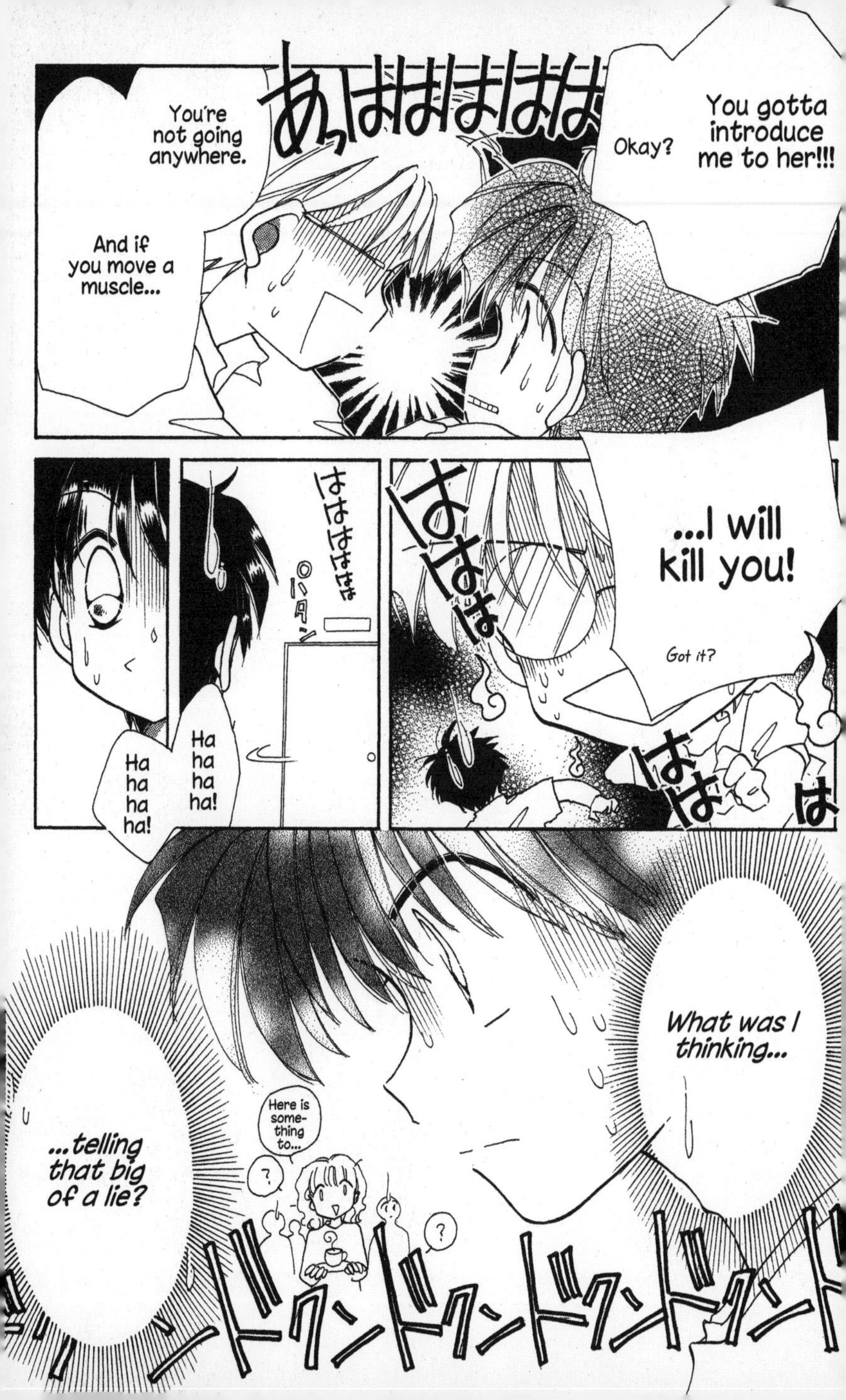
You gotta introduce me to her!!!
Okay?
あっはははははは
You're not going anywhere.
And if you move a muscle...
...I will kill you!
Got it?
ははは
はは
は
はははははは
パタン
Ha ha ha ha!
Ha ha ha ha!
What was I thinking...
...telling that big of a lie?
Here is some-thing to...
?
?
ドクンドクンドクンドクン

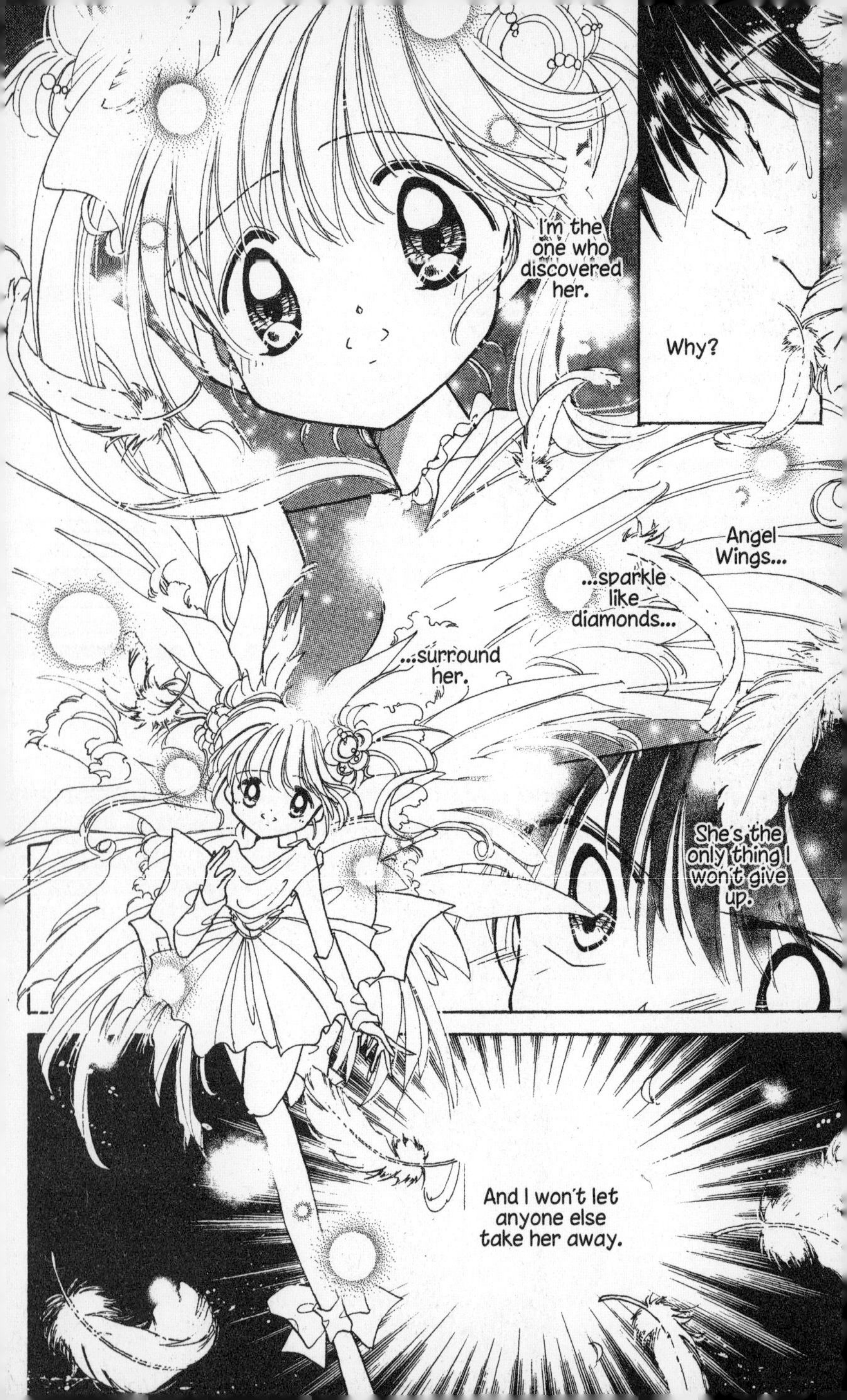
Why?
I'm the one who discovered her.
Angel Wings...
...sparkle like diamonds...
...surround her.
She's the only thing I won't give up.
And I won't let anyone else take her away.

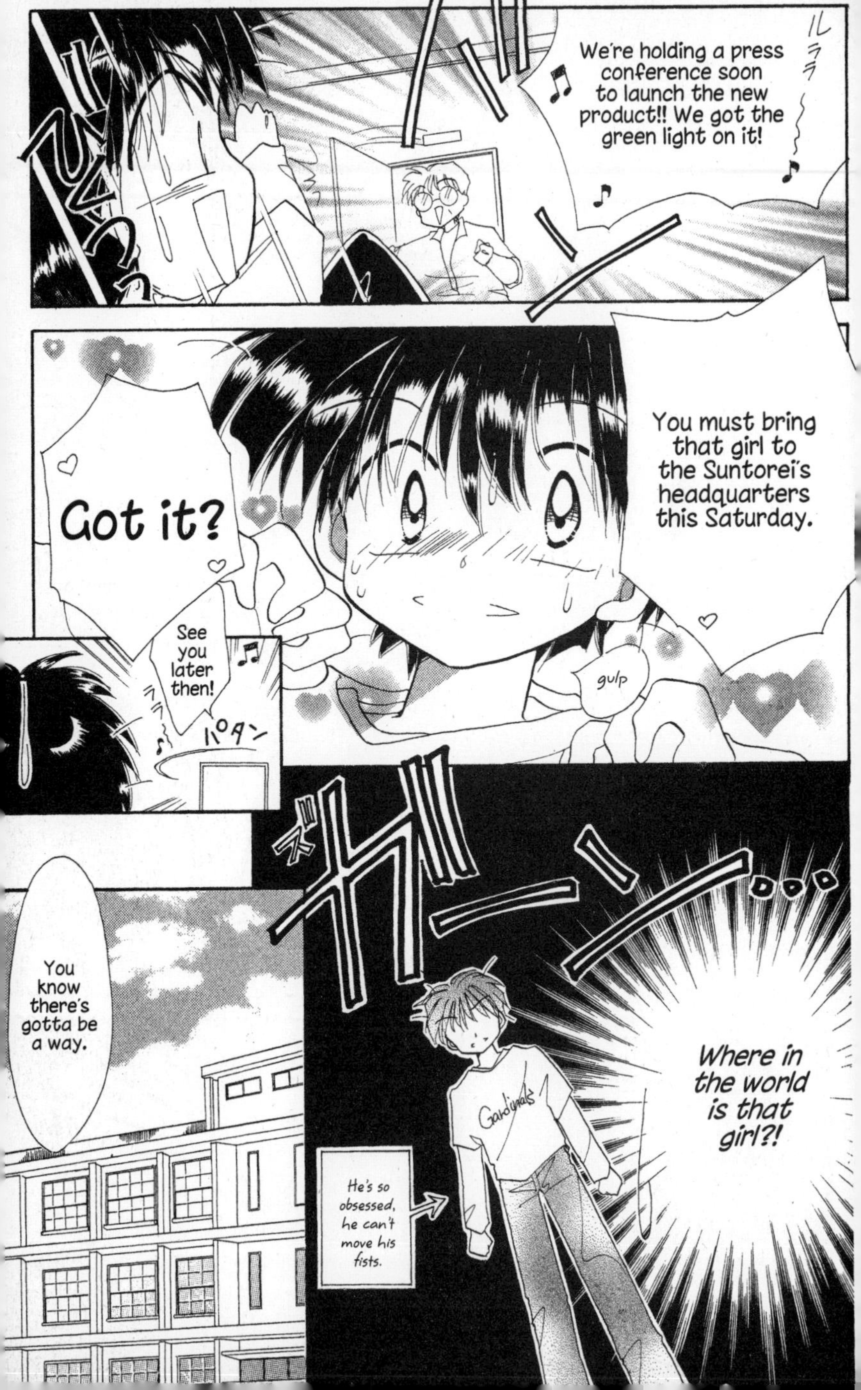
ルララ
We're holding a press conference soon to launch the new product!! We got the green light on it!
You must bring that girl to the Suntorei's headquarters this Saturday.
Got it?
gulp
See you later then!
ララ
パタン
ズガーン...
Where in the world is that girl?!
He's so obsessed, he can't move his fists.
You know there's gotta be a way.

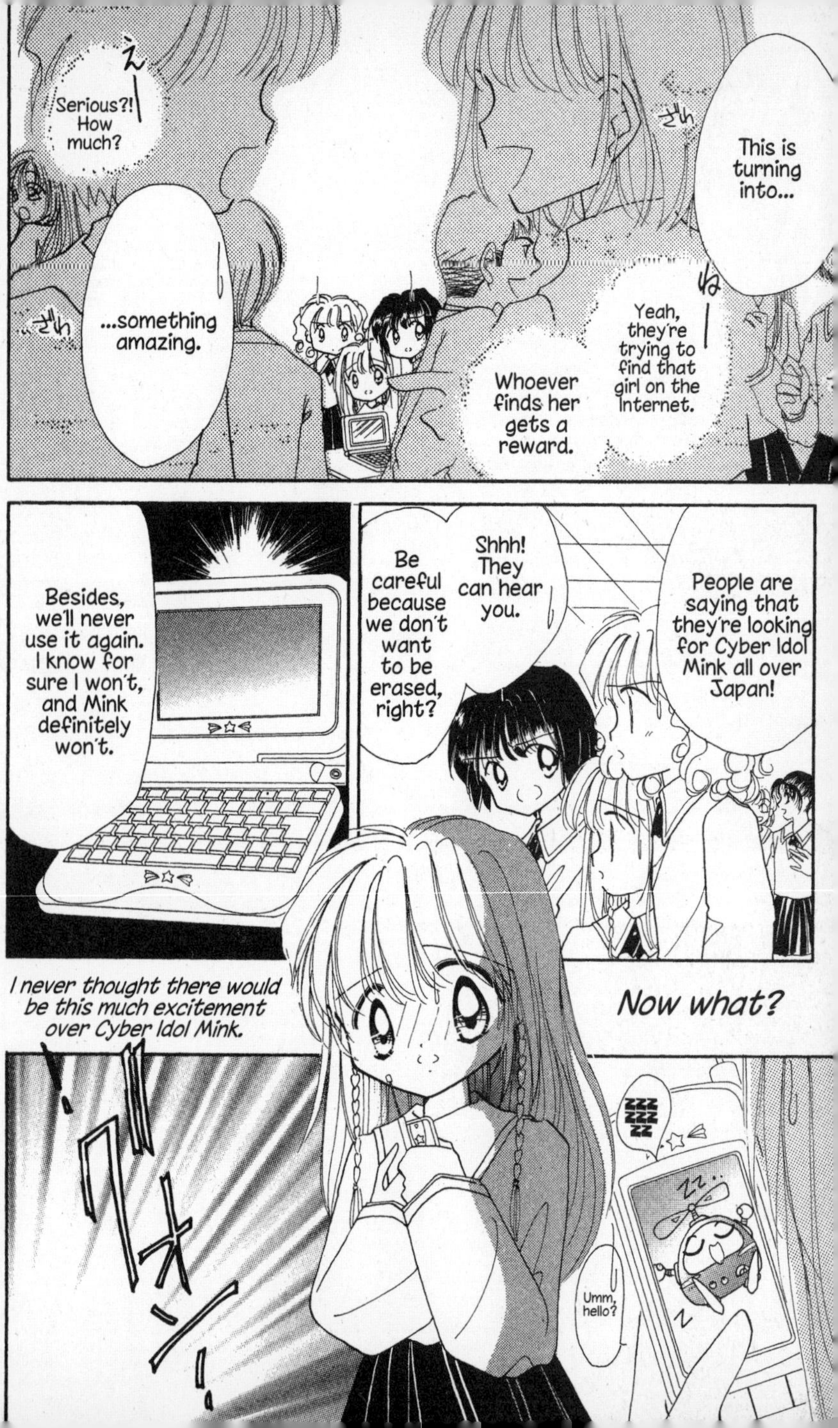
This is turning into...
Yeah, they're trying to find that girl on the Internet.
Whoever finds her gets a reward.
Serious?! How much?
...something amazing.
People are saying that they're looking for Cyber Idol Mink all over Japan!
Shhh! They can hear you.
Be careful because we don't want to be erased, right?
Besides, we'll never use it again. I know for sure I won't, and Mink definitely won't.
Now what?
ZZZ ZZZ ZZ
Umm, hello?
I never thought there would be this much excitement over Cyber Idol Mink.

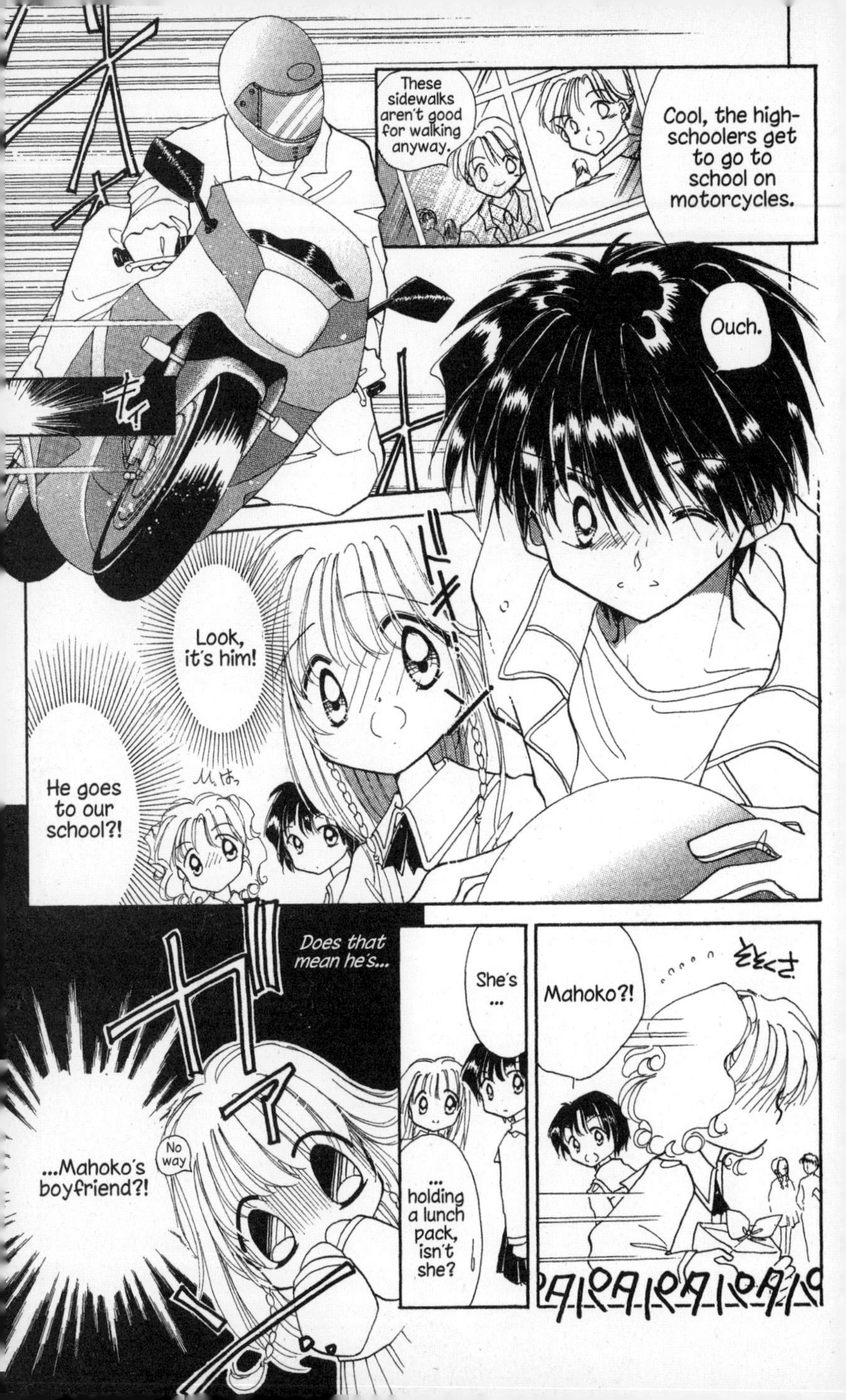
Cool, the high-schoolers get to go to school on motorcycles.
These sidewalks aren't good for walking anyway.
Ouch.
Look, it's him!
He goes to our school?!
Mahoko?!
She's ...
... holding a lunch pack, isn't she?
Does that mean he's...
No way
...Mahoko's boyfriend?!

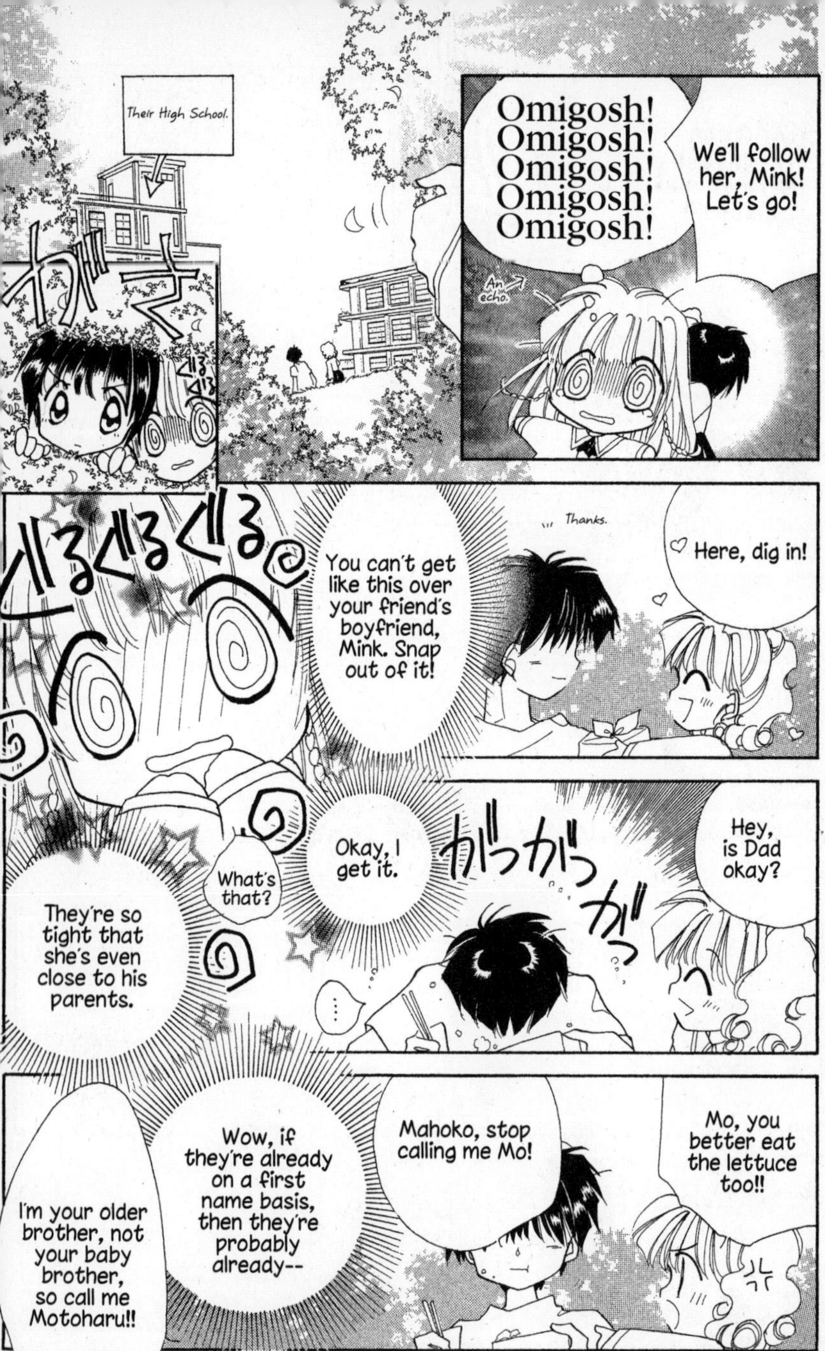
We'll follow her, Mink! Let's go!
Omigosh! Omigosh! Omigosh! Omigosh! Omigosh!
An echo.
Their High School.
Here, dig in!
Thanks.
You can't get like this over your friend's boyfriend, Mink. Snap out of it!
ぐるぐるぐる
Hey, is Dad okay?
がつがつ
Okay, I get it.
What's that?
They're so tight that she's even close to his parents.
...
Mo, you better eat the lettuce too!!
Mahoko, stop calling me Mo!
Wow, if they're already on a first name basis, then they're probably already--
I'm your older brother, not your baby brother, so call me Motoharu!!

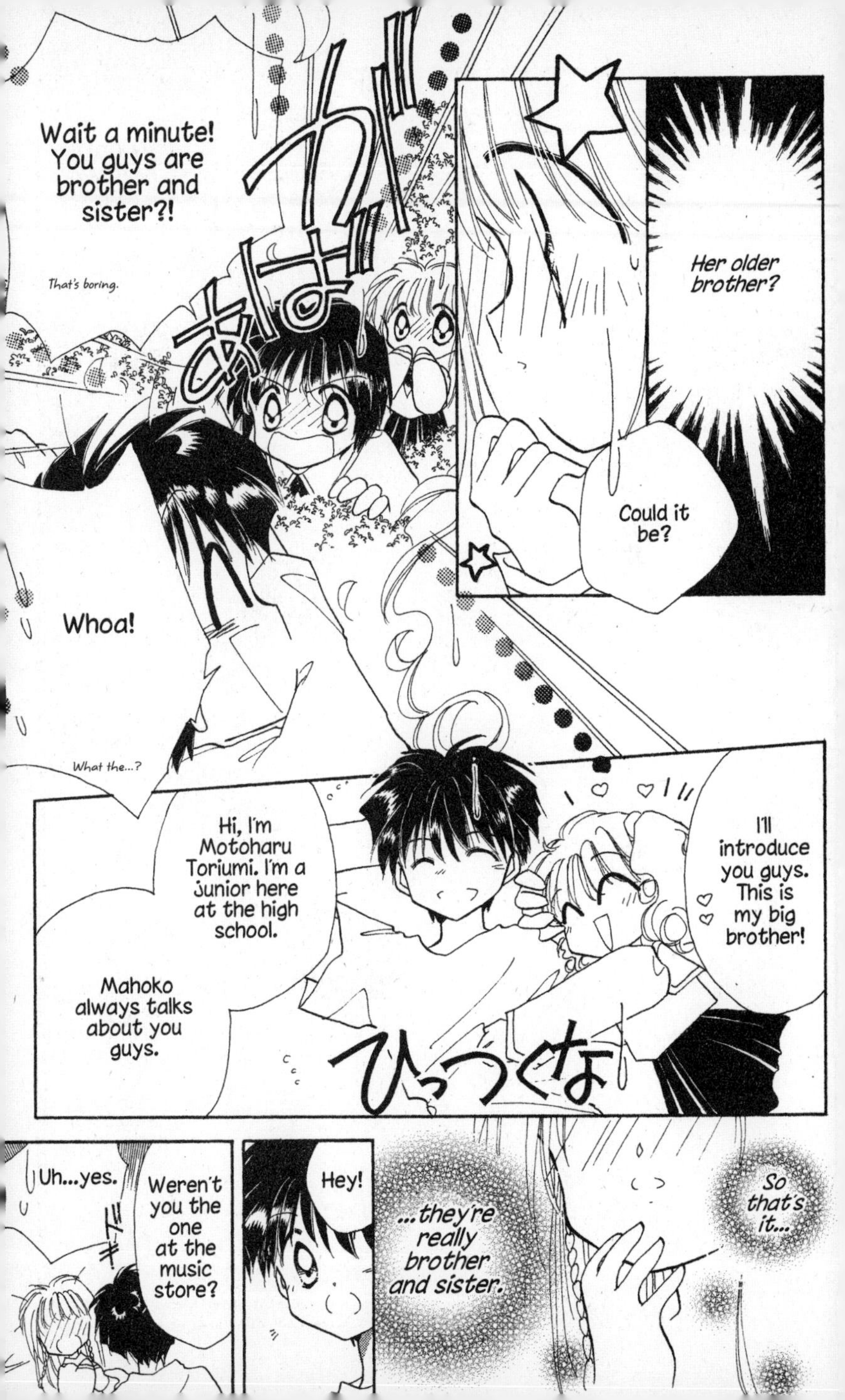

Her older brother?
Could it be?
Wait a minute! You guys are brother and sister?!
That's boring.
Whoa!
What the...?
I'll introduce you guys. This is my big brother!
Hi, I'm Motoharu Toriumi. I'm a junior here at the high school.
Mahoko always talks about you guys.
ひっつくな
So that's it...
...they're really brother and sister.
Hey!
Weren't you the one at the music store?
Uh...yes.

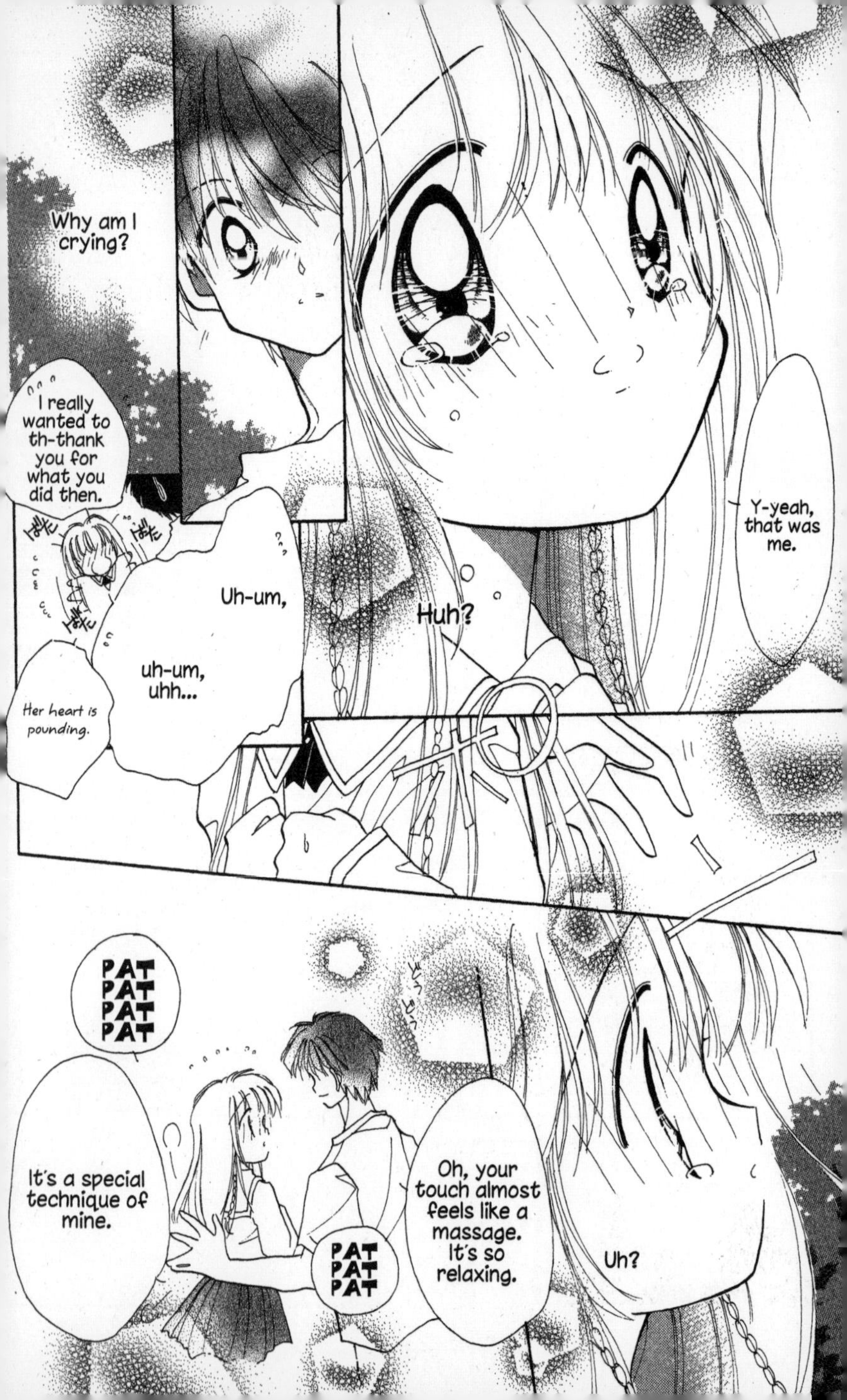

Y-yeah, that was me.
Huh?
Why am I crying?
I really wanted to th-thank you for what you did then.
Uh-um,
uh-um, uhh...
Her heart is pounding.
Uh?
Oh, your touch almost feels like a massage. It's so relaxing.
PAT PAT PAT
PAT PAT PAT PAT
It's a special technique of mine.

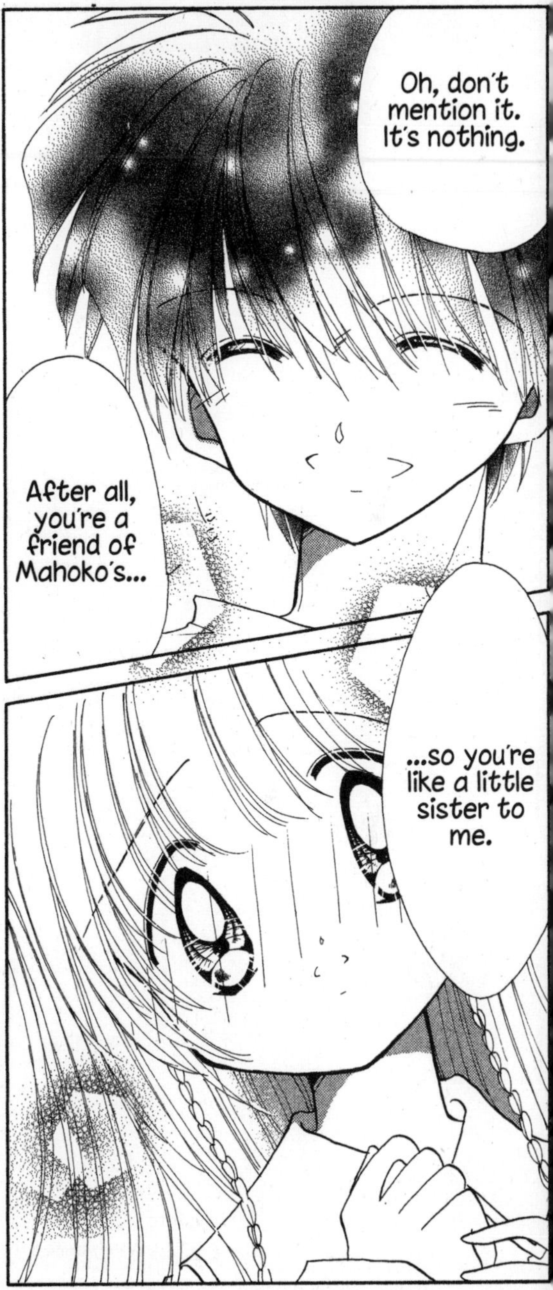
Oh, don't mention it. It's nothing.
After all, you're a friend of Mahoko's...
...so you're like a little sister to me.

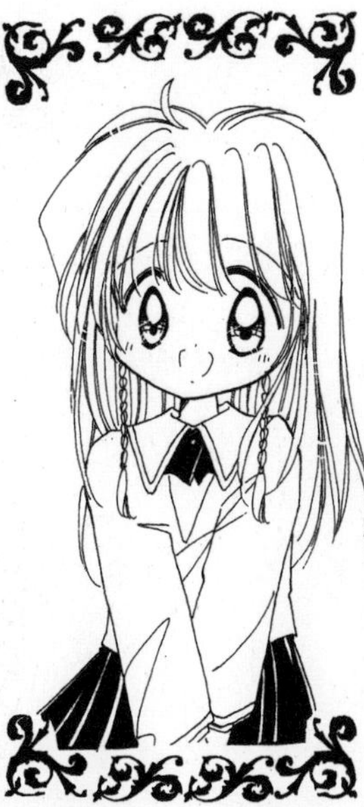

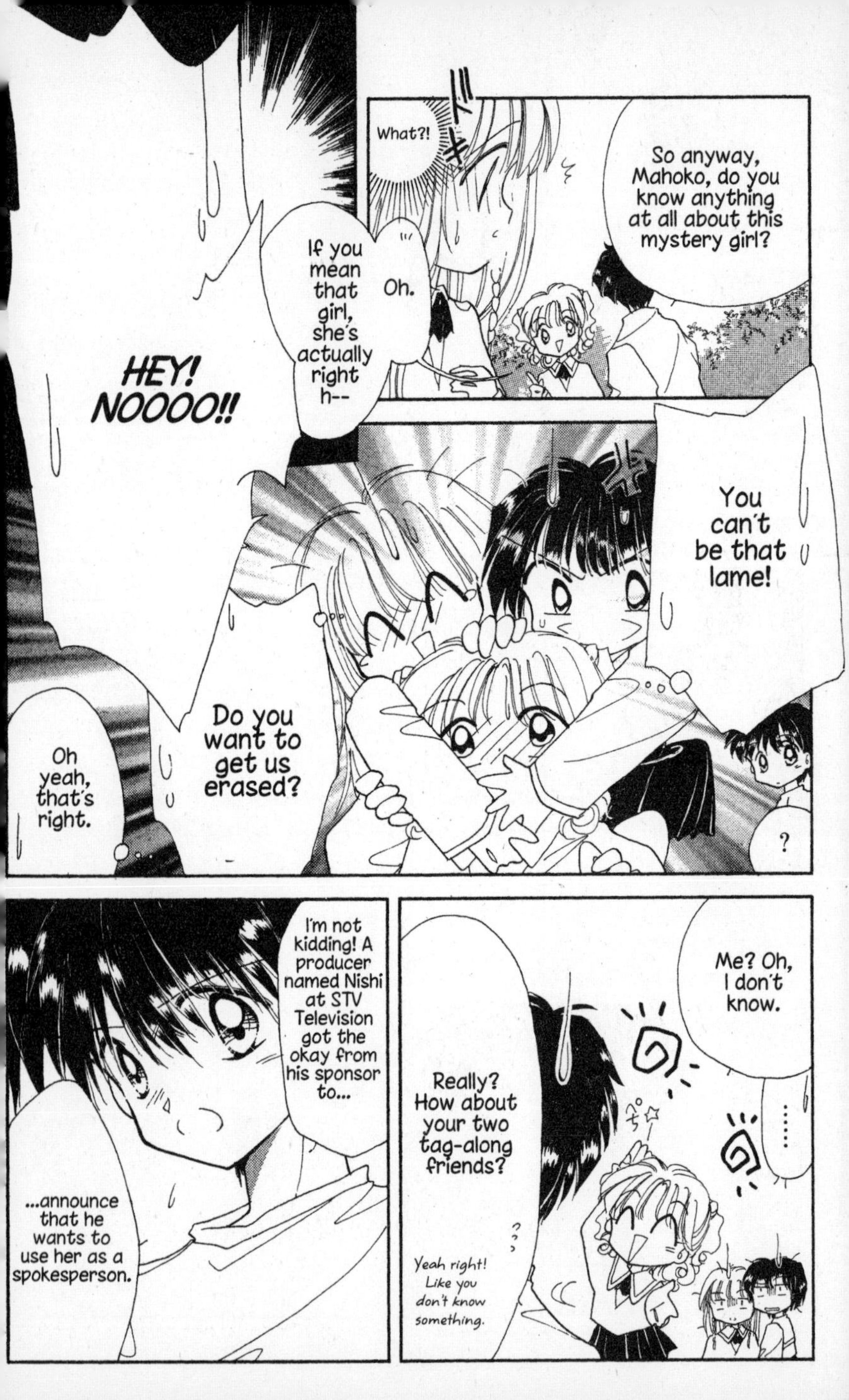

So anyway, Mahoko, do you know anything at all about this mystery girl?
What?!
Oh.
If you mean that girl, she's actually right h--
You can't be that lame!
?
HEY! NOOOO!!
Do you want to get us erased?
Oh yeah, that's right.
Me? Oh, I don't know.
......
Really? How about your two tag-along friends?
Yeah right! Like you don't know something.
I'm not kidding! A producer named Nishi at STV Television got the okay from his sponsor to...
...announce that he wants to use her as a spokesperson.

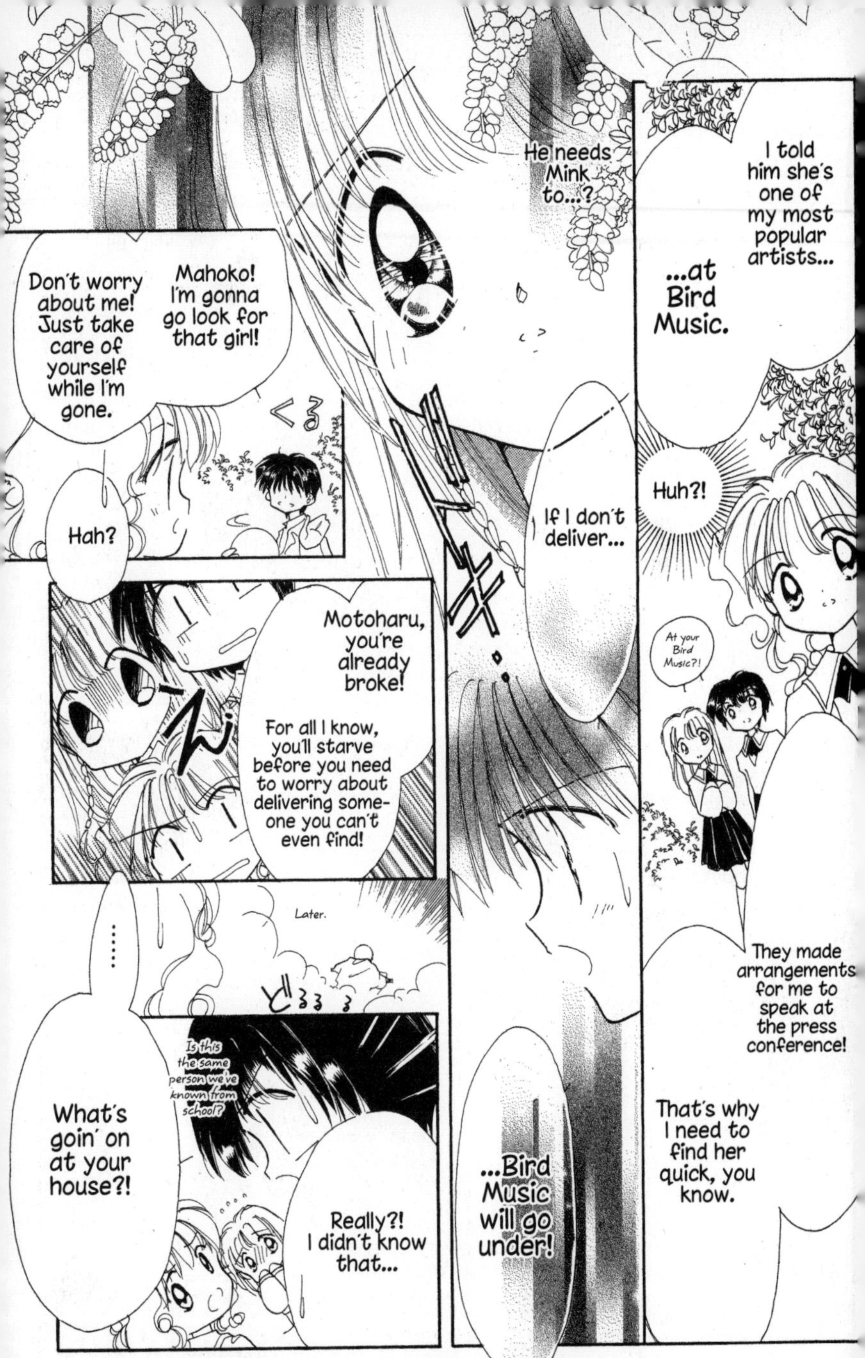
I told him she's one of my most popular artists...
...at Bird Music.
Huh?!
At your Bird Music?!
They made arrangements for me to speak at the press conference!
That's why I need to find her quick, you know.
He needs Mink to...?
If I don't deliver...
...Bird Music will go under!
Mahoko! I'm gonna go look for that girl!
Don't worry about me! Just take care of yourself while I'm gone.
Hah?
Motoharu, you're already broke!
For all I know, you'll starve before you need to worry about delivering someone you can't even find!
Later.
......
Really?! I didn't know that...
Is this the same person we've known from school?
What's goin' on at your house?!

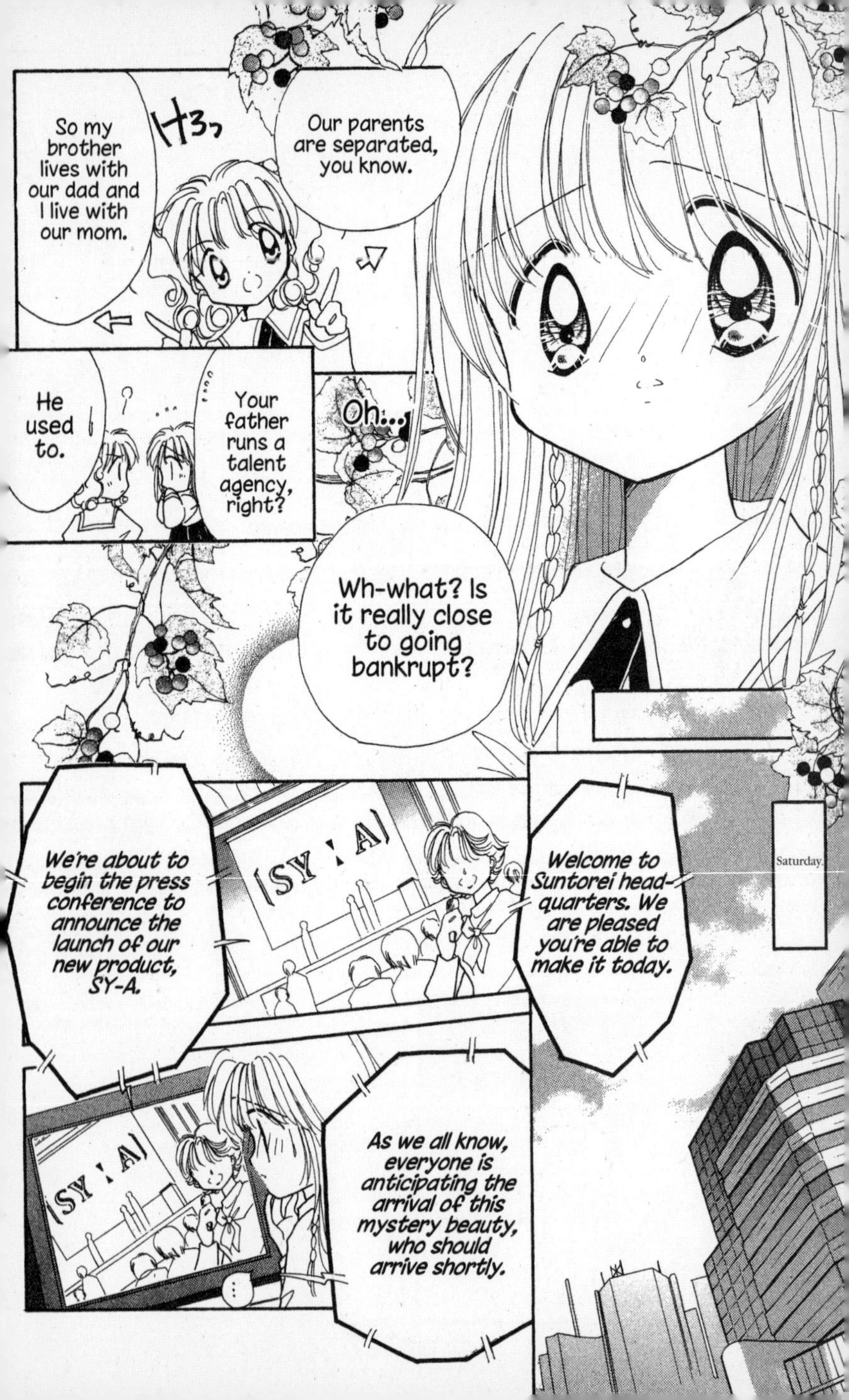
Our parents are separated, you know.
So my brother lives with our dad and I live with our mom.
Your father runs a talent agency, right?
He used to.
Oh...
Wh-what? Is it really close to going bankrupt?
Saturday.
Welcome to Suntorei head-quarters. We are pleased you're able to make it today.
We're about to begin the press conference to announce the launch of our new product, SY-A.
SY A
As we all know, everyone is anticipating the arrival of this mystery beauty, who should arrive shortly.
SY A
...

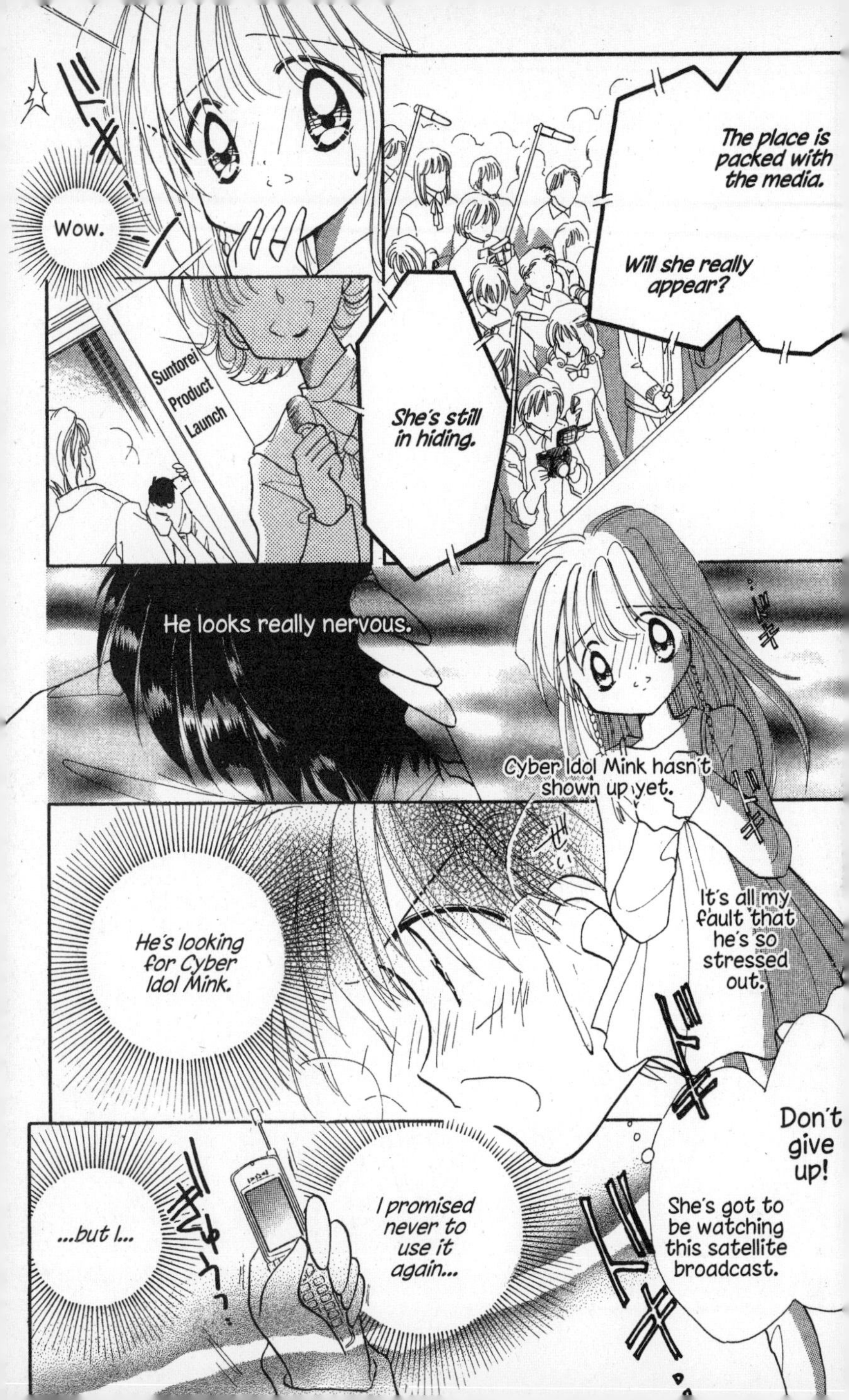
The place is packed with the media.
Will she really appear?
Wow.
Suntorei Product Launch
She's still in hiding.
He looks really nervous.
Cyber Idol Mink hasn't shown up yet.
It's all my fault that he's so stressed out.
He's looking for Cyber Idol Mink.
Don't give up!
She's got to be watching this satellite broadcast.
I promised never to use it again...
...but I...

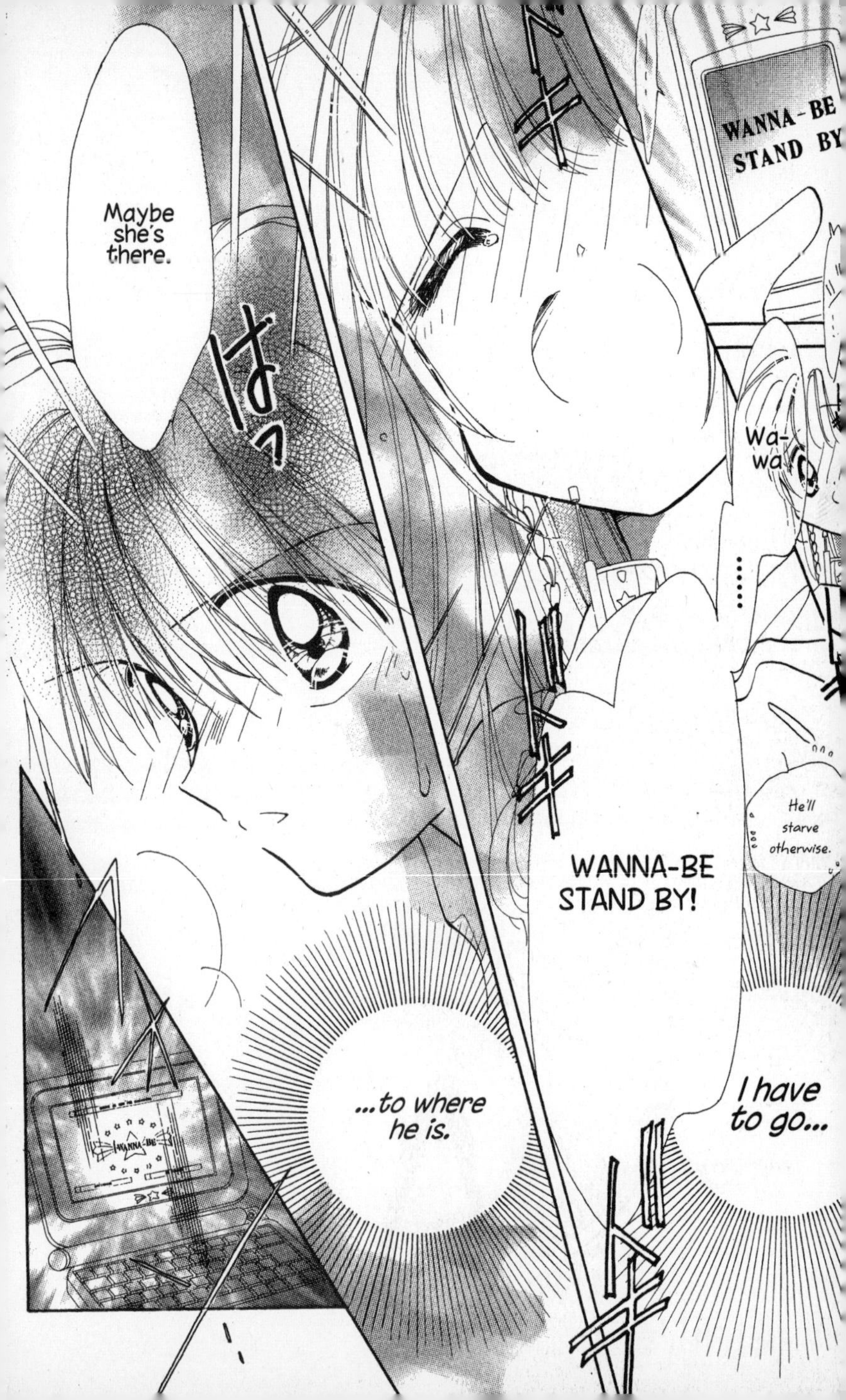
WANNA-BE STAND BY
Wa-wa
......
He'll starve otherwise.
WANNA-BE STAND BY!
I have to go...
Maybe she's there.
はっ
...to where he is.

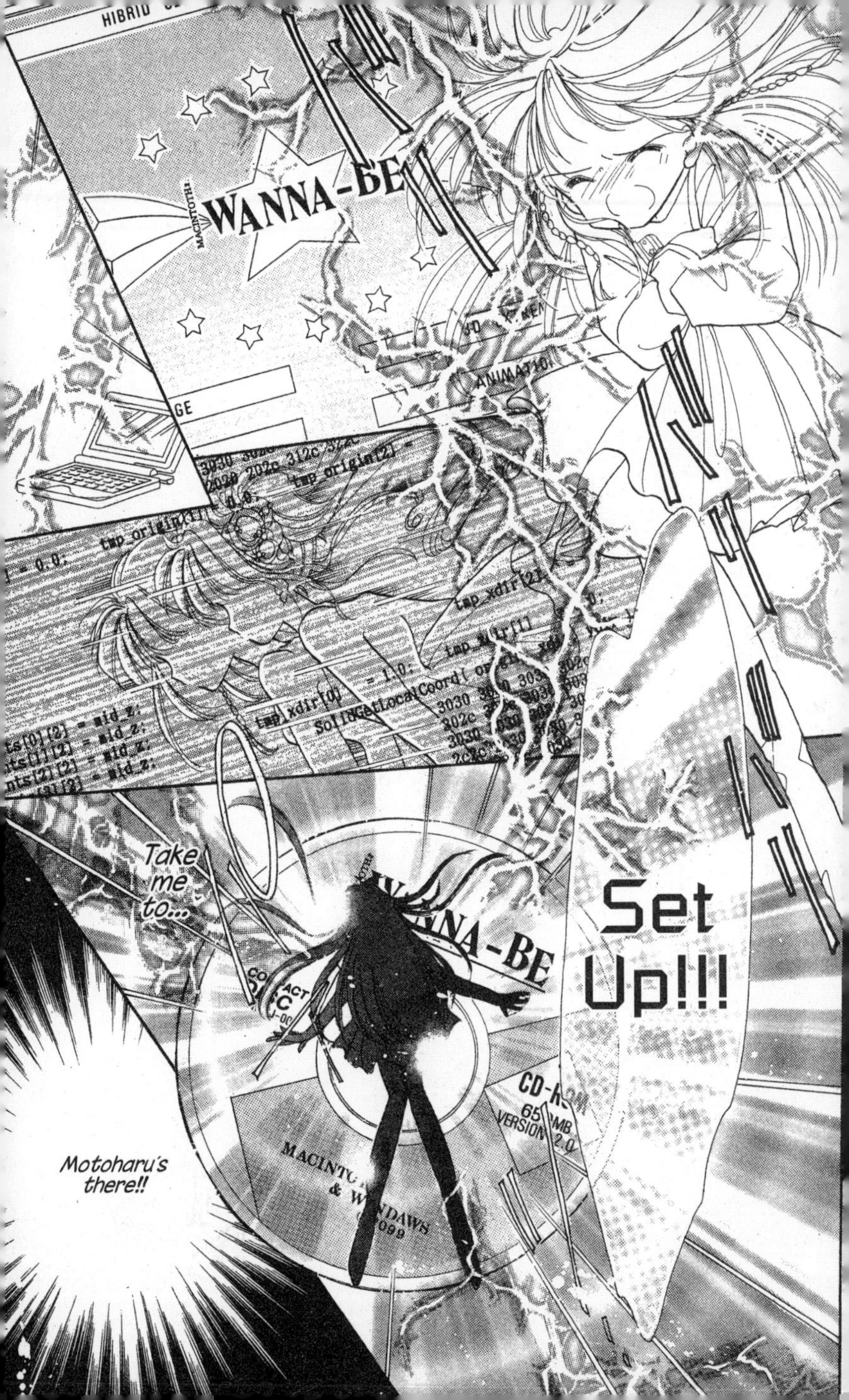
Set Up!!!
Take me to...
Motoharu's there!!

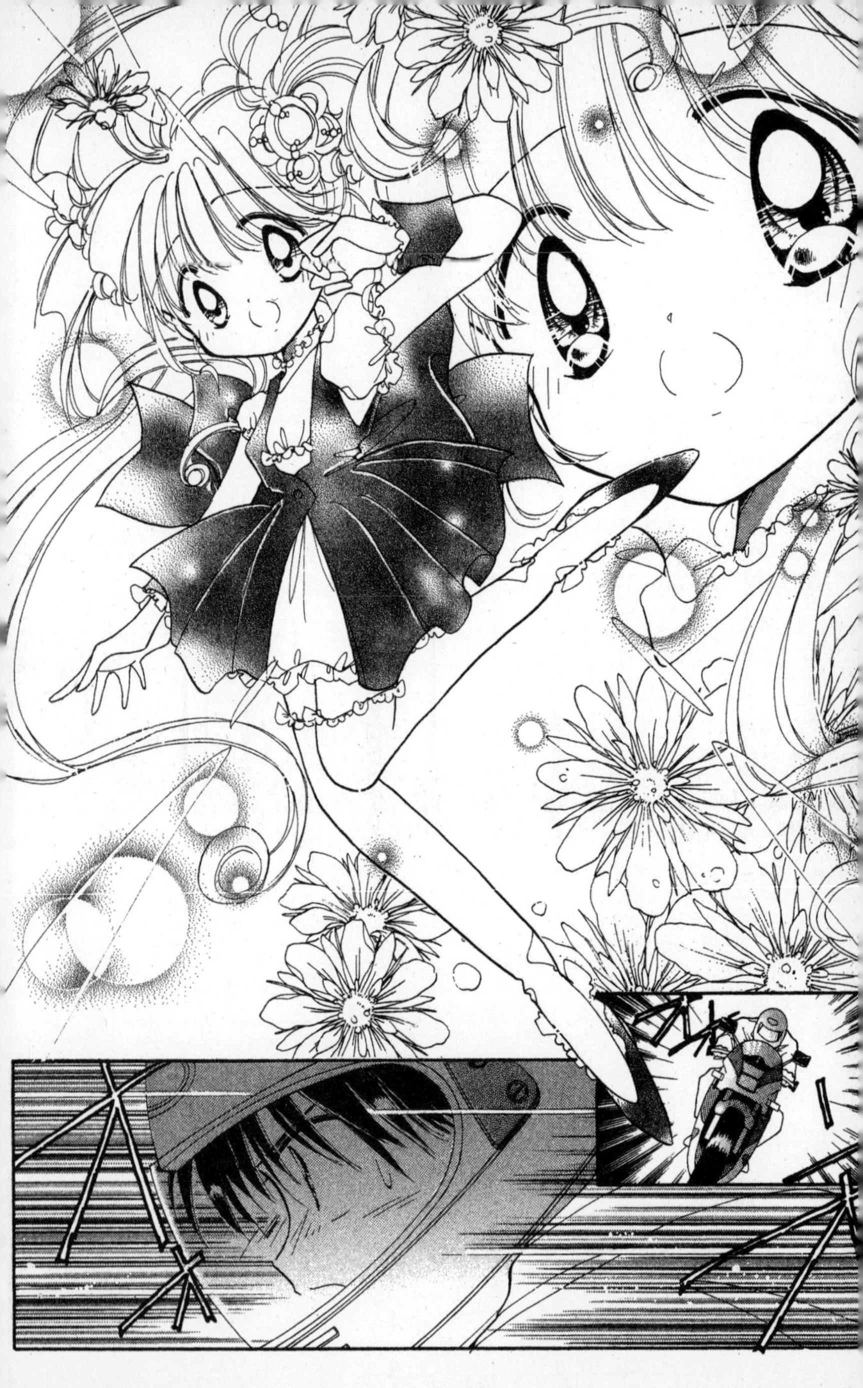

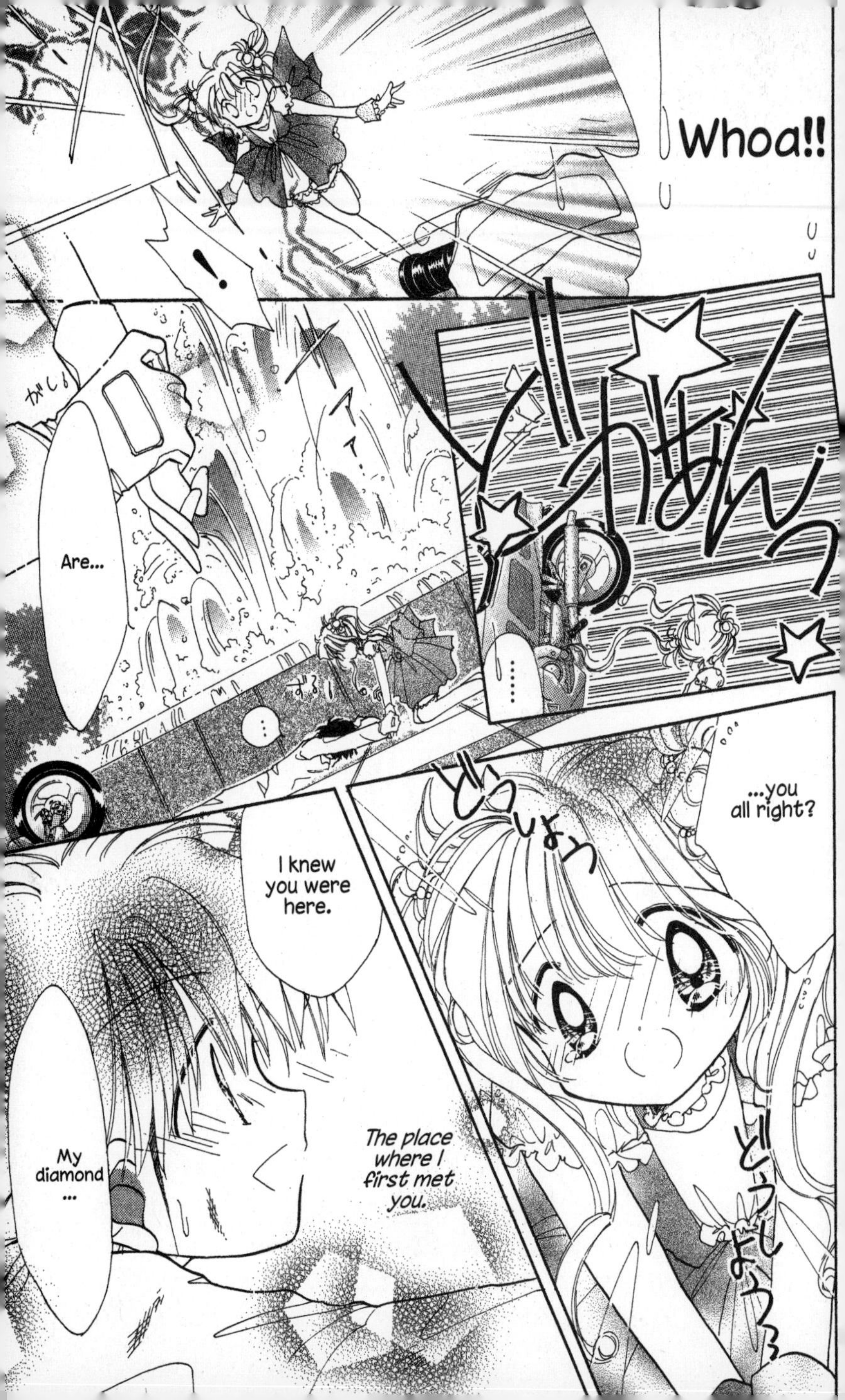
Whoa!!
!
......
Are...
...
...you all right?
I knew you were here.
The place where I first met you.
My diamond ...

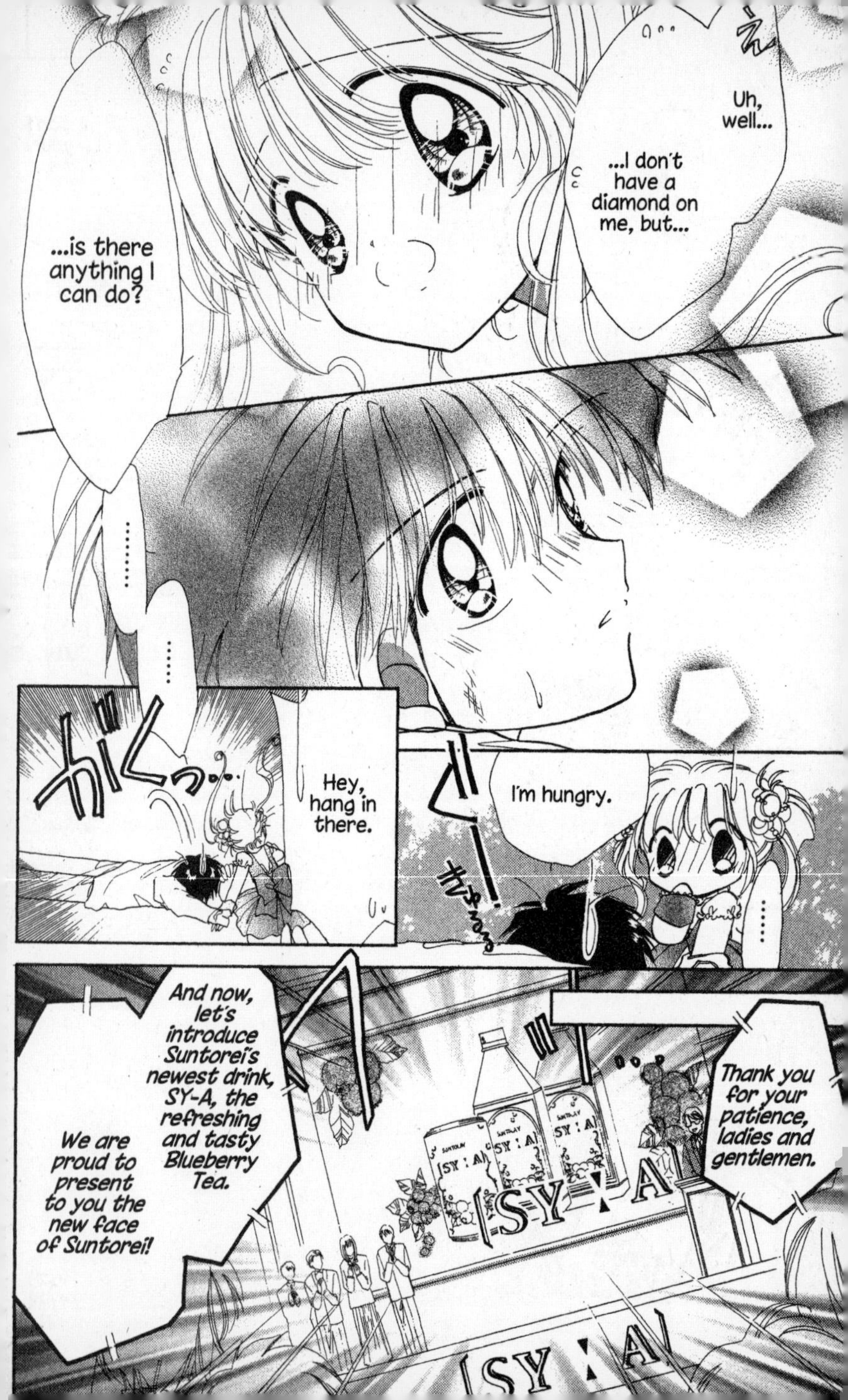
え
Uh, well...
...I don't have a diamond on me, but...
...is there anything I can do?
......
......
......
I'm hungry.
がくっ...
Hey, hang in there.
Thank you for your patience, ladies and gentlemen.
And now, let's introduce Suntorei's newest drink, SY-A, the refreshing and tasty Blueberry Tea.
We are proud to present to you the new face of Suntorei!
SY : A

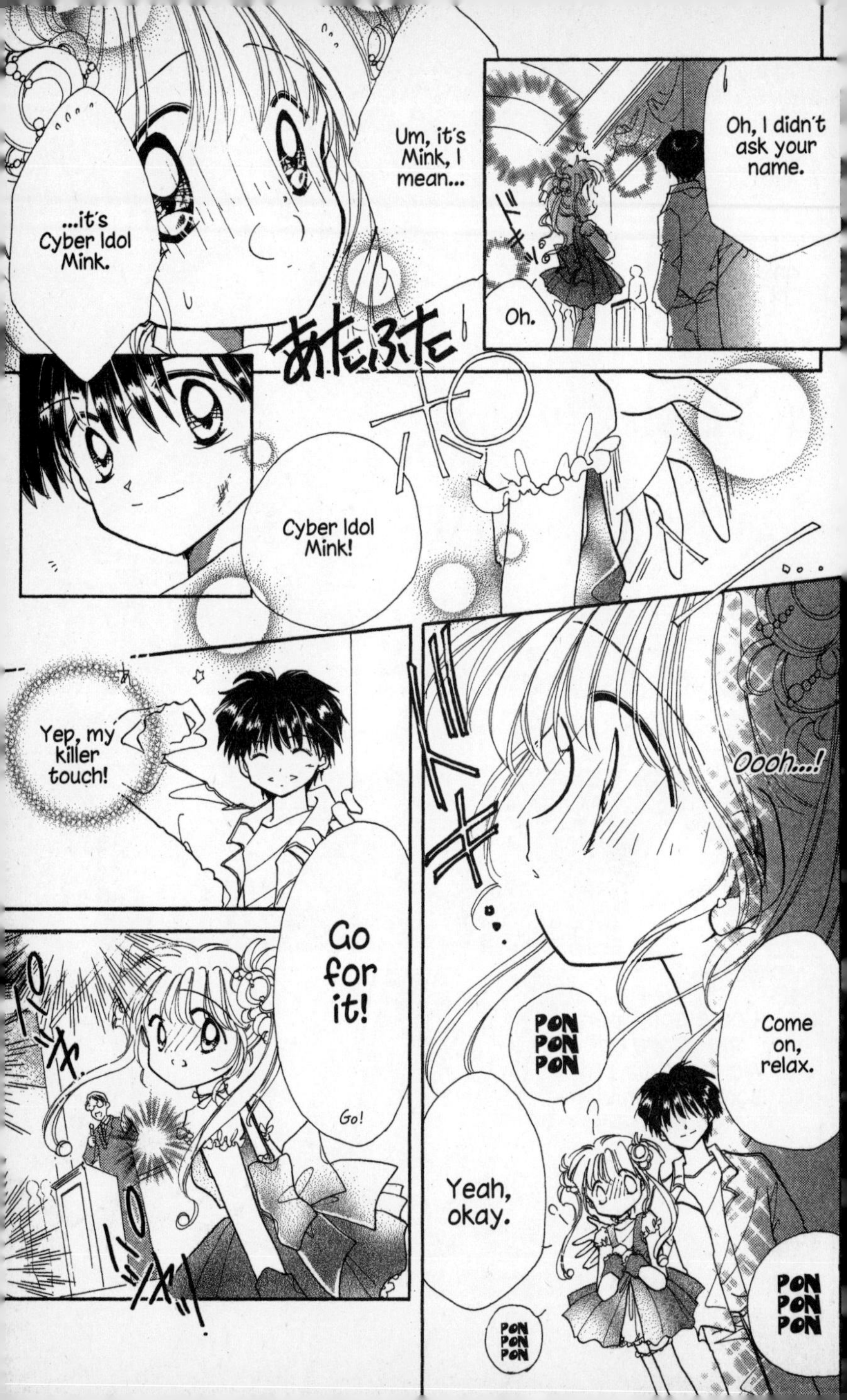
Oh, I didn't ask your name.
Oh.
Um, it's Mink, I mean...
...it's Cyber Idol Mink.
あたふた
Cyber Idol Mink!
Oooh...!
Come on, relax.
PON PON PON
Yeah, okay.
PON PON PON
PON PON PON
Yep, my killer touch!
Go for it!
Go!

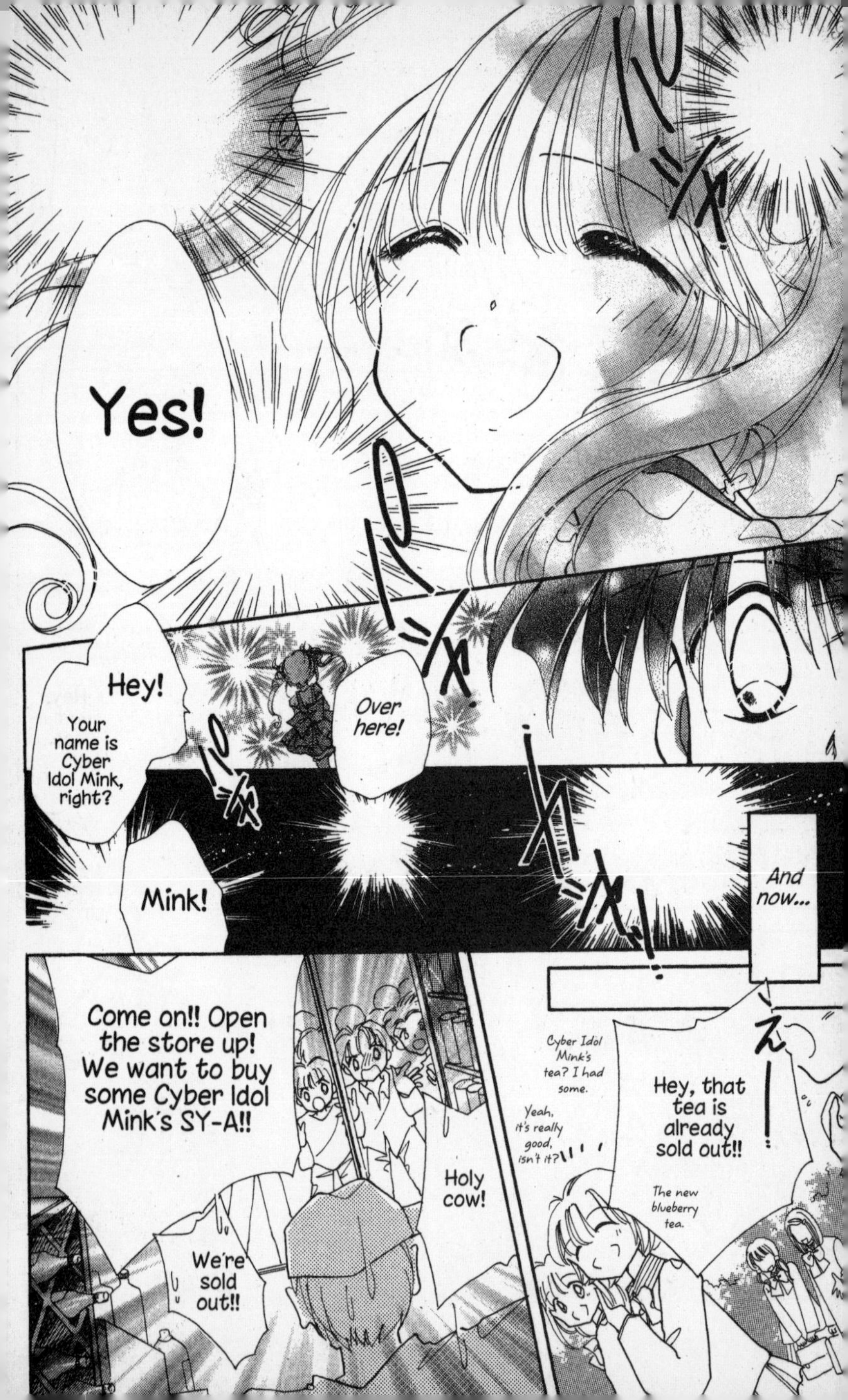
Yes!
Over here!
Hey!
Your name is Cyber Idol Mink, right?
And now...
Mink!
Hey, that tea is already sold out!!
Cyber Idol Mink's tea? I had some.
Yeah, it's really good, isn't it?
The new blueberry tea.
Holy cow!
Come on!! Open the store up! We want to buy some Cyber Idol Mink's SY-A!!
We're sold out!!

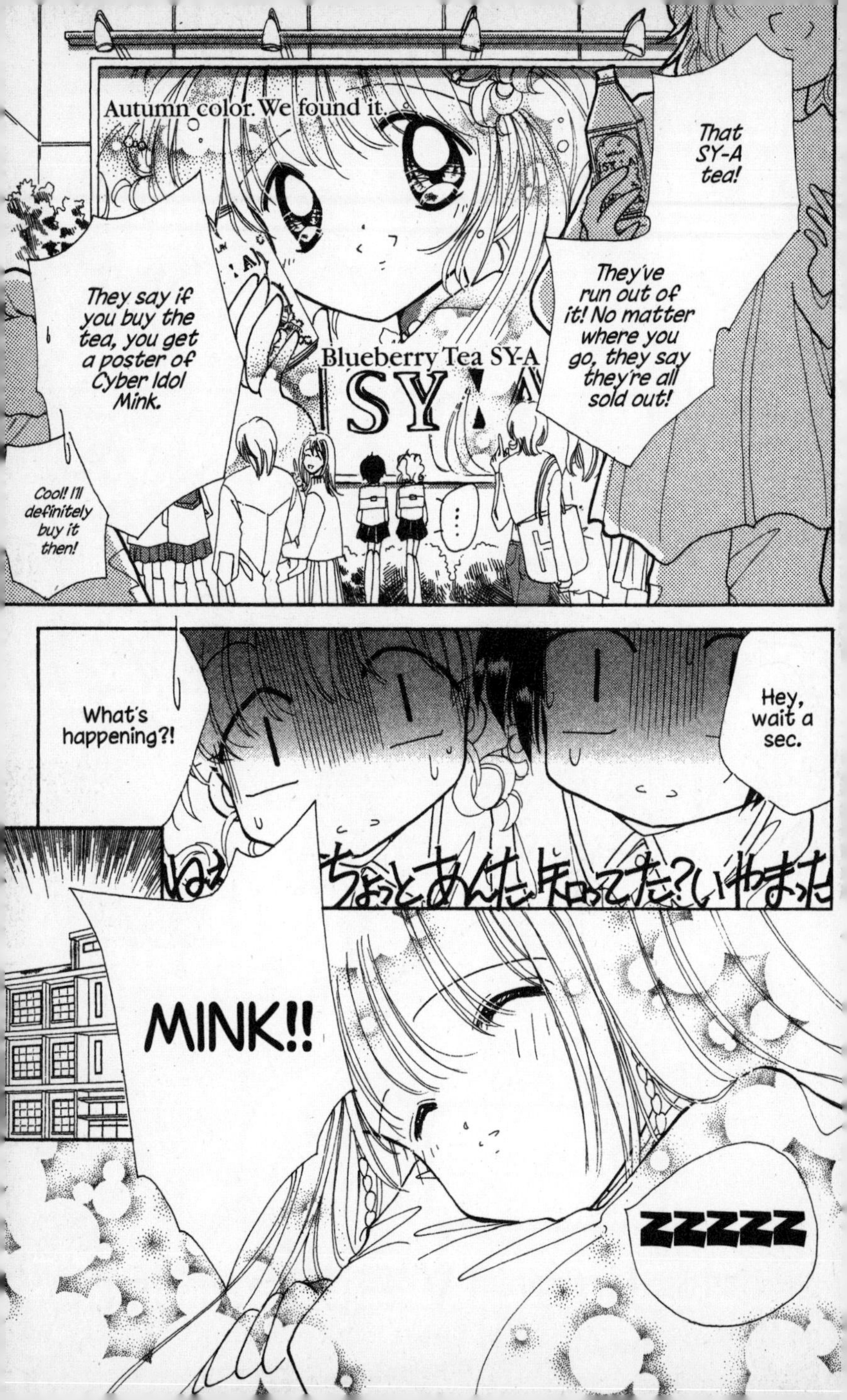
That SY-A tea!
They've run out of it! No matter where you go, they say they're all sold out!
Autumn color. We found it.
They say if you buy the tea, you get a poster of Cyber Idol Mink.
Blueberry Tea SY-A
Cool! I'll definitely buy it then!
...
Hey, wait a sec.
What's happening?!
ちょっとあんた知ってた？いやまった
MINK!!
ZZZZZ

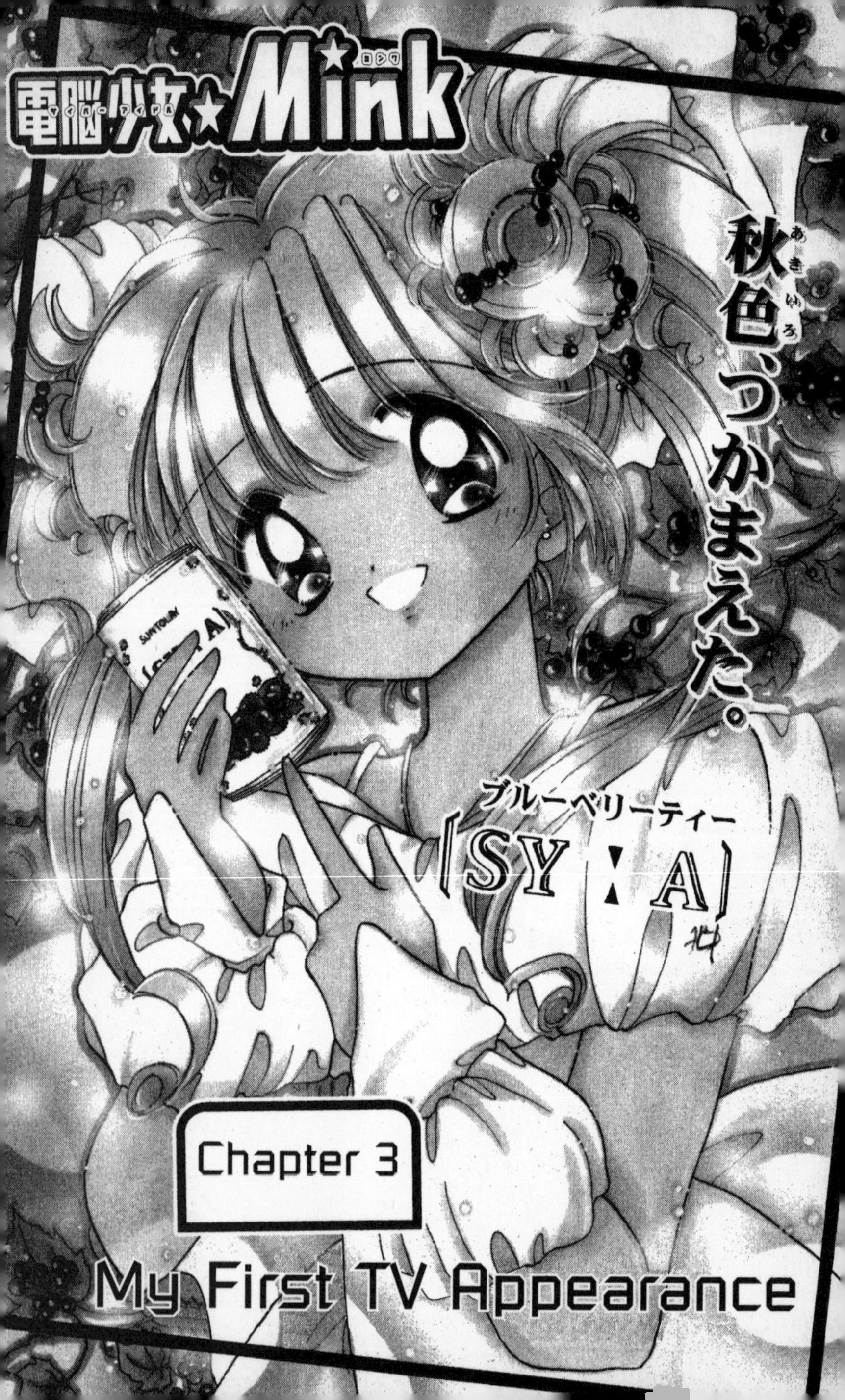
電脳少女★Mink
秋色、つかまえた。
ブルーベリーティー
「SY:A」
Chapter 3
My First TV Appearance

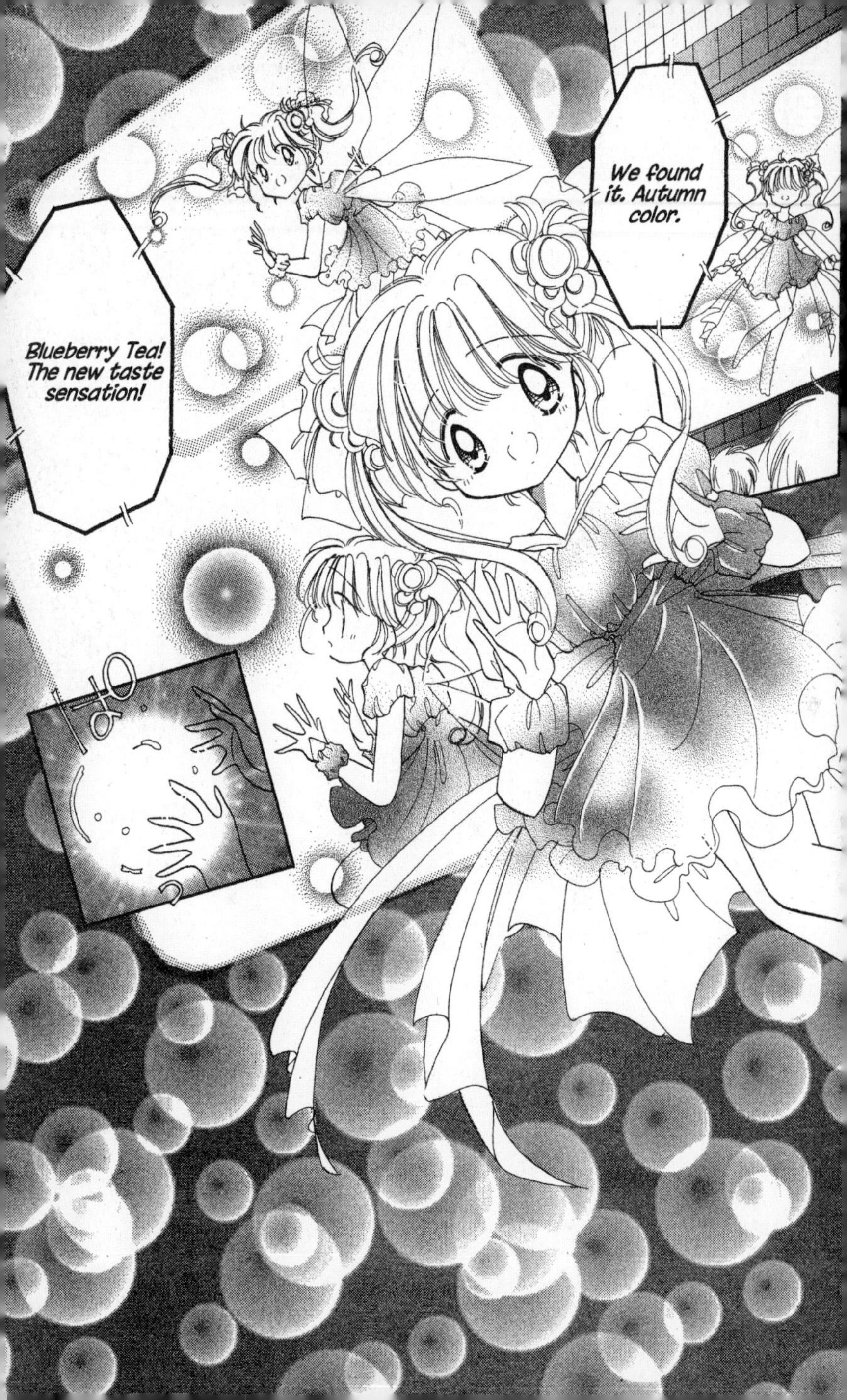
We found it. Autumn color.
Blueberry Tea! The new taste sensation!

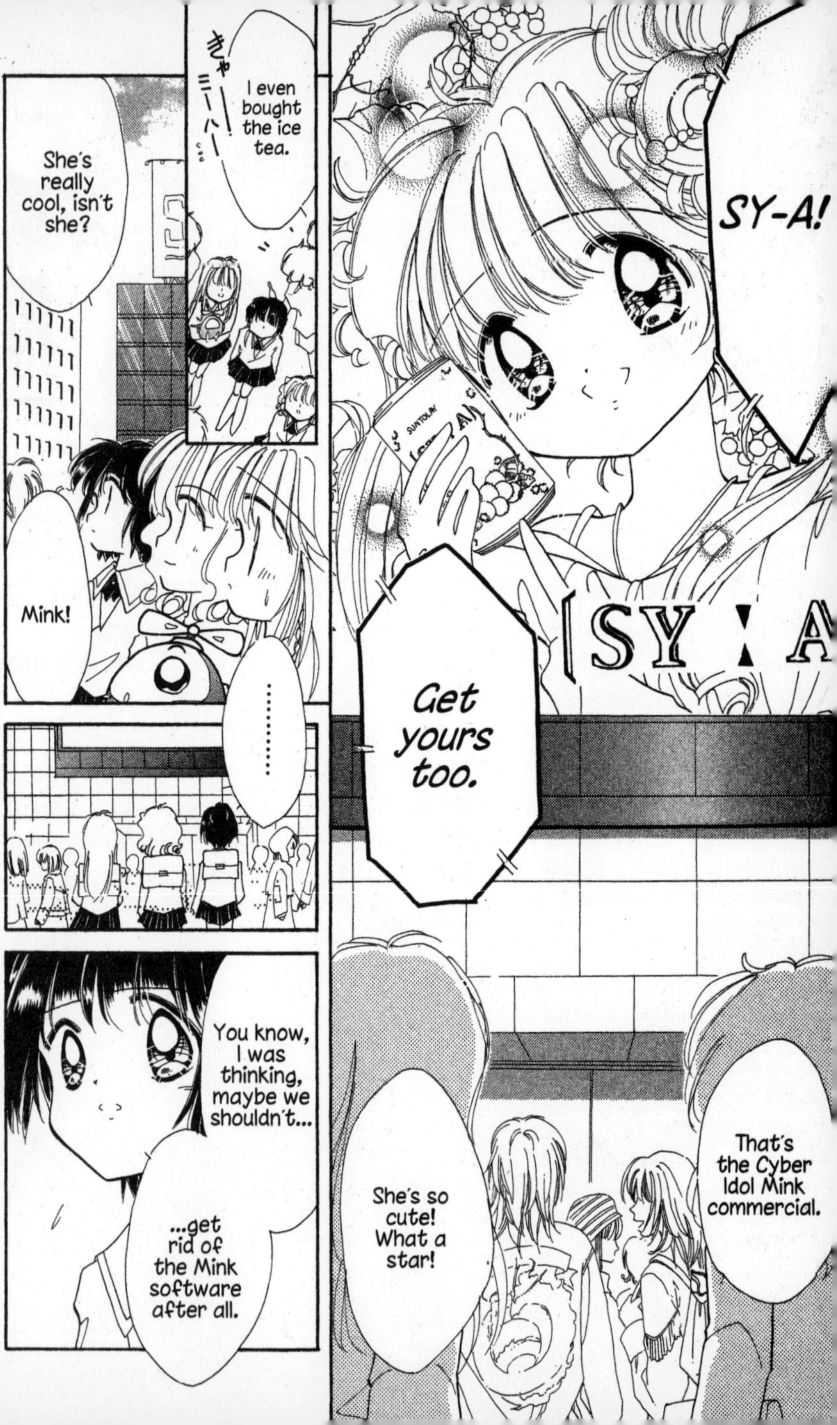
SY-A!
SY A
Get yours too.
That's the Cyber Idol Mink commercial.
She's so cute! What a star!
I even bought the ice tea.
きゃー ミーハー…
She's really cool, isn't she?
……
Mink!
You know, I was thinking, maybe we shouldn't...
...get rid of the Mink software after all.

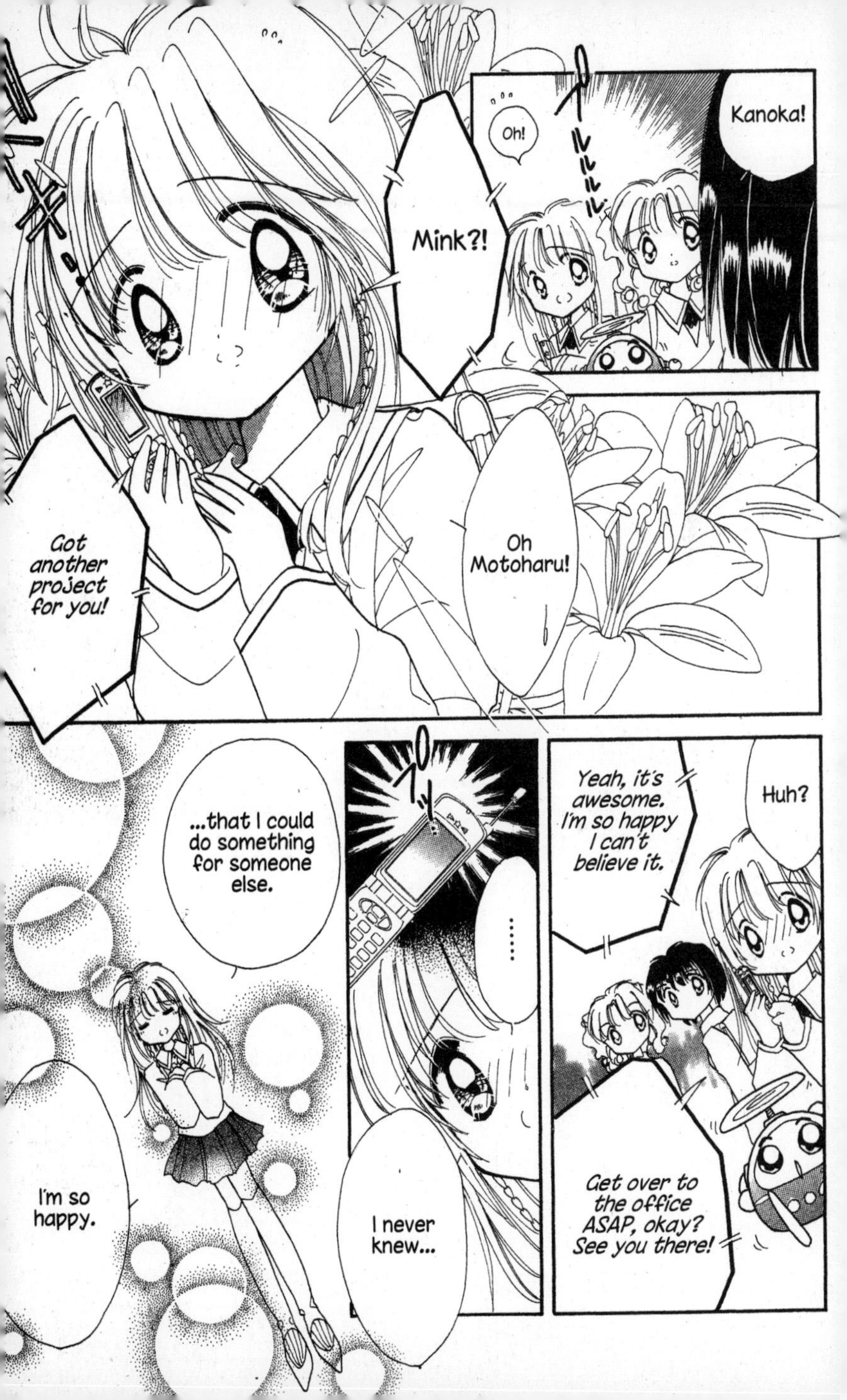
Kanoka!
Oh!
Oh Motoharu!
Mink?!
Got another project for you!
Huh?
Yeah, it's awesome. I'm so happy I can't believe it.
Get over to the office ASAP, okay? See you there!
......
I never knew...
...that I could do something for someone else.
I'm so happy.

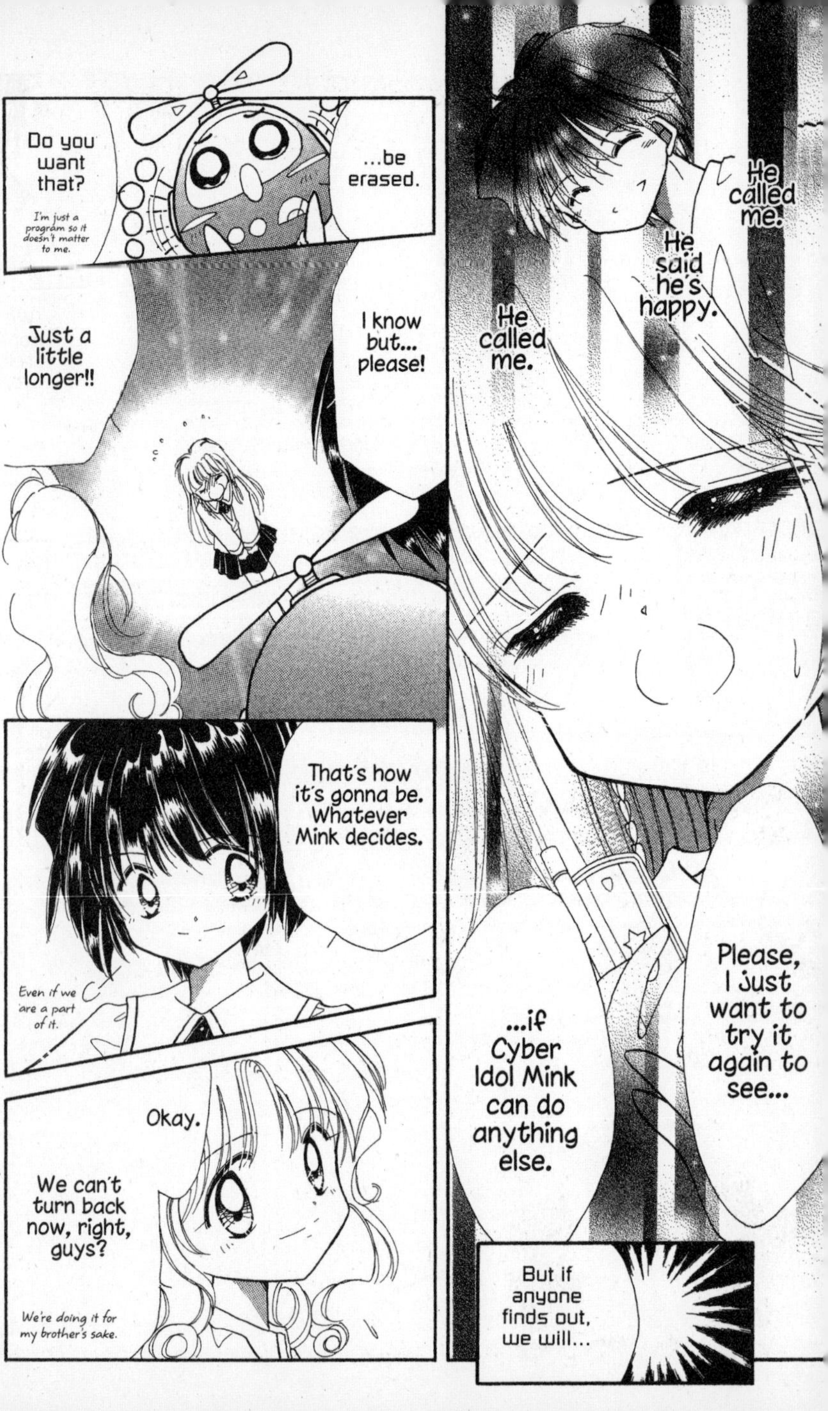
He called me.
He said he's happy.
He called me.
Please, I just want to try it again to see...
...if Cyber Idol Mink can do anything else.
But if anyone finds out, we will...
...be erased.
Do you want that?
I'm just a program so it doesn't matter to me.
I know but... please!
Just a little longer!!
That's how it's gonna be. Whatever Mink decides.
Even if we are a part of it.
Okay.
We can't turn back now, right, guys?
We're doing it for my brother's sake.

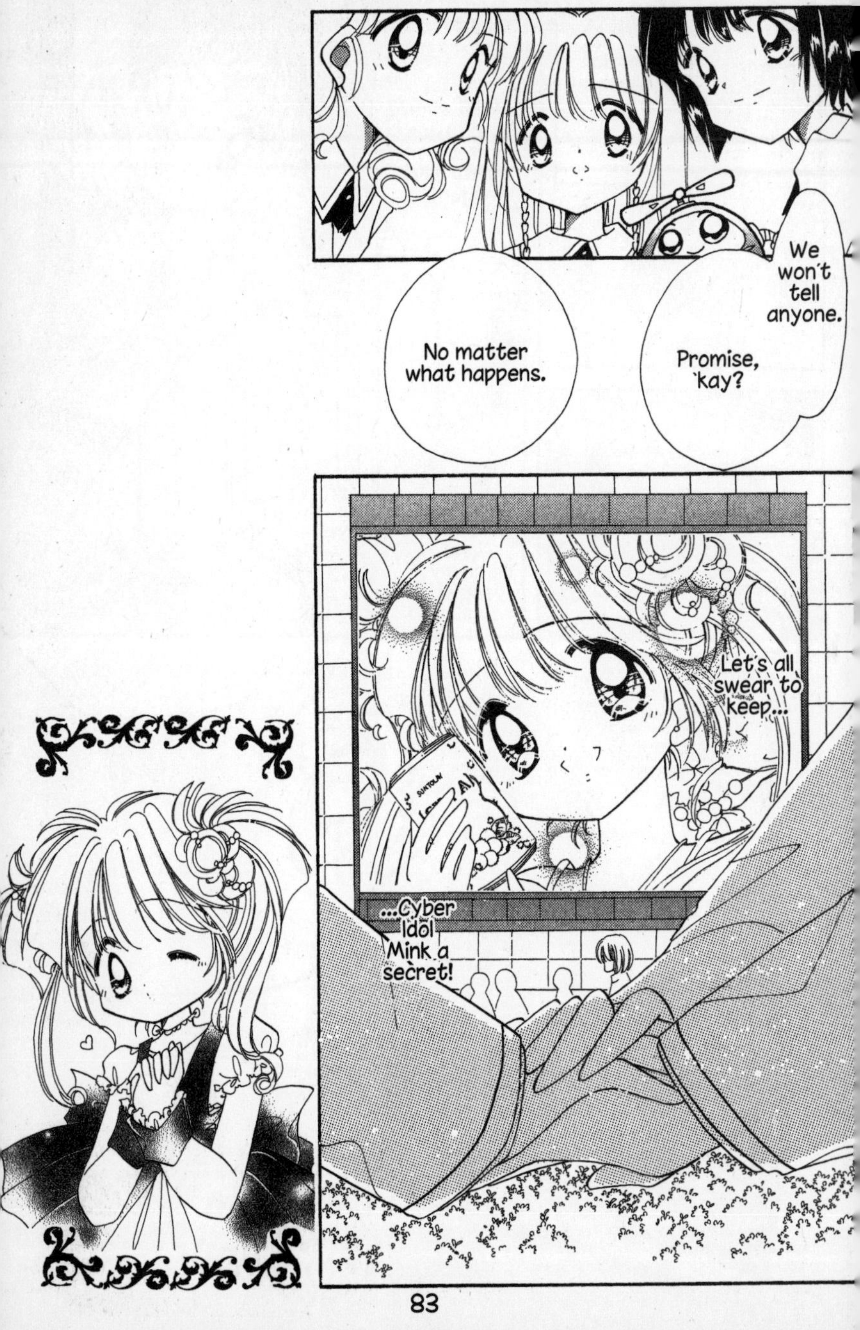
We won't tell anyone.
Promise, `kay?
No matter what happens.
Let's all swear to keep...
...Cyber Idol Mink a secret!

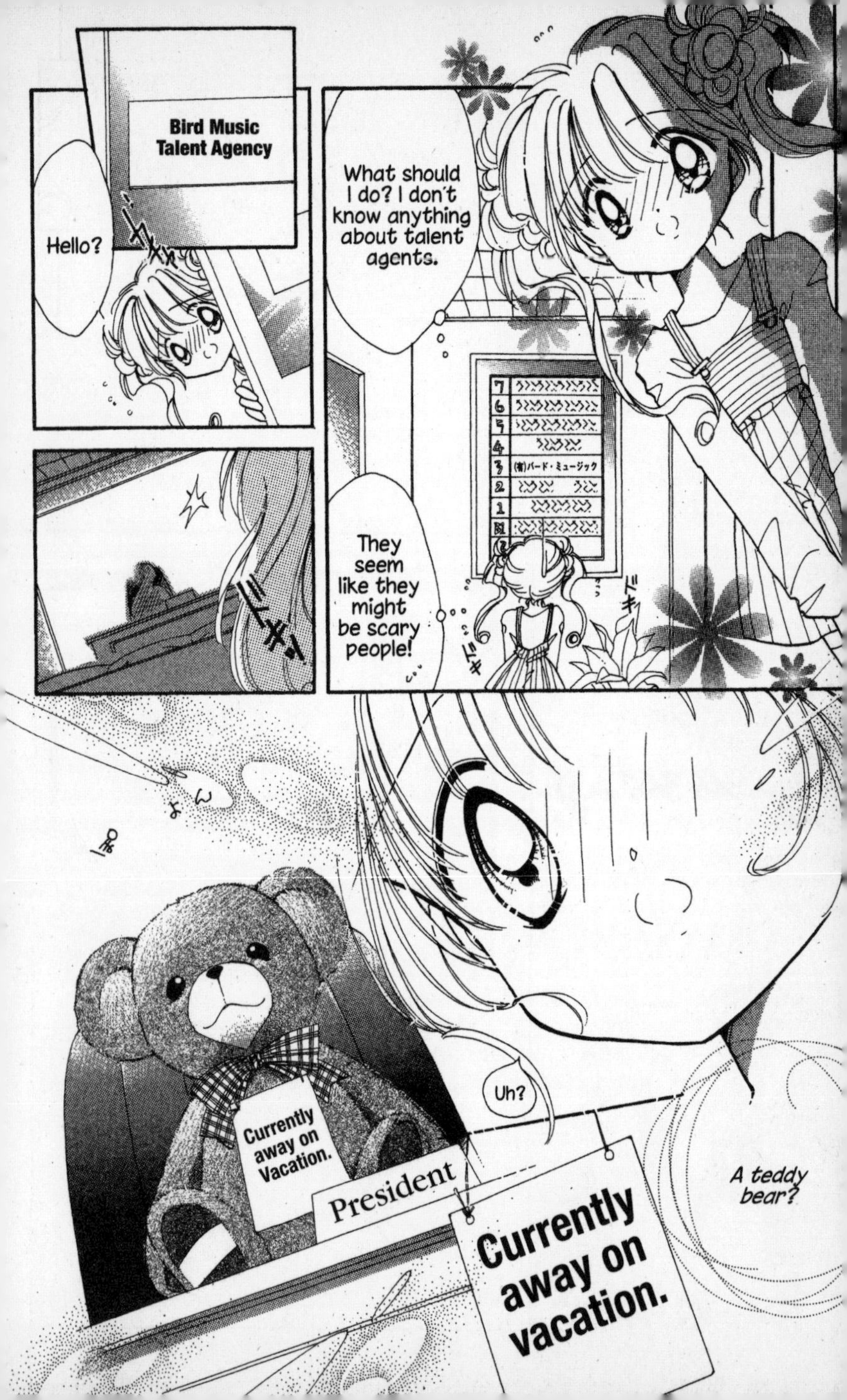
What should I do? I don't know anything about talent agents.
(有)バード・ミュージック
They seem like they might be scary people!
Bird Music Talent Agency
Hello?
Uh?
A teddy bear?
Currently away on Vacation.
President
Currently away on vacation.

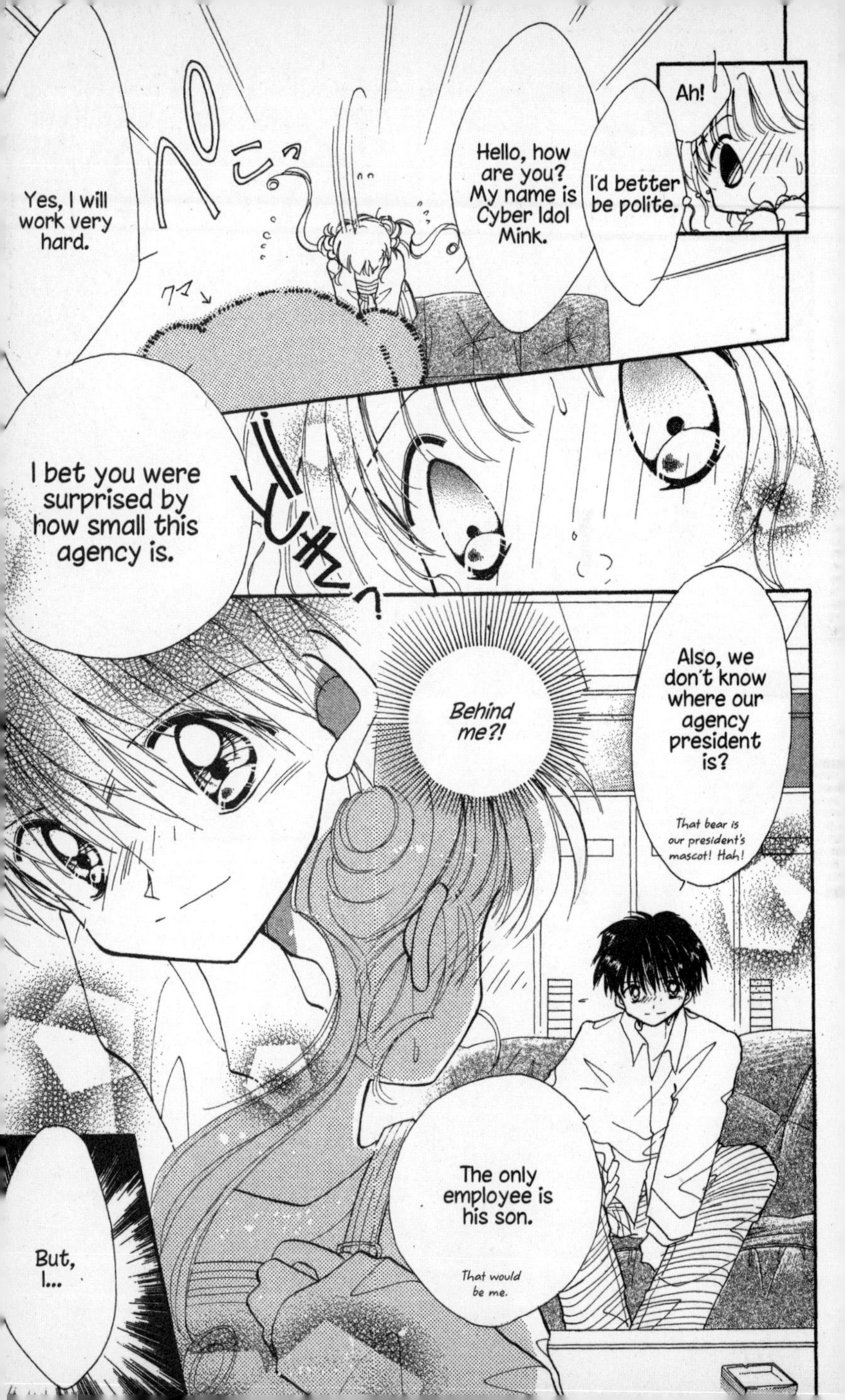
Ah!
I'd better be polite.
Hello, how are you? My name is Cyber Idol Mink.
Yes, I will work very hard.
I bet you were surprised by how small this agency is.
Also, we don't know where our agency president is?
That bear is our president's mascot! Hah!
Behind me?!
The only employee is his son.
That would be me.
But, I...

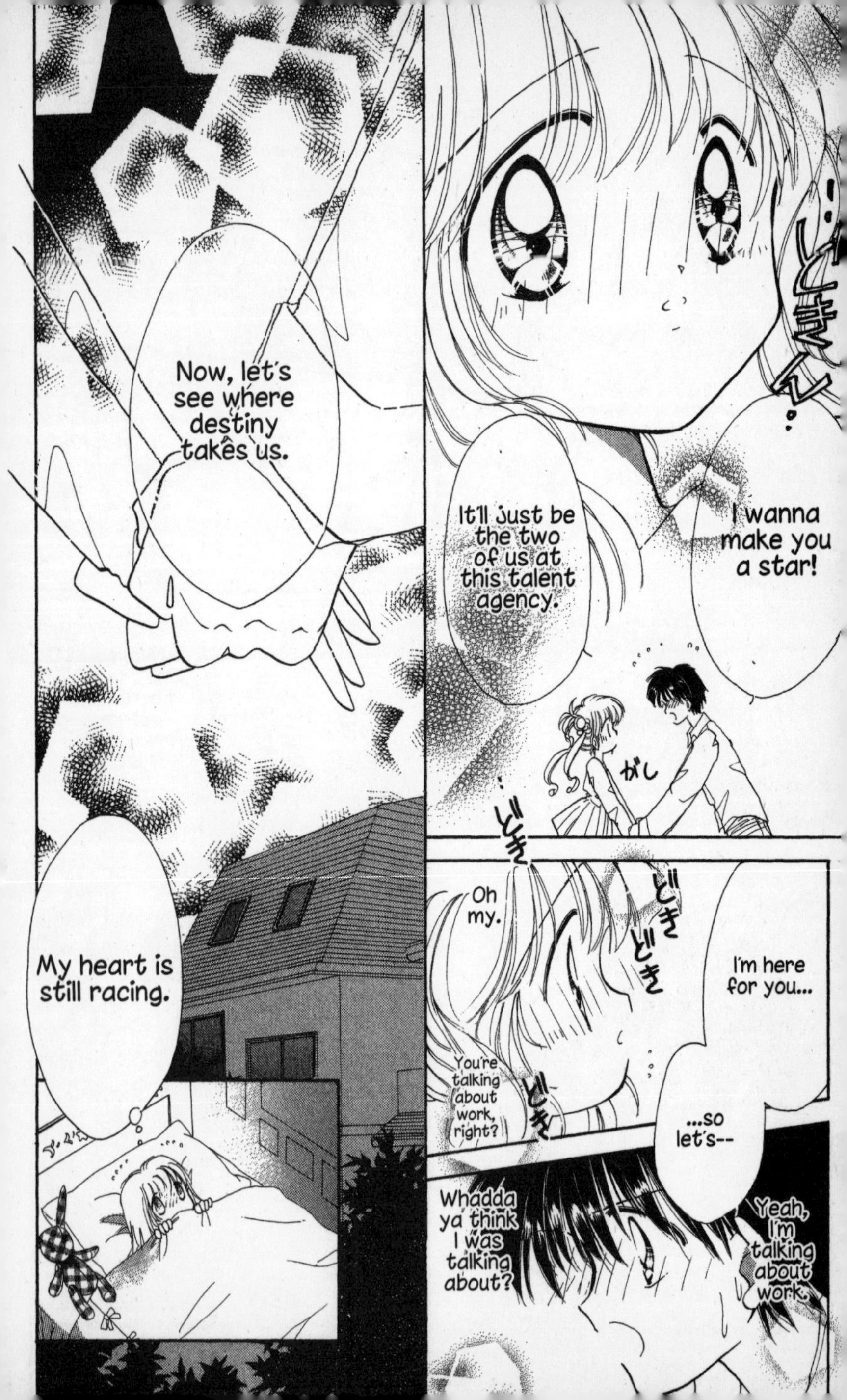
I wanna make you a star!
It'll just be the two of us at this talent agency.
がし
どき
I'm here for you...
Oh my.
どき
どき
...so let's--
You're talking about work, right?
どき
Yeah, I'm talking about work.
Whadda ya think I was talking about?
Now, let's see where destiny takes us.
My heart is still racing.

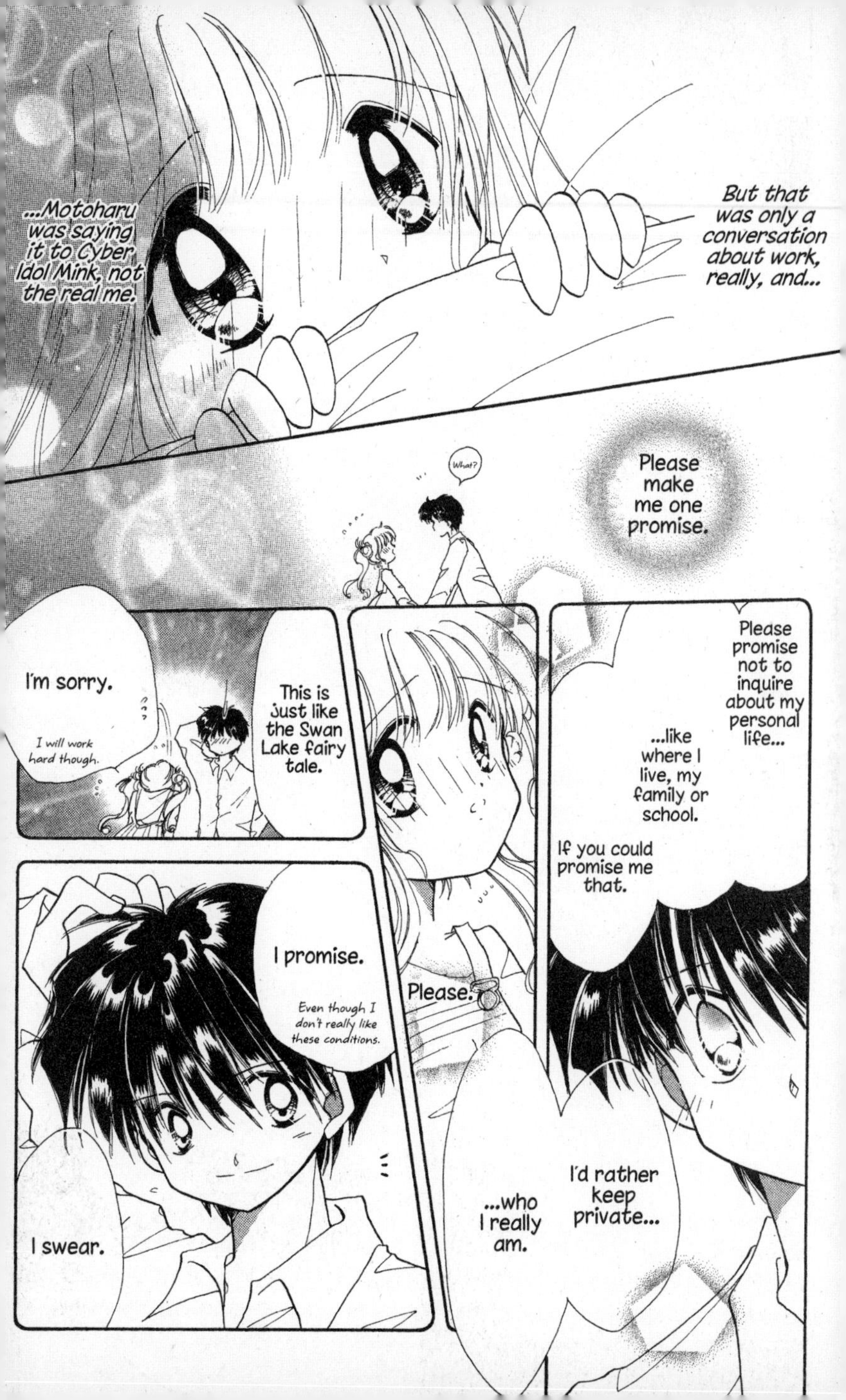

But that was only a conversation about work, really, and...
...Motoharu was saying it to Cyber Idol Mink, not the real me.
Please make me one promise.
What?
Please promise not to inquire about my personal life...
...like where I live, my family or school.
If you could promise me that.
Please.
I'd rather keep private...
...who I really am.
This is just like the Swan Lake fairy tale.
I'm sorry.
I will work hard though.
I promise.
Even though I don't really like these conditions.
I swear.

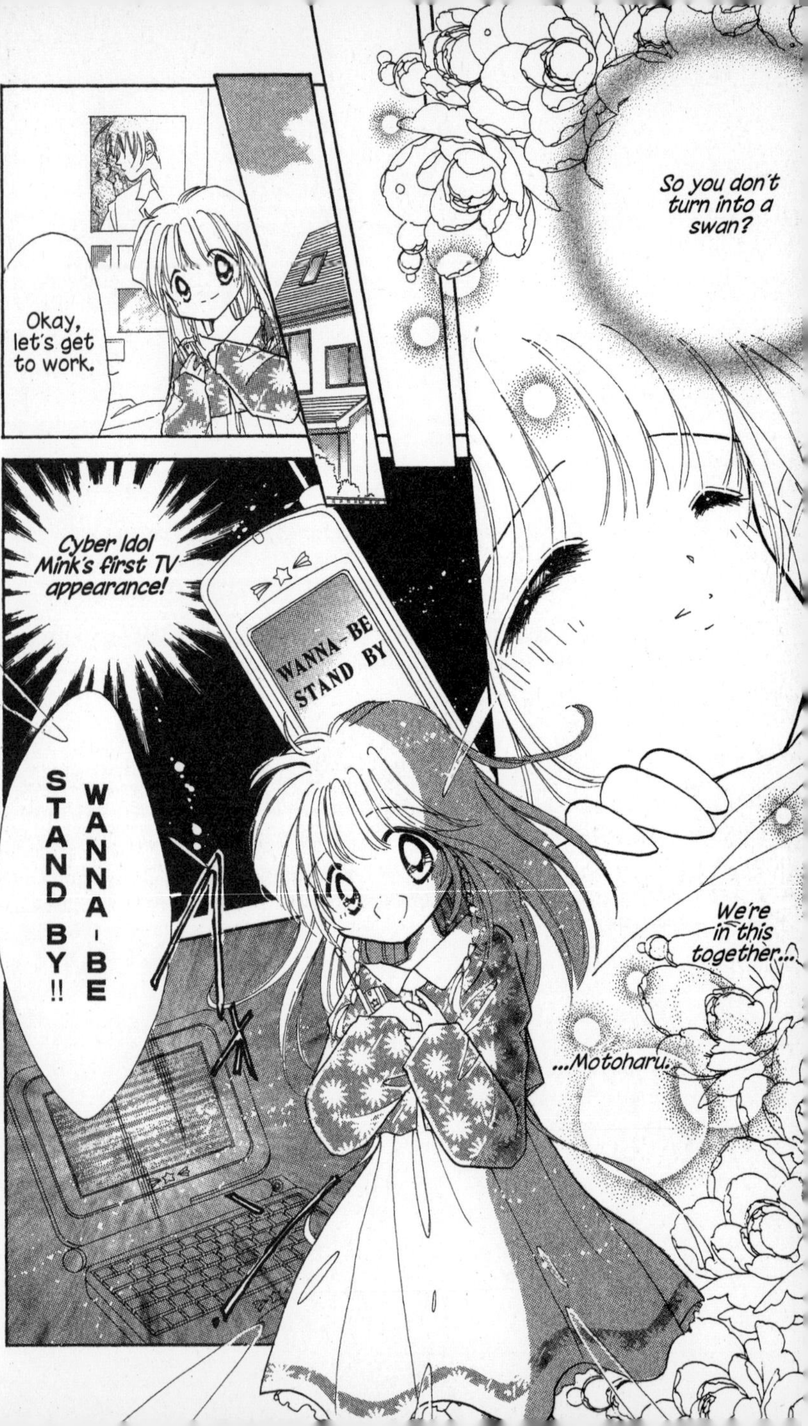
So you don't turn into a swan?
We're in this together...
...Motoharu.
Okay, let's get to work.
Cyber Idol Mink's first TV appearance!
WANNA-BE STAND BY
WANNA-BE STAND BY!!

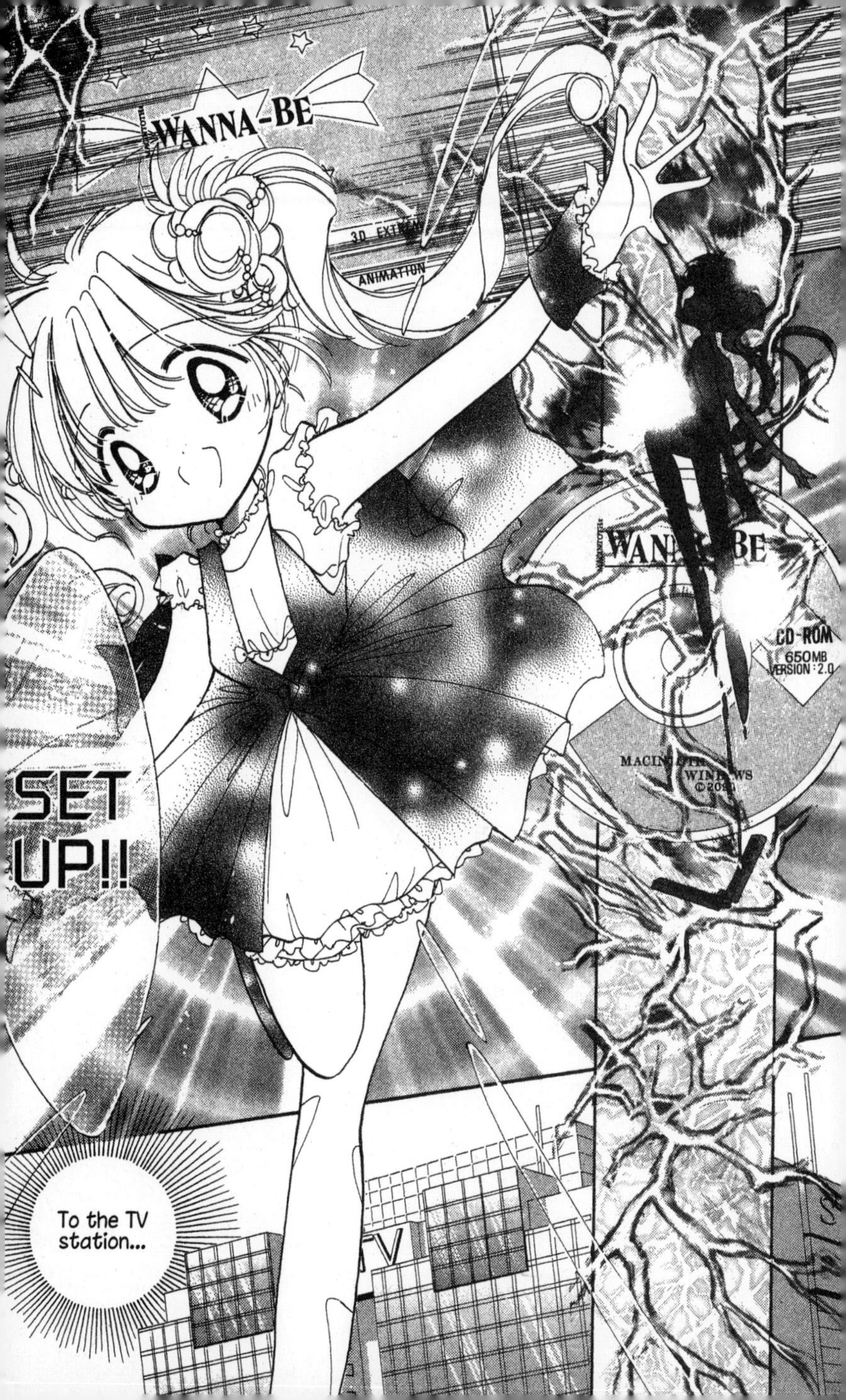
WANNA-BE
ANIMATION
CD-ROM
650MB
VERSION : 2.0
SET UP!!
TV
To the TV station...

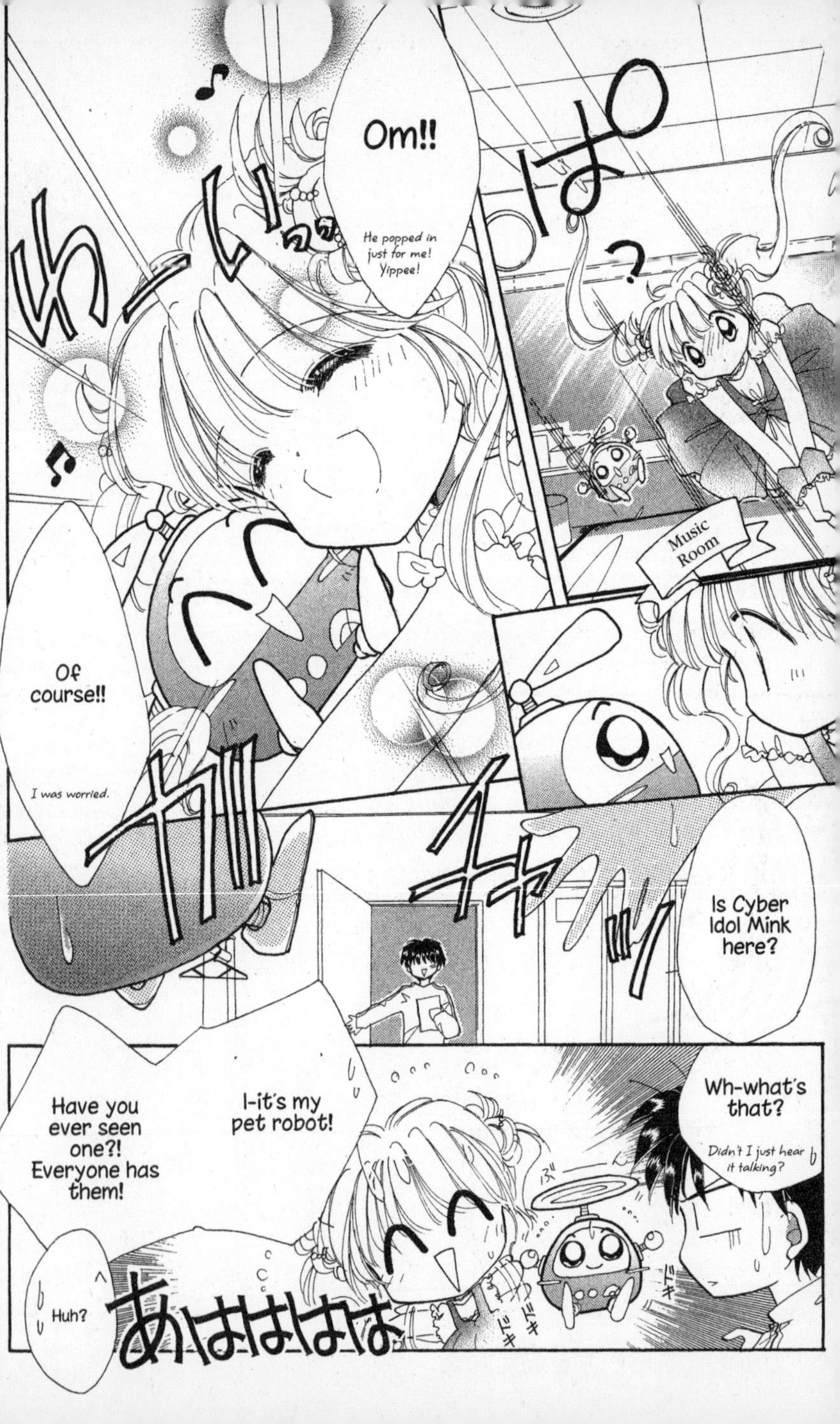

Om!!
He popped in just for me! Yippee!
Music Room
Of course!!
I was worried.
Is Cyber Idol Mink here?
Wh-what's that?
Didn't I just hear it talking?
I-it's my pet robot!
Have you ever seen one?! Everyone has them!
Huh?

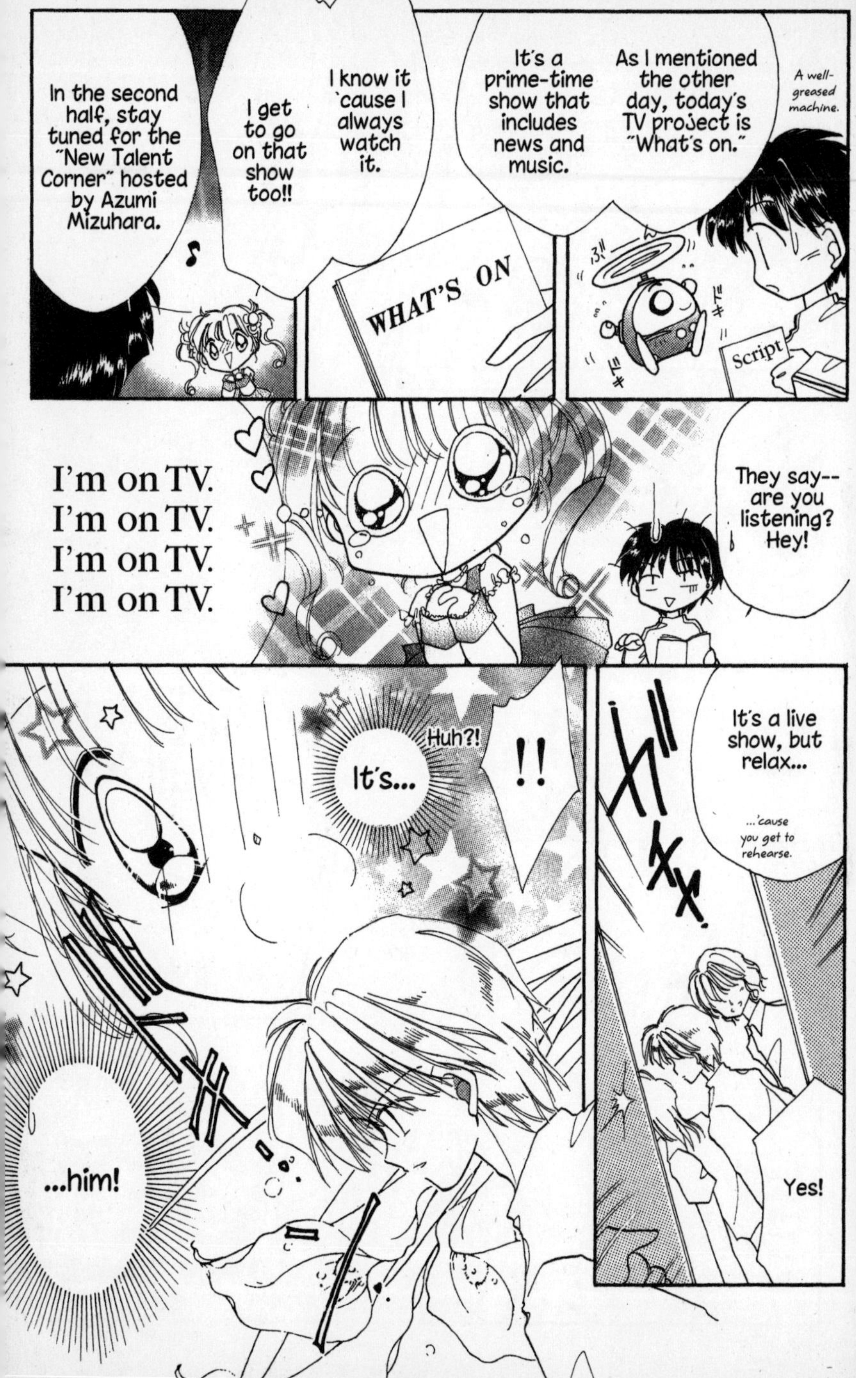
A well-greased machine.
As I mentioned the other day, today's TV project is "What's on."
Script
It's a prime-time show that includes news and music.
WHAT'S ON
I know it 'cause I always watch it.
I get to go on that show too!!
In the second half, stay tuned for the "New Talent Corner" hosted by Azumi Mizuhara.
They say-- are you listening? Hey!
I'm on TV.
I'm on TV.
I'm on TV.
I'm on TV.
It's a live show, but relax...
...'cause you get to rehearse.
Yes!
!!
Huh?!
It's...
...him!

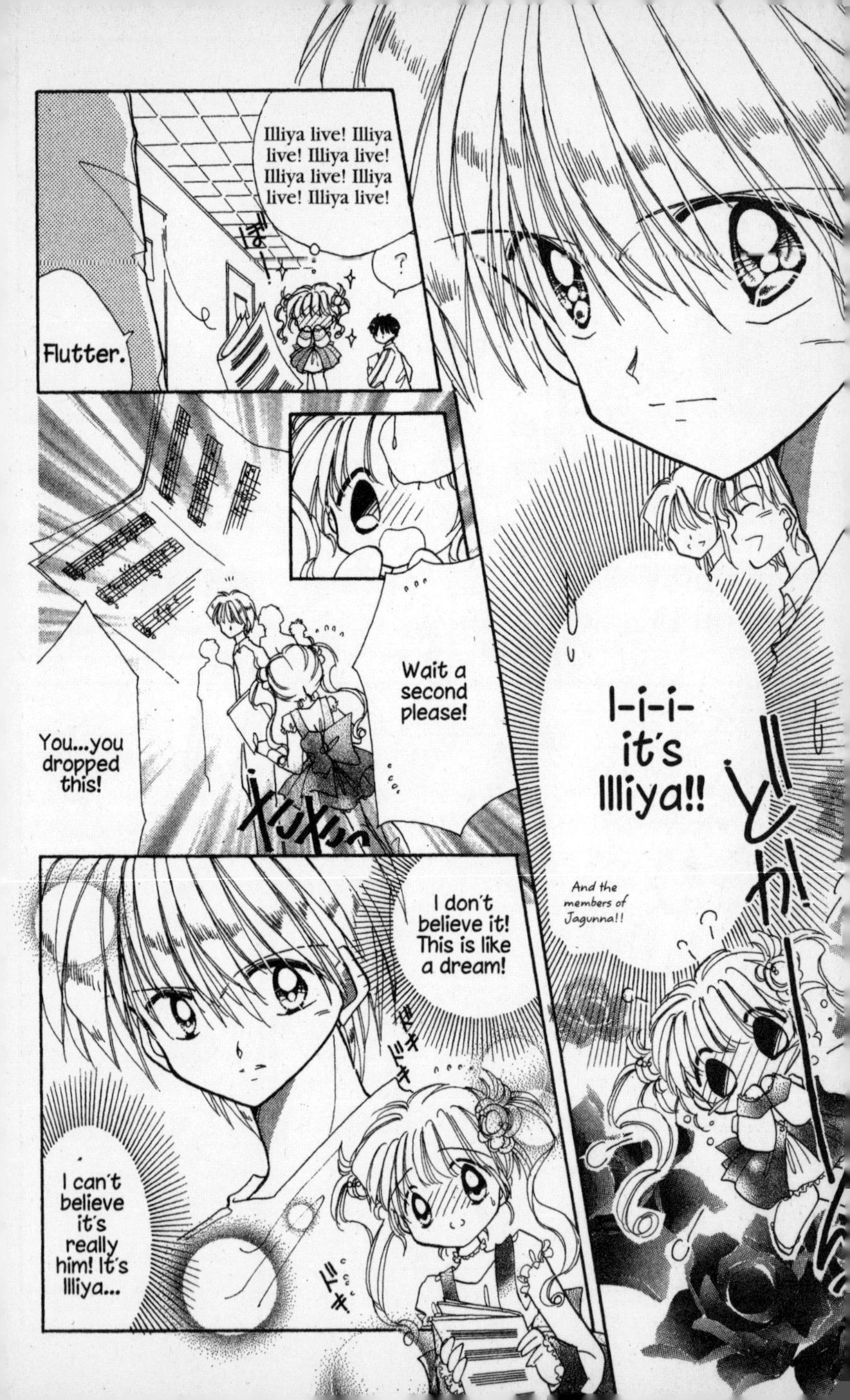
I-i-i-it's Illiya!!
And the members of Jagunna!!
Illiya live! Illiya live! Illiya live! Illiya live! Illiya live! Illiya live!
Flutter.
Wait a second please!
You...you dropped this!
I don't believe it! This is like a dream!
I can't believe it's really him! It's Illiya...

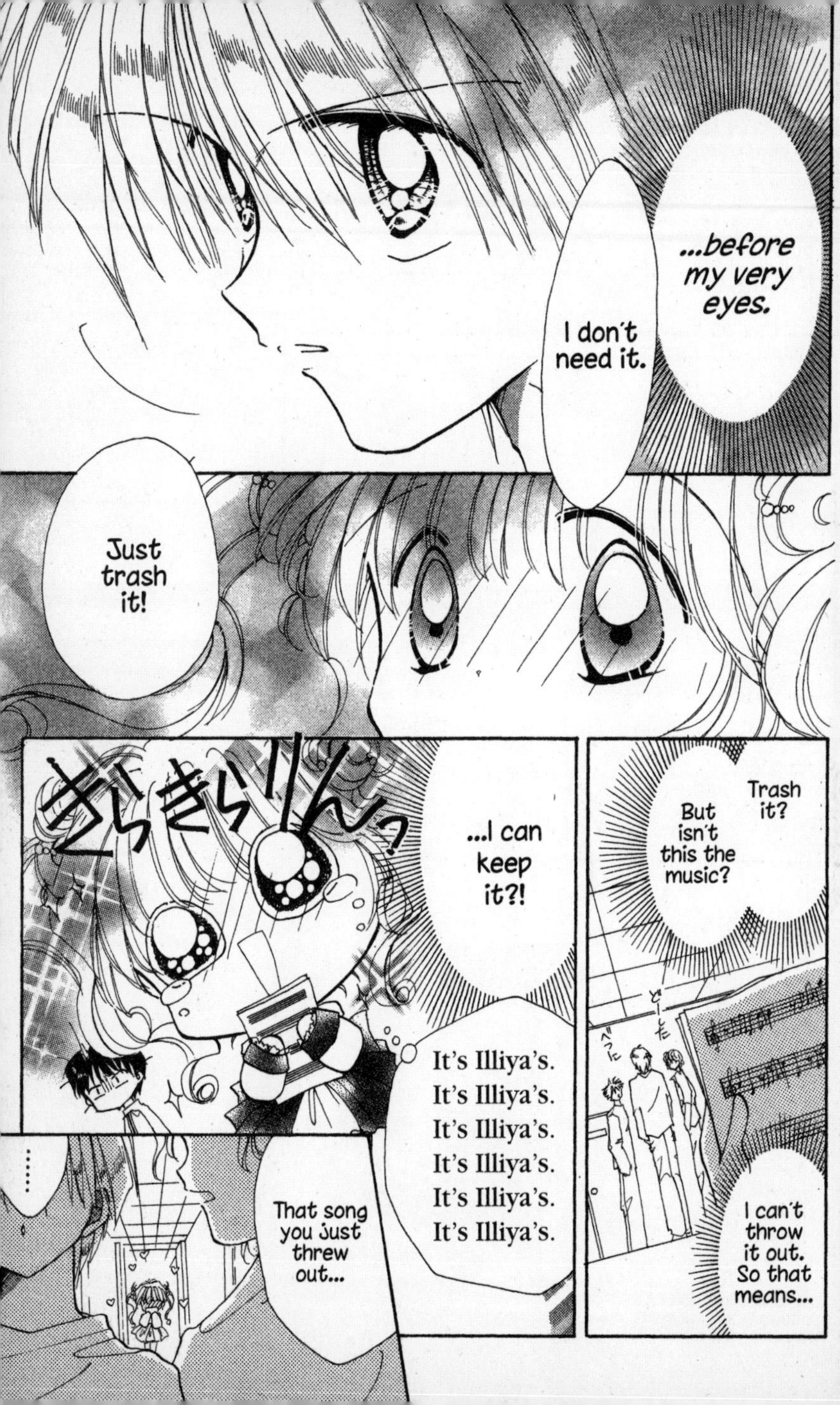

...before my very eyes.
I don't need it.
Just trash it!
Trash it?
But isn't this the music?
どーした
べつに
I can't throw it out. So that means...
...I can keep it?!
きらきらりんっ
It's Illiya's.
It's Illiya's.
It's Illiya's.
It's Illiya's.
It's Illiya's.
It's Illiya's.
That song you just threw out...
......

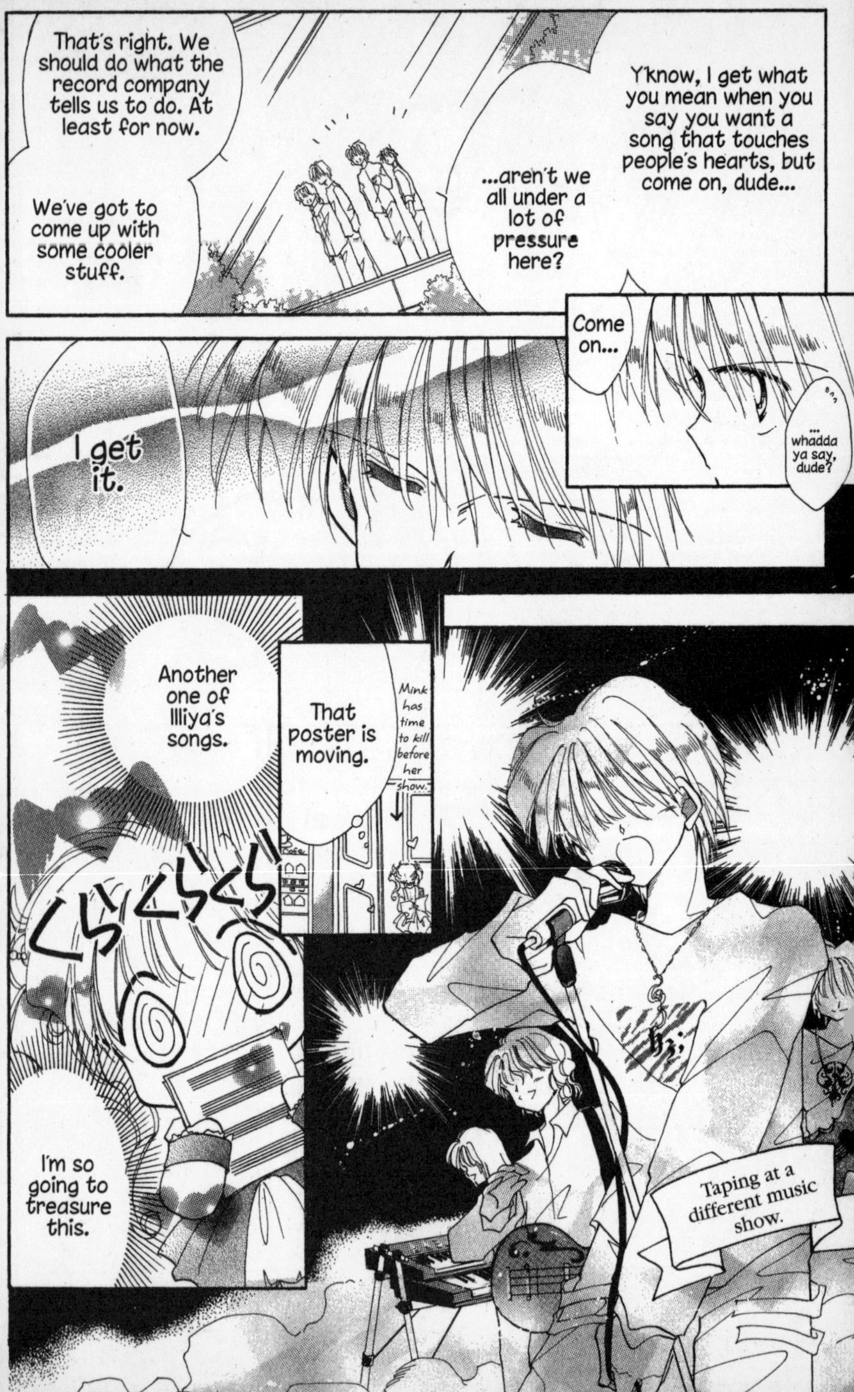
Y'know, I get what you mean when you say you want a song that touches people's hearts, but come on, dude...
...aren't we all under a lot of pressure here?
That's right. We should do what the record company tells us to do. At least for now.
We've got to come up with some cooler stuff.
Come on...
...whadda ya say, dude?
I get it.
Taping at a different music show.
That poster is moving.
Mink has time to kill before her show.
Another one of Illiya's songs.
くらくらくら
I'm so going to treasure this.

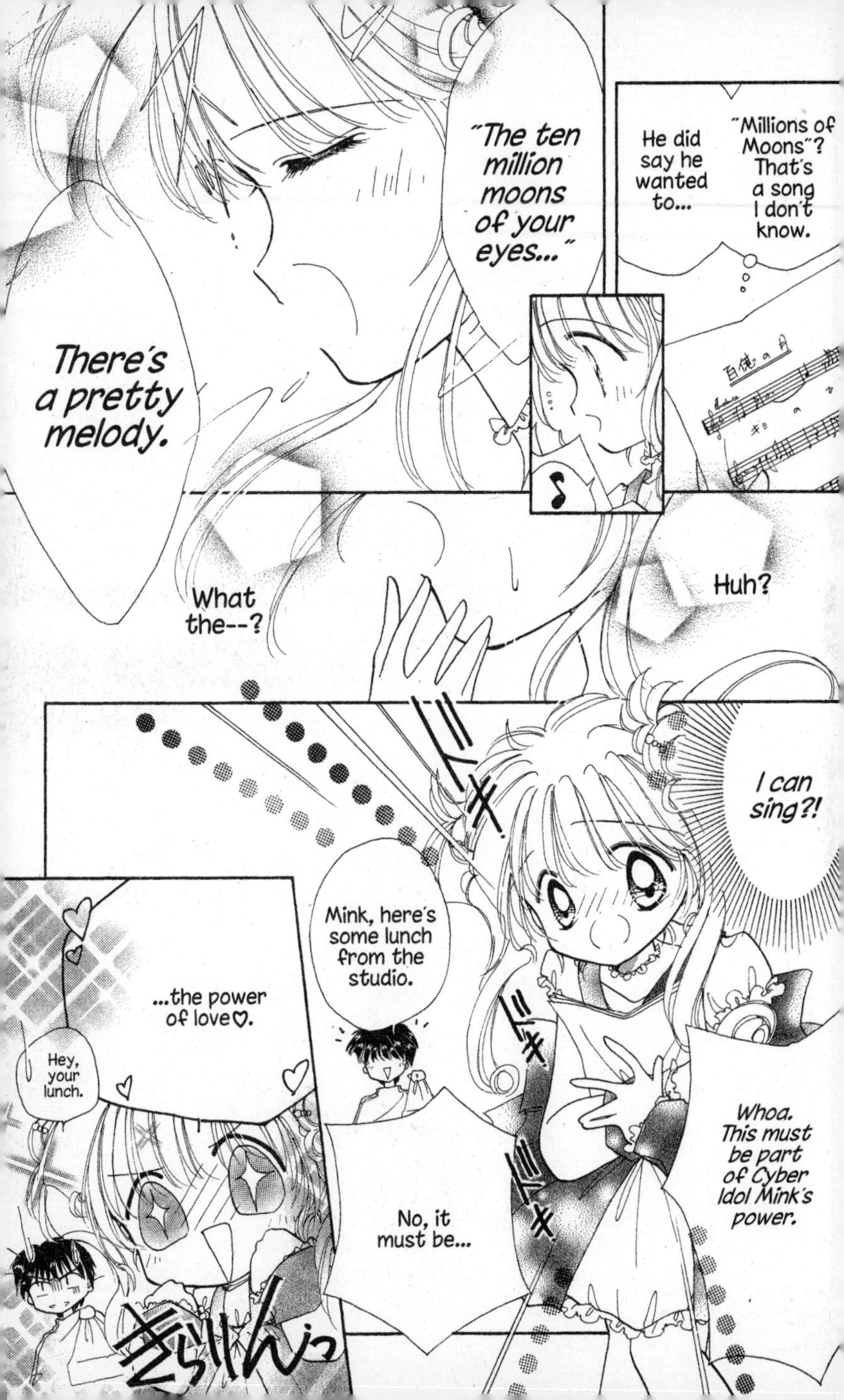
"Millions of Moons"? That's a song I don't know.
He did say he wanted to...
百億の月
"The ten million moons of your eyes..."
There's a pretty melody.
Huh?
What the--?
I can sing?!
ドキ
Whoa. This must be part of Cyber Idol Mink's power.
No, it must be...
Mink, here's some lunch from the studio.
...the power of love♡.
Hey, your lunch.
きらりんっ

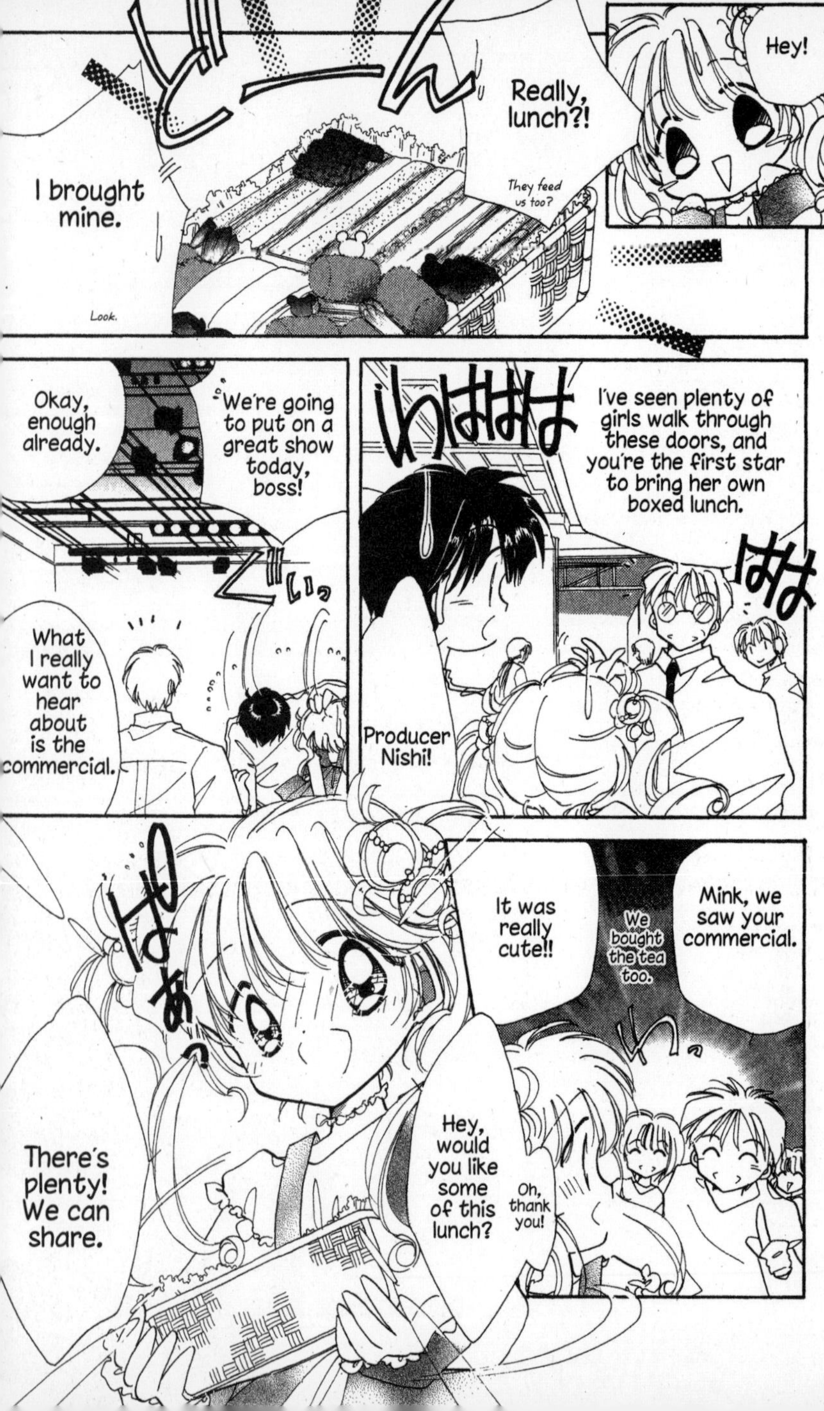

Hey!
どーん
Really, lunch?!
They feed us too?
I brought mine.
Look.
わははは
I've seen plenty of girls walk through these doors, and you're the first star to bring her own boxed lunch.
はは
Producer Nishi!
We're going to put on a great show today, boss!
Okay, enough already.
ぐいっ
What I really want to hear about is the commercial.
Mink, we saw your commercial.
We bought the tea too.
It was really cute!!
わっ
Hey, would you like some of this lunch?
Oh, thank you!
はあっ
There's plenty! We can share.

Mink Rap!!

Q: When you buy manga pens, do you buy the pen tip separately from the pen shaft?

A: For me, I buy them separately. I rarely buy pen shafts because I usually hold on to them for long periods of time. The one I'm using now, I've had for five or six years! Pen tips wear out so I buy lots of them. I suggest changing the pen tips when they run out 'cause it's really hard to write with, okay? By the way, I use "G" pens, round-tip pens and school pens. The brand is Zebra.

Many elementary and middle-school students send me letters with questions about manga production. I'll do my best to answer these, since there's so much I don't know about production either! I often don't know who to ask myself!

-Megumi

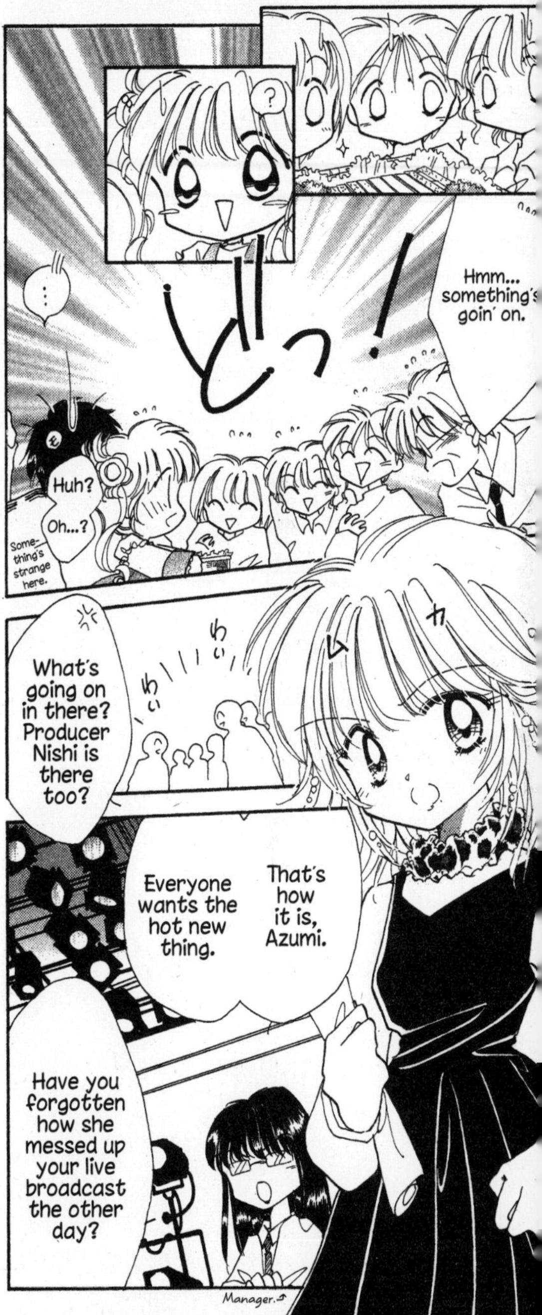
?
Hmm... something's goin' on.
...
Huh?
Oh...?
Something's strange here.
What's going on in there? Producer Nishi is there too?
That's how it is, Azumi.
Everyone wants the hot new thing.
Have you forgotten how she messed up your live broadcast the other day?
Manager.

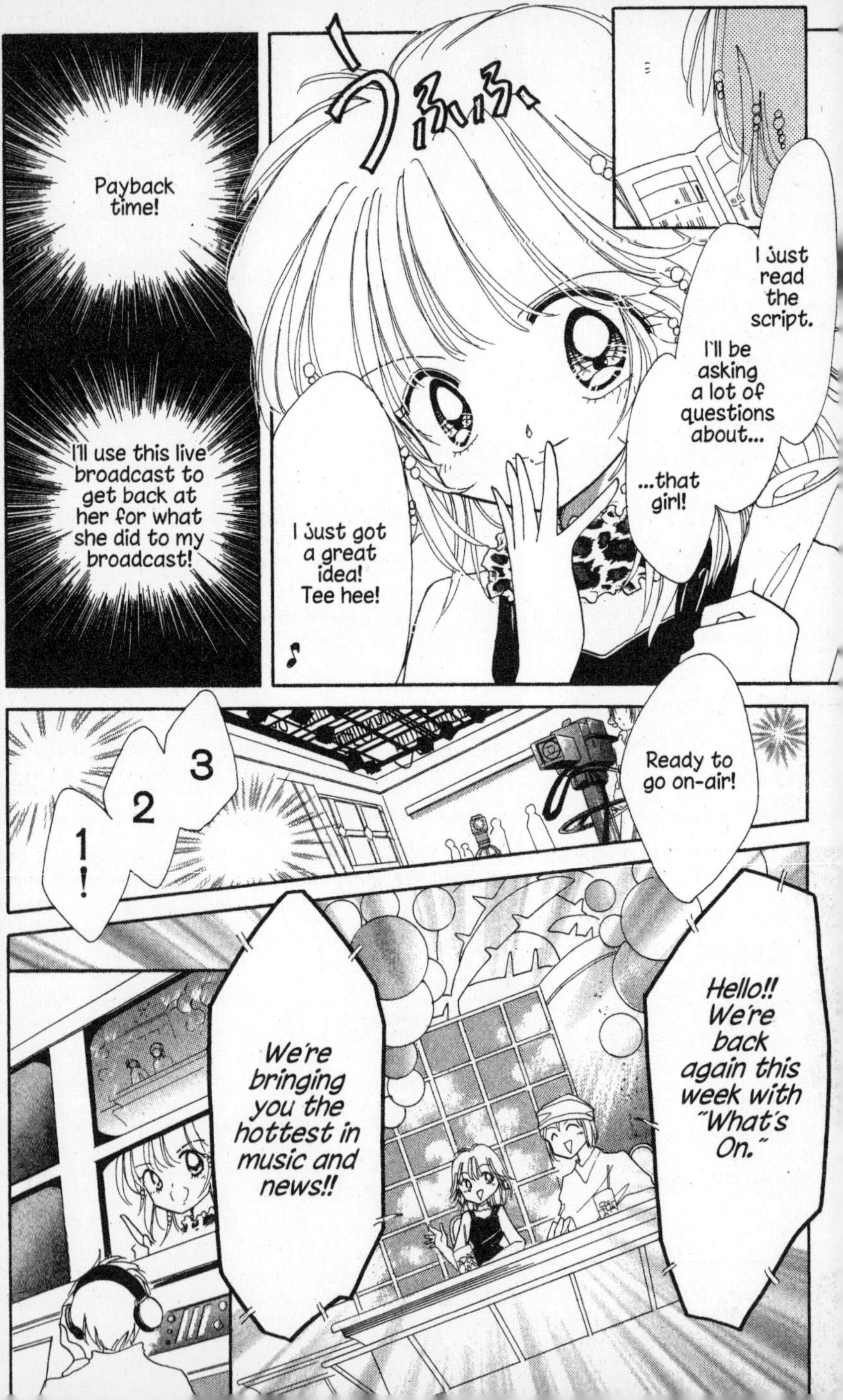
I just read the script.
I'll be asking a lot of questions about...
...that girl!
うふふ
I just got a great idea! Tee hee!
Payback time!
I'll use this live broadcast to get back at her for what she did to my broadcast!
Ready to go on-air!
3
2
1!
Hello!! We're back again this week with "What's On."
We're bringing you the hottest in music and news!!

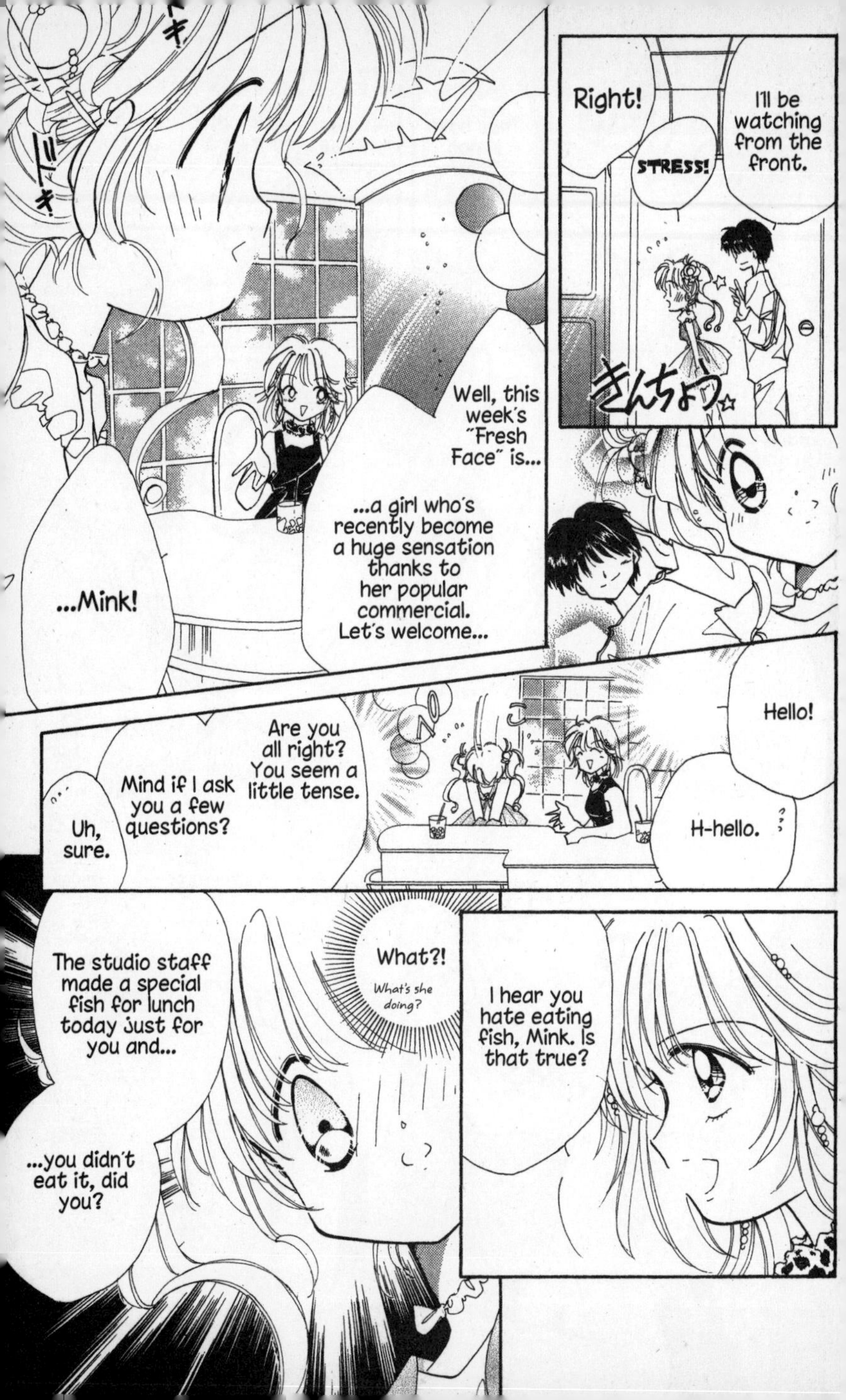

I'll be watching from the front.
Right!
STRESS!
きんちょう☆
Well, this week's "Fresh Face" is...
...a girl who's recently become a huge sensation thanks to her popular commercial. Let's welcome...
...Mink!
ドキ
Hello!
H-hello.
Are you all right? You seem a little tense.
Mind if I ask you a few questions?
Uh, sure.
I hear you hate eating fish, Mink. Is that true?
What?!
What's she doing?
The studio staff made a special fish for lunch today just for you and...
...you didn't eat it, did you?

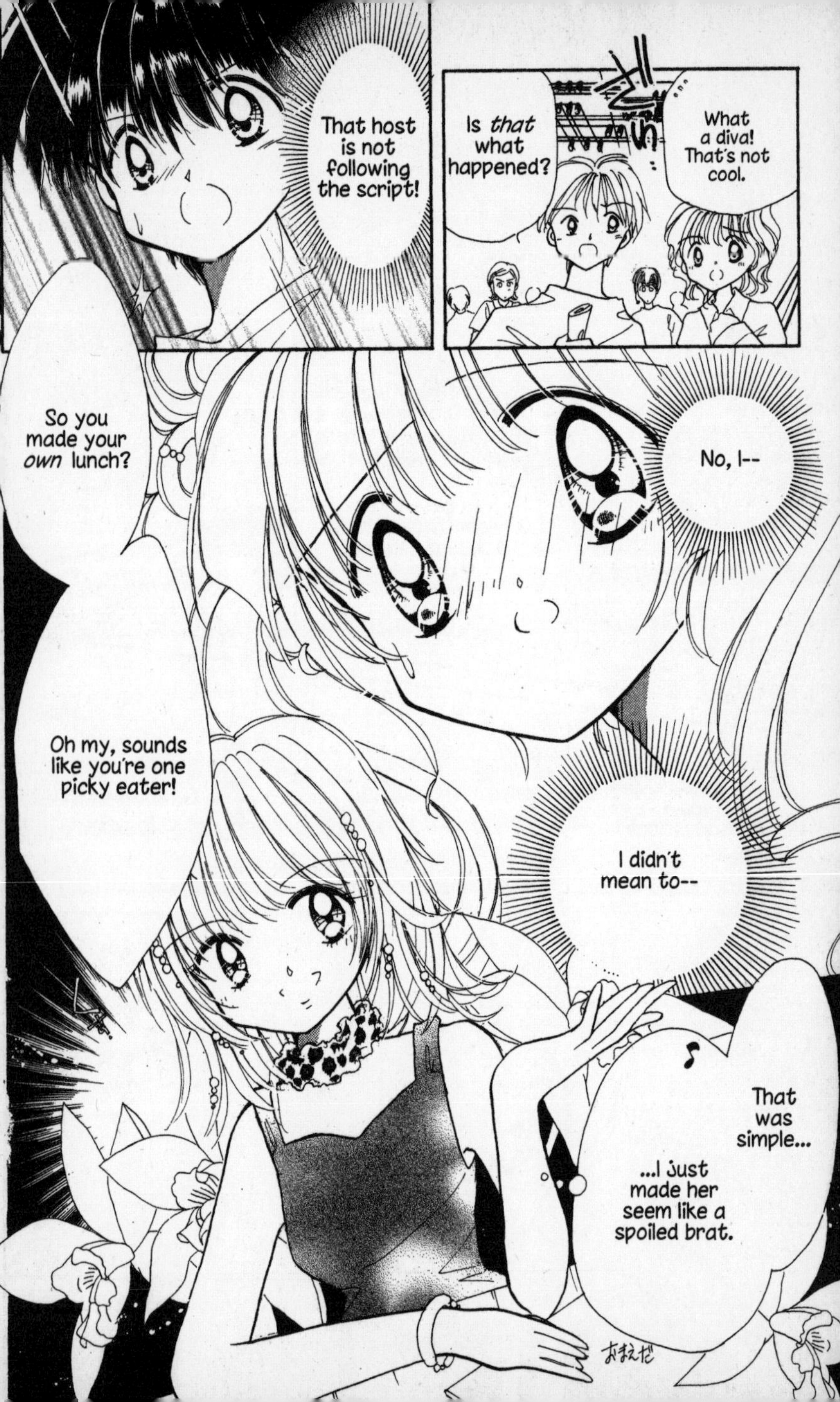
What a diva! That's not cool.
Is *that* what happened?
That host is not following the script!
No, I--
So you made your *own* lunch?
I didn't mean to--
Oh my, sounds like you're one picky eater!
That was simple...
...I just made her seem like a spoiled brat.
おまえだ

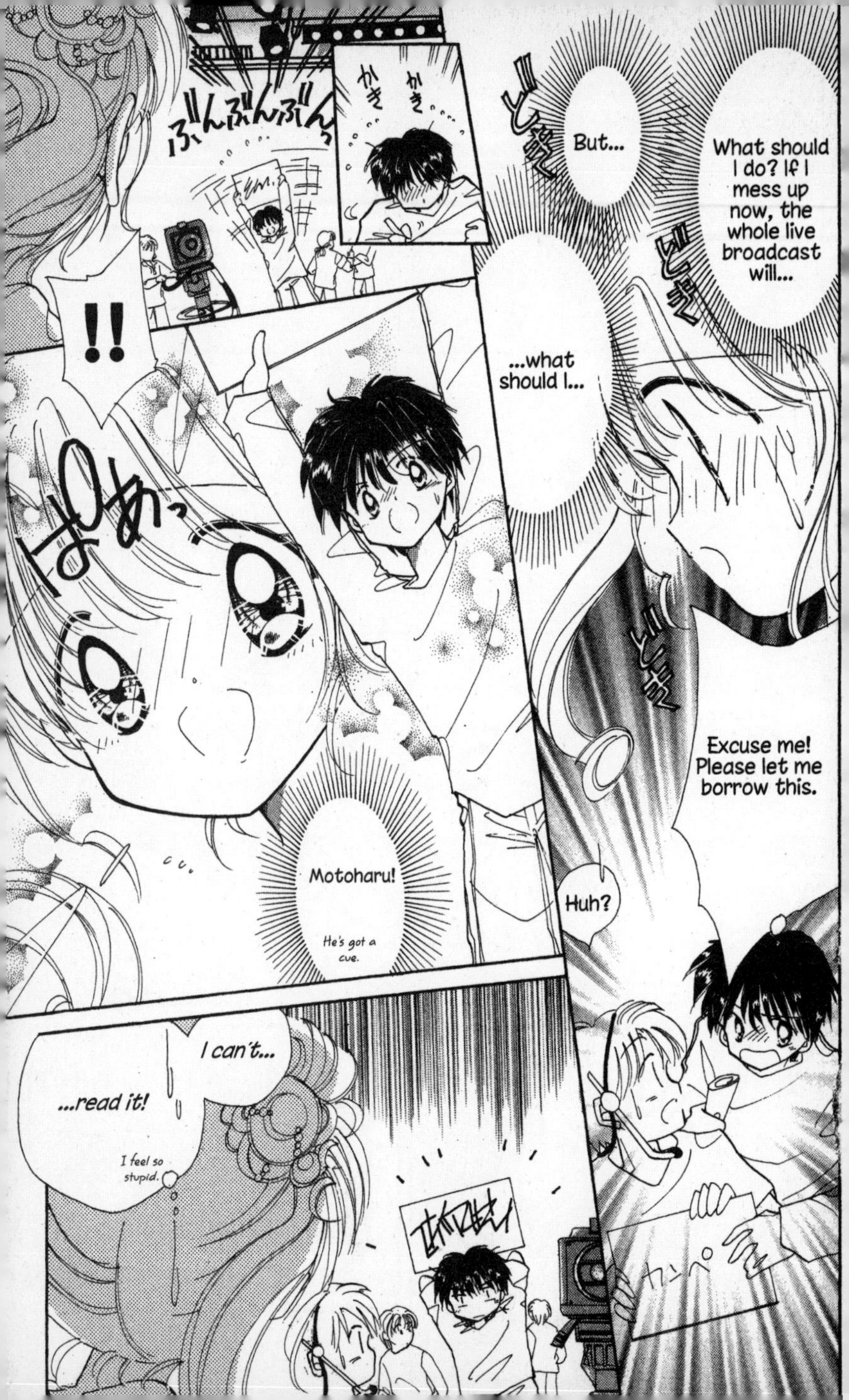
What should I do? If I mess up now, the whole live broadcast will...
But...
...what should I...
Excuse me! Please let me borrow this.
Huh?
かき かき
ぶんぶんぶん
!!
ぱあっ
Motoharu!
He's got a cue.
I can't...
...read it!
I feel so stupid.

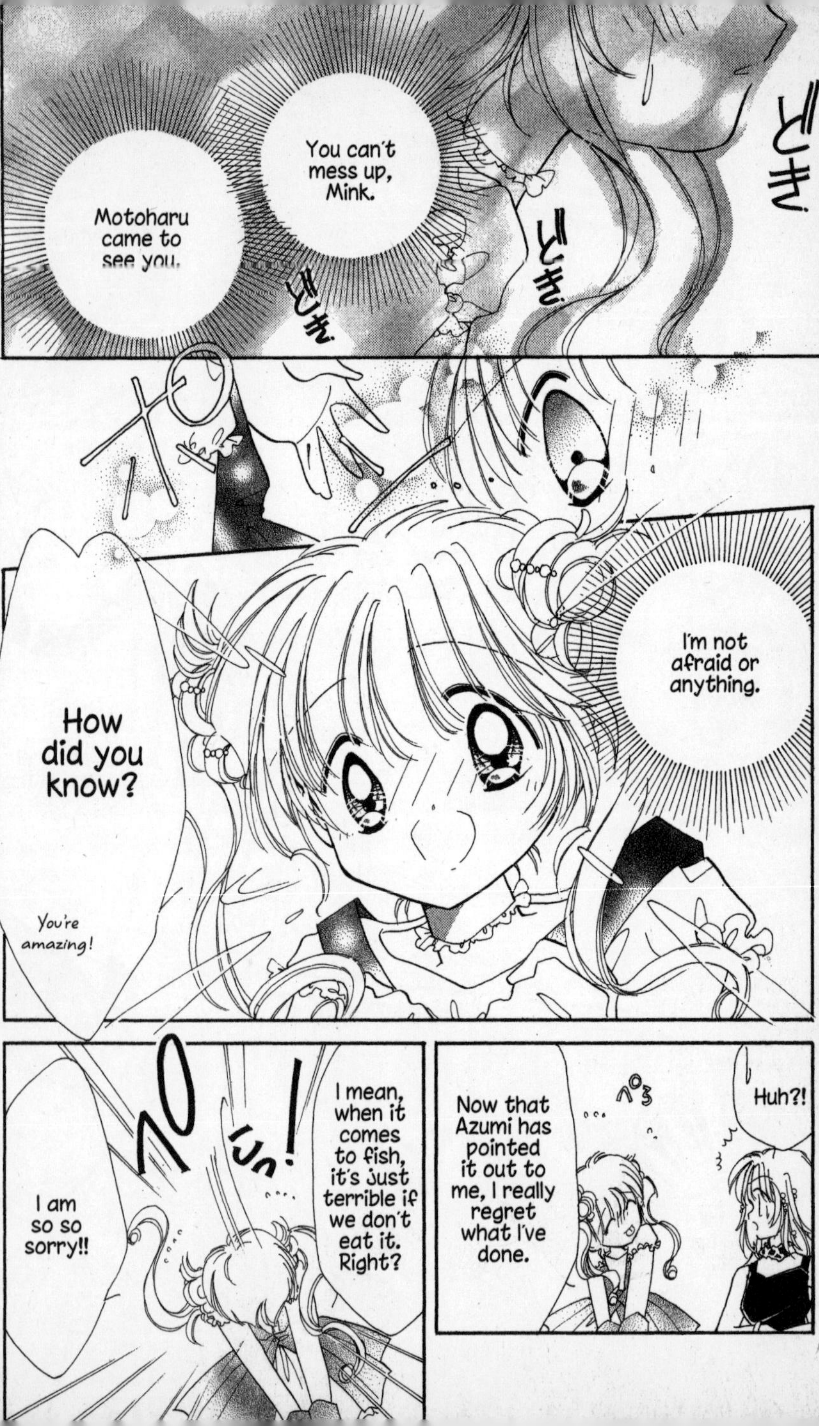
どき
You can't mess up, Mink.
どき
Motoharu came to see you.
どき
I'm not afraid or anything.
How did you know?
You're amazing!
Huh?!
Now that Azumi has pointed it out to me, I really regret what I've done.
I mean, when it comes to fish, it's just terrible if we don't eat it. Right?
I am so so sorry!!

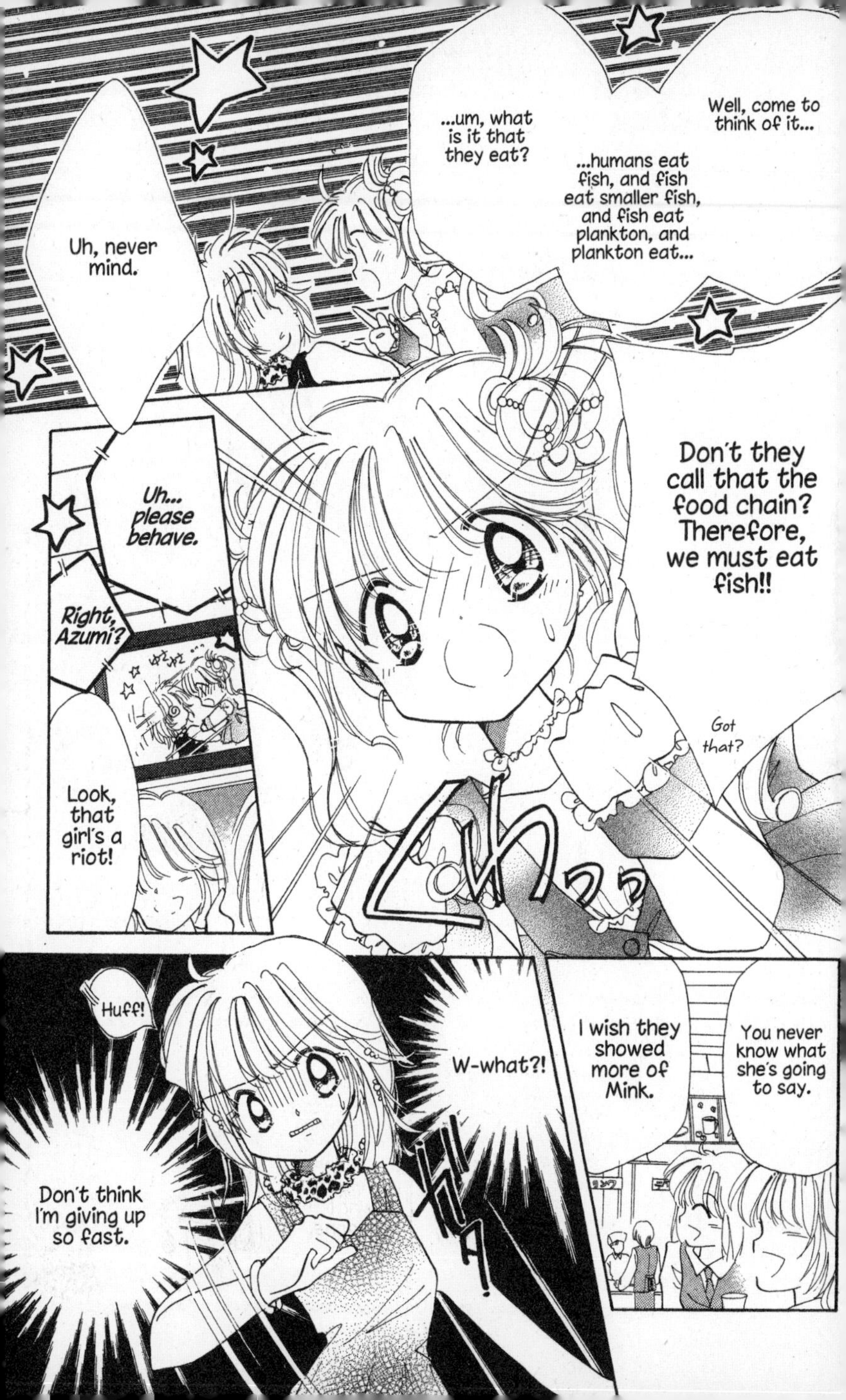
Well, come to think of it...
...humans eat fish, and fish eat smaller fish, and fish eat plankton, and plankton eat...
...um, what is it that they eat?
Uh, never mind.
Don't they call that the food chain? Therefore, we must eat fish!!
Got that?
Uh... please behave.
Right, Azumi?
Look, that girl's a riot!
You never know what she's going to say.
I wish they showed more of Mink.
W-what?!
Huff!
Don't think I'm giving up so fast.

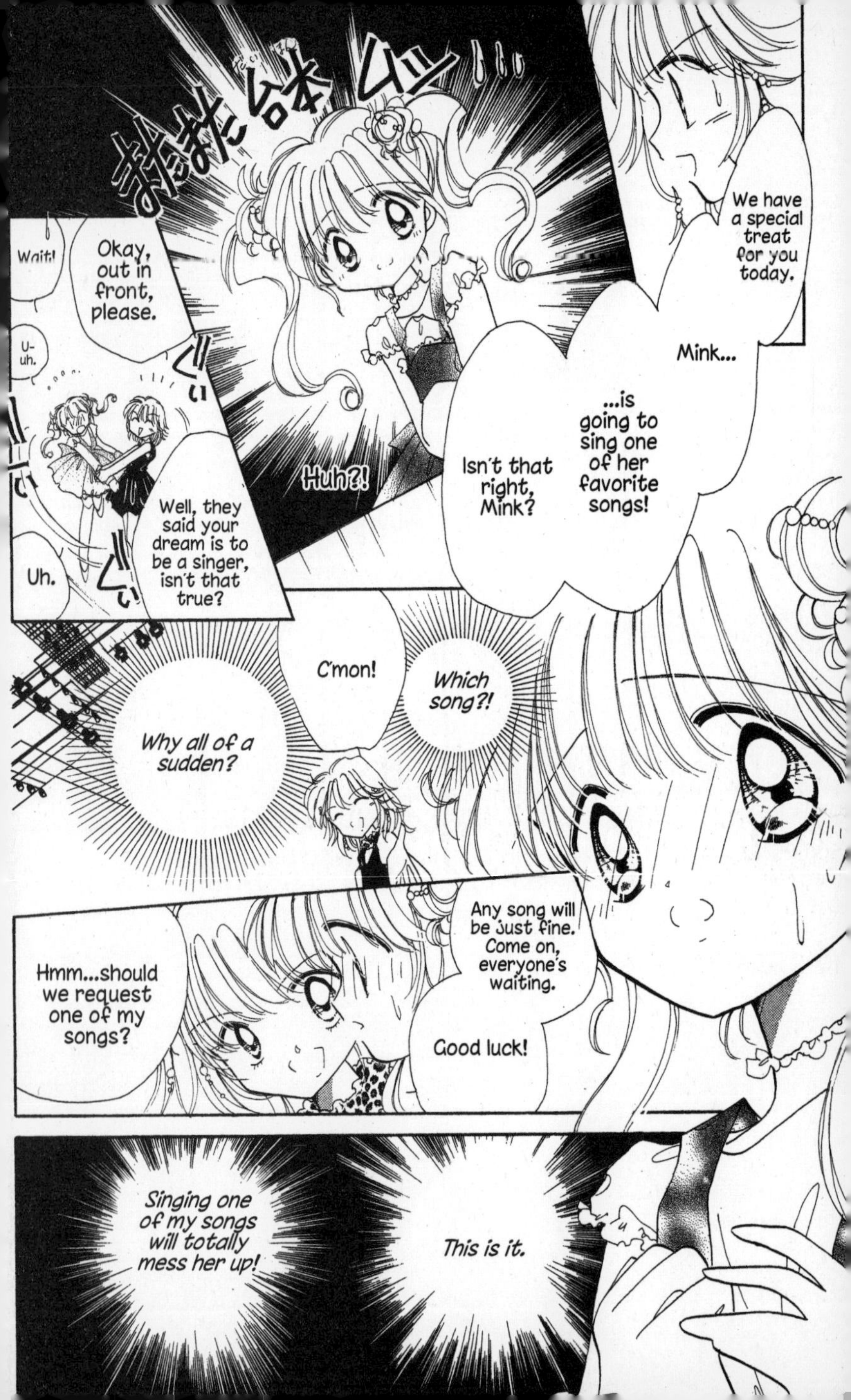

We have a special treat for you today.
Mink...
...is going to sing one of her favorite songs!
Isn't that right, Mink?
Huh?!
Okay, out in front, please.
Wait!
U-uh.
Well, they said your dream is to be a singer, isn't that true?
Uh.
C'mon!
Which song?!
Why all of a sudden?
Any song will be just fine. Come on, everyone's waiting.
Good luck!
Hmm...should we request one of my songs?
This is it.
Singing one of my songs will totally mess her up!

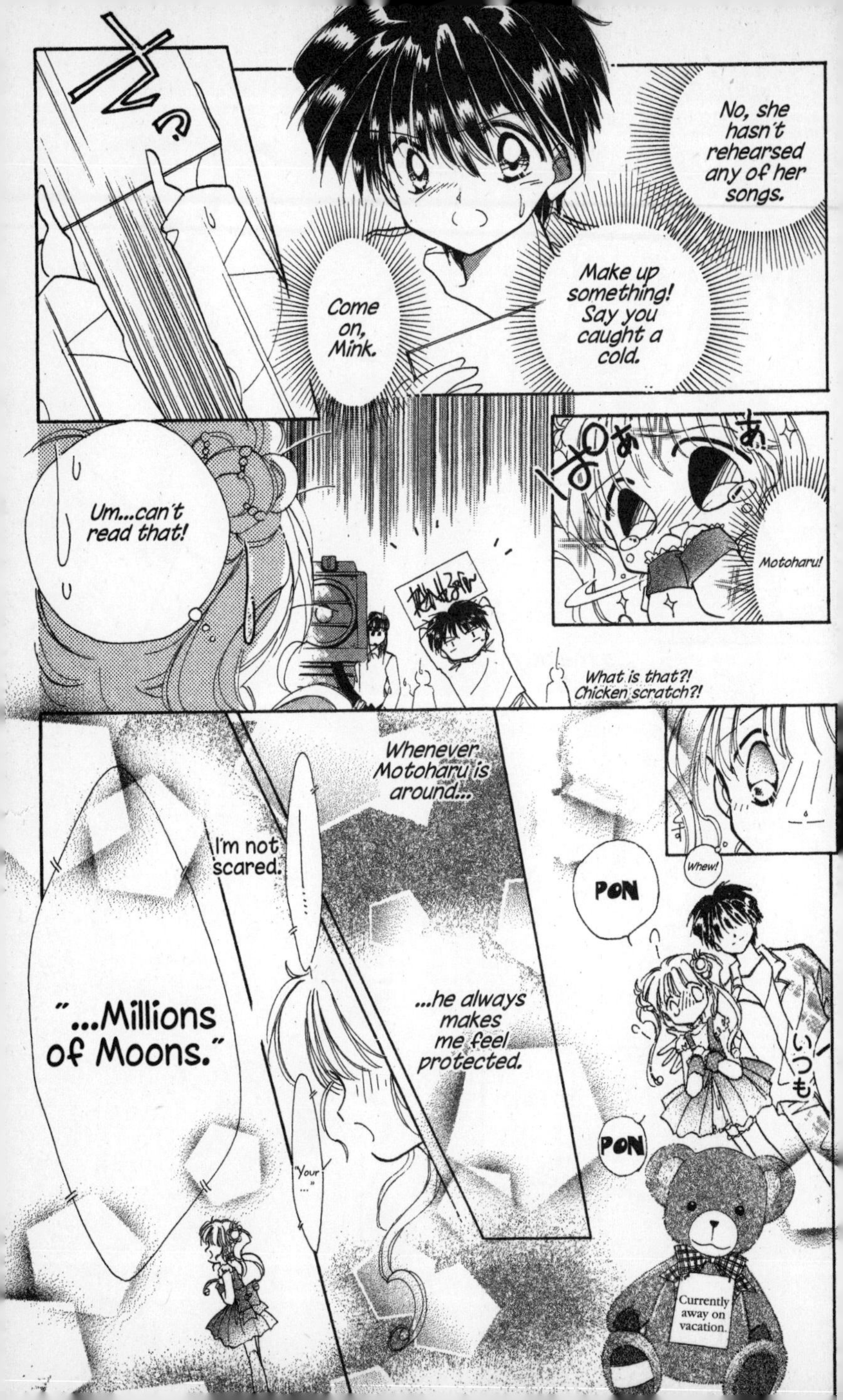
No, she hasn't rehearsed any of her songs.
Make up something! Say you caught a cold.
Come on, Mink.
Motoharu!
Um...can't read that!
What is that?! Chicken scratch?!
Whew!
PON
いつも
PON
Currently away on vacation.
Whenever Motoharu is around...
I'm not scared.
...he always makes me feel protected.
"Your ..."
"...Millions of Moons."

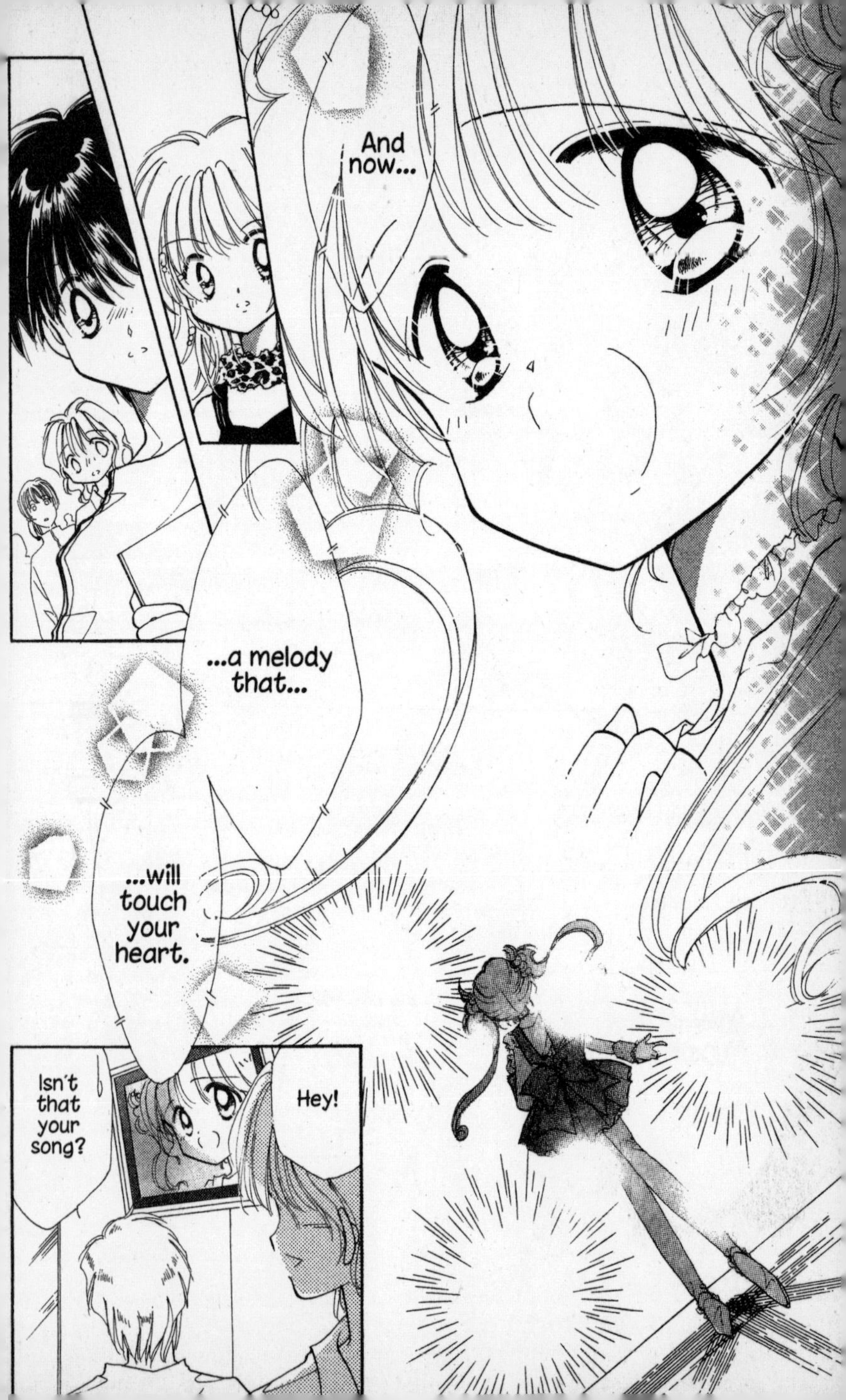
And now...
...a melody that...
...will touch your heart.
Hey!
Isn't that your song?

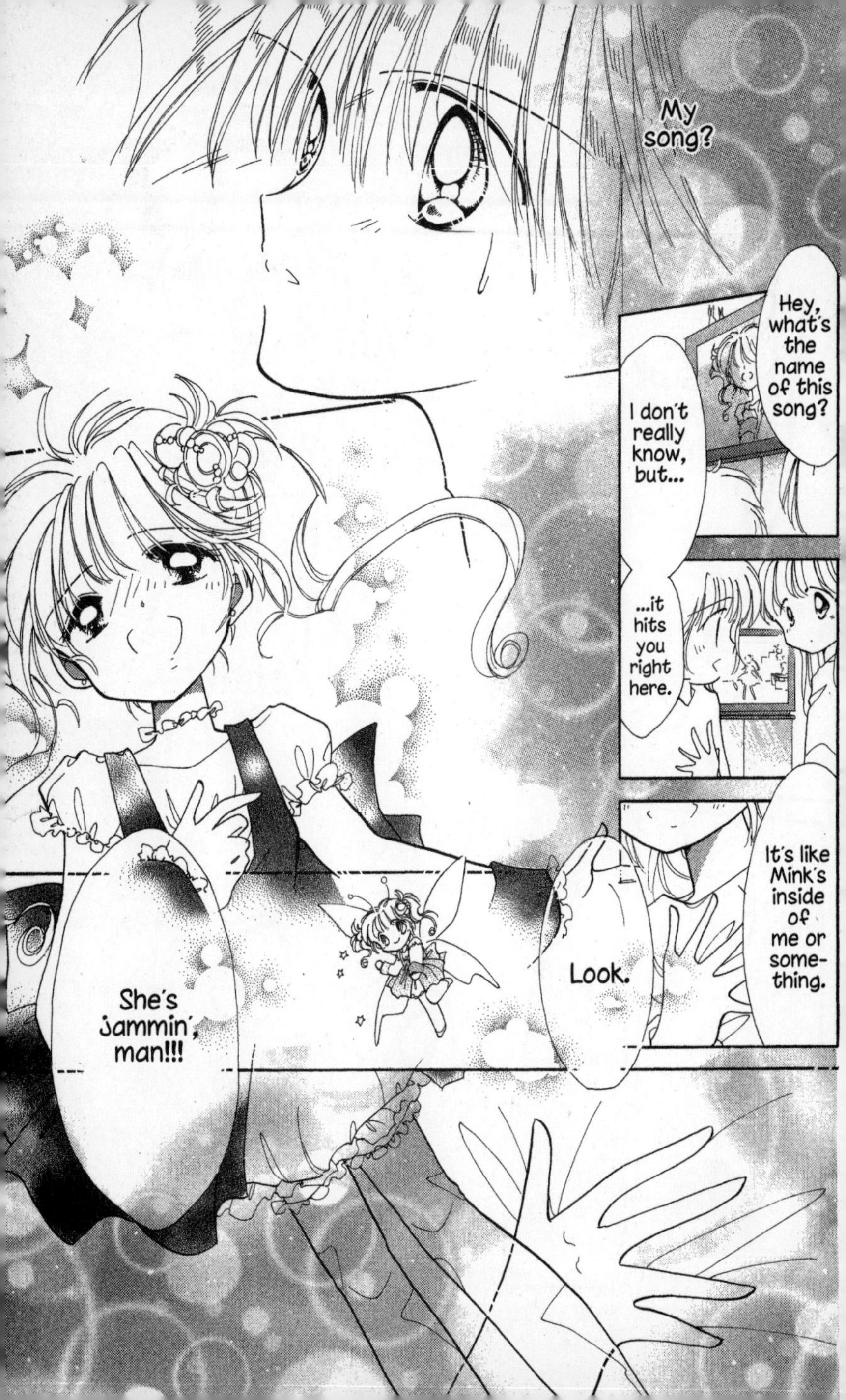
My song?
Hey, what's the name of this song?
I don't really know, but...
...it hits you right here.
It's like Mink's inside of me or something.
Look.
She's jammin', man!!!

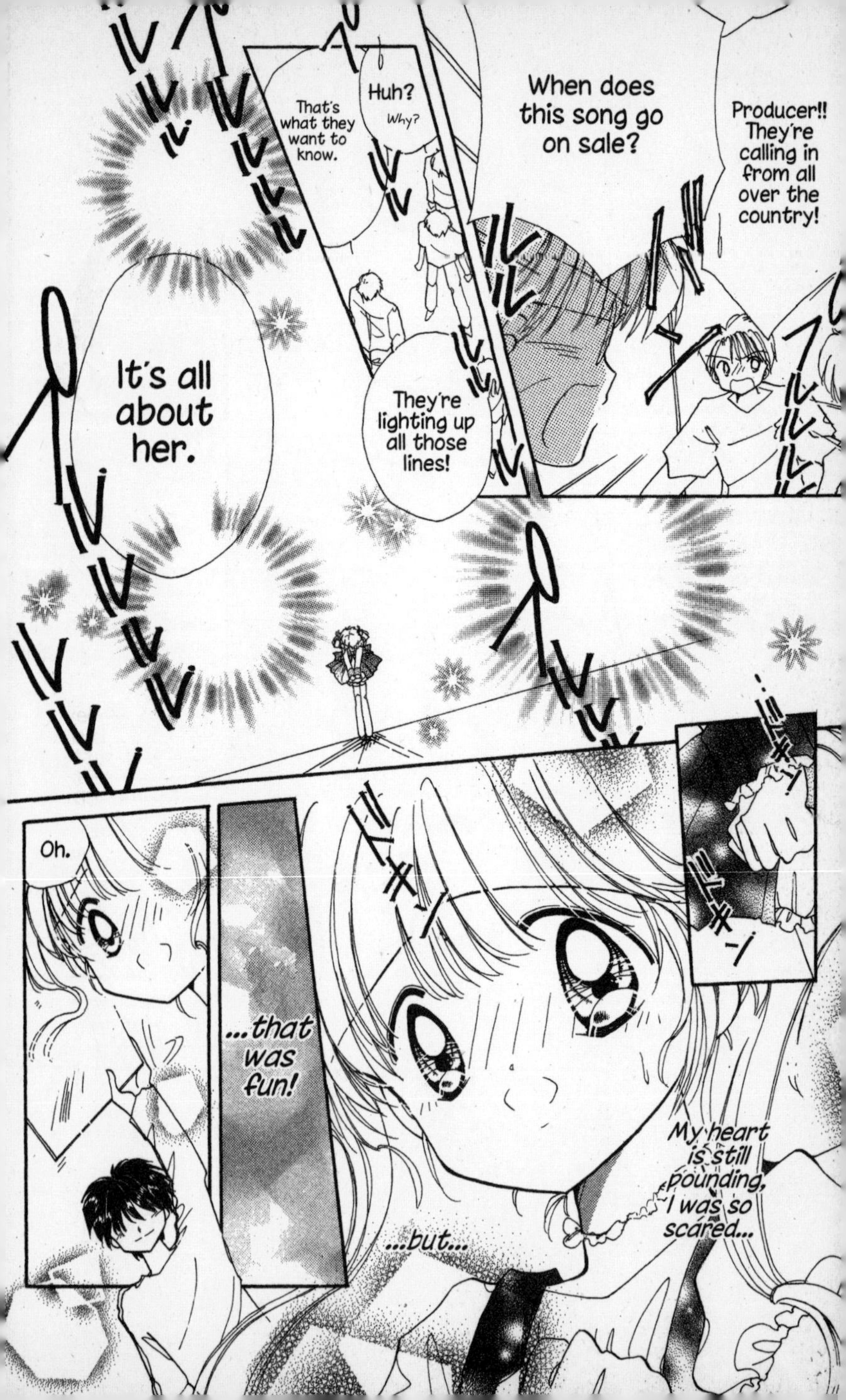
Producer!! They're calling in from all over the country!
When does this song go on sale?
Huh?
Why?
That's what they want to know.
They're lighting up all those lines!
It's all about her.
My heart is still pounding, I was so scared...
...but...
...that was fun!
Oh.

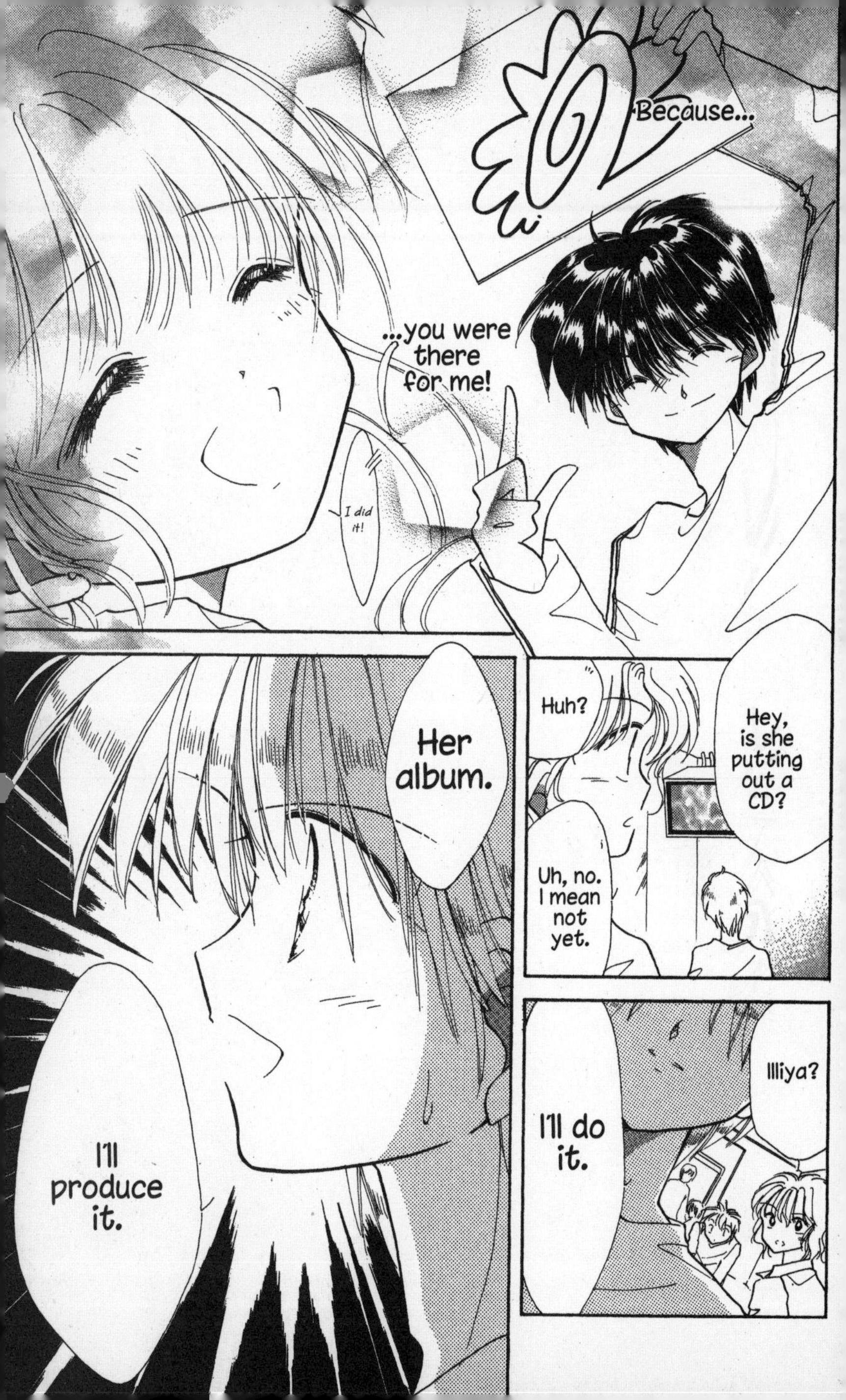
Because...
...you were there for me!
I did it!
Hey, is she putting out a CD?
Huh?
Uh, no. I mean not yet.
Illiya?
I'll do it.
Her album.
I'll produce it.

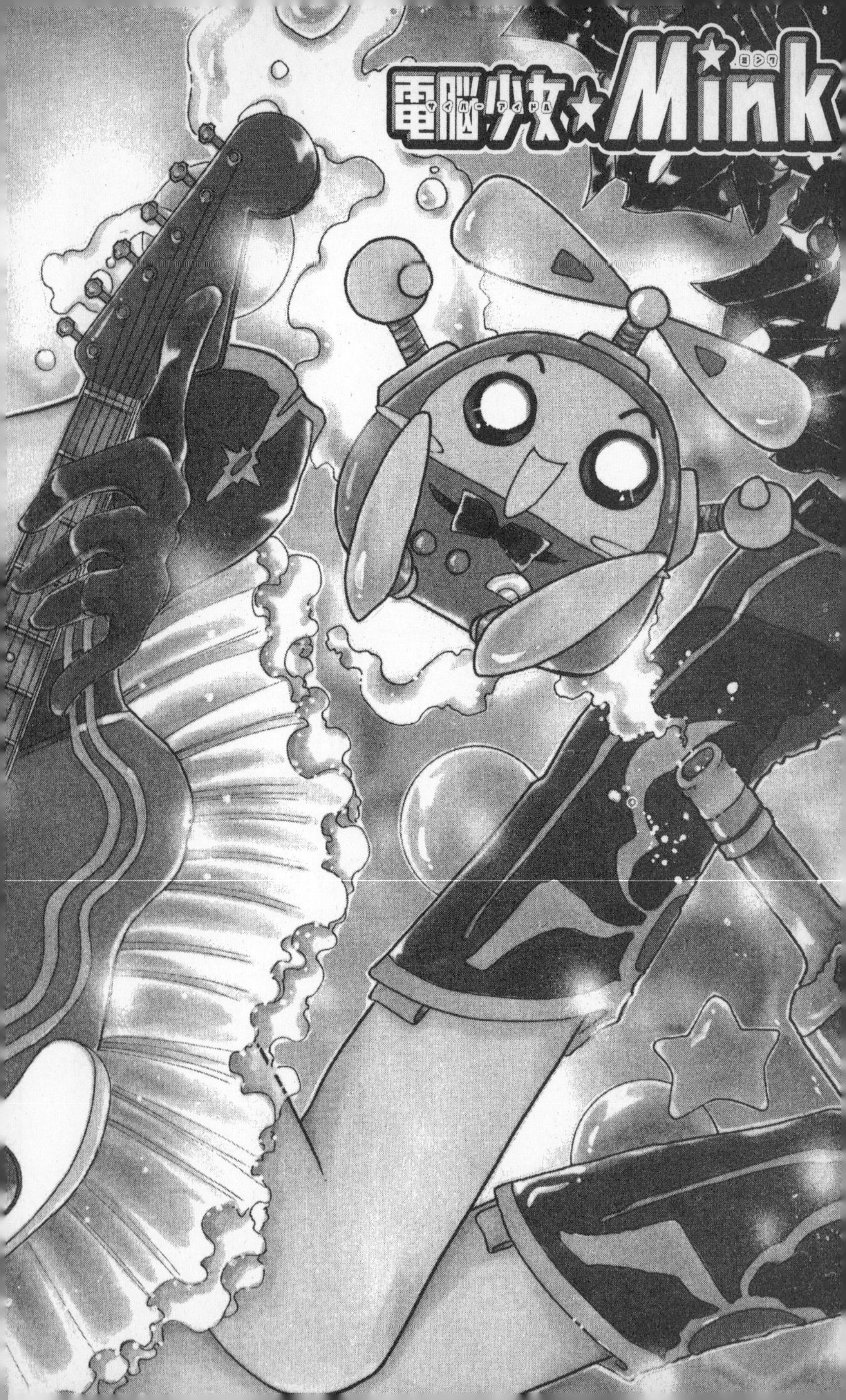
電脳少女☆Mink
サイバーアイドル
ミンク

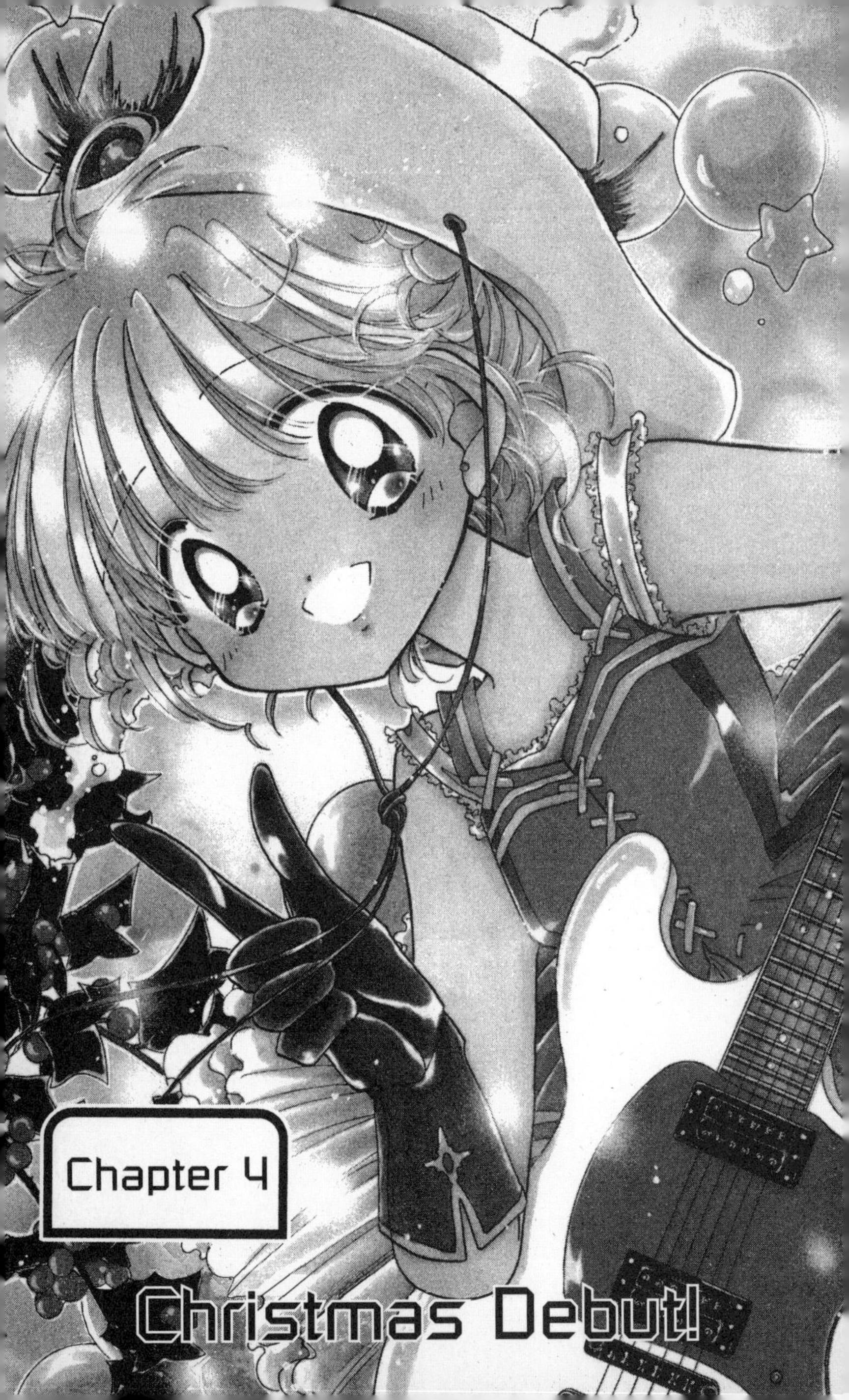
Chapter 4
Christmas Debut!

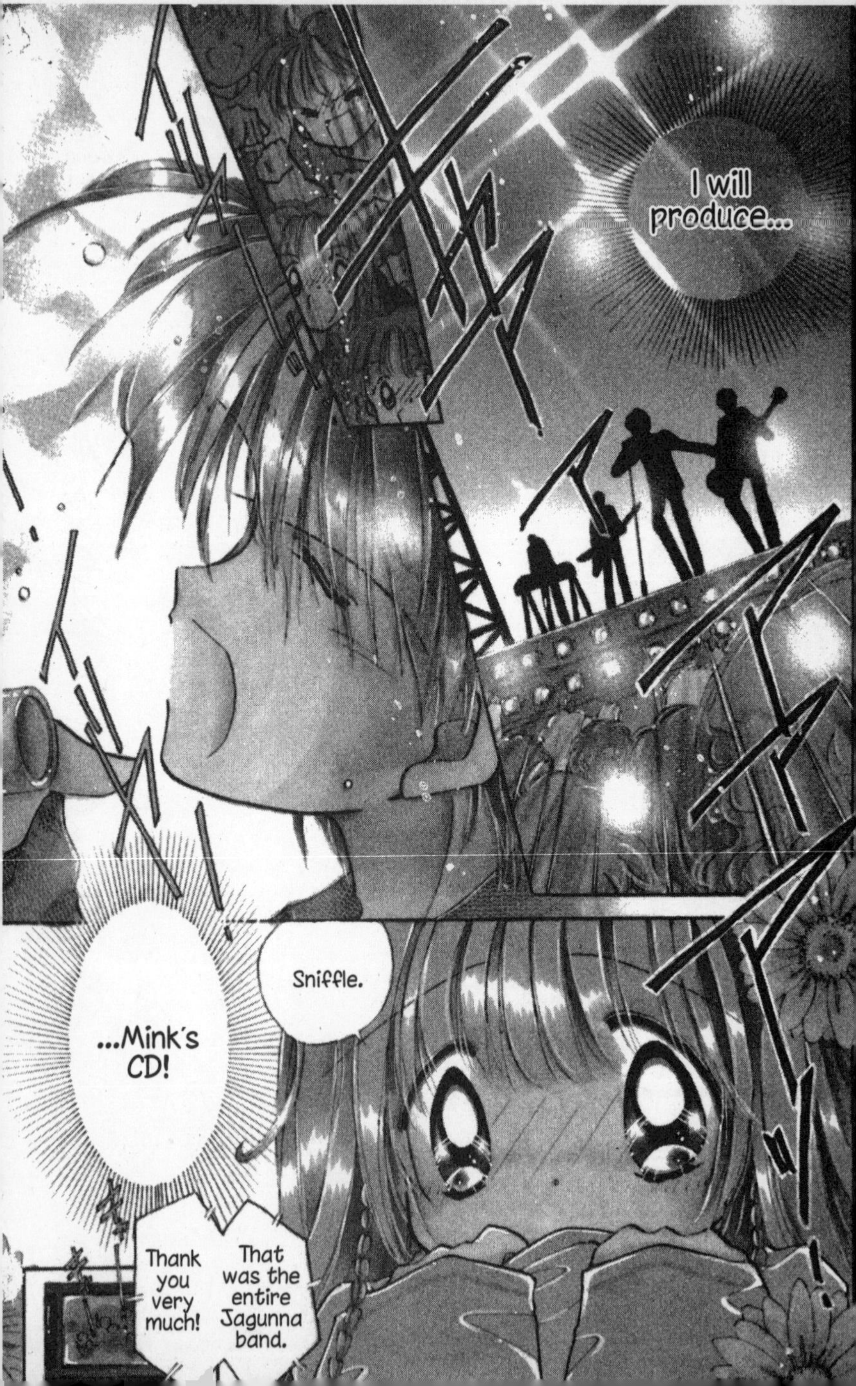
I will produce...
Sniffle.
...Mink's CD!
That was the entire Jagunna band.
Thank you very much!

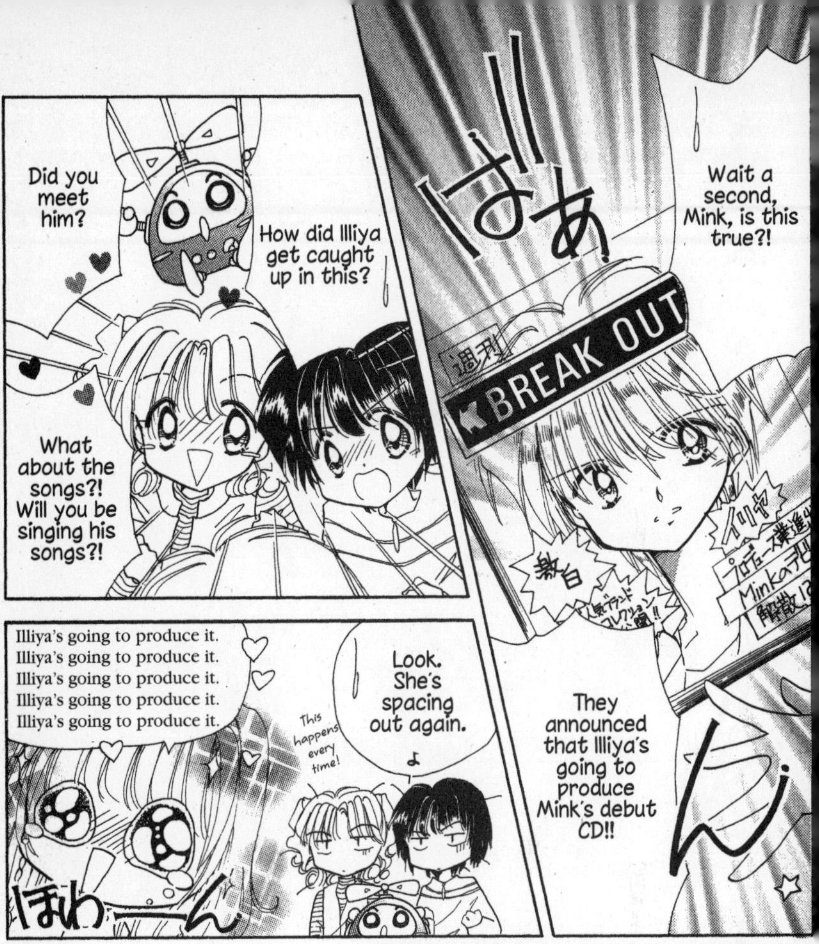
Wait a second, Mink, is this true?!
ばあ
週刊
BREAK OUT
激白
They announced that Illiya's going to produce Mink's debut CD!!
ん
How did Illiya get caught up in this?
Did you meet him?
What about the songs?! Will you be singing his songs?!
Look. She's spacing out again.
This happens every time!
Illiya's going to produce it.
Illiya's going to produce it.
Illiya's going to produce it.
Illiya's going to produce it.
Illiya's going to produce it.
ほわーん

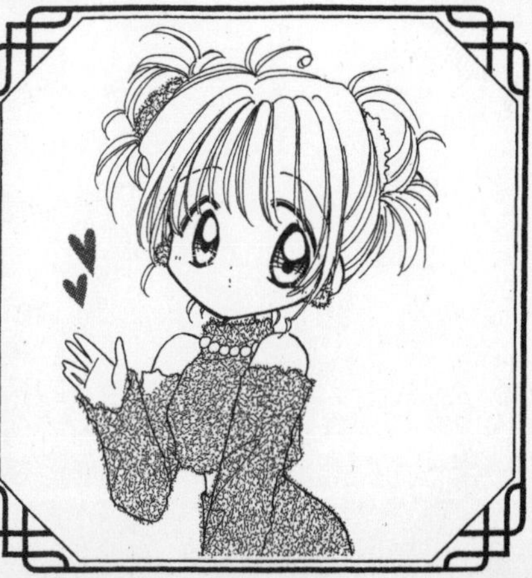

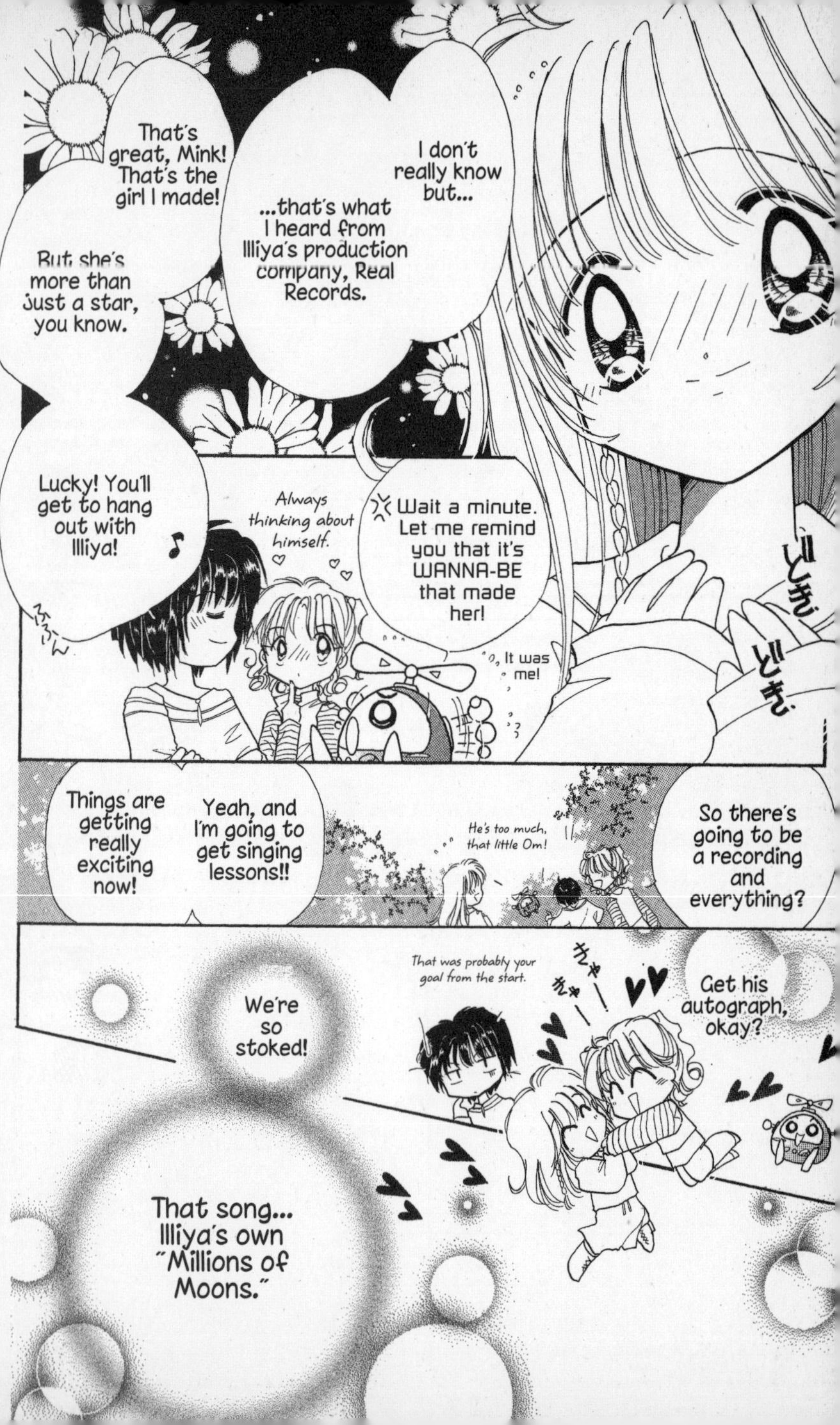
I don't really know but...
...that's what I heard from Illiya's production company, Real Records.
That's great, Mink! That's the girl I made!
But she's more than just a star, you know.
Wait a minute. Let me remind you that it's WANNA-BE that made her!
It was me!
Always thinking about himself.
Lucky! You'll get to hang out with Illiya!
So there's going to be a recording and everything?
He's too much, that little Om!
Yeah, and I'm going to get singing lessons!!
Things are getting really exciting now!
Get his autograph, okay?
きゃー
きゃー
That was probably your goal from the start.
We're so stoked!
That song... Illiya's own "Millions of Moons."

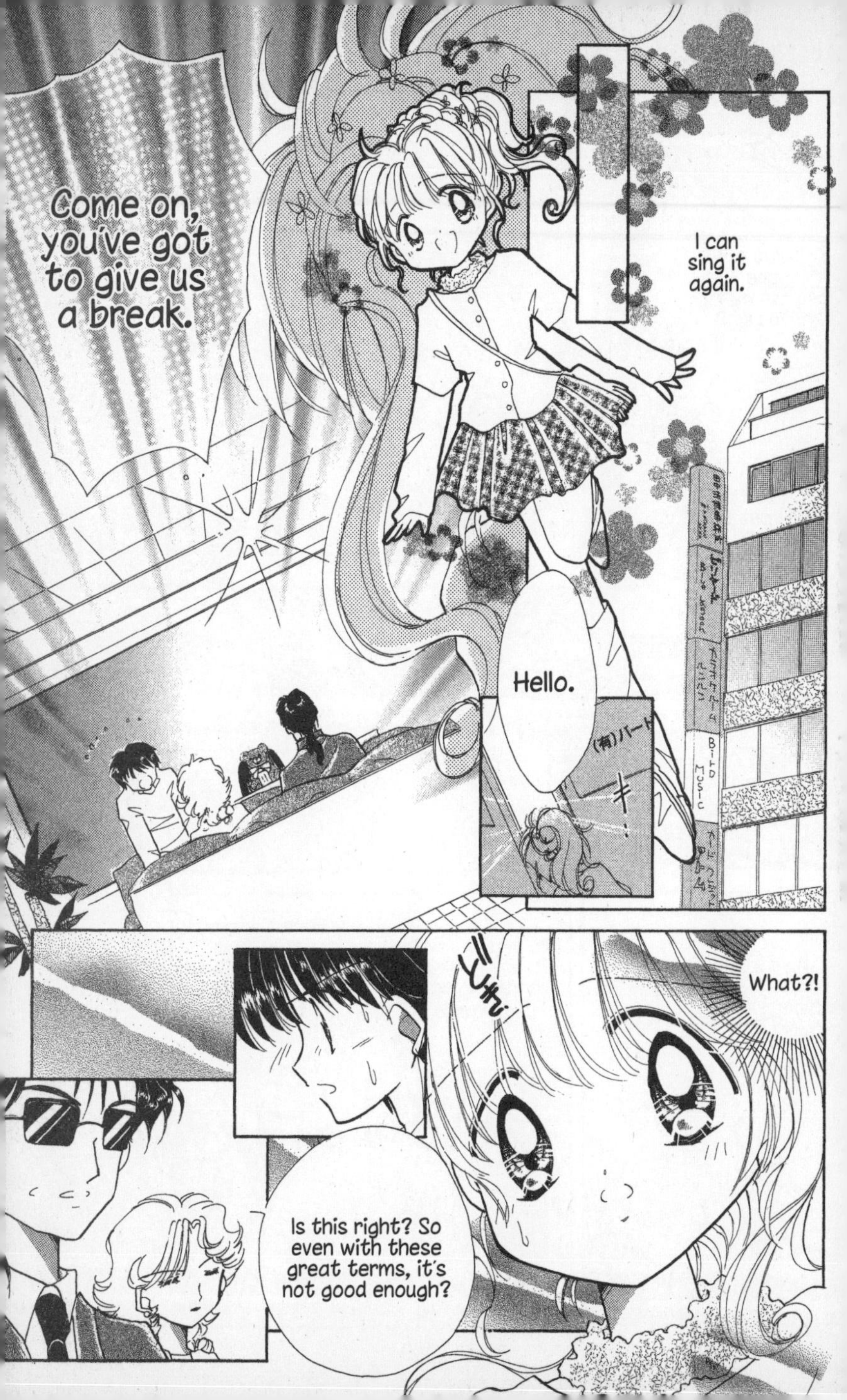
I can sing it again.
Hello.
Come on, you've got to give us a break.
What?!
Is this right? So even with these great terms, it's not good enough?

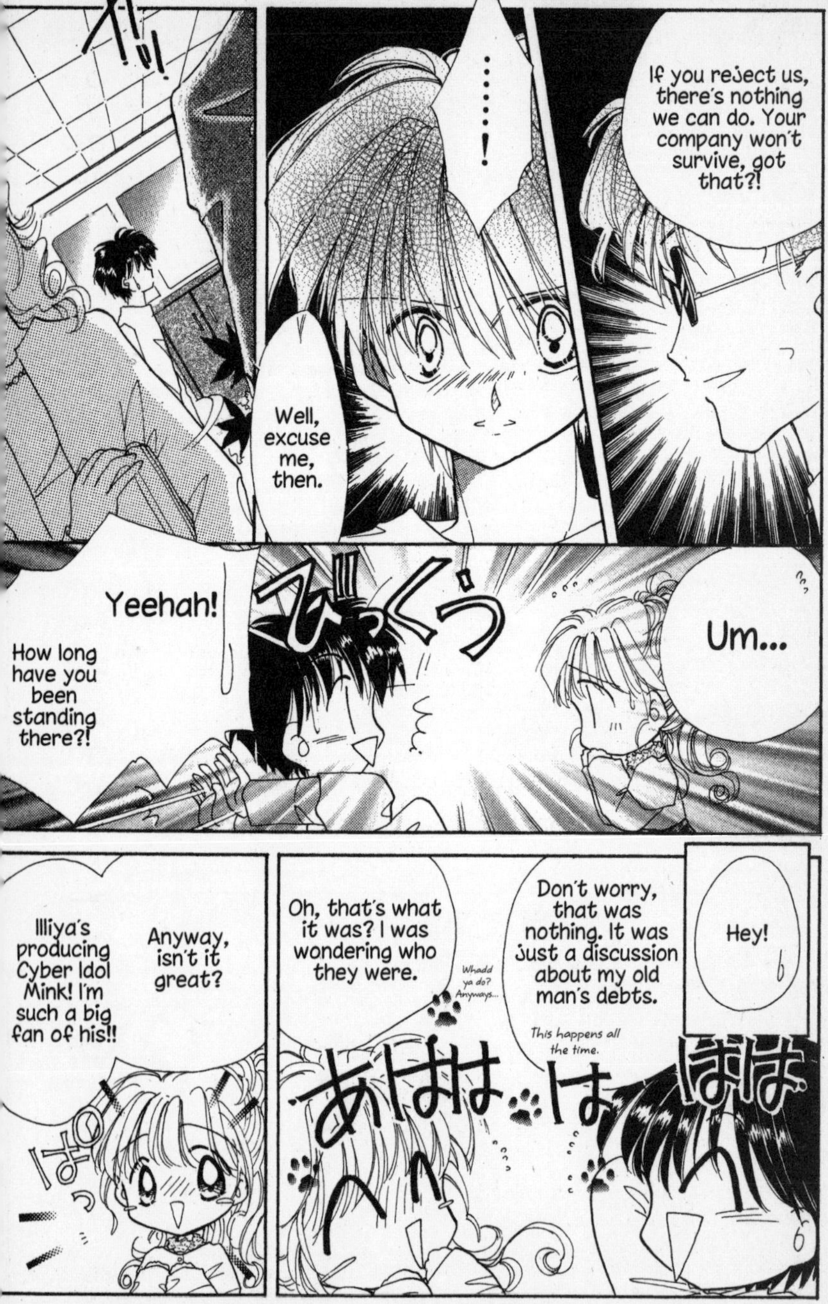
If you reject us, there's nothing we can do. Your company won't survive, got that?!
......!
Well, excuse me, then.
Um...
びっくぅ
Yeehah!
How long have you been standing there?!
Hey!
Don't worry, that was nothing. It was just a discussion about my old man's debts.
This happens all the time.
Oh, that's what it was? I was wondering who they were.
Whadd ya do? Anyways...
Anyway, isn't it great?
Illiya's producing Cyber Idol Mink! I'm such a big fan of his!!

Mink Rap!

My Favorite Songs!

"Songs of Love" by Gardens

"That Paper Airplane Crossing a Cloudy Sky" by 19

"Making a Beeline" by Miho Komatsu

"Next to You" and "Wish" by Hitomi

"Before Dawn" by Sugashikao

"Heart of the Night" by Nanase Aikawa

"Isn't She Cute?" by Mission

"Lovesong" by Something Else

"Squall" by Eiko Matsumoto

"Love's Lovestar" by The Brilliant Green

"Paradise" by Yuki Uchida

PS: I've noticed that most of these singles start with guitar solos.

-Megumi

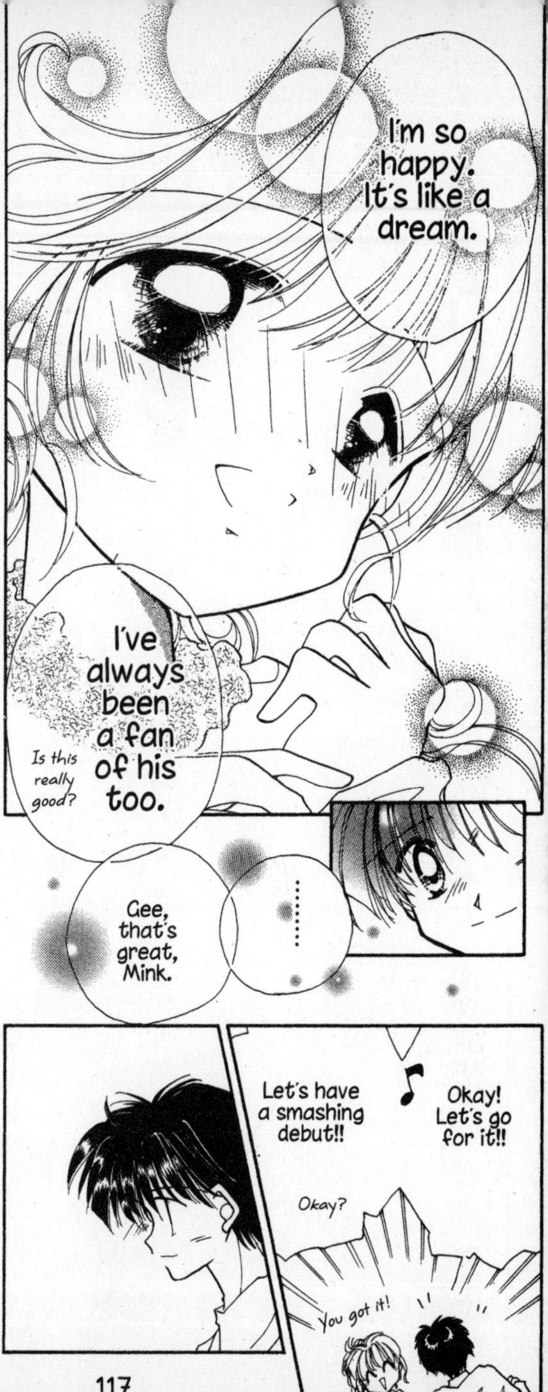

I'm so happy. It's like a dream.
I've always been a fan of his too.
Is this really good?
......
Gee, that's great, Mink.
Okay! Let's go for it!!
Let's have a smashing debut!!
Okay?
You got it!

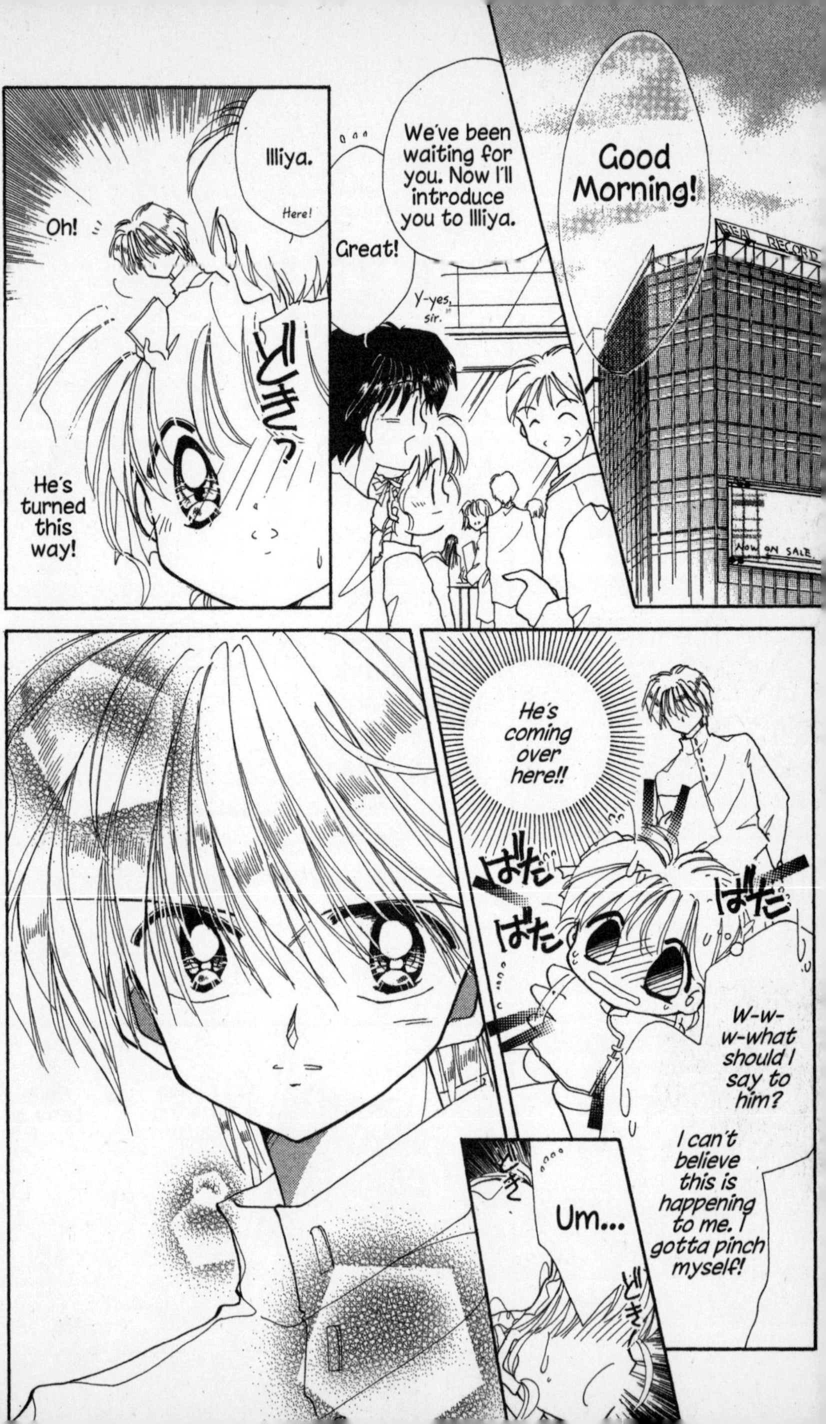
Good Morning!
REAL RECORD
NOW ON SALE
We've been waiting for you. Now I'll introduce you to Illiya.
Great!
Y-yes, sir.
Illiya.
Here!
Oh!
どきっ
He's turned this way!
He's coming over here!!
ばた
ばた
ばた
W-w-w-what should I say to him?
I can't believe this is happening to me. I gotta pinch myself!
どき
Um...
どき

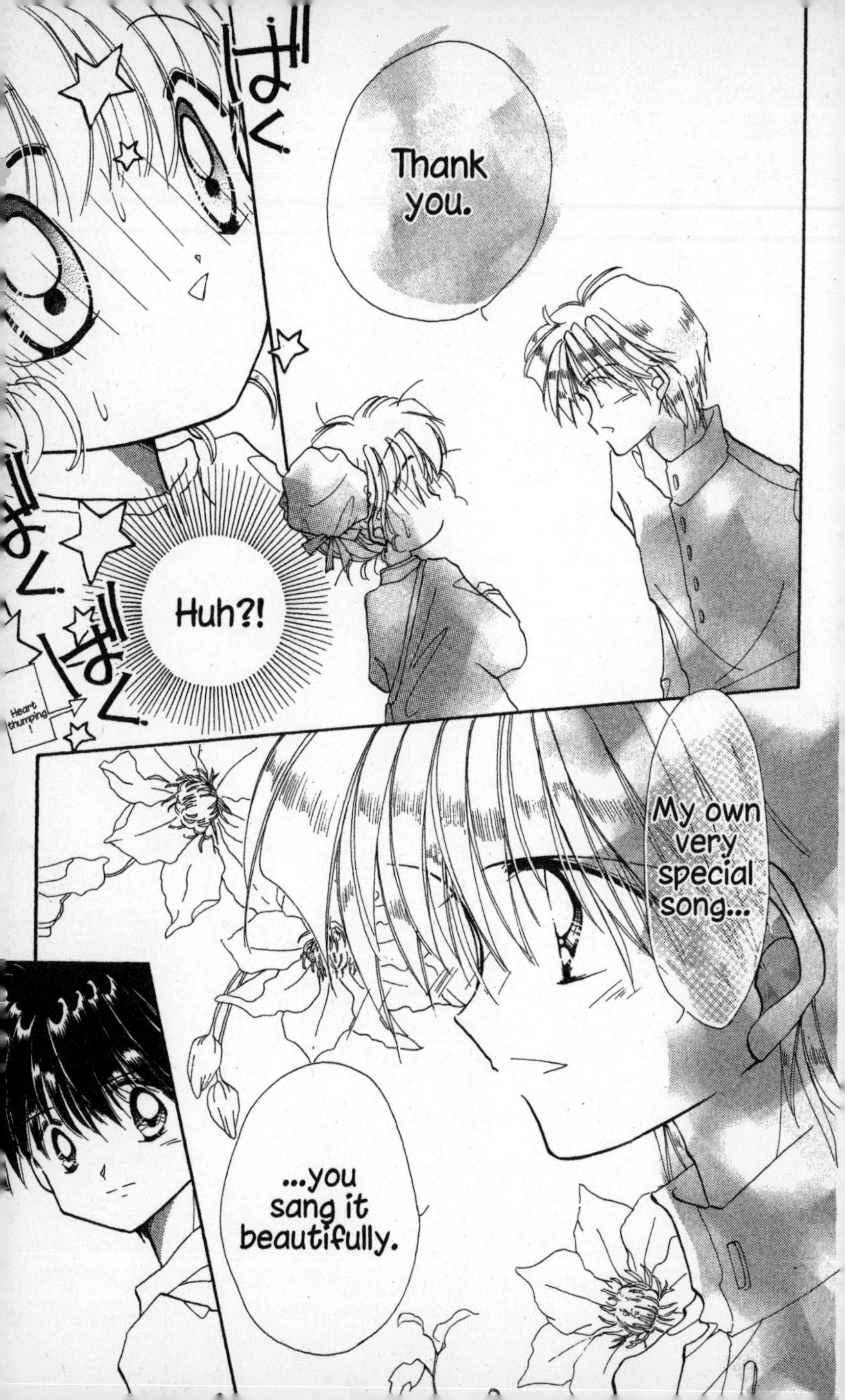
Thank you.
ばく
Huh?!
ばく
ばく
Heart thumping!
My own very special song...
...you sang it beautifully.

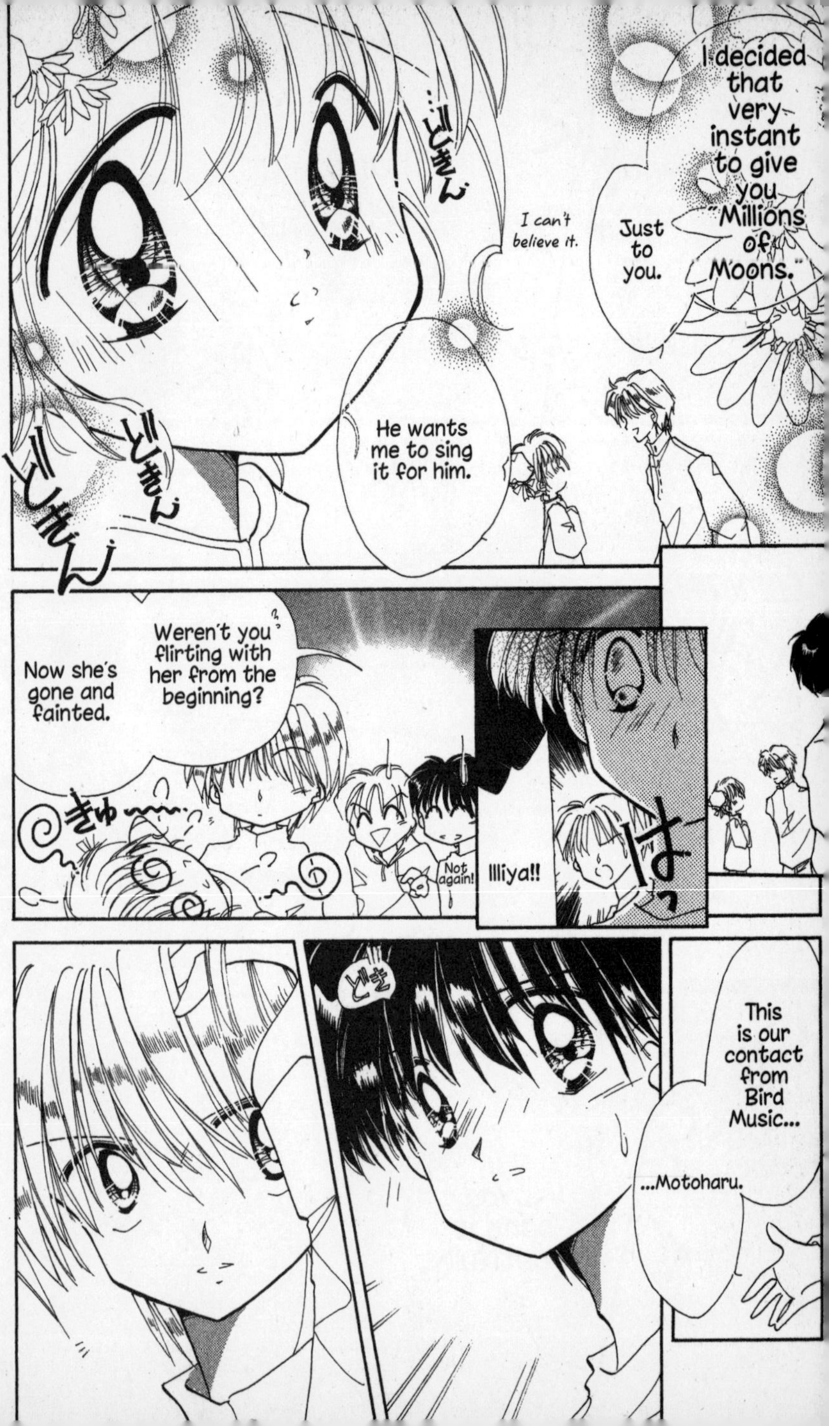
I decided that very instant to give you "Millions of Moons."
Just to you.
I can't believe it.
…どきん
He wants me to sing it for him.
どきん
どきん
Illiya!!
は
Weren't you flirting with her from the beginning?
Now she's gone and fainted.
Not again!
きゅ~~~
This is our contact from Bird Music...
...Motoharu.
どき

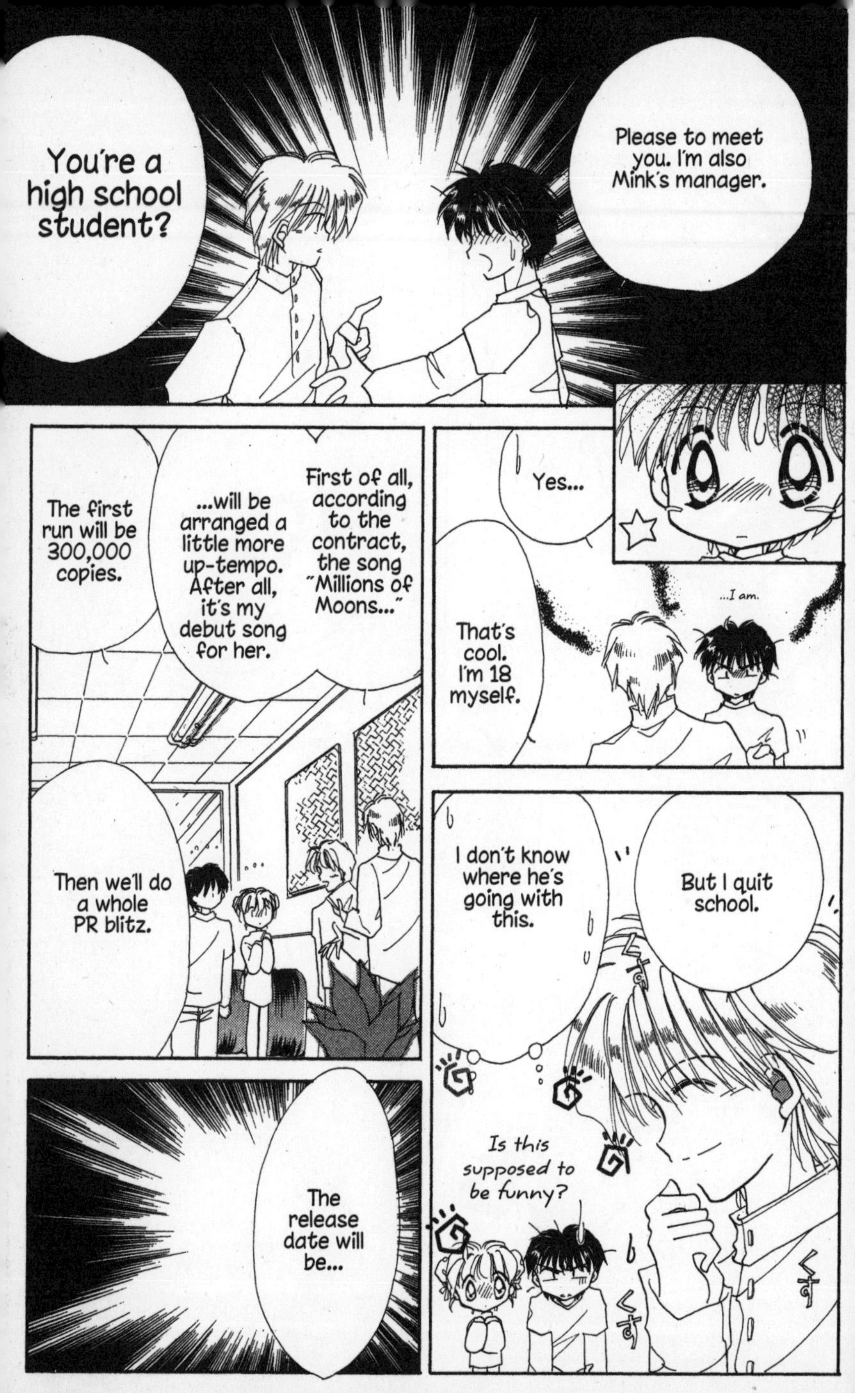
Please to meet you. I'm also Mink's manager.
You're a high school student?
Yes...
...I am.
That's cool. I'm 18 myself.
But I quit school.
I don't know where he's going with this.
Is this supposed to be funny?
First of all, according to the contract, the song "Millions of Moons..."
...will be arranged a little more up-tempo. After all, it's my debut song for her.
The first run will be 300,000 copies.
Then we'll do a whole PR blitz.
The release date will be...

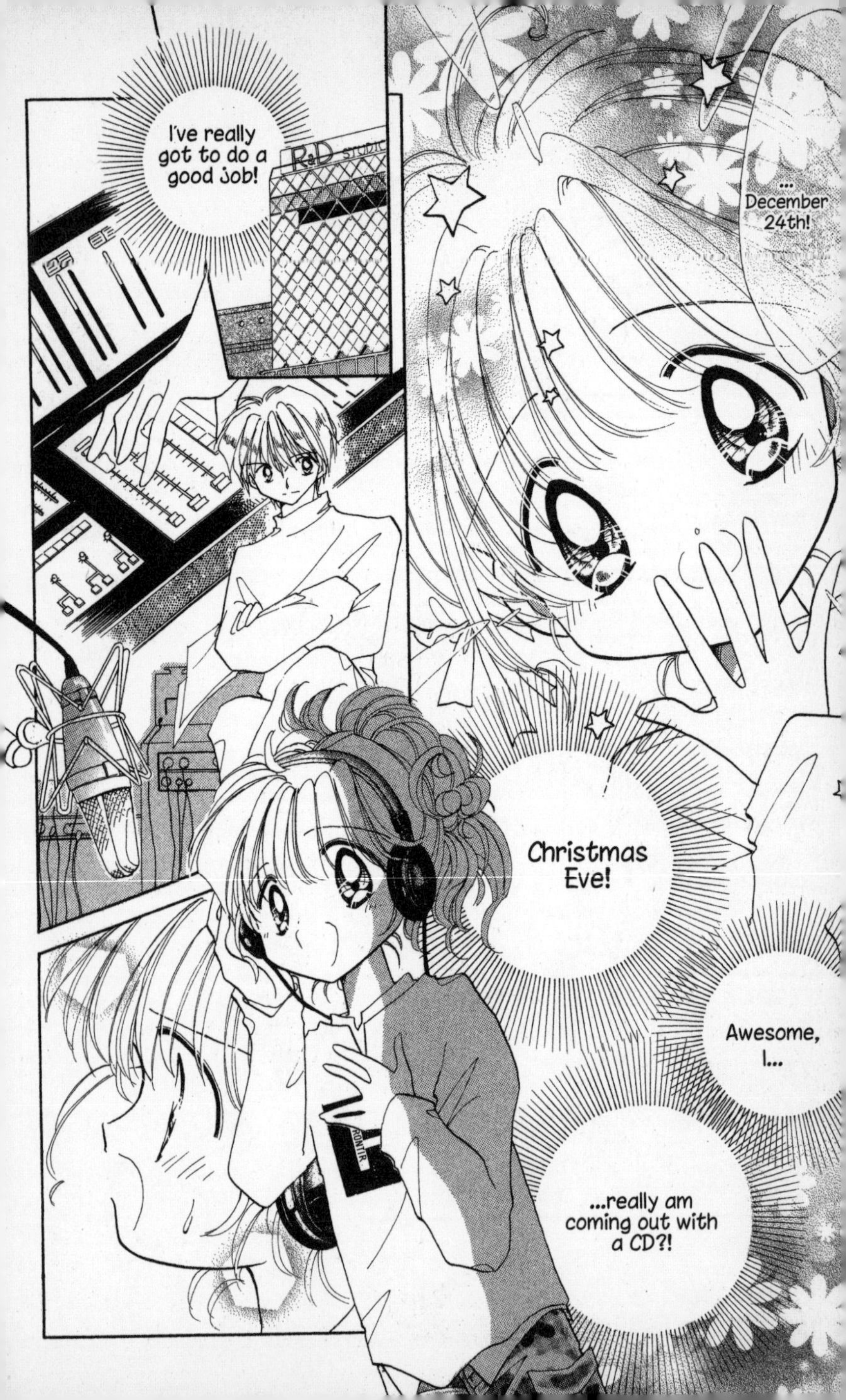
...December 24th!
Christmas Eve!
Awesome, I...
...really am coming out with a CD?!
I've really got to do a good job!
R&D STUDIO
FRONTIER

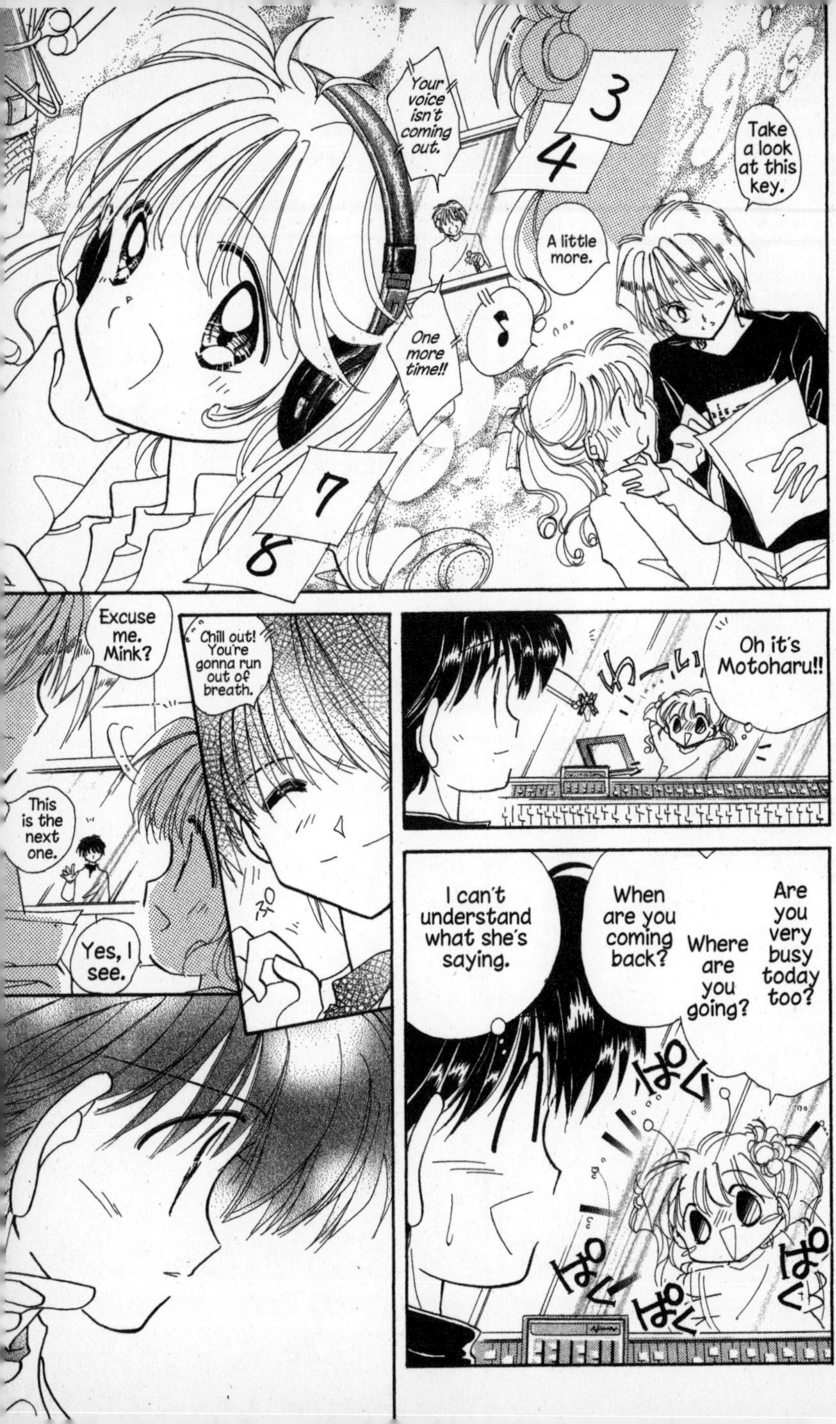
Take a look at this key.
Your voice isn't coming out.
A little more.
One more time!!
Oh it's Motoharu!!
Are you very busy today too?
Where are you going?
When are you coming back?
I can't understand what she's saying.
Chill out! You're gonna run out of breath.
Excuse me. Mink?
This is the next one.
Yes, I see.

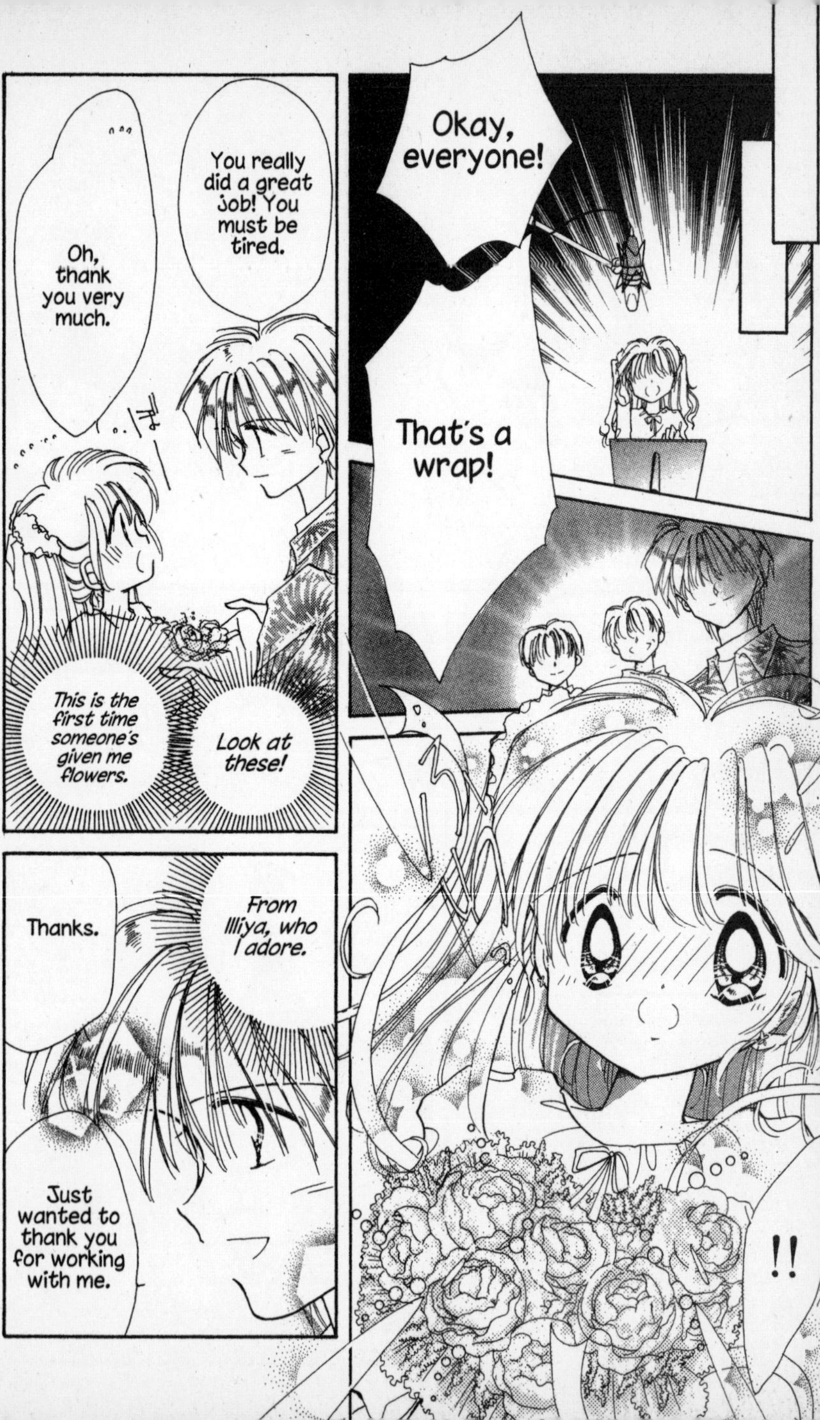

Okay, everyone!
That's a wrap!
!!
You really did a great job! You must be tired.
Oh, thank you very much.
Look at these!
This is the first time someone's given me flowers.
From Illiya, who I adore.
Thanks.
Just wanted to thank you for working with me.

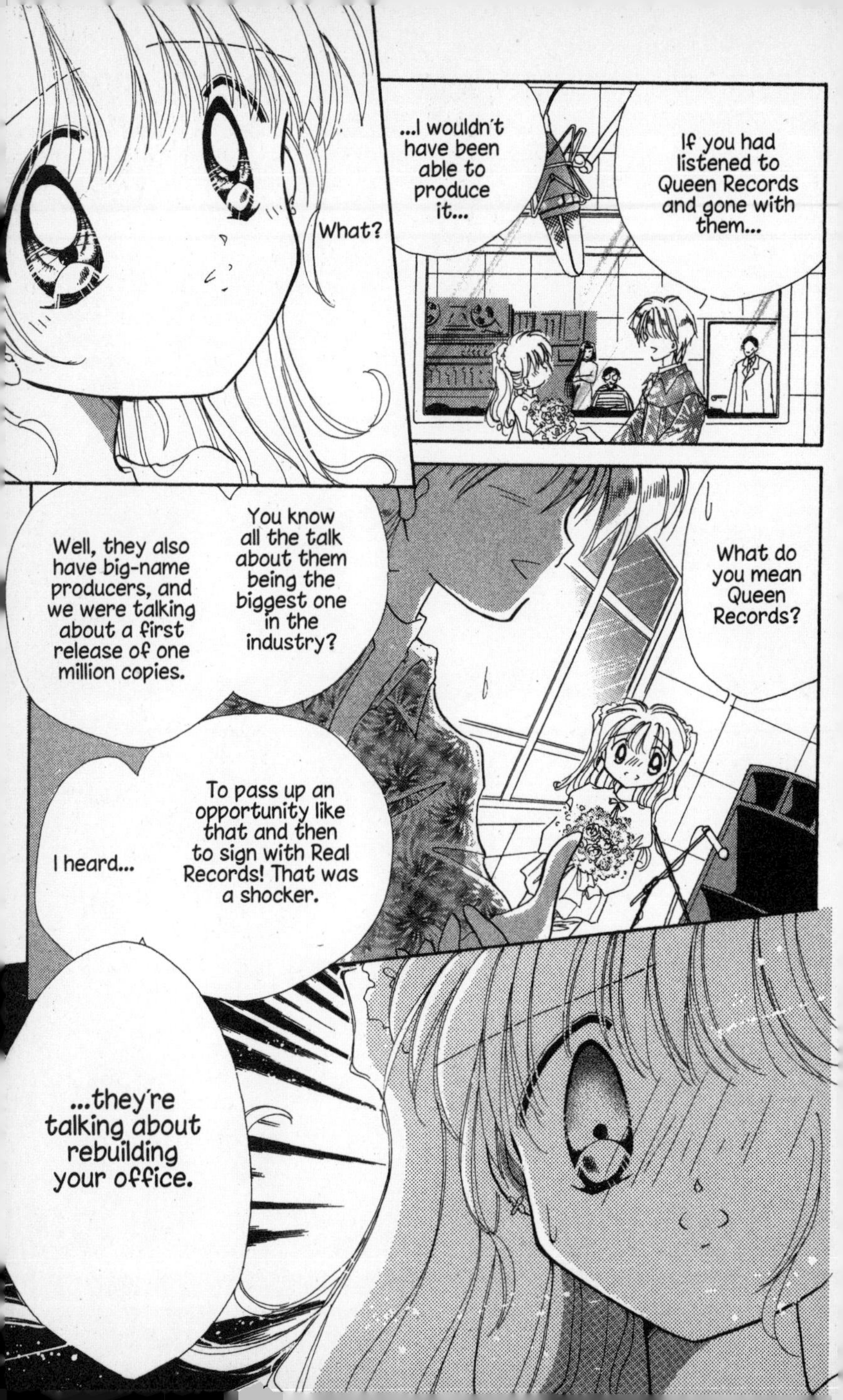
If you had listened to Queen Records and gone with them...
...I wouldn't have been able to produce it...
What?
What do you mean Queen Records?
You know all the talk about them being the biggest one in the industry?
Well, they also have big-name producers, and we were talking about a first release of one million copies.
To pass up an opportunity like that and then to sign with Real Records! That was a shocker.
I heard...
...they're talking about rebuilding your office.

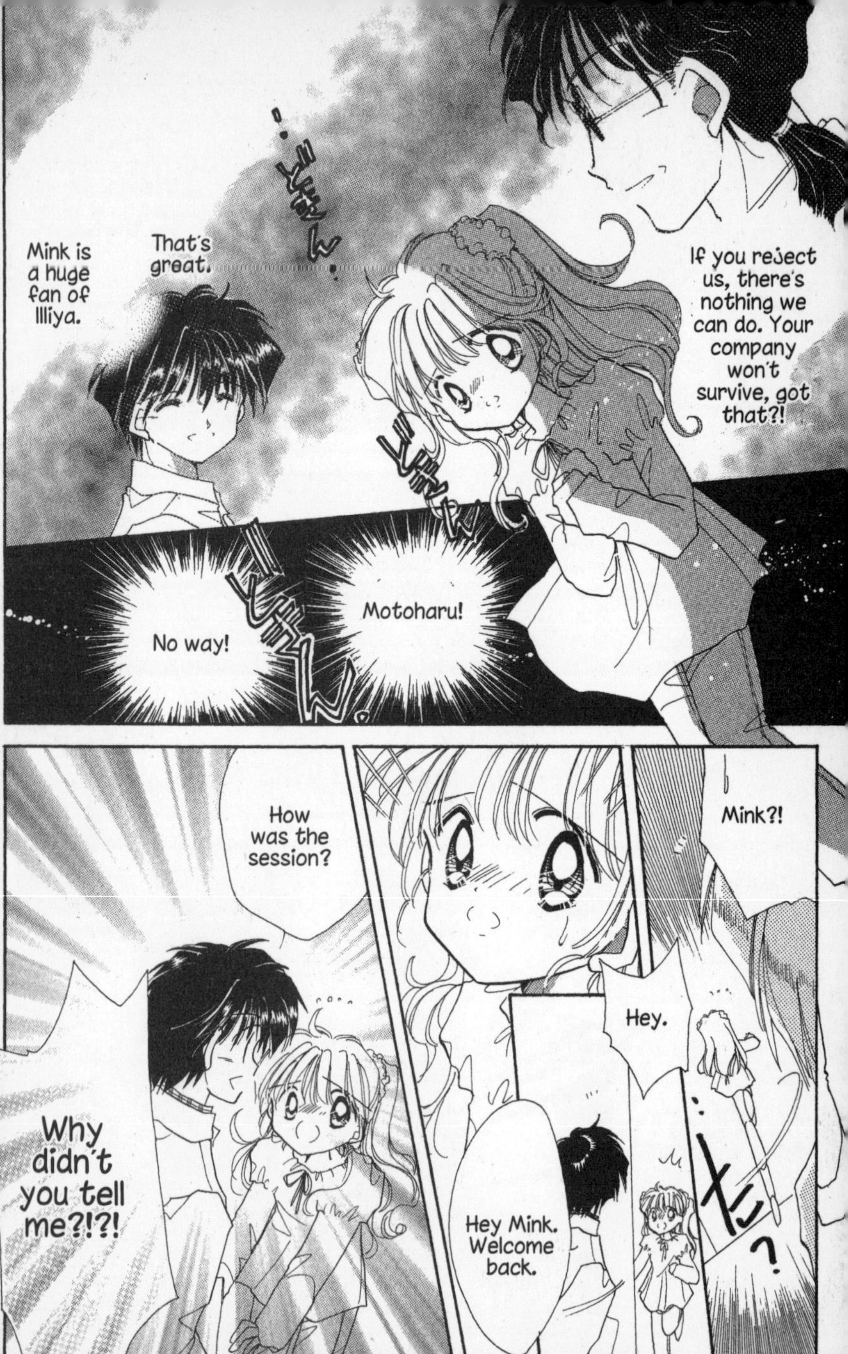
If you reject us, there's nothing we can do. Your company won't survive, got that?!
That's great.
Mink is a huge fan of Illiya.
Motoharu!
No way!
Mink?!
Hey.
Hey Mink. Welcome back.
How was the session?
Why didn't you tell me?!?!

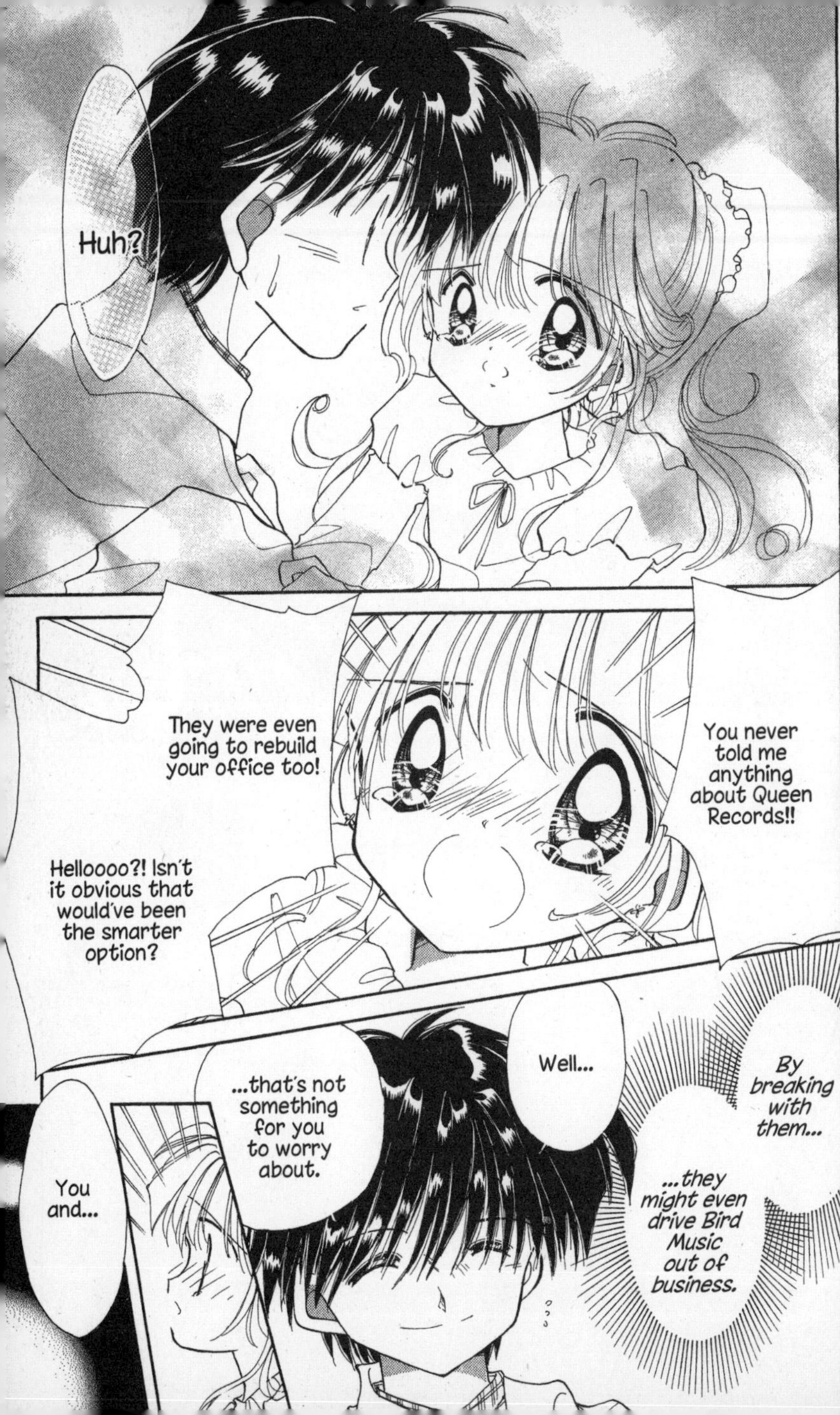
Huh?
You never told me anything about Queen Records!!
They were even going to rebuild your office too!
Helloooo?! Isn't it obvious that would've been the smarter option?
By breaking with them...
...they might even drive Bird Music out of business.
Well...
...that's not something for you to worry about.
You and...

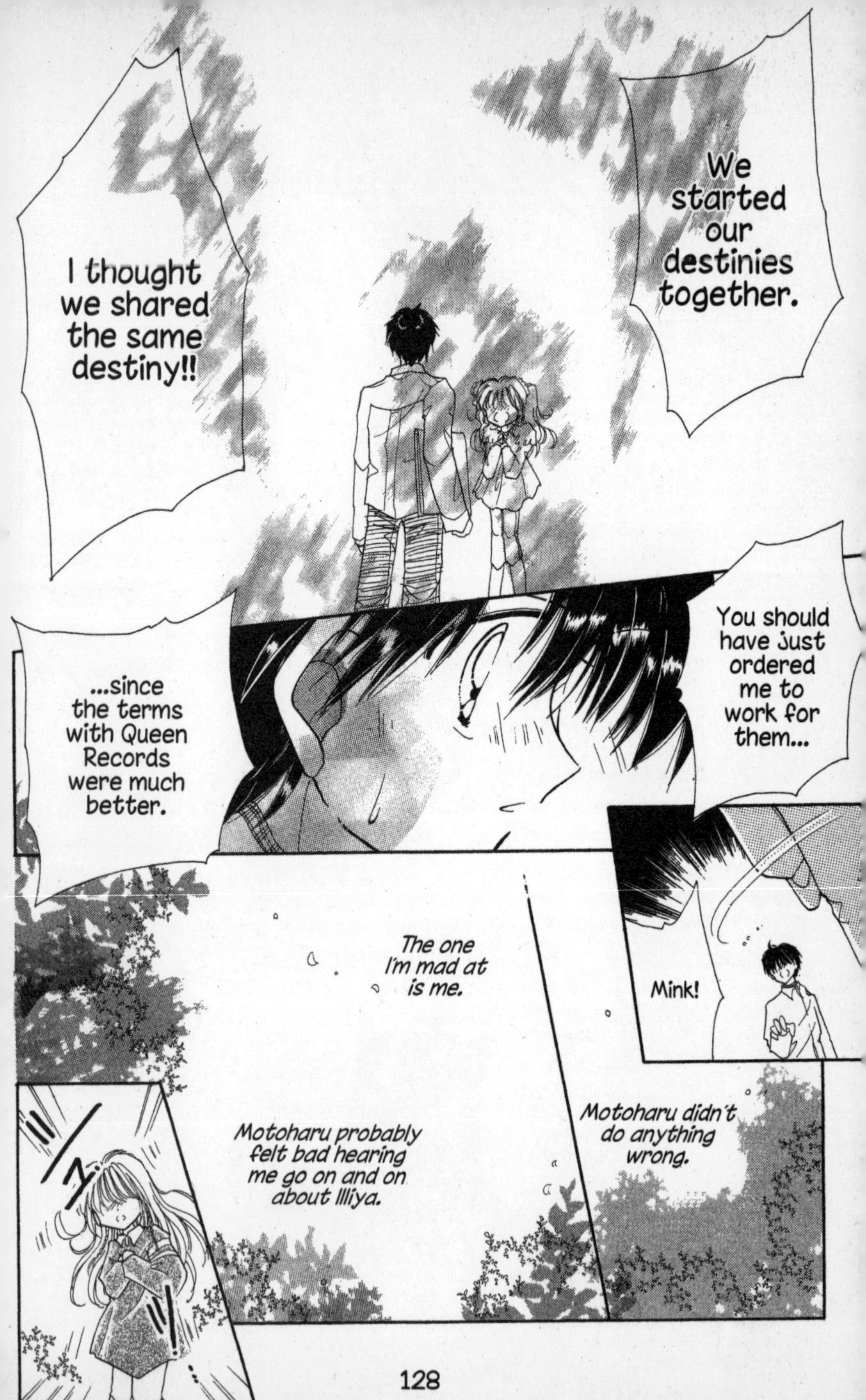
We started our destinies together.
I thought we shared the same destiny!!
You should have just ordered me to work for them...
...since the terms with Queen Records were much better.
Mink!
The one I'm mad at is me.
Motoharu didn't do anything wrong.
Motoharu probably felt bad hearing me go on and on about Illiya.

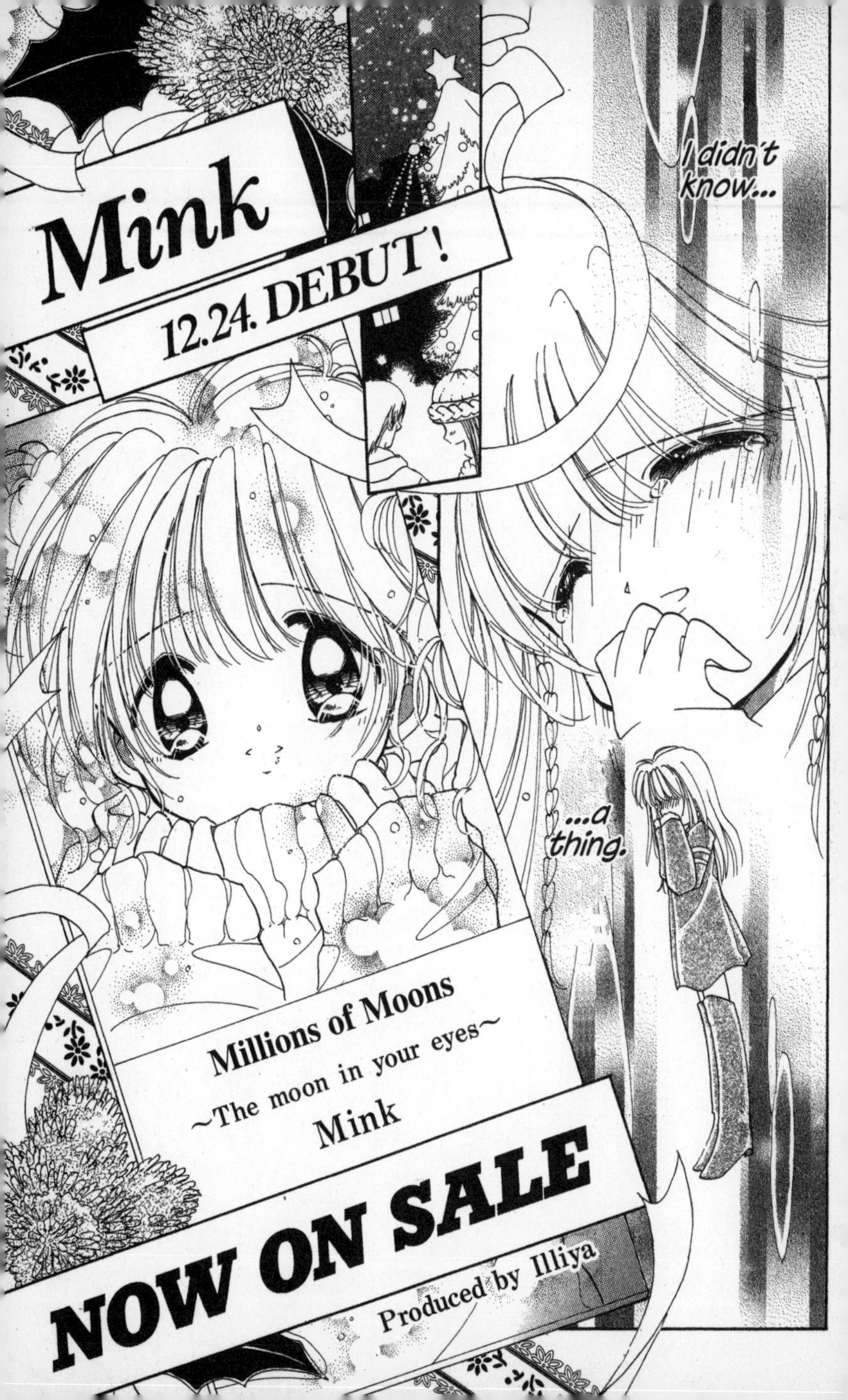
I didn't know...
...a thing.
Mink
12.24. DEBUT!
Millions of Moons
~The moon in your eyes~
Mink
NOW ON SALE
Produced by Illiya

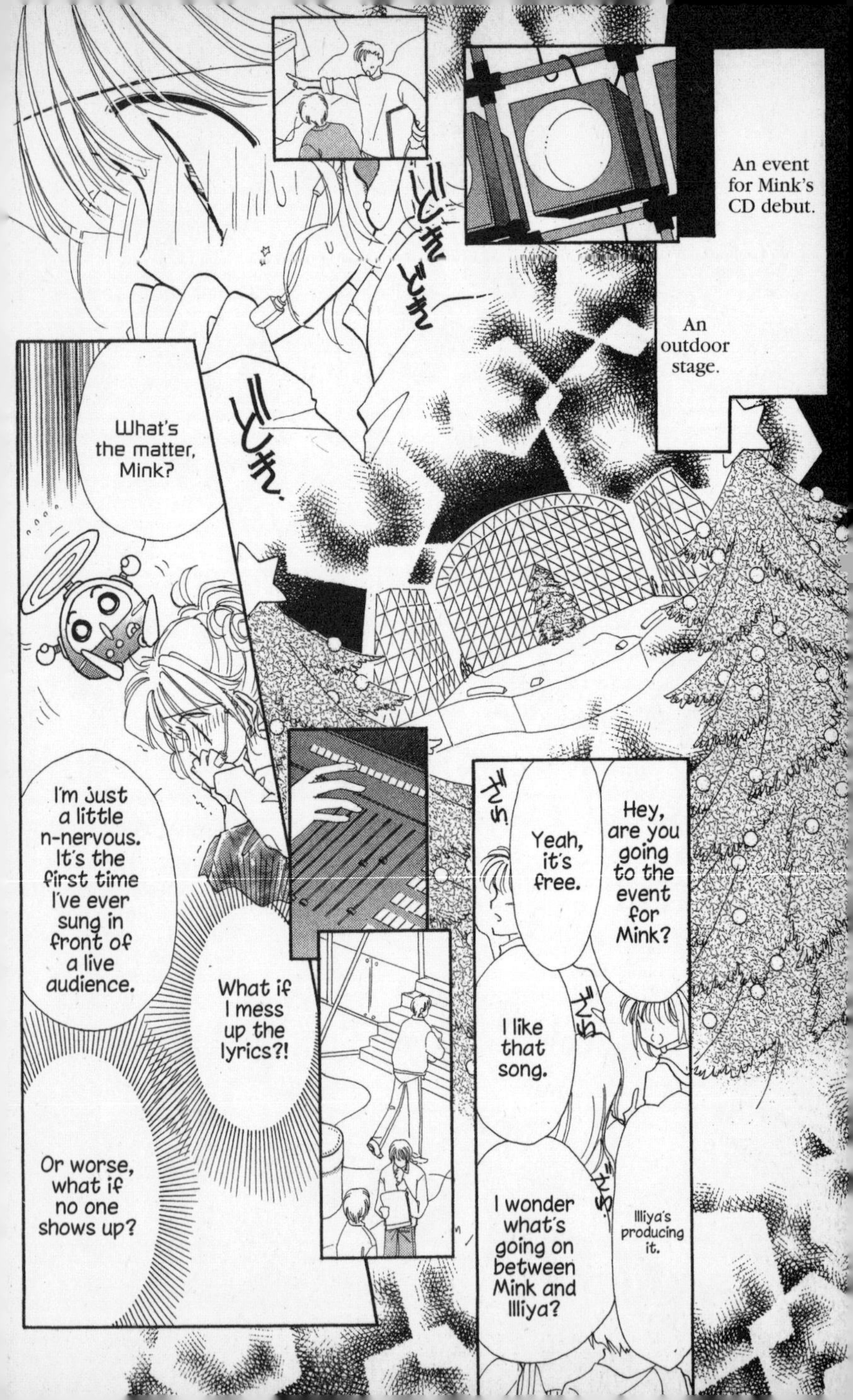
An event for Mink's CD debut.
An outdoor stage.
Hey, are you going to the event for Mink?
Yeah, it's free.
I like that song.
Illiya's producing it.
I wonder what's going on between Mink and Illiya?
What's the matter, Mink?
I'm just a little n-nervous. It's the first time I've ever sung in front of a live audience.
What if I mess up the lyrics?!
Or worse, what if no one shows up?

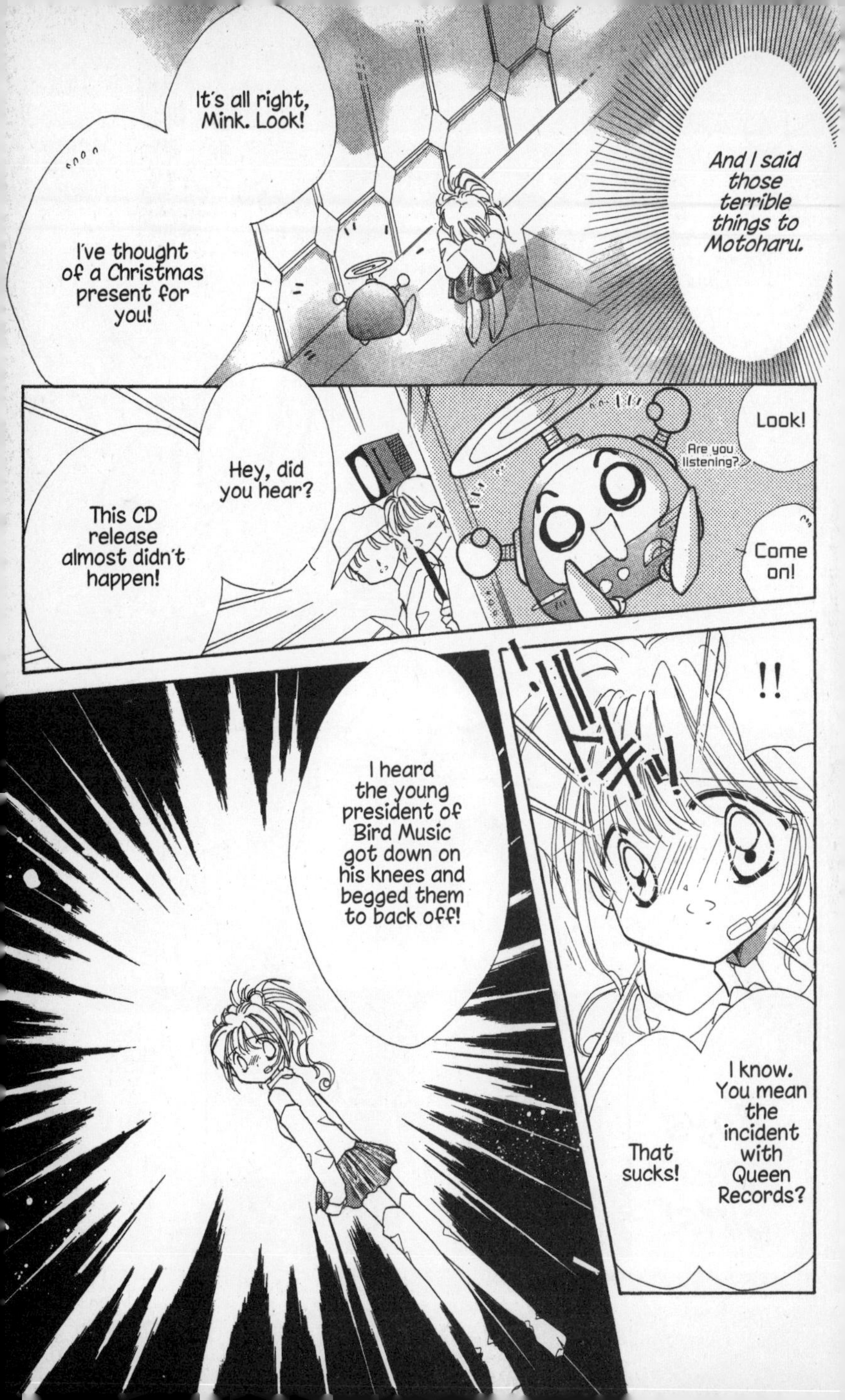
And I said those terrible things to Motoharu.
It's all right, Mink. Look!
I've thought of a Christmas present for you!
Look!
Are you listening?
Come on!
Hey, did you hear?
This CD release almost didn't happen!
!!
ドキッ!
I know. You mean the incident with Queen Records?
That sucks!
I heard the young president of Bird Music got down on his knees and begged them to back off!

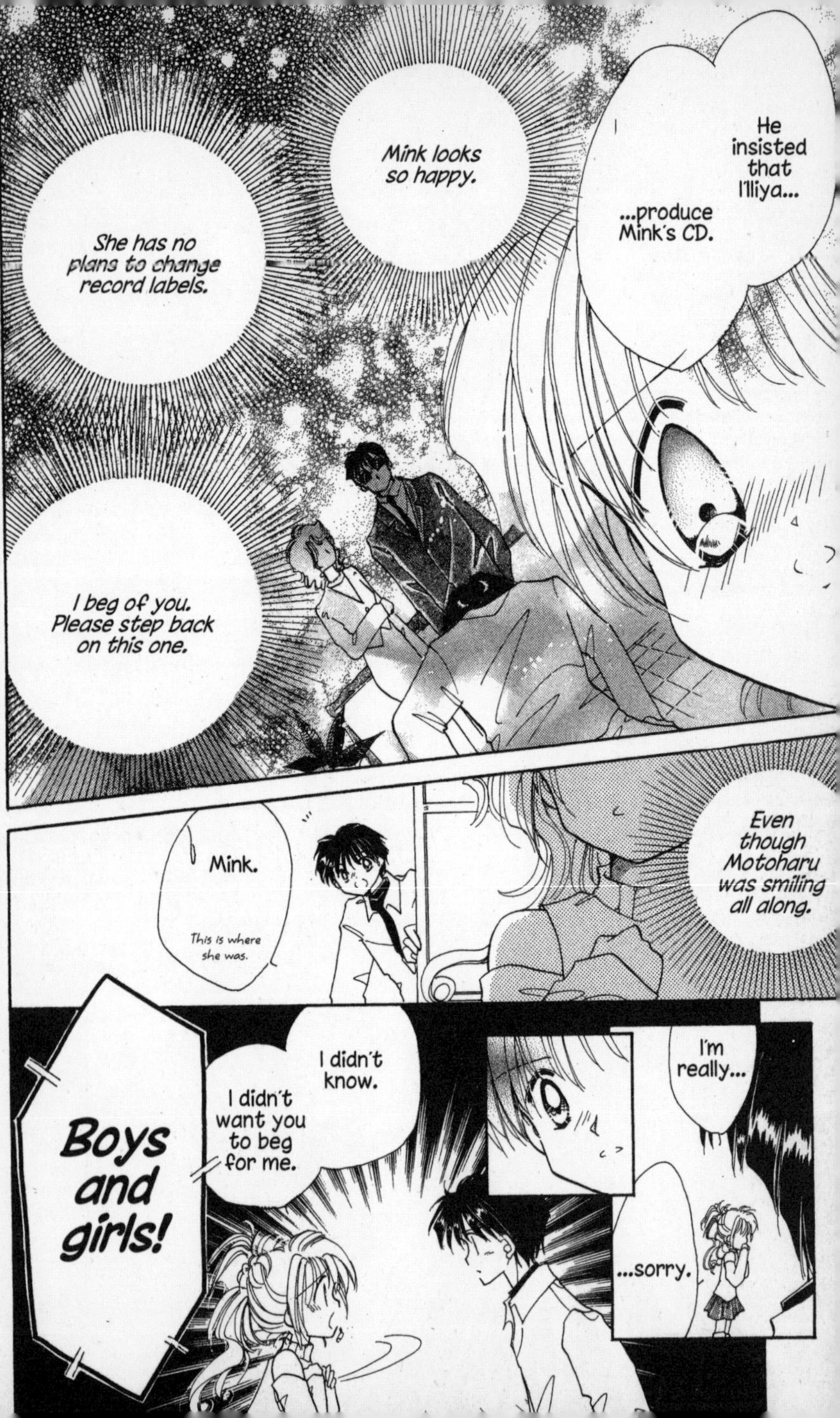
He insisted that I'lliya...
...produce Mink's CD.
Mink looks so happy.
She has no plans to change record labels.
I beg of you. Please step back on this one.
Even though Motoharu was smiling all along.
Mink.
This is where she was.
I'm really...
...sorry.
I didn't know.
I didn't want you to beg for me.
Boys and girls!

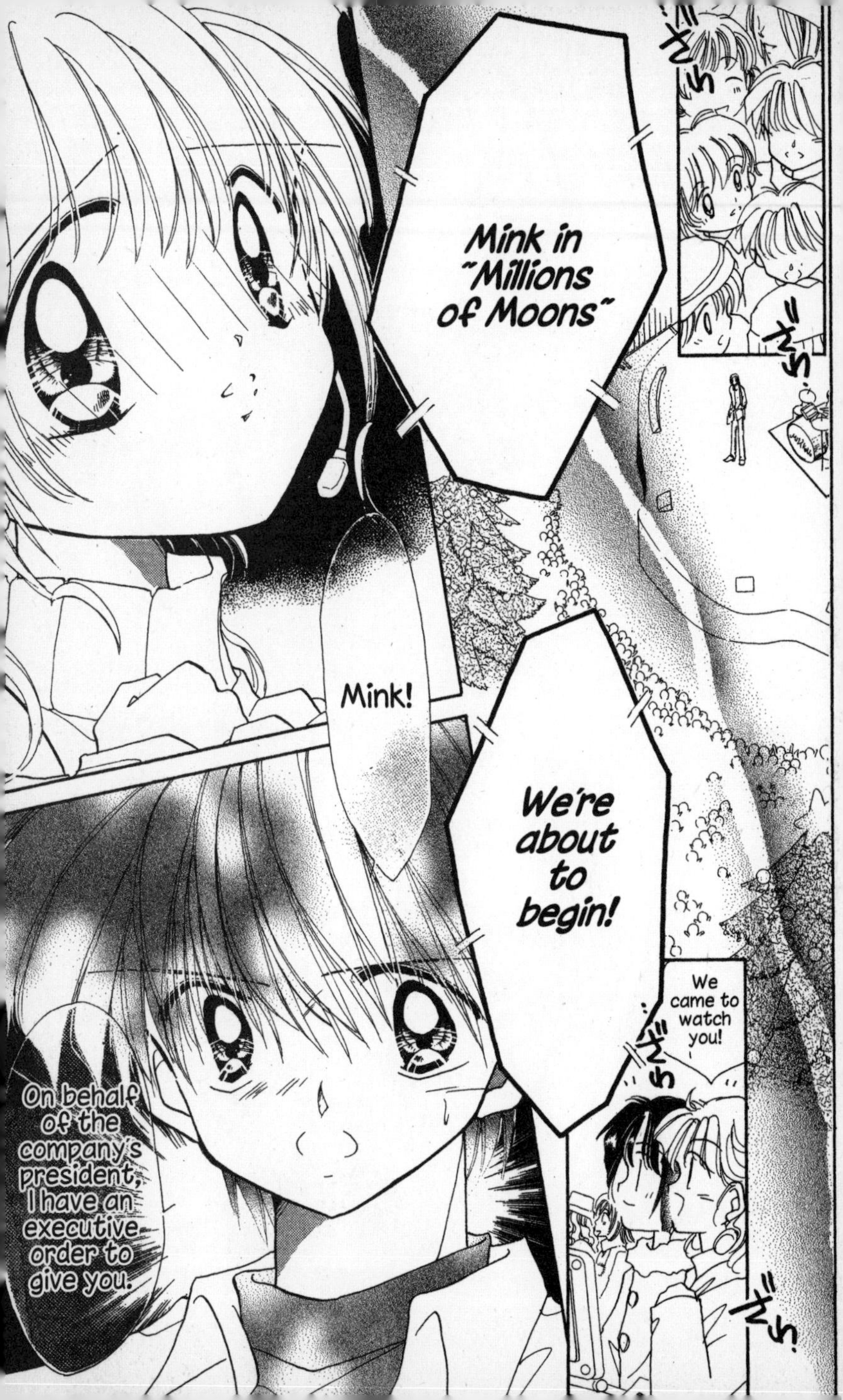
Mink in ~Millions of Moons~
We're about to begin!
Mink!
We came to watch you!
On behalf of the company's president, I have an executive order to give you.

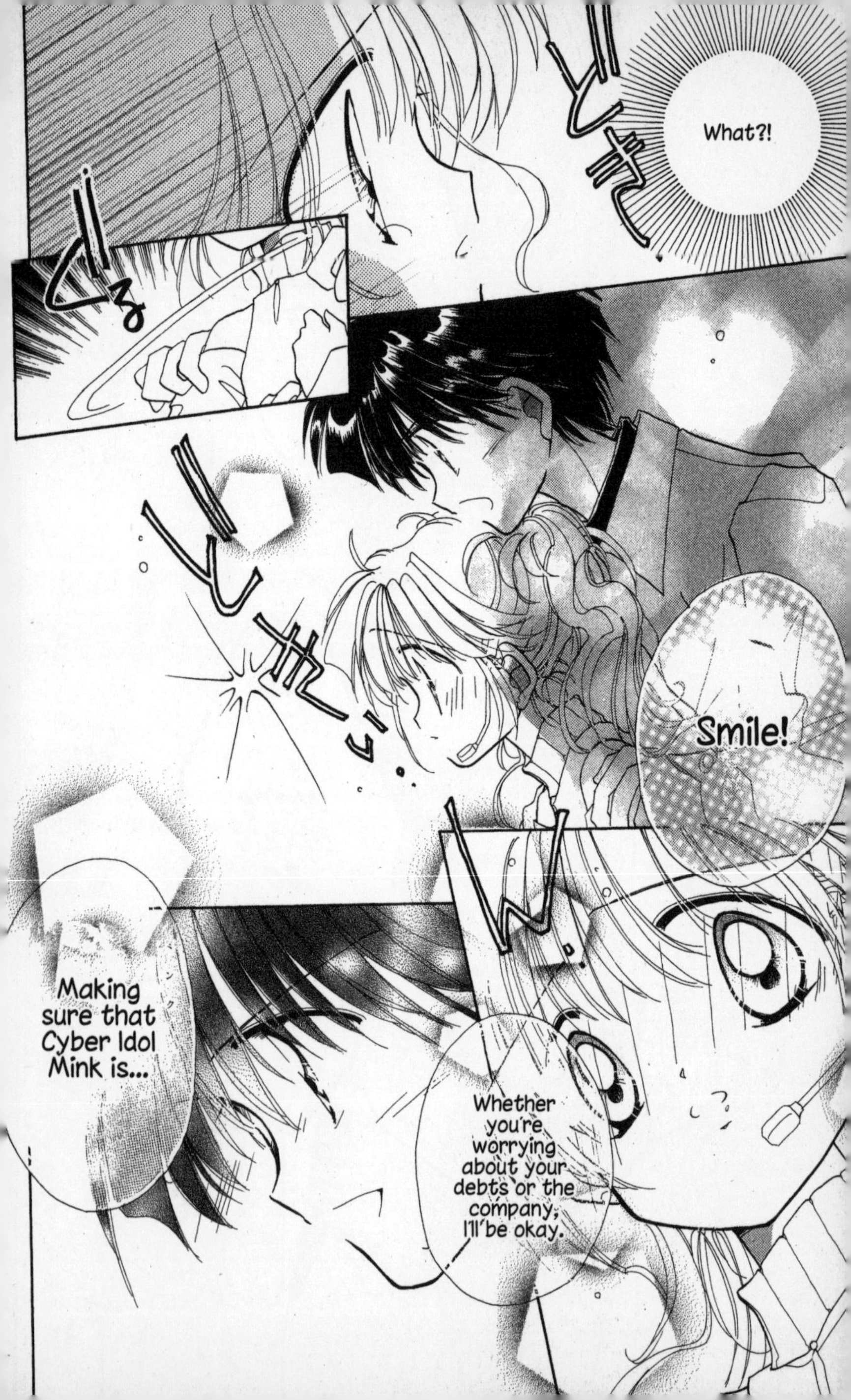
What?!
Smile!
Whether you're worrying about your debts or the company, I'll be okay.
Making sure that Cyber Idol Mink is...

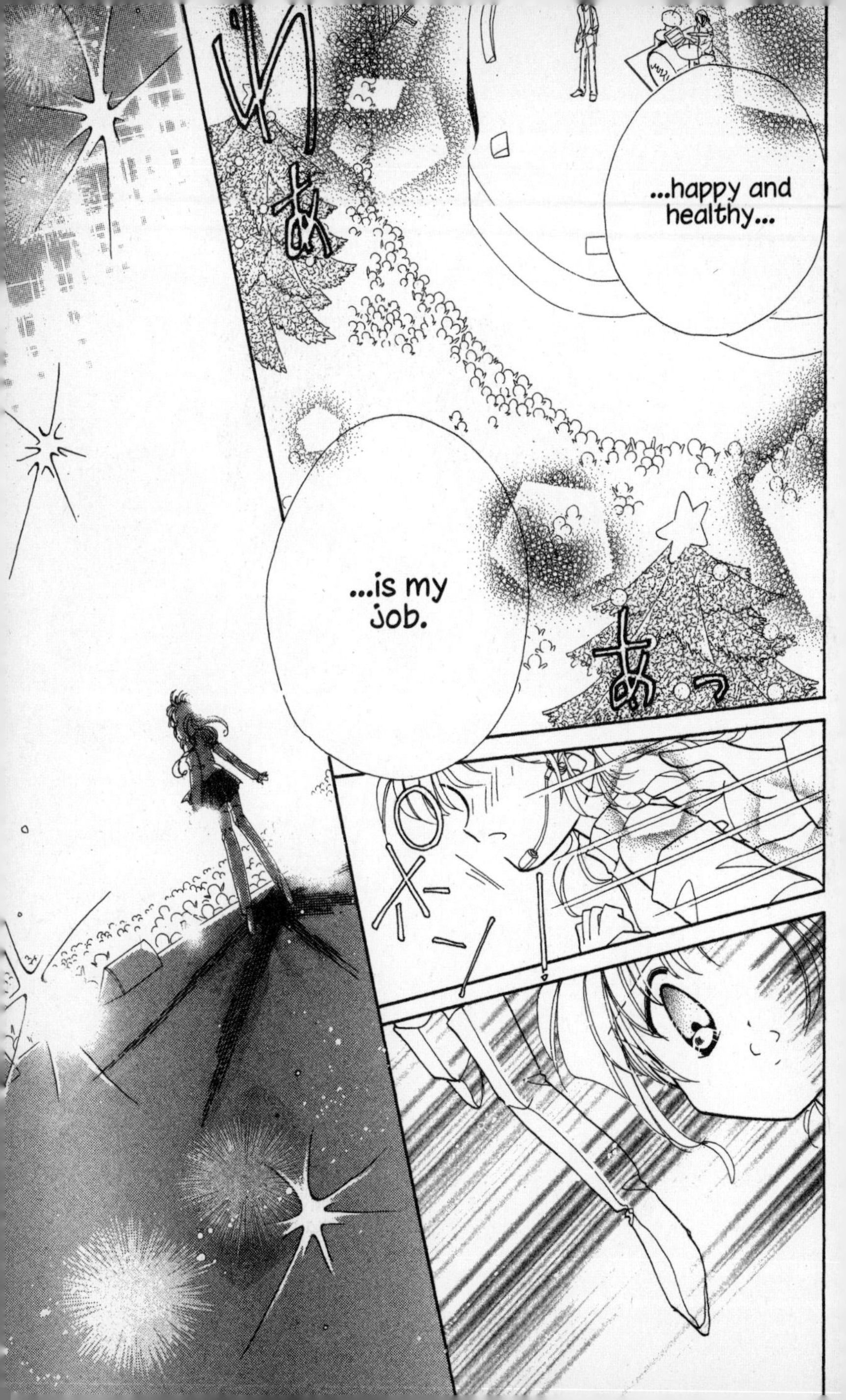
...happy and healthy...
...is my job.
あっ

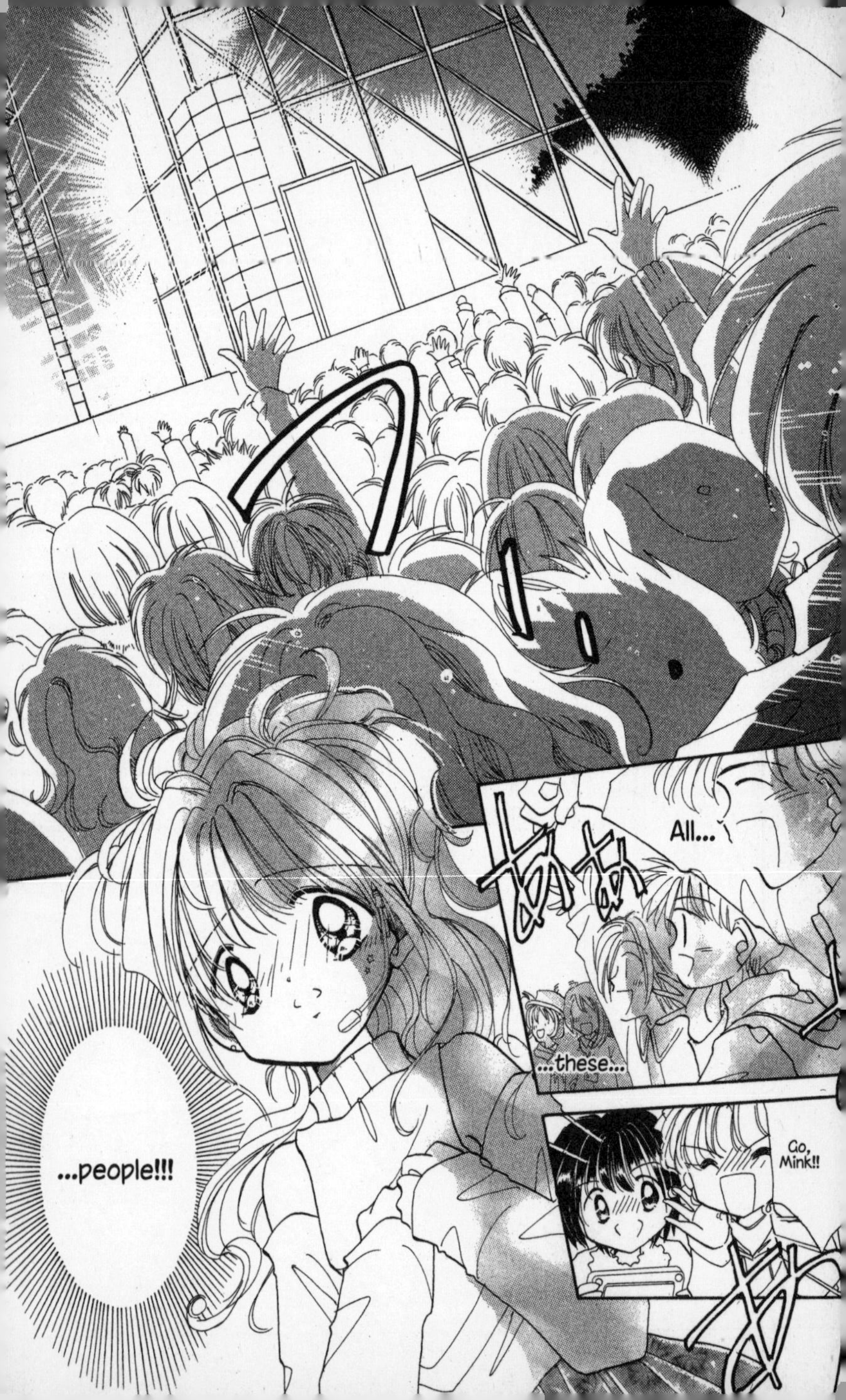
All...
...these...
Go, Mink!!
...people!!!

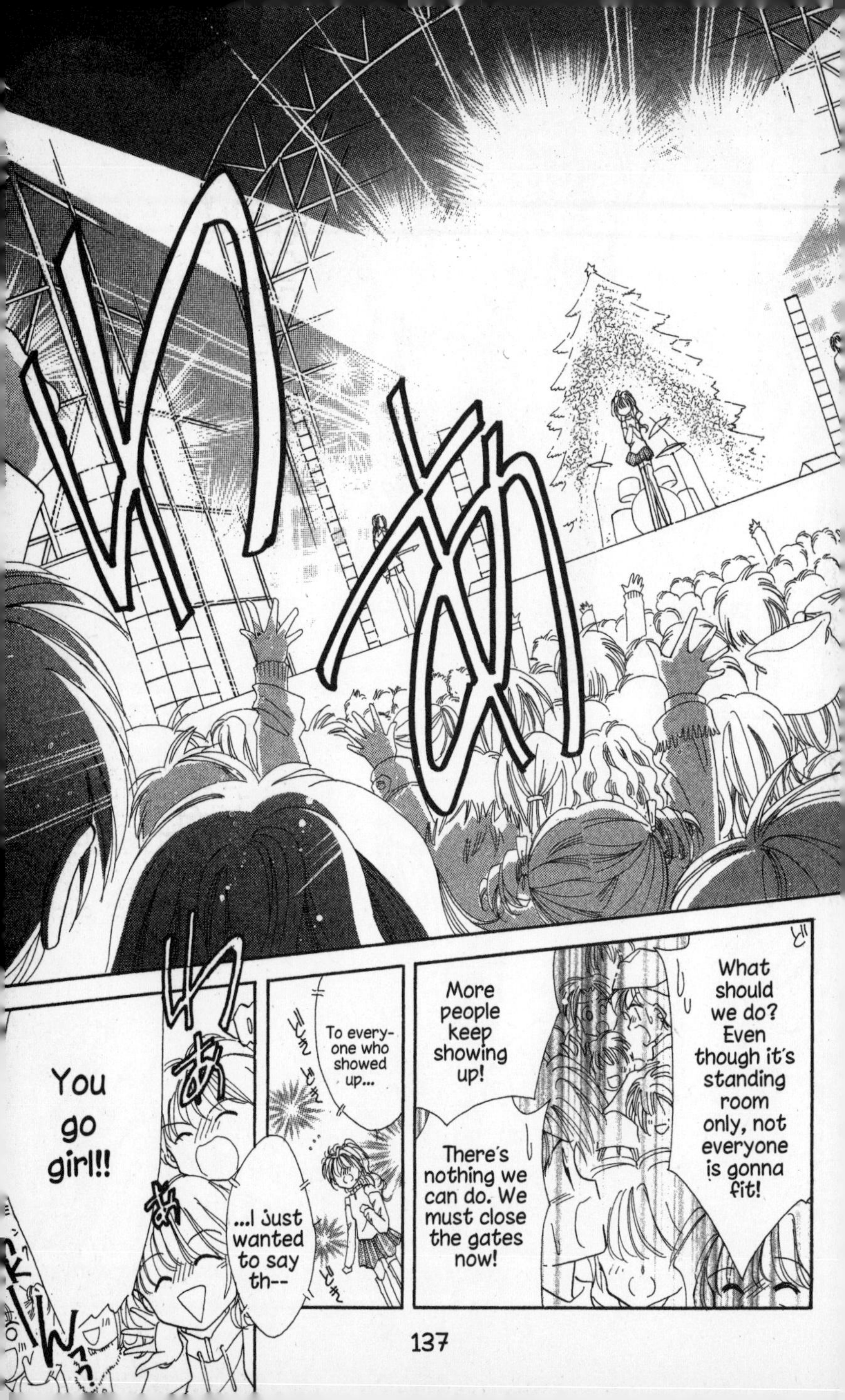
What should we do? Even though it's standing room only, not everyone is gonna fit!
More people keep showing up!
There's nothing we can do. We must close the gates now!
To every-one who showed up...
...I just wanted to say th--
You go girl!!

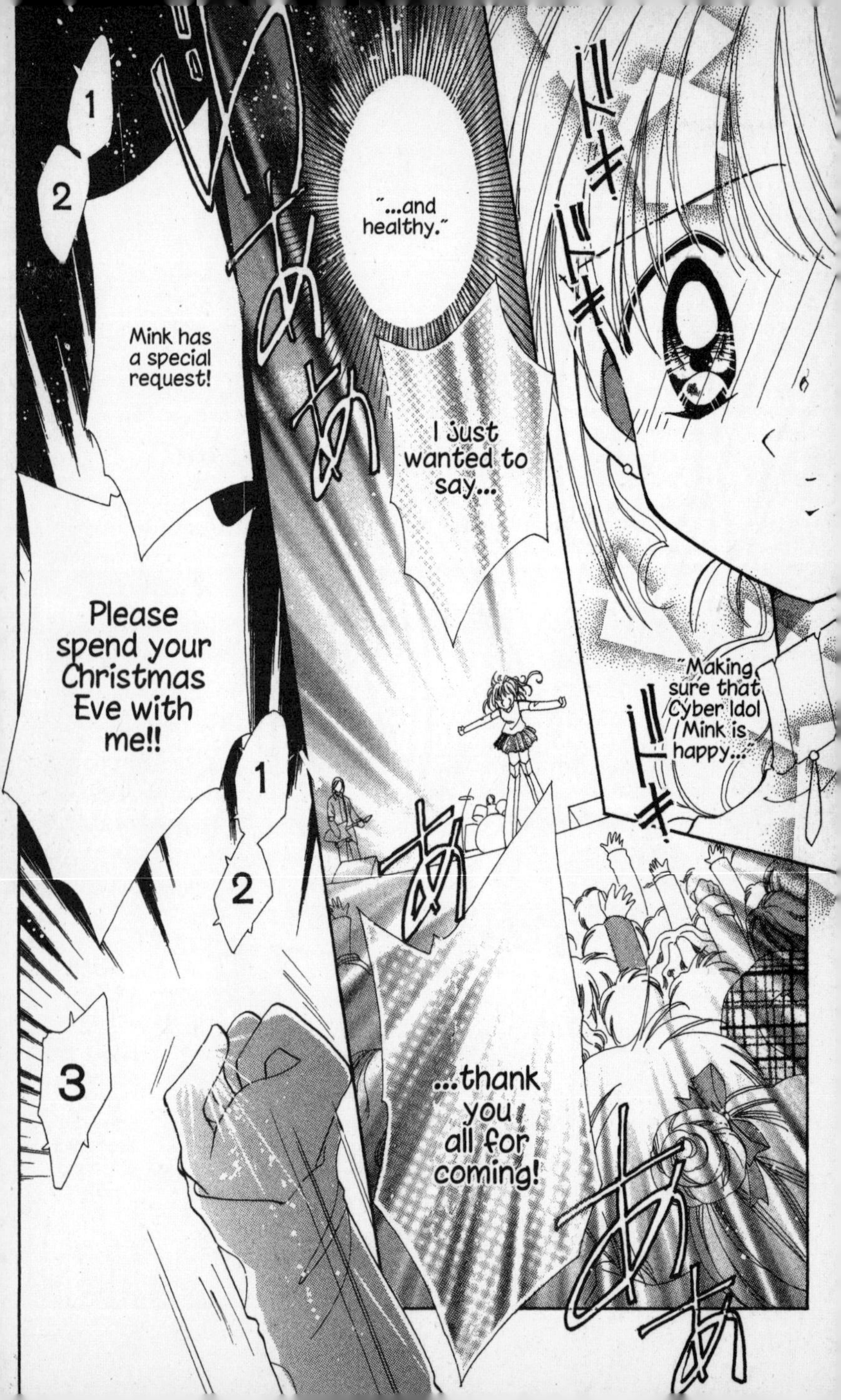
"Making sure that Cyber Idol Mink is happy..."
"...and healthy."
I just wanted to say...
...thank you all for coming!
1
2
Mink has a special request!
Please spend your Christmas Eve with me!!
1
2
3

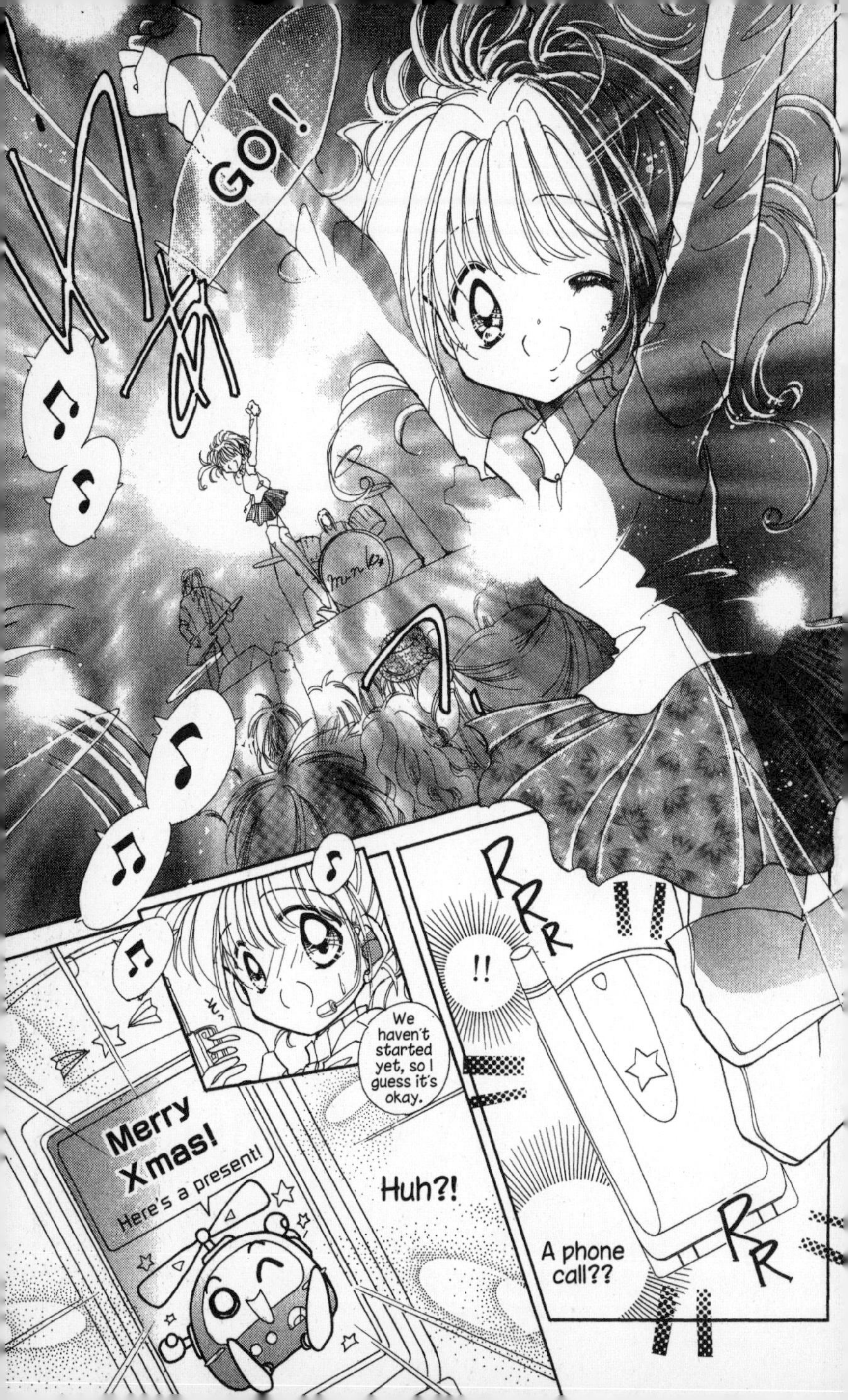
GO!
♫ ♪
♪ ♫
RRR
!!
A phone call??
RR
♫ ♪
We haven't started yet, so I guess it's okay.
Huh?!
Merry Xmas!
Here's a present!

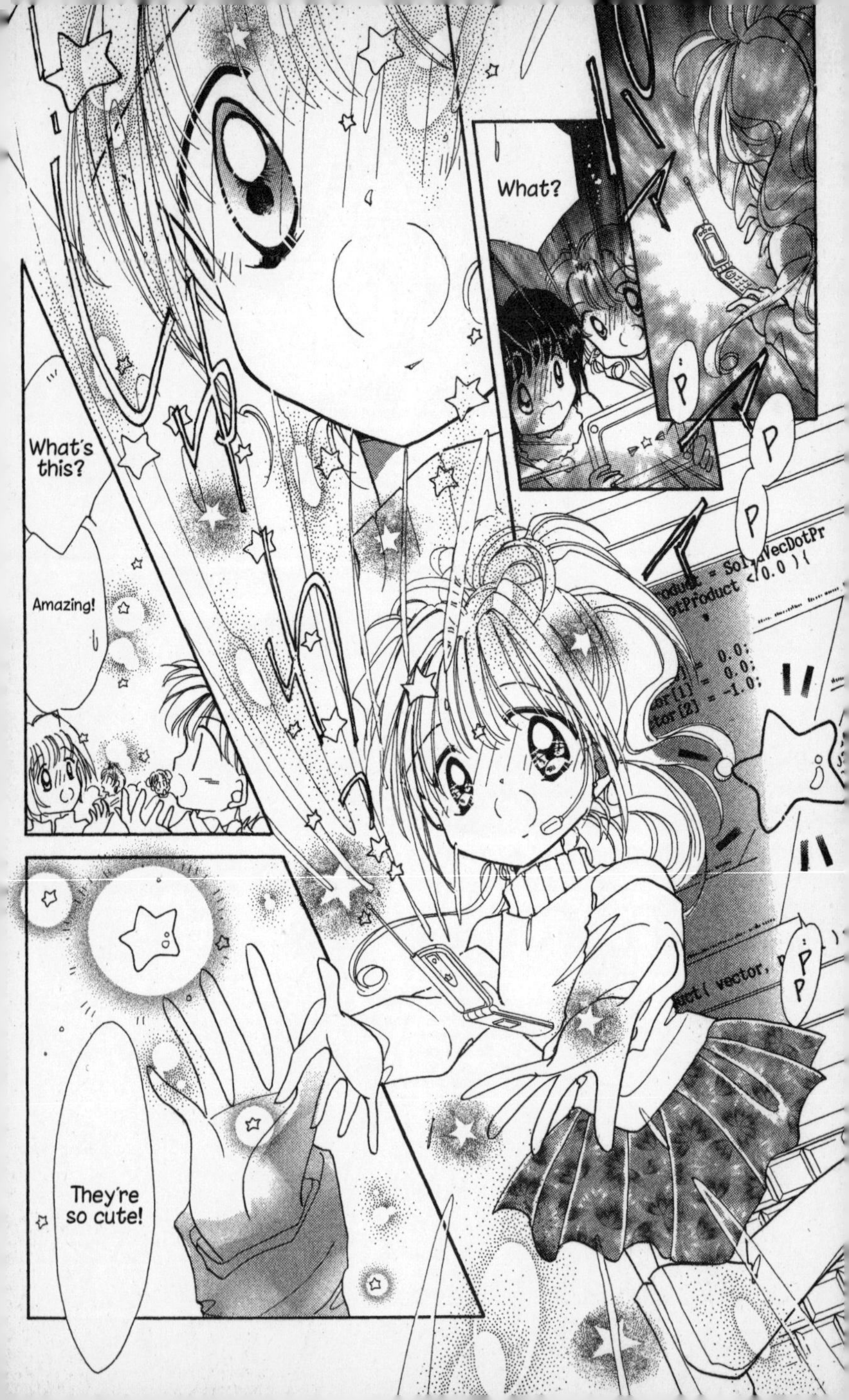
What?
What's this?
Amazing!
They're so cute!

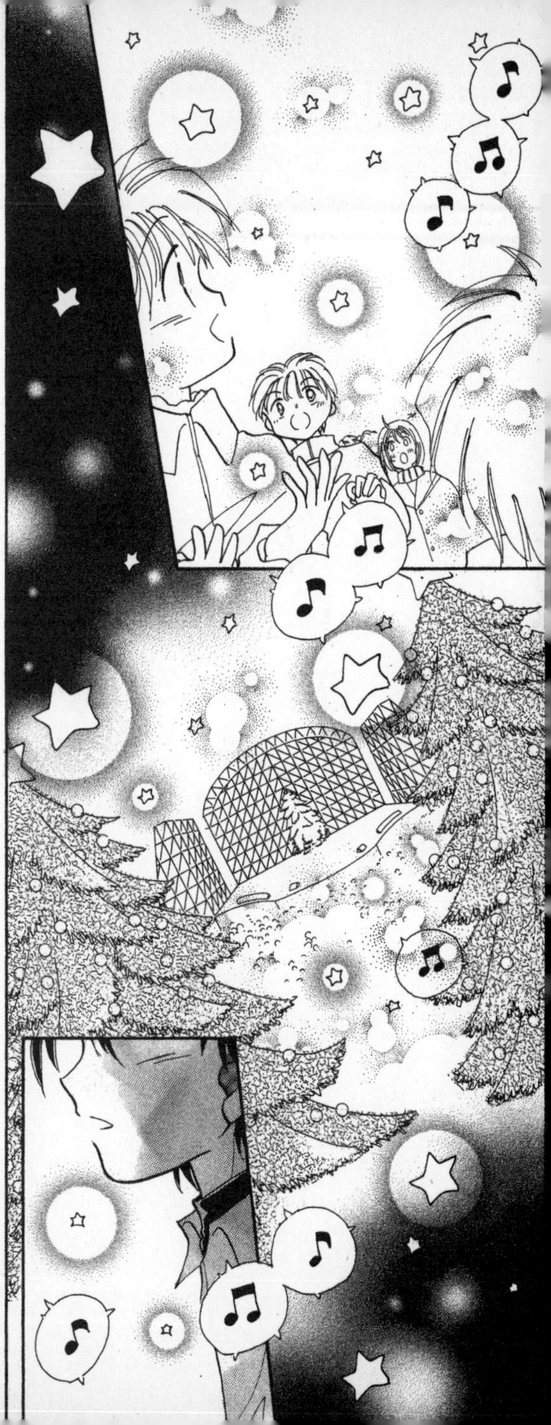

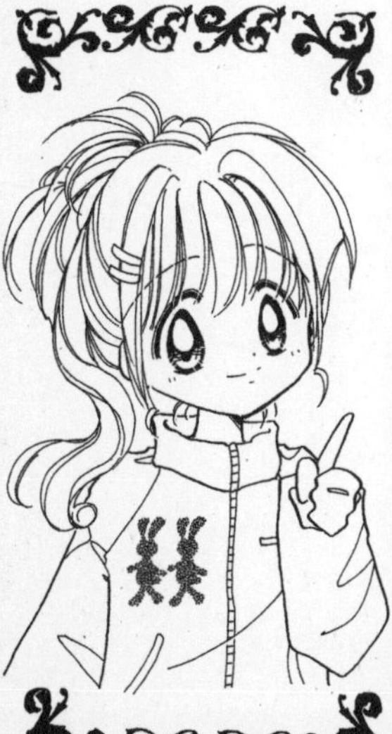

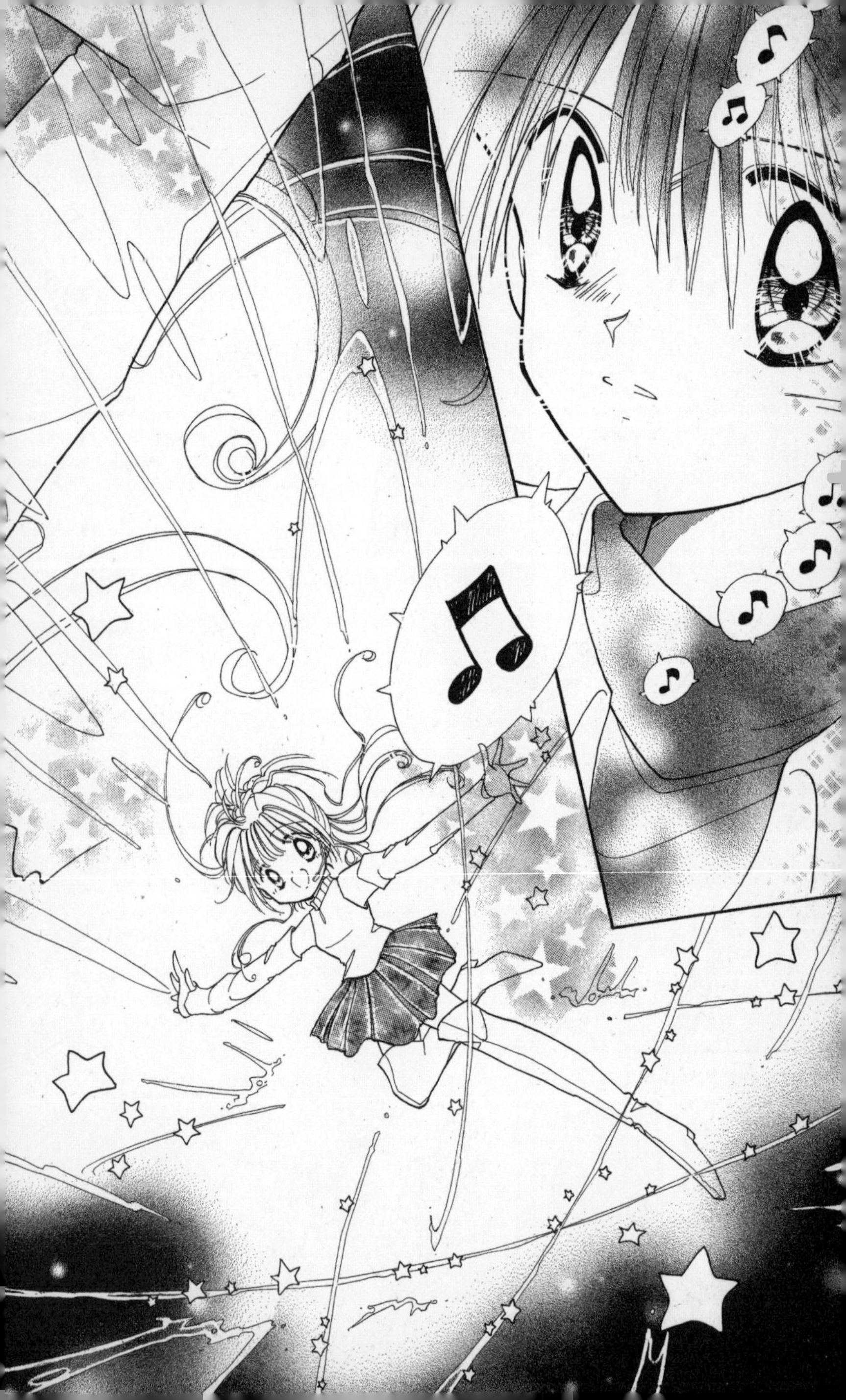

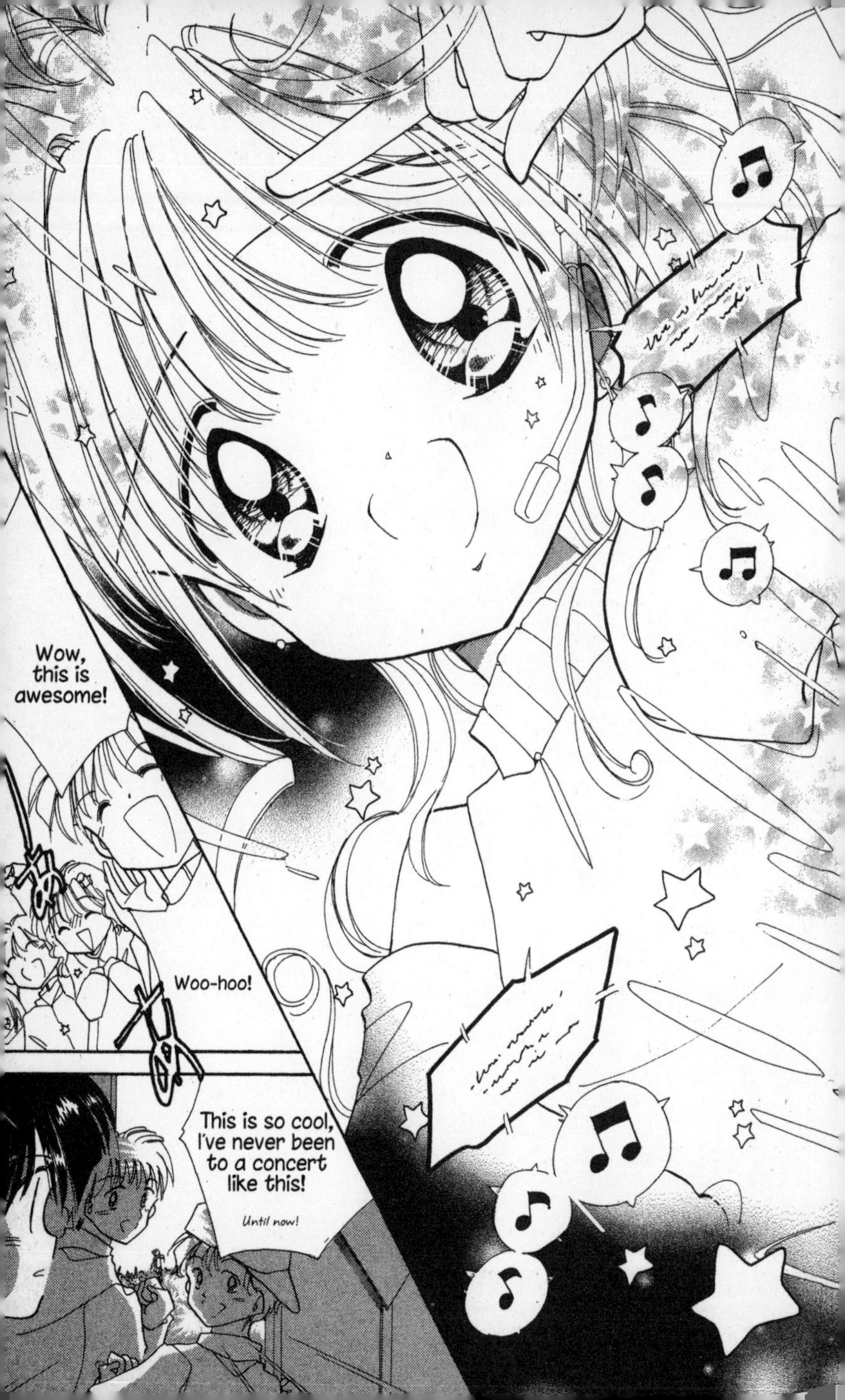
Wow, this is awesome!
Woo-hoo!
This is so cool, I've never been to a concert like this!
Until now!

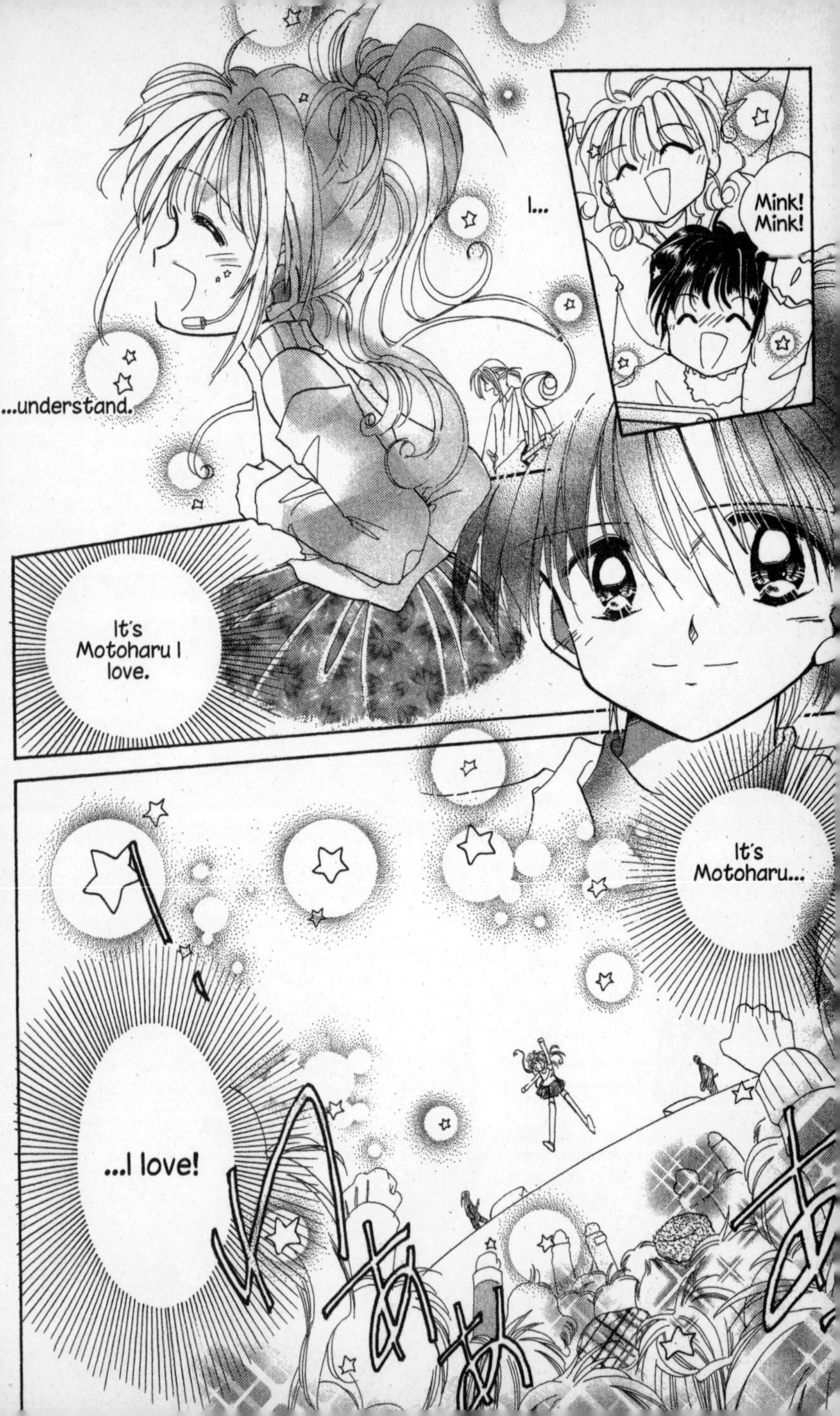
Mink! Mink!
I...
...understand.
It's Motoharu I love.
It's Motoharu...
...I love!

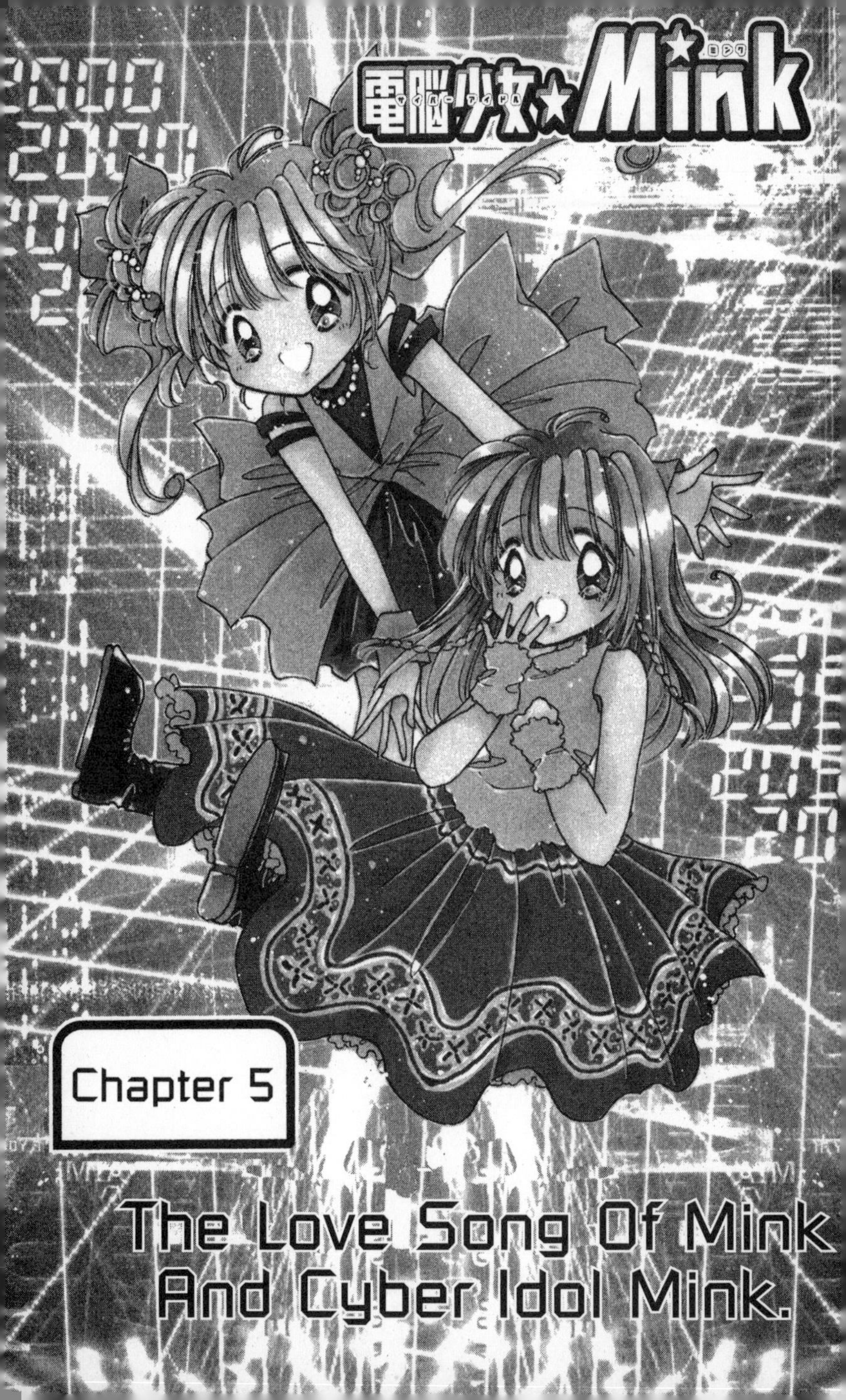
電脳少女★Mink
Chapter 5
The Love Song Of Mink
And Cyber Idol Mink.

Mink Rap!!

This is the kind of question a lot of
people have sent in so I'm trying to
summarize and answer it now.

Q: Are there special classes or
formal training to become a manga
artist? If so, what kind of school
provides this type of training?
Did you have to take any classes?

A: This is hard to answer. The
reason is that to become a manga
artist, the actual "study" is really
practicing on your own. I went to a
regular elementary school, middle
school and high school, and then
right into a vocational school. And to
be honest, it didn't have much to do
with manga cartooning at all! Then I
worked in an office for a while doing
administrative stuff. The best form
of training is reading panels in
magazines. I've heard there are
manga/cartooning schools, but I
don't know much about them--sorry!
Although I have taken a class on
it (but it was back in elementary
school). I have to admit that I never
finished the course, but I did pick up
hands-on techniques, manga jargon
and the know-how in the field. The
key is to keep drawing!

-Megumi

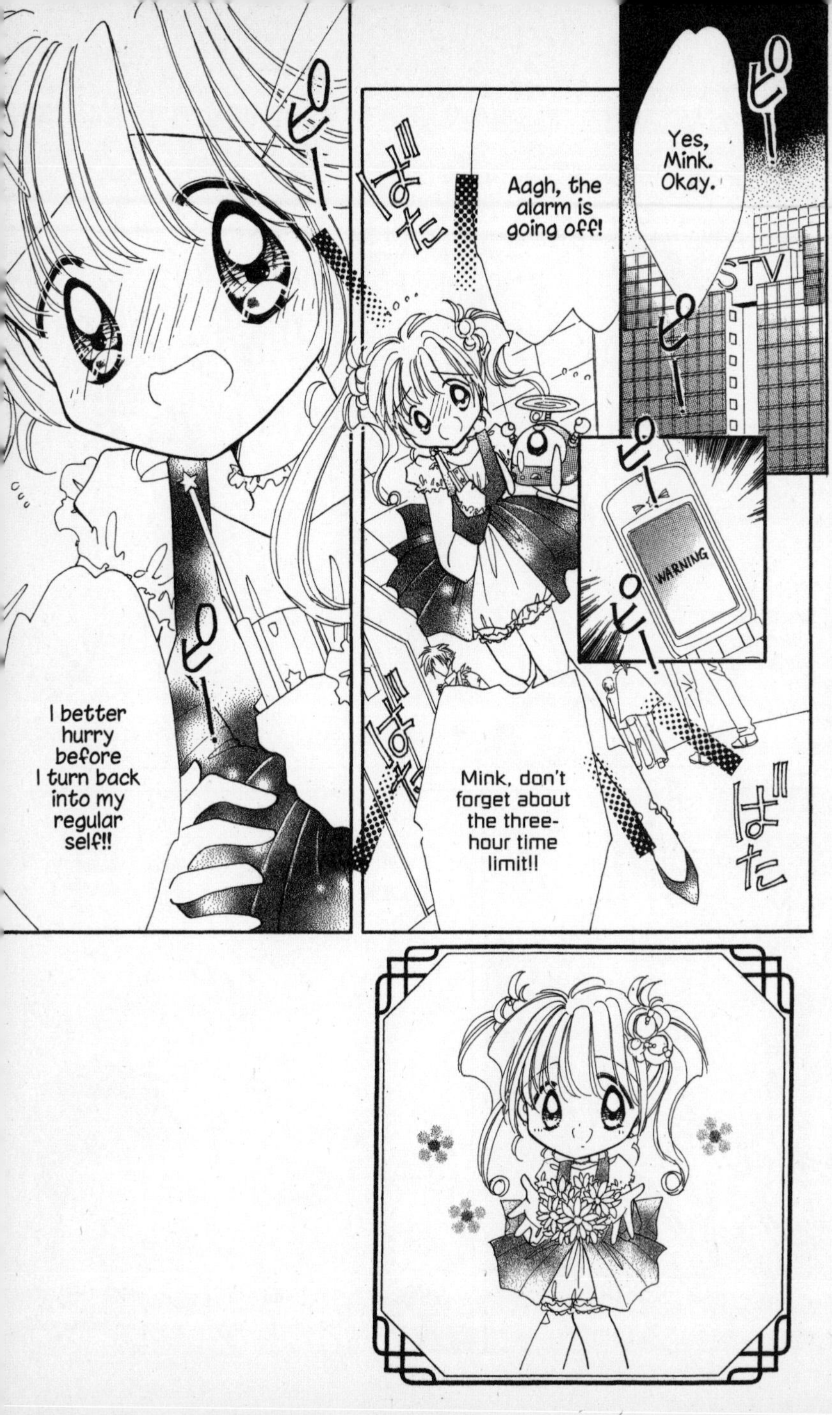

Yes, Mink. Okay.
STV
WARNING
Aagh, the alarm is going off!
Mink, don't forget about the three-hour time limit!!
I better hurry before I turn back into my regular self!!

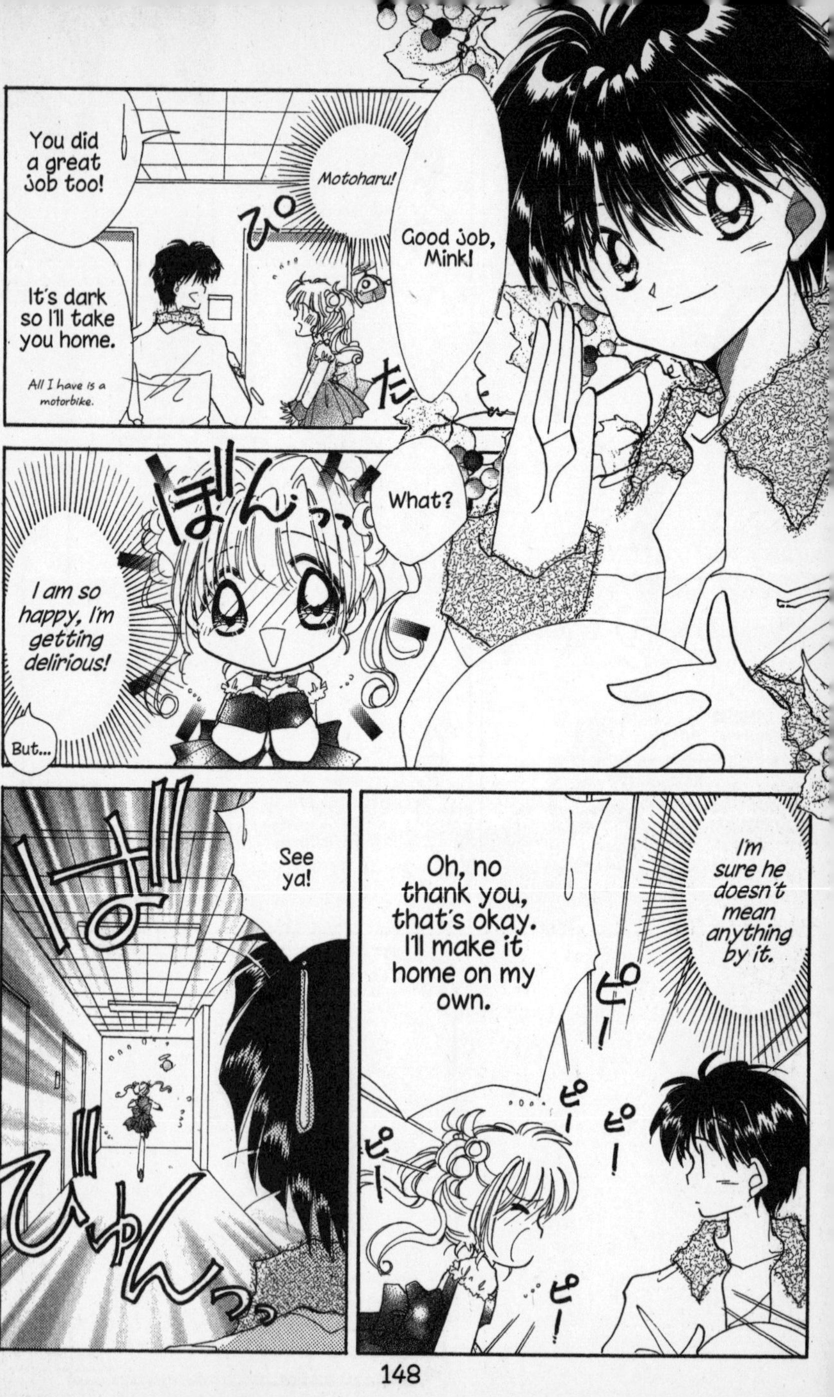
Good job, Mink!
Motoharu!
ぴ
You did a great job too!
It's dark so I'll take you home.
All I have is a motorbike.
た
What?
ぽんっっ
I am so happy, I'm getting delirious!
But...
I'm sure he doesn't mean anything by it.
Oh, no thank you, that's okay. I'll make it home on my own.
ピー! ピー! ピー! ピー! ピー!
See ya!
ぱ
ひゅんっっ

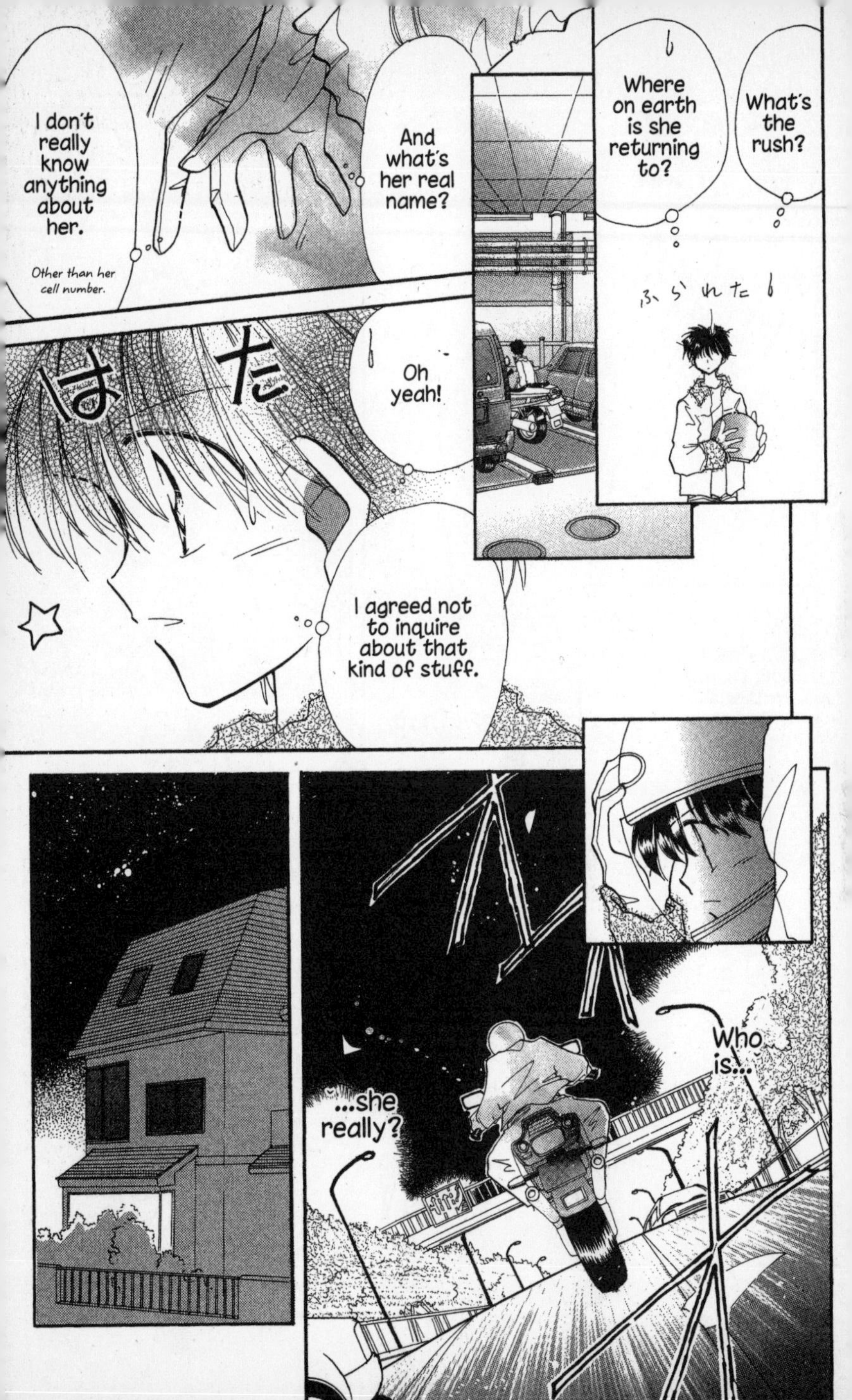
What's the rush?
Where on earth is she returning to?
ふられた
And what's her real name?
I don't really know anything about her.
Other than her cell number.
はた
Oh yeah!
I agreed not to inquire about that kind of stuff.
Who is...
...she really?

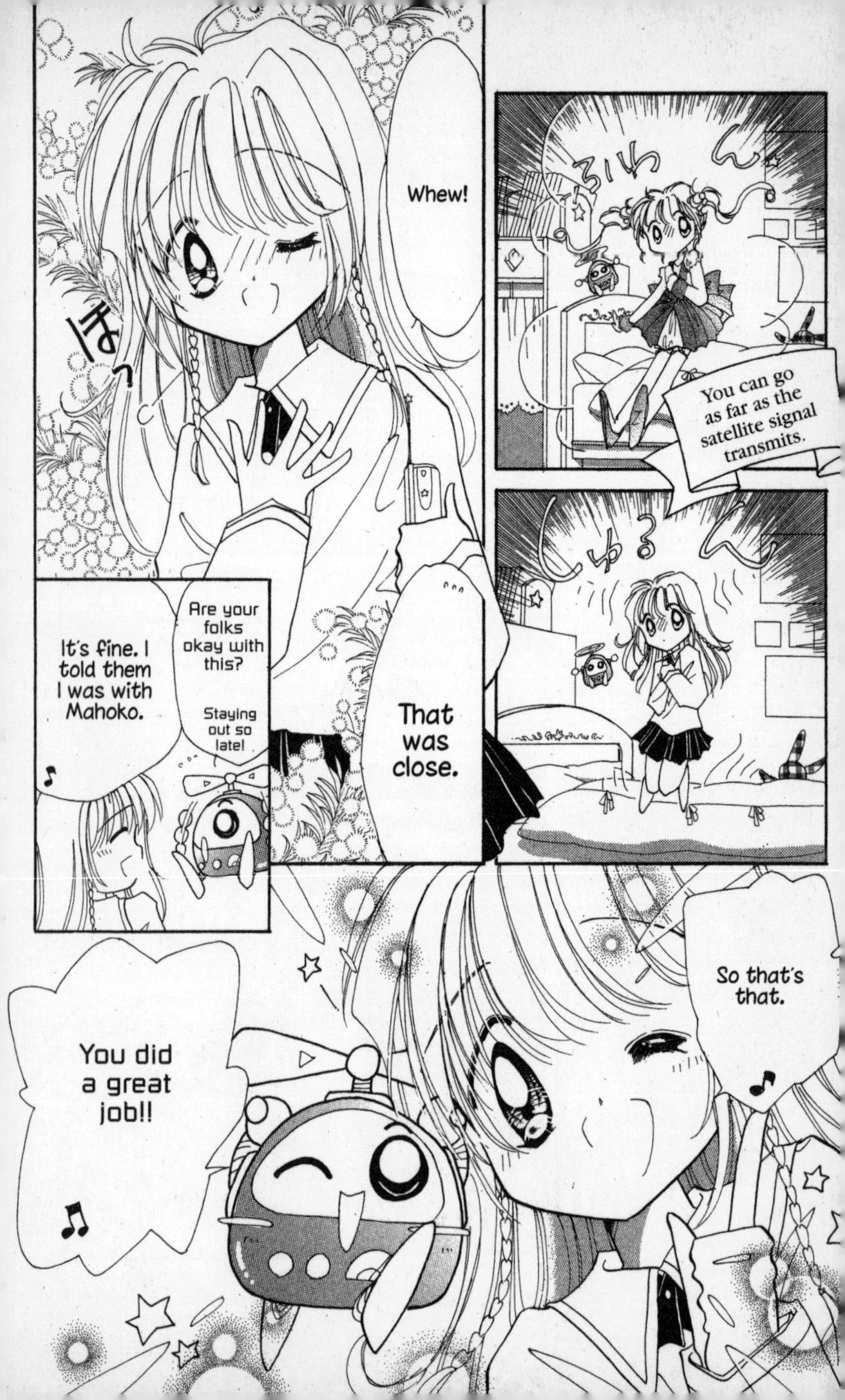

You can go as far as the satellite signal transmits.
しゅるん
Whew!
ほっ
That was close.
Are your folks okay with this?
Staying out so late!
It's fine. I told them I was with Mahoko.
So that's that.
You did a great job!!

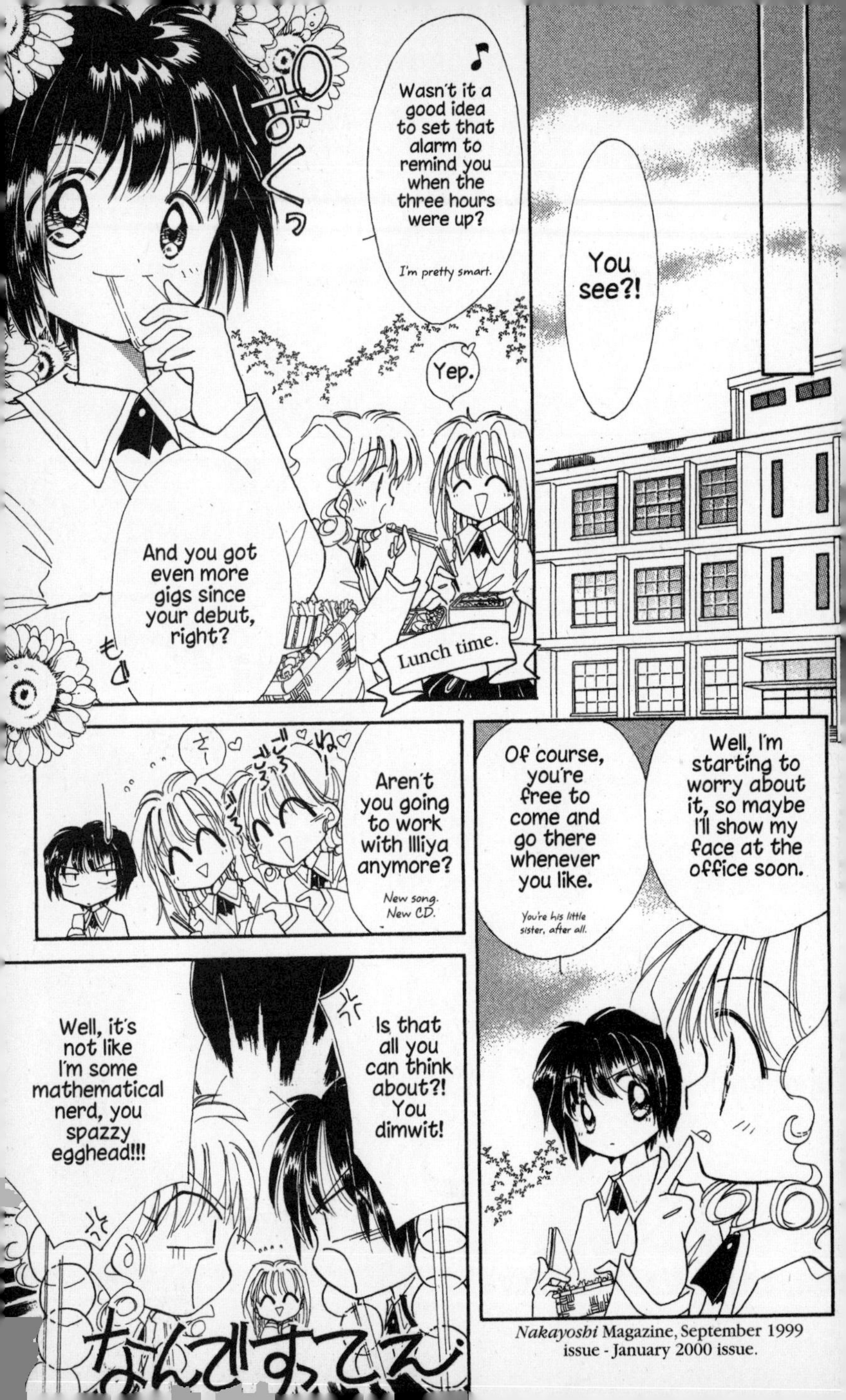
You see?!
Wasn't it a good idea to set that alarm to remind you when the three hours were up?
I'm pretty smart.
Yep.
And you got even more gigs since your debut, right?
Lunch time.
Well, I'm starting to worry about it, so maybe I'll show my face at the office soon.
Of course, you're free to come and go there whenever you like.
You're his little sister, after all.
Aren't you going to work with Illiya anymore?
New song. New CD.
Is that all you can think about?! You dimwit!
Well, it's not like I'm some mathematical nerd, you spazzy egghead!!!
なんですってぇ

Nakayoshi Magazine, September 1999 issue - January 2000 issue.

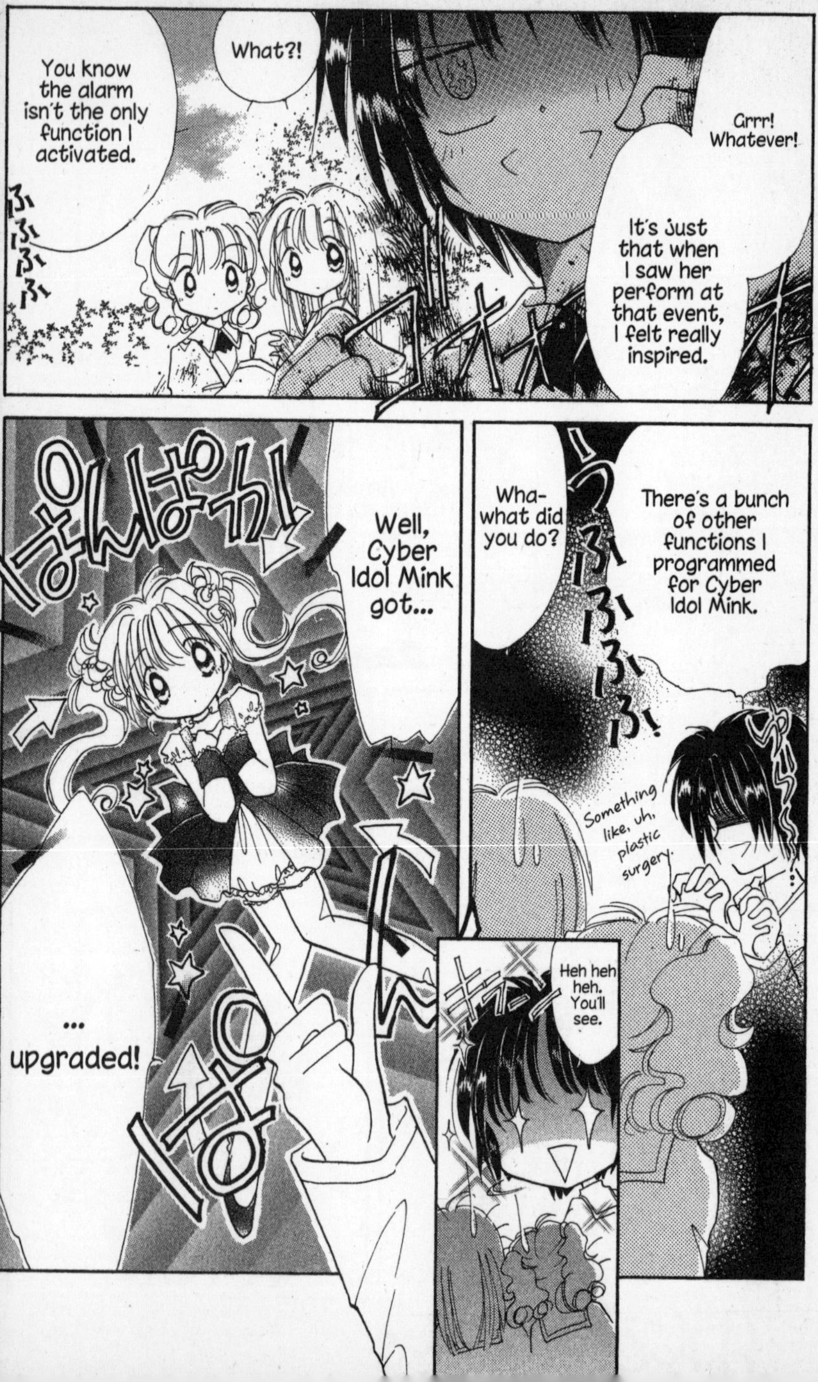

Grrr! Whatever!
It's just that when I saw her perform at that event, I felt really inspired.
What?!
You know the alarm isn't the only function I activated.
ふふふふ
There's a bunch of other functions I programmed for Cyber Idol Mink.
Wha-what did you do?
うふふふふ!
Something like, uh, plastic surgery.
Heh heh heh. You'll see.
Well, Cyber Idol Mink got...
... upgraded!

Mink Rap!!

These are the albums I listened to while working on this manga:

Strange Fruits by Chara

Life-Time and *Weary Flower* by Grapevine

Fiore and *Fiore II* by Arisa Mitsuki

Cure by Tohko

Cruise Record 1995-2000 by Globe

LOVEppears and *Appears* by Ayumi Hamasaki

Cicada by Noriyuki Makihara

Wait--that's not a lot of albums this time. Maybe because there were a lot of songs on each one!

It was really a shame about Noriyuki Makihara* but I still love his songs even now. I'll always like his music.

-Megumi

*Editor's Note: Pop singer who got into some legal trouble.

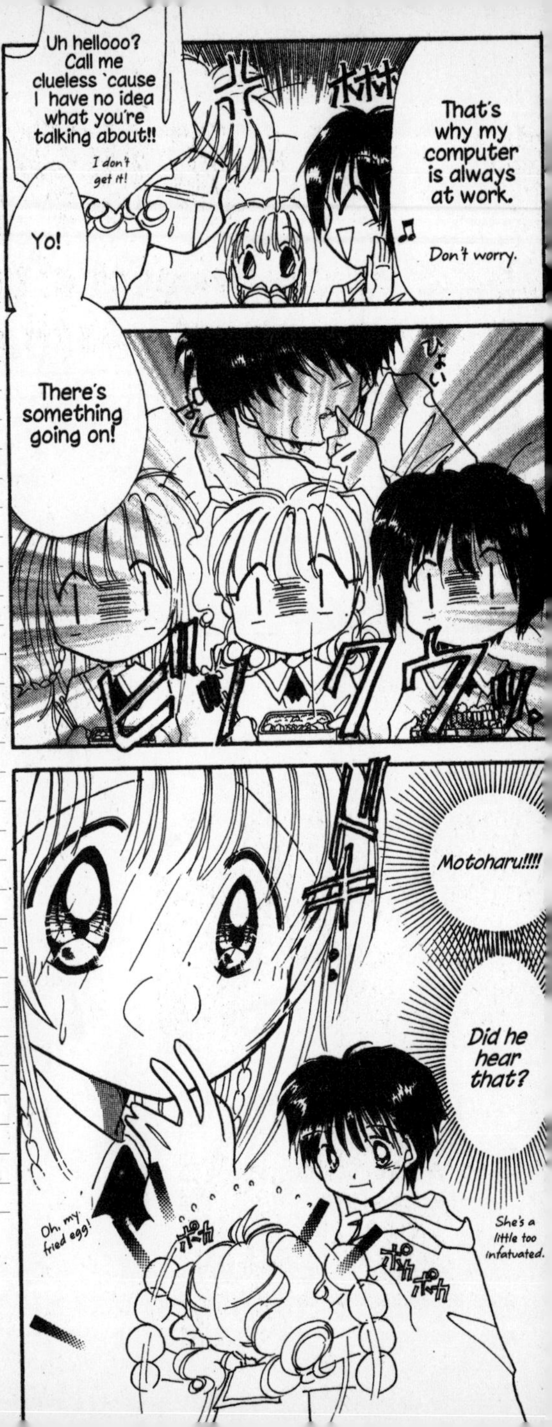

That's why my computer is always at work.
Don't worry.
Uh hellooo? Call me clueless `cause I have no idea what you're talking about!!
I don't get it!
Yo!
There's something going on!
Motoharu!!!!
Did he hear that?
She's a little too infatuated.
Oh, my fried egg!

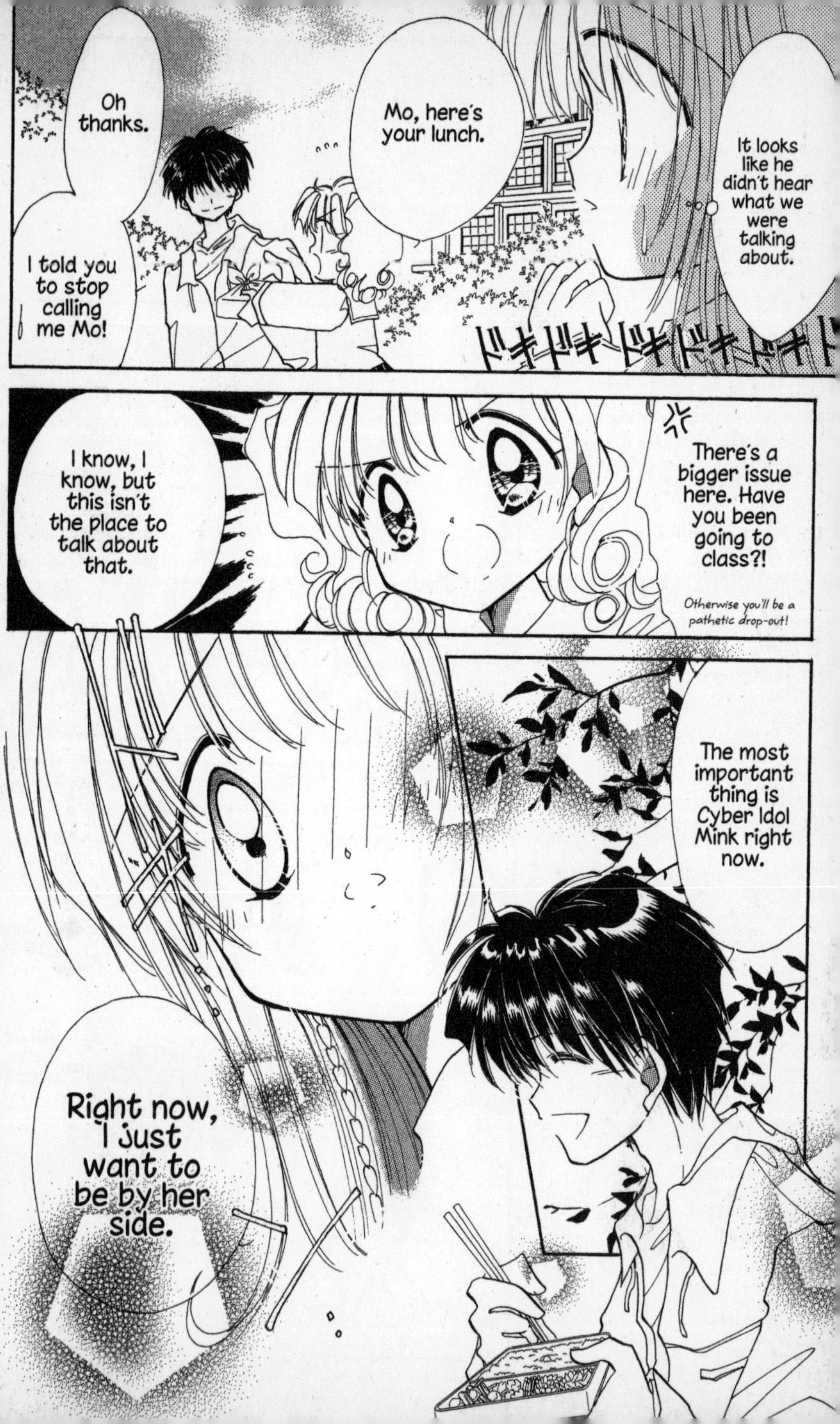
It looks like he didn't hear what we were talking about.
ドキドキドキドキドキド
Mo, here's your lunch.
Oh thanks.
I told you to stop calling me Mo!
There's a bigger issue here. Have you been going to class?!
Otherwise you'll be a pathetic drop-out!
I know, I know, but this isn't the place to talk about that.
The most important thing is Cyber Idol Mink right now.
Right now, I just want to be by her side.

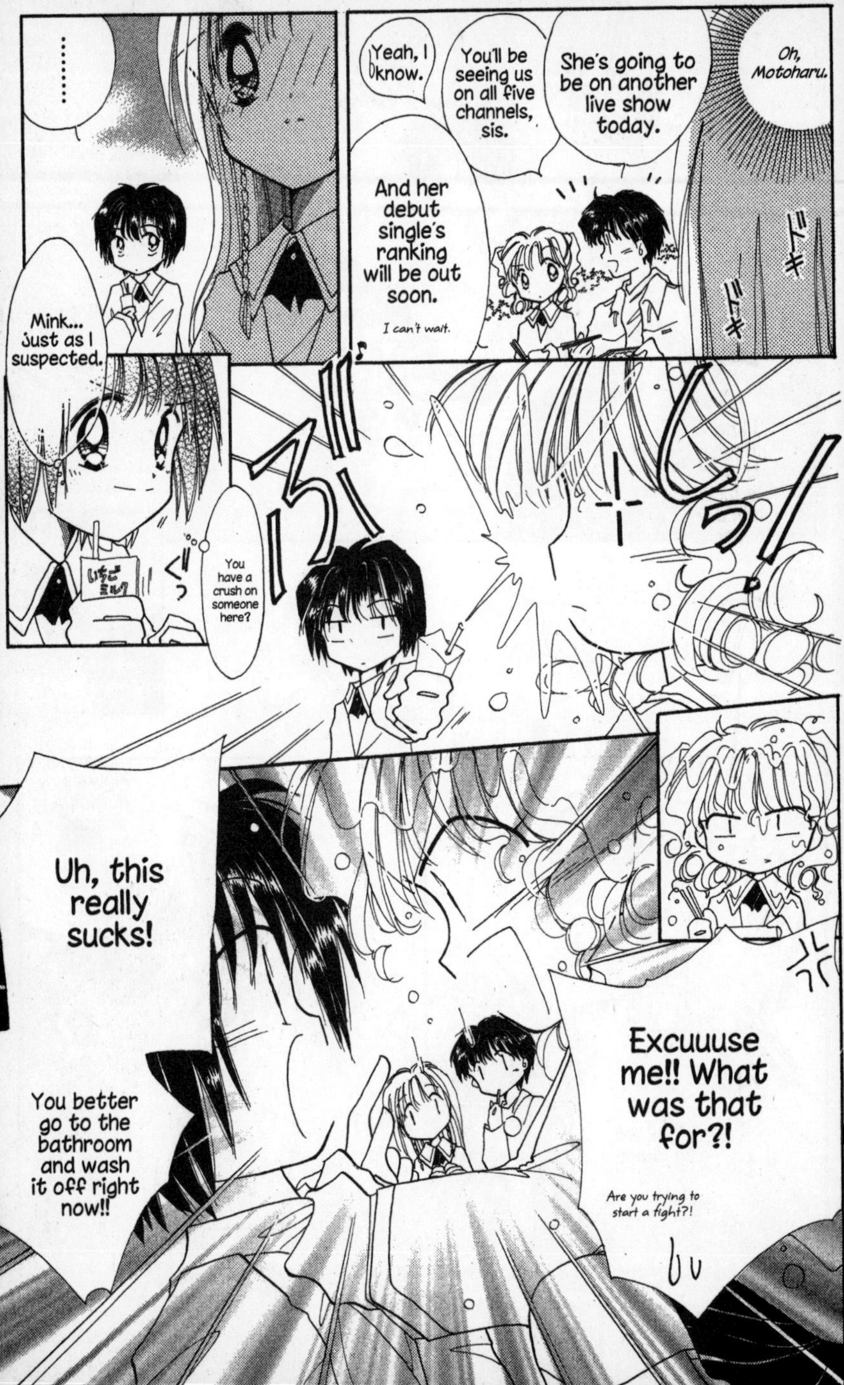
Oh, Motoharu.
She's going to be on another live show today.
You'll be seeing us on all five channels, sis.
Yeah, I know.
And her debut single's ranking will be out soon.
I can't wait.
ドキ ドキ
……
Mink... Just as I suspected.
いちごミルク
You have a crush on someone here?
Excuuuse me!! What was that for?!
Are you trying to start a fight?!
Uh, this really sucks!
You better go to the bathroom and wash it off right now!!

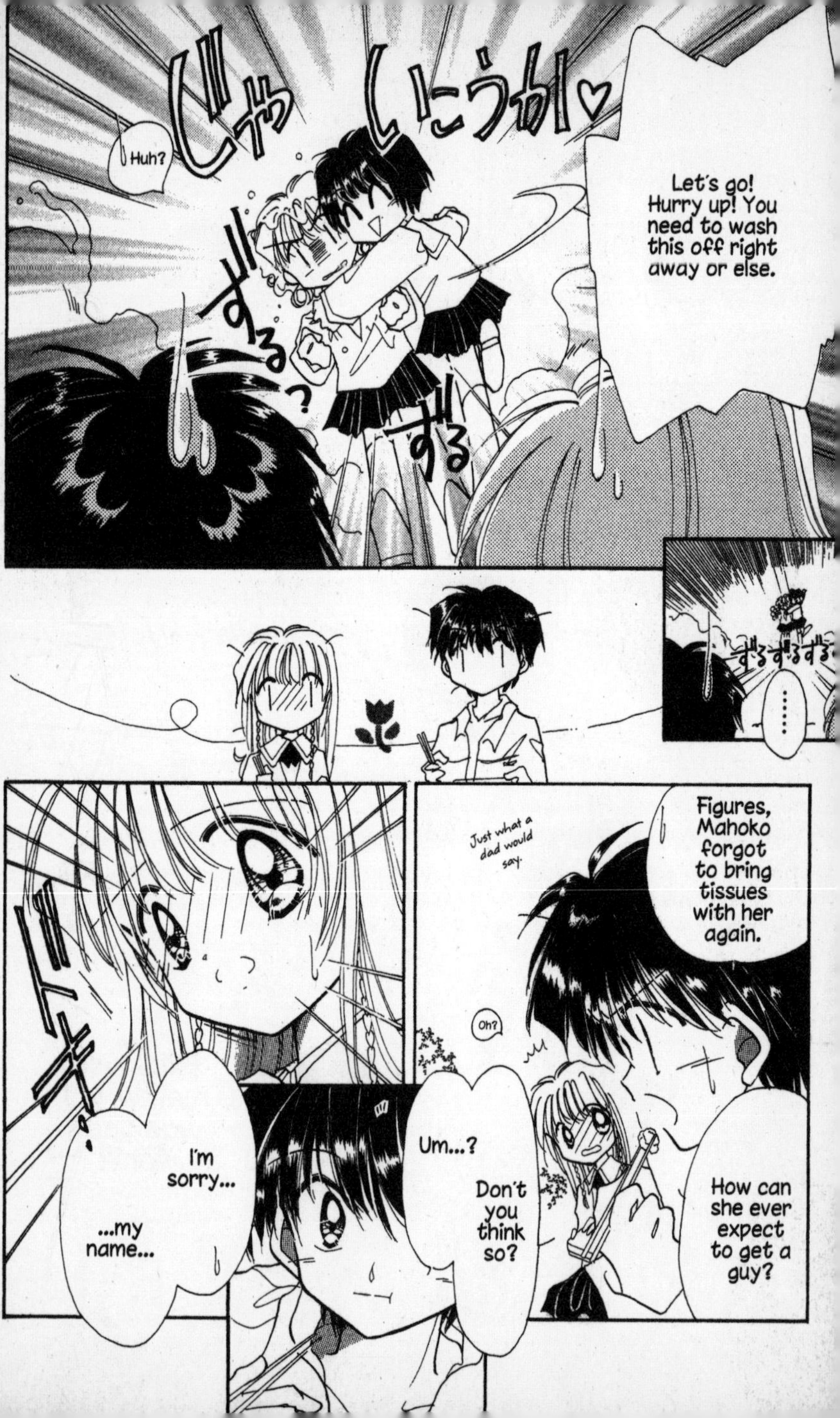
Let's go! Hurry up! You need to wash this off right away or else.
じゃ いこうか!♡
Huh?
ずる
?
ずる
ずるずるずる
......
Figures, Mahoko forgot to bring tissues with her again.
Just what a dad would say.
Oh?
How can she ever expect to get a guy?
Um...?
Don't you think so?
I'm sorry...
...my name...

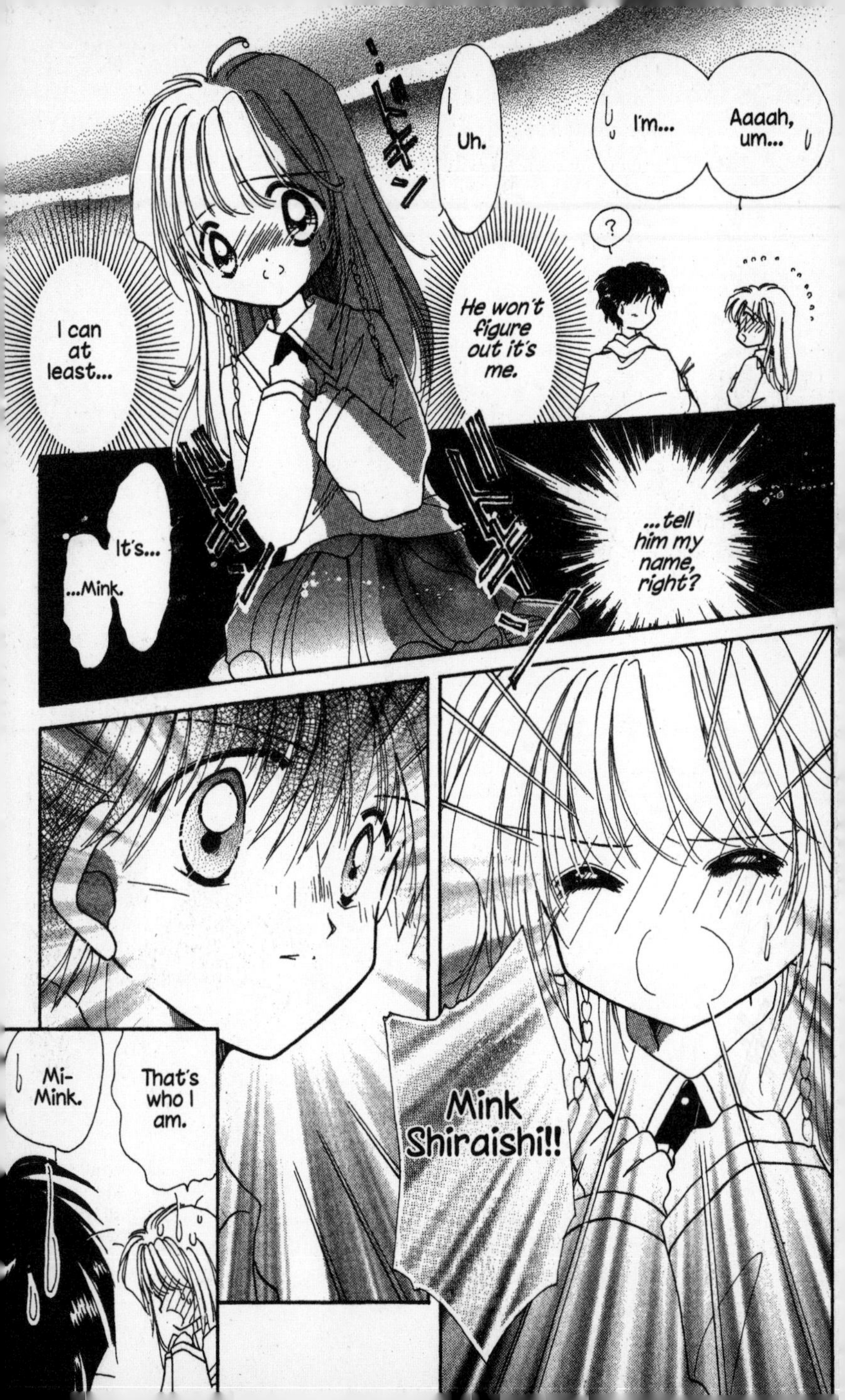

Aaaah, um...
I'm...
?
Uh.
He won't figure out it's me.
I can at least...
...tell him my name, right?
It's...
...Mink.
Mink Shiraishi!!
That's who I am.
Mi-Mink.

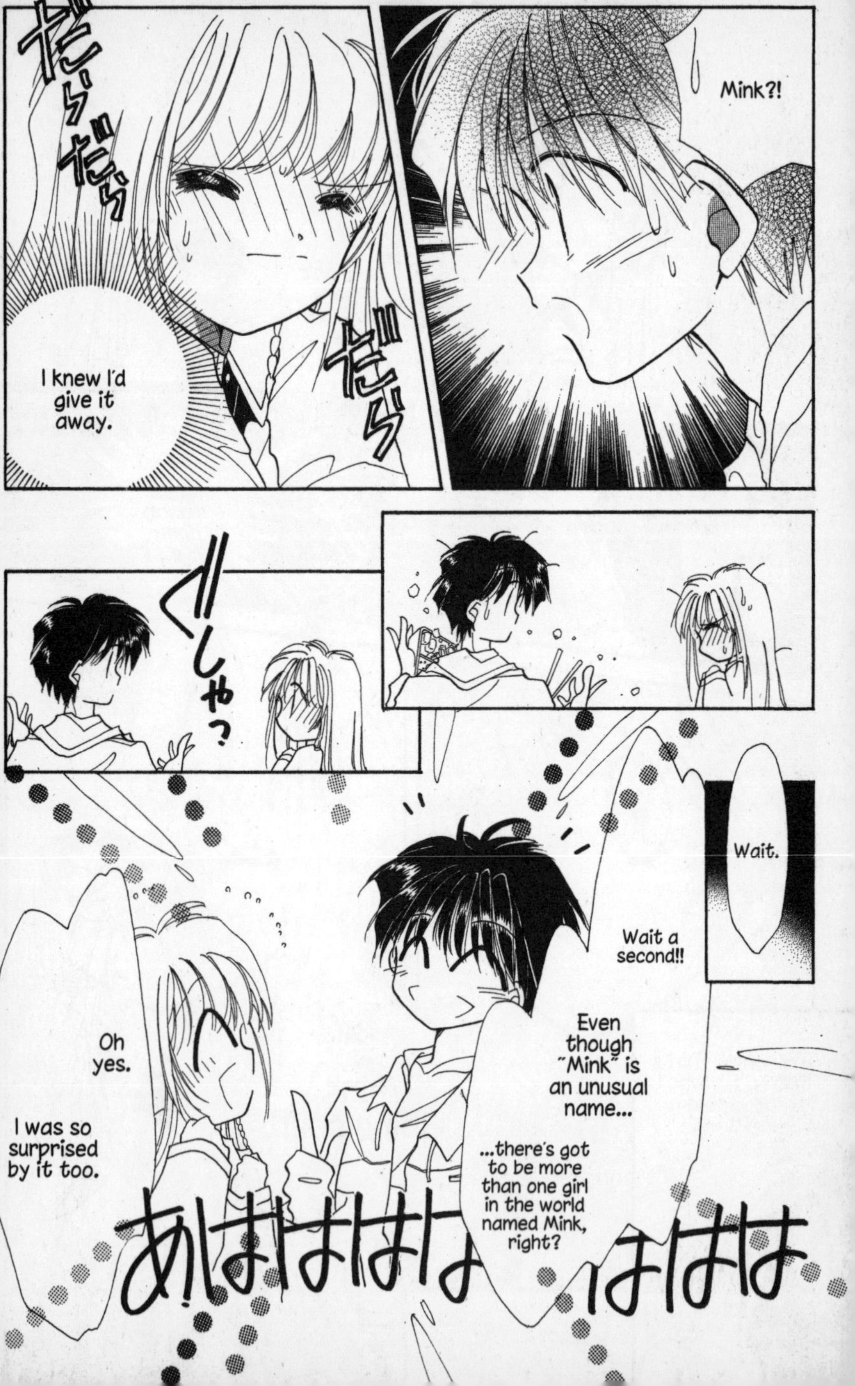
Mink?!
だらだら
I knew I'd give it away.
だら
くしゃっ
Wait.
Wait a second!!
Even though "Mink" is an unusual name...
...there's got to be more than one girl in the world named Mink, right?
Oh yes.
I was so surprised by it too.
あははははははは

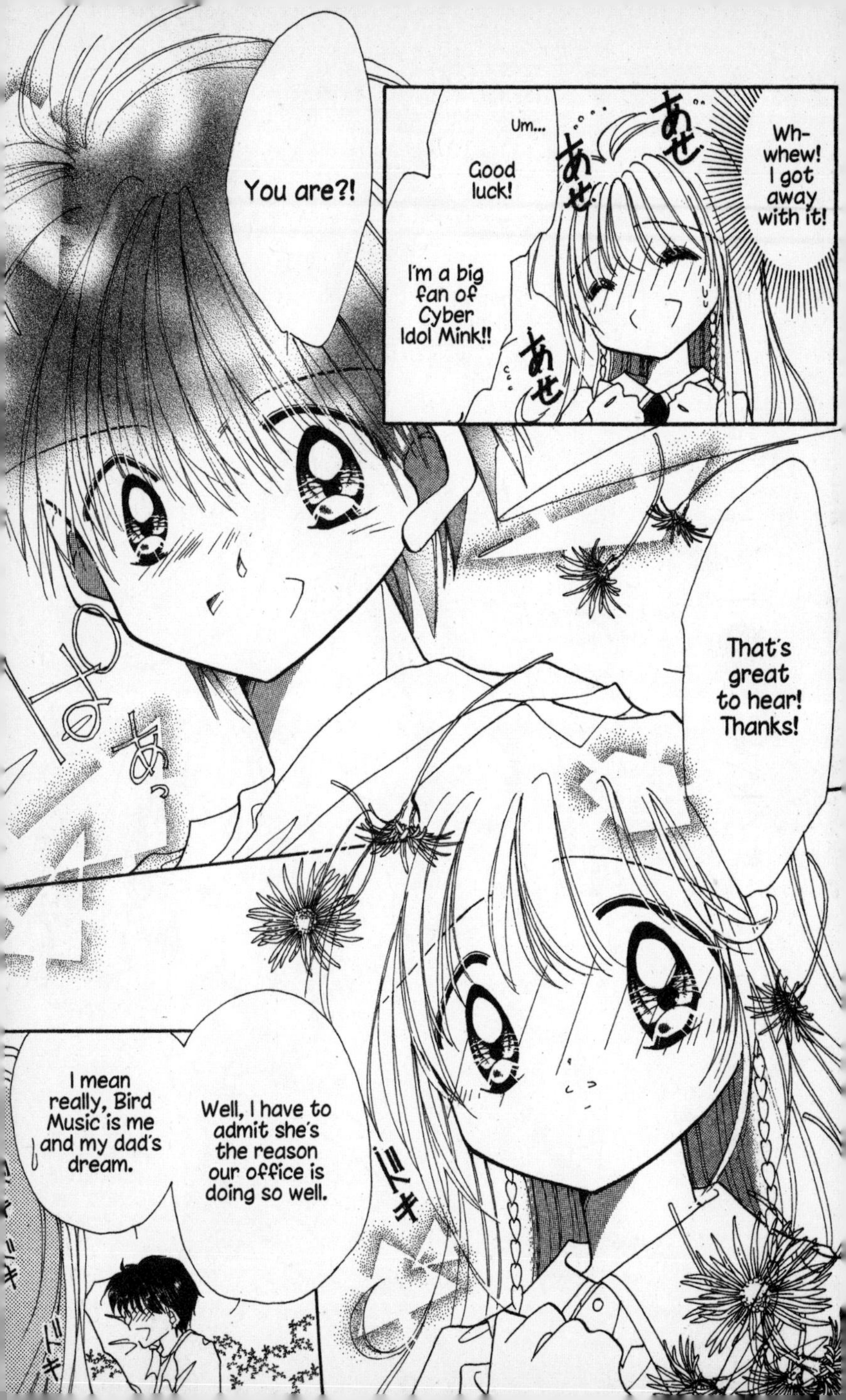

Wh-whew! I got away with it!
あせ
あせ
Um...
Good luck!
I'm a big fan of Cyber Idol Mink!!
あせ
You are?!
はあっ
That's great to hear! Thanks!
ドキ
Well, I have to admit she's the reason our office is doing so well.
I mean really, Bird Music is me and my dad's dream.
ドキ

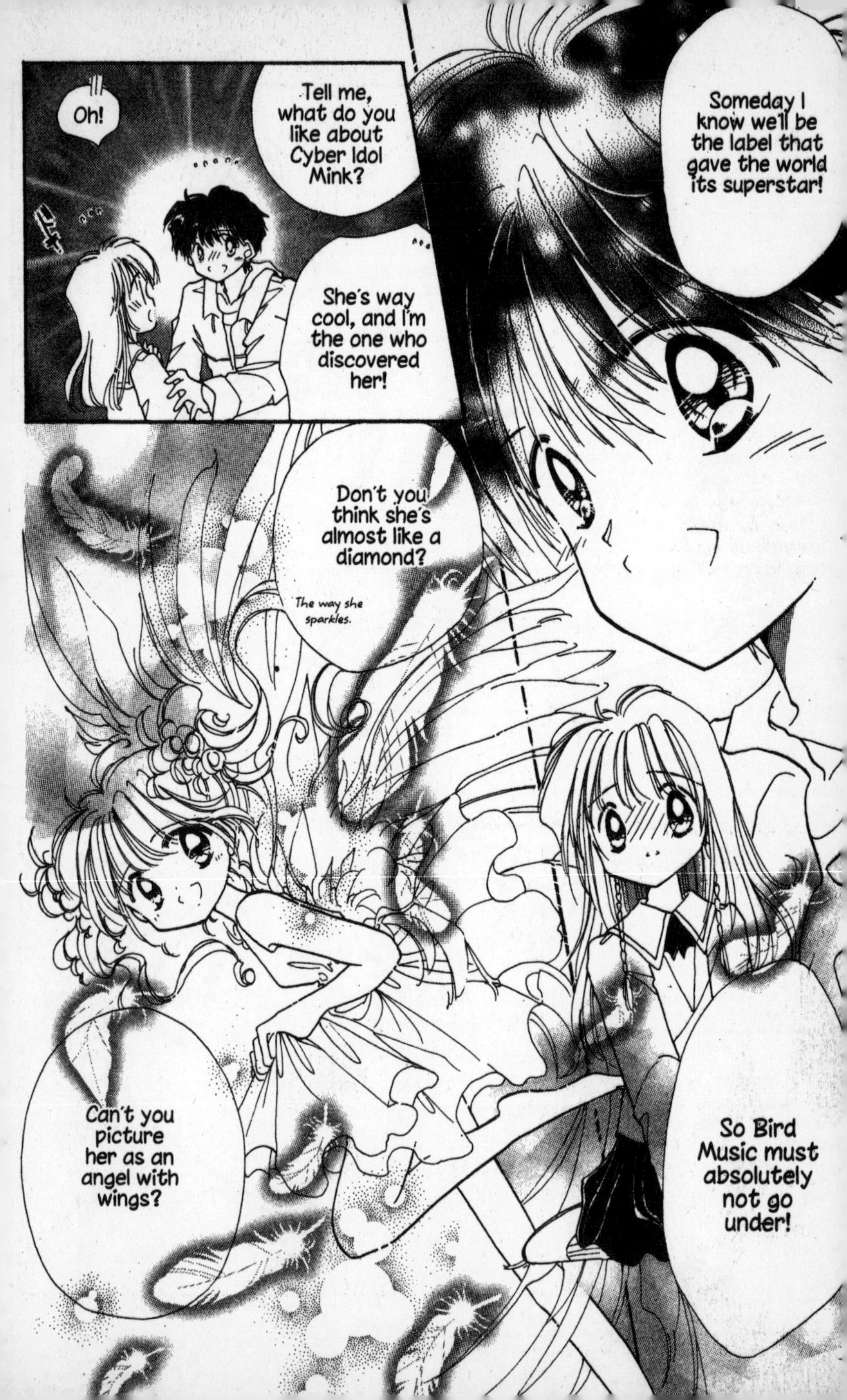
Someday I know we'll be the label that gave the world its superstar!
Tell me, what do you like about Cyber Idol Mink?
Oh!
She's way cool, and I'm the one who discovered her!
Don't you think she's almost like a diamond?
The way she sparkles.
So Bird Music must absolutely not go under!
Can't you picture her as an angel with wings?

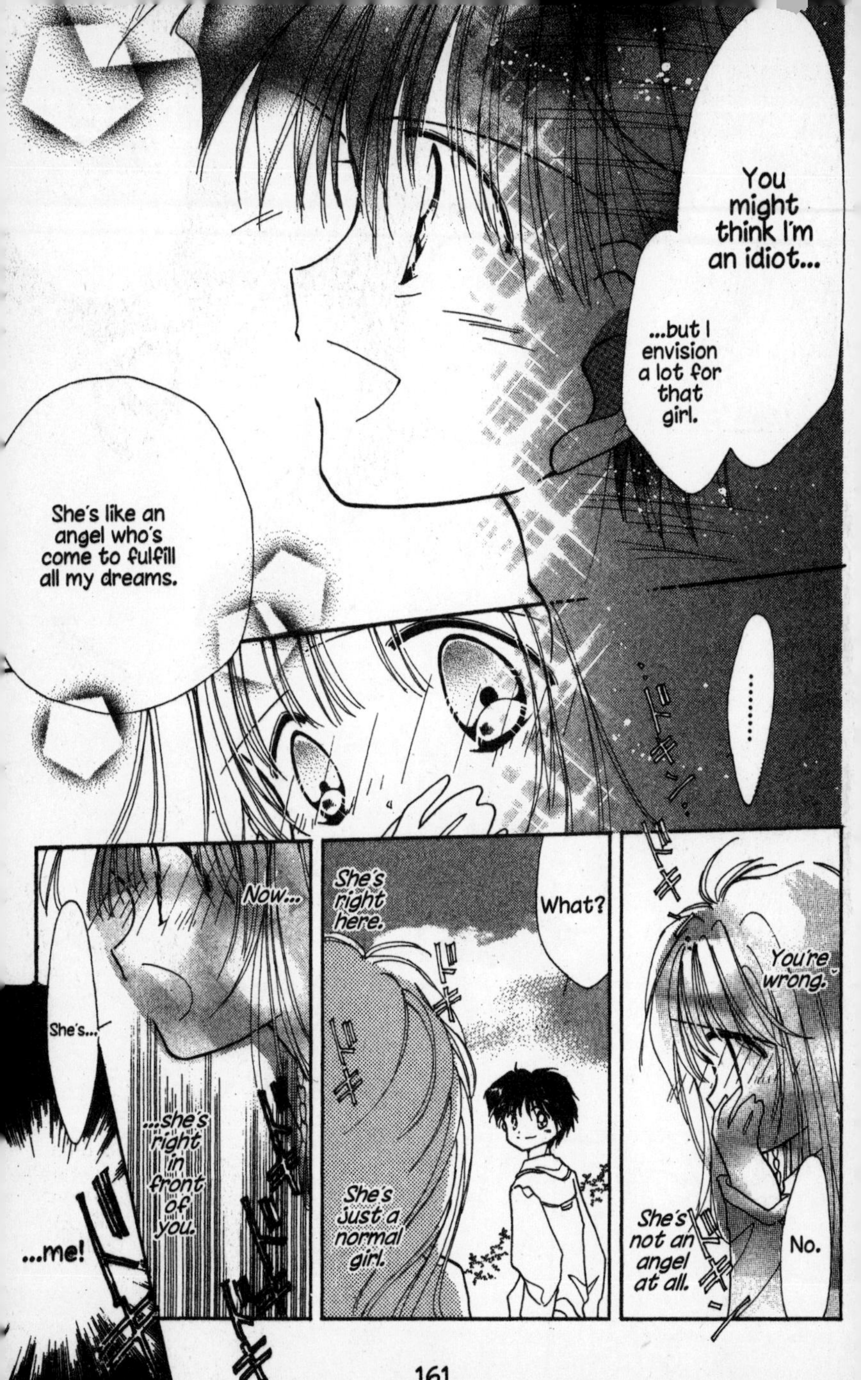
You might think I'm an idiot...
...but I envision a lot for that girl.
She's like an angel who's come to fulfill all my dreams.
......
You're wrong.
No.
She's not an angel at all.
What?
She's right here.
She's just a normal girl.
Now...
She's...
...she's right in front of you.
...me!

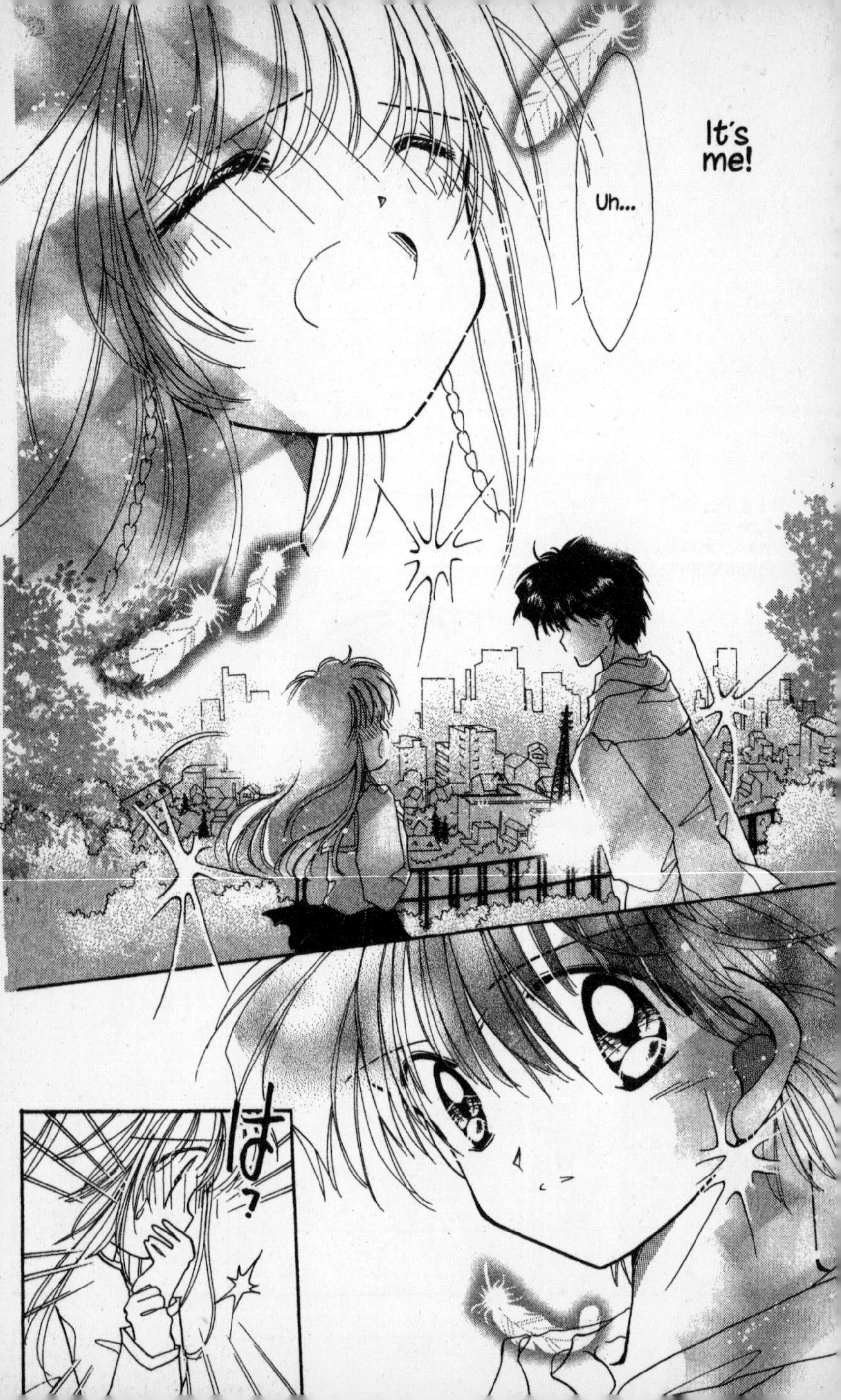
It's me!
Uh...
はっ

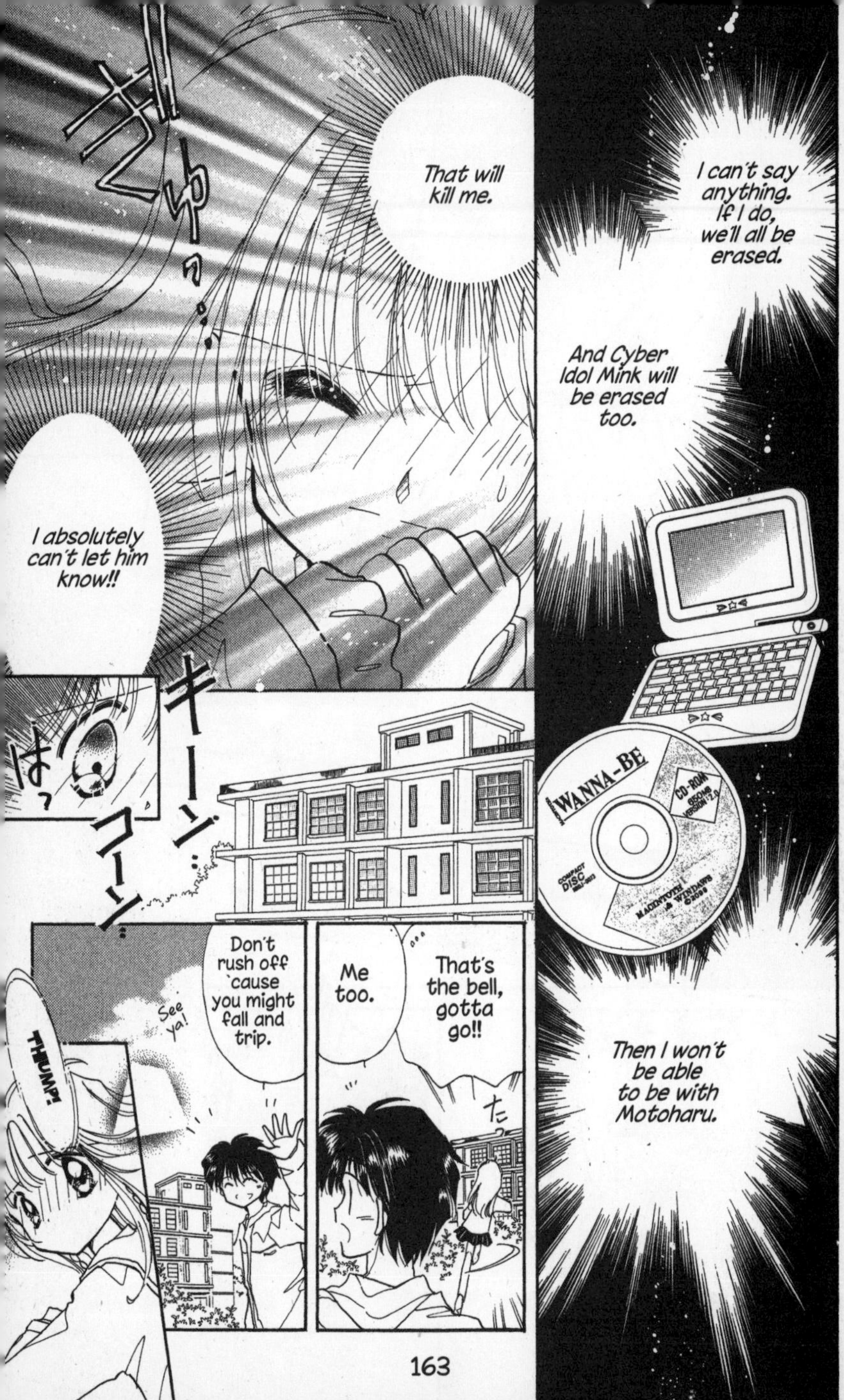
I can't say anything. If I do, we'll all be erased.
And Cyber Idol Mink will be erased too.
WANNA-BE
CD-ROM
Then I won't be able to be with Motoharu.
That will kill me.
I absolutely can't let him know!!
はっ
キーンコーン
That's the bell, gotta go!!
Me too.
たっ
Don't rush off 'cause you might fall and trip.
See ya!
THUMP!

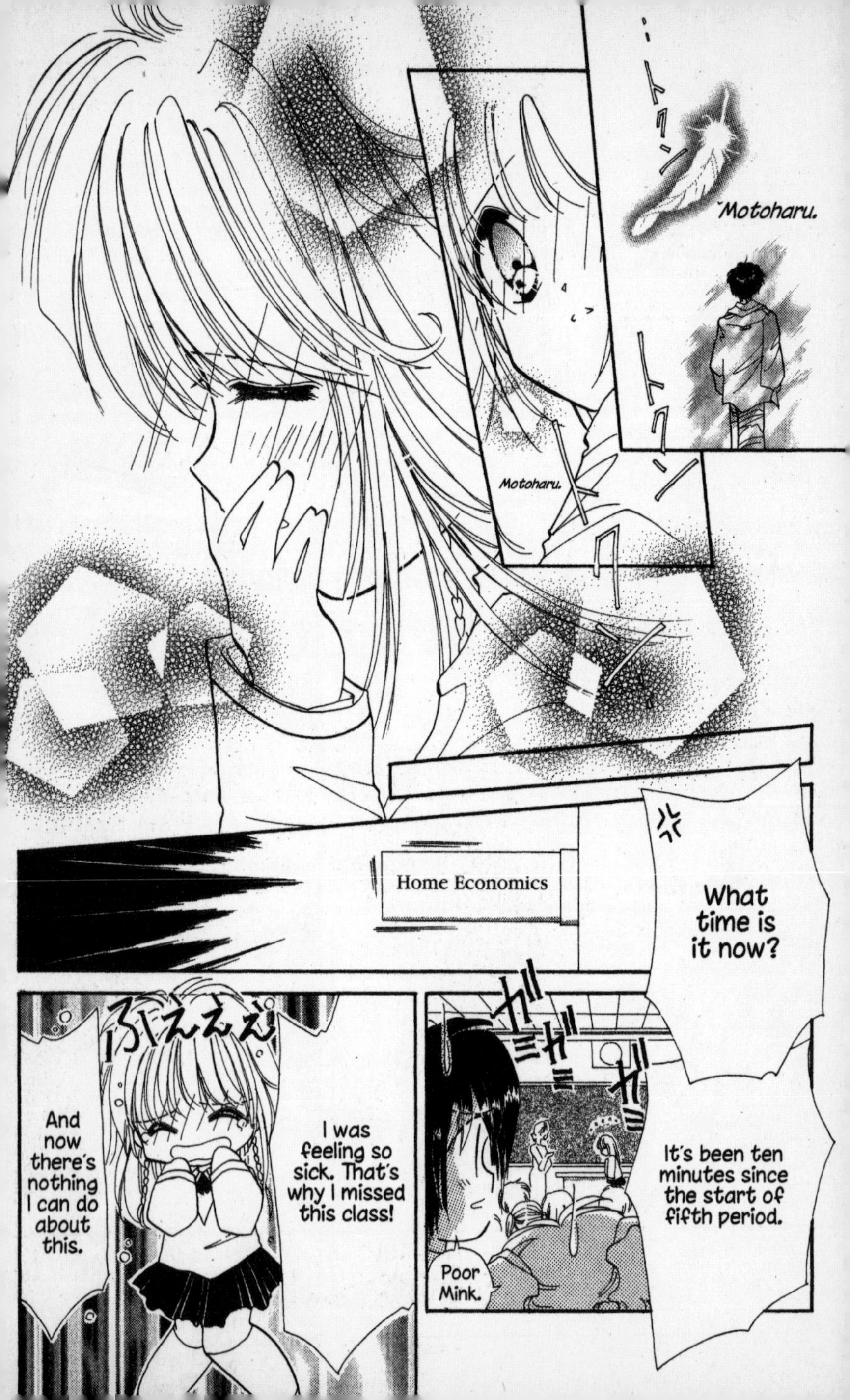
…トクン
Motoharu.
トクン
Motoharu.
トクン
What time is it now?
Home Economics
ガ ガ ガ
It's been ten minutes since the start of fifth period.
Poor Mink.
ふえええ
I was feeling so sick. That's why I missed this class!
And now there's nothing I can do about this.

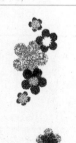

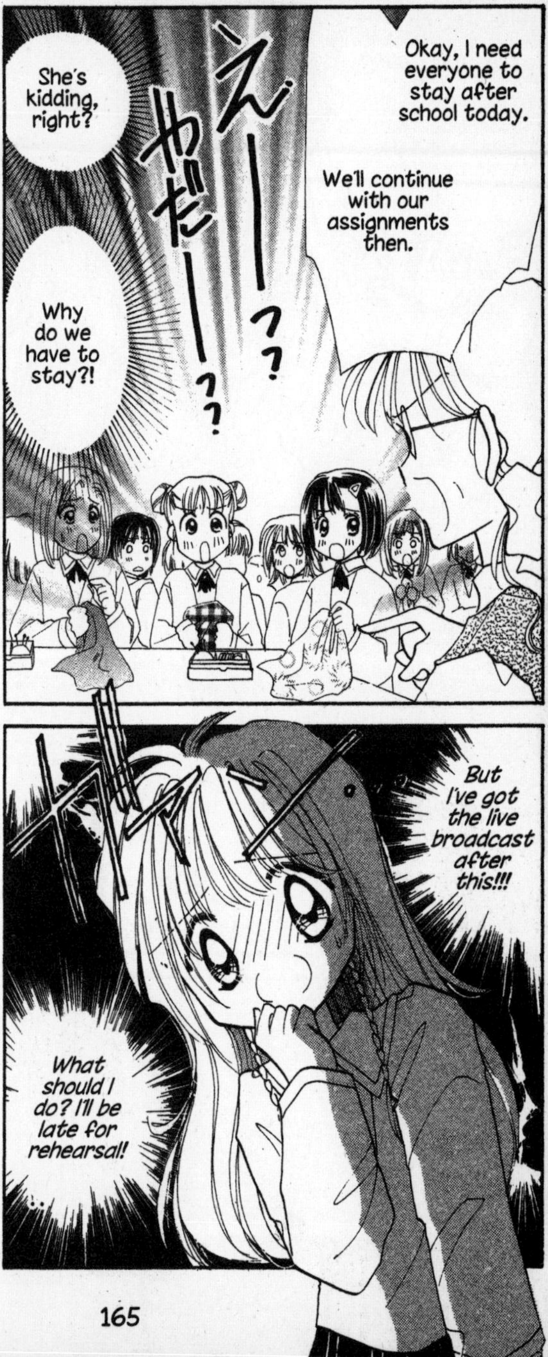
Okay, I need everyone to stay after school today.
We'll continue with our assignments then.
えーーっ??
やだーーっ??
She's kidding, right?
Why do we have to stay?!
But I've got the live broadcast after this!!!
What should I do? I'll be late for rehearsal!

Mink Rap!!

Special thanks to:

Miyuki Okazaki
Miwa Ishioka
Harumi Azima

As always, thanks to you, the reader!

-Megumi

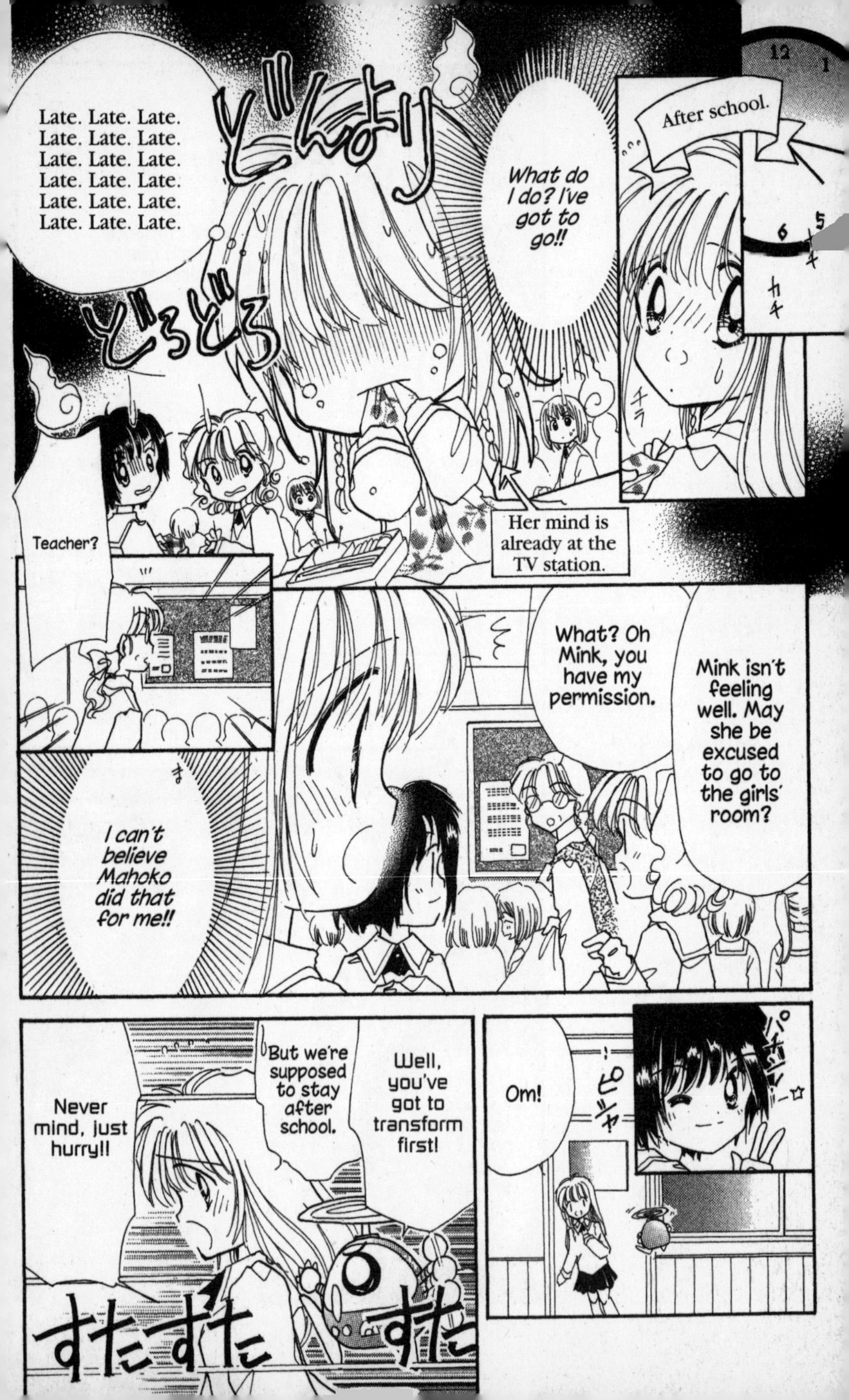
After school.
カチ
チラ
What do I do? I've got to go!!
どんより
どろどろ
Late. Late. Late. Late. Late. Late. Late. Late. Late. Late. Late. Late. Late. Late. Late. Late. Late. Late.
Her mind is already at the TV station.
Teacher?
Mink isn't feeling well. May she be excused to go to the girls' room?
What? Oh Mink, you have my permission.
I can't believe Mahoko did that for me!!
パチン☆
ピシャ
Om!
Well, you've got to transform first!
But we're supposed to stay after school.
Never mind, just hurry!!
すたすた すたすた

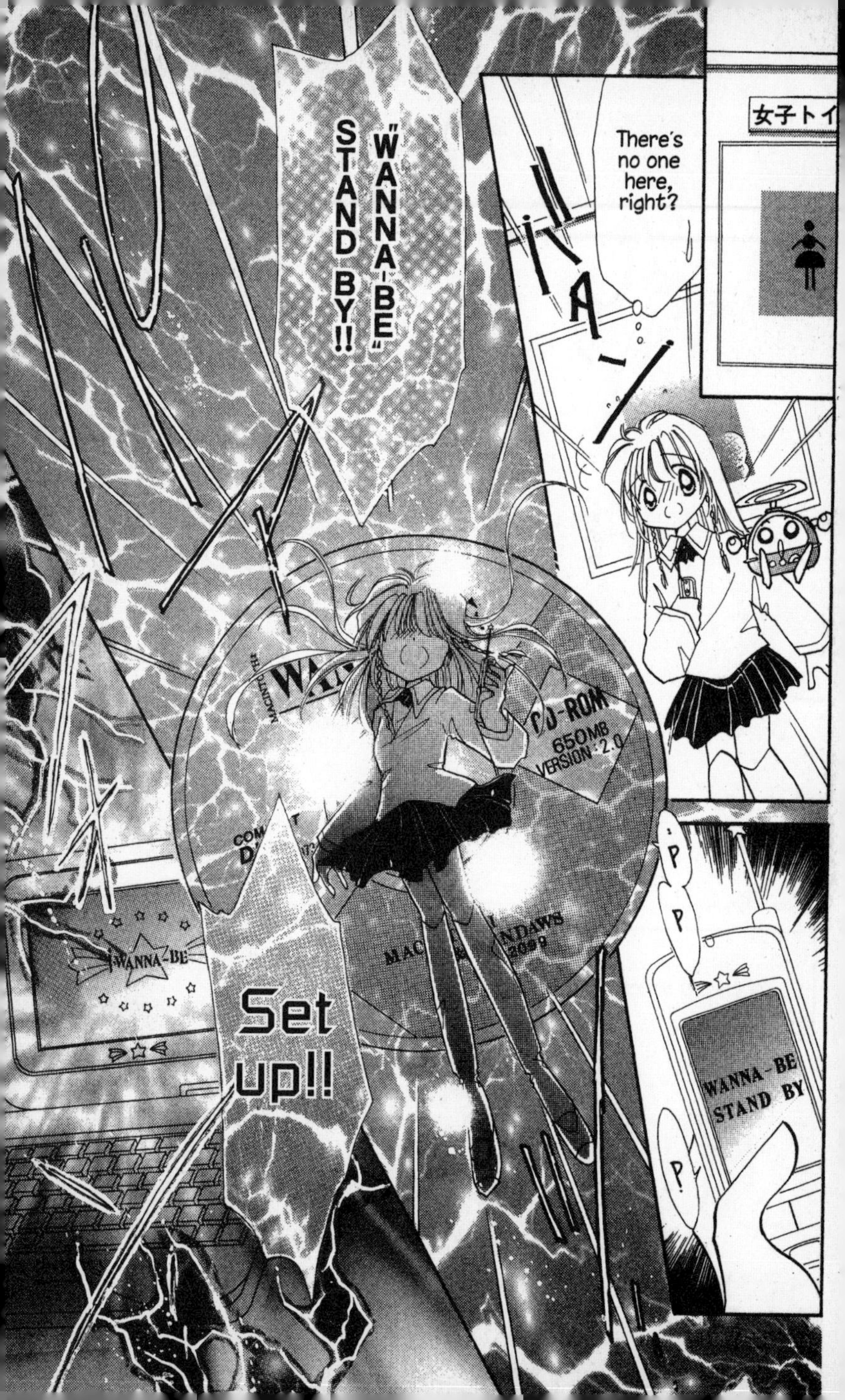
女子トイ
There's no one here, right?
P
P
P
WANNA-BE STAND BY
"WANNA-BE" STAND BY!!
CD-ROM 650MB VERSION: 2.0
WANNA-BE
Set up!!

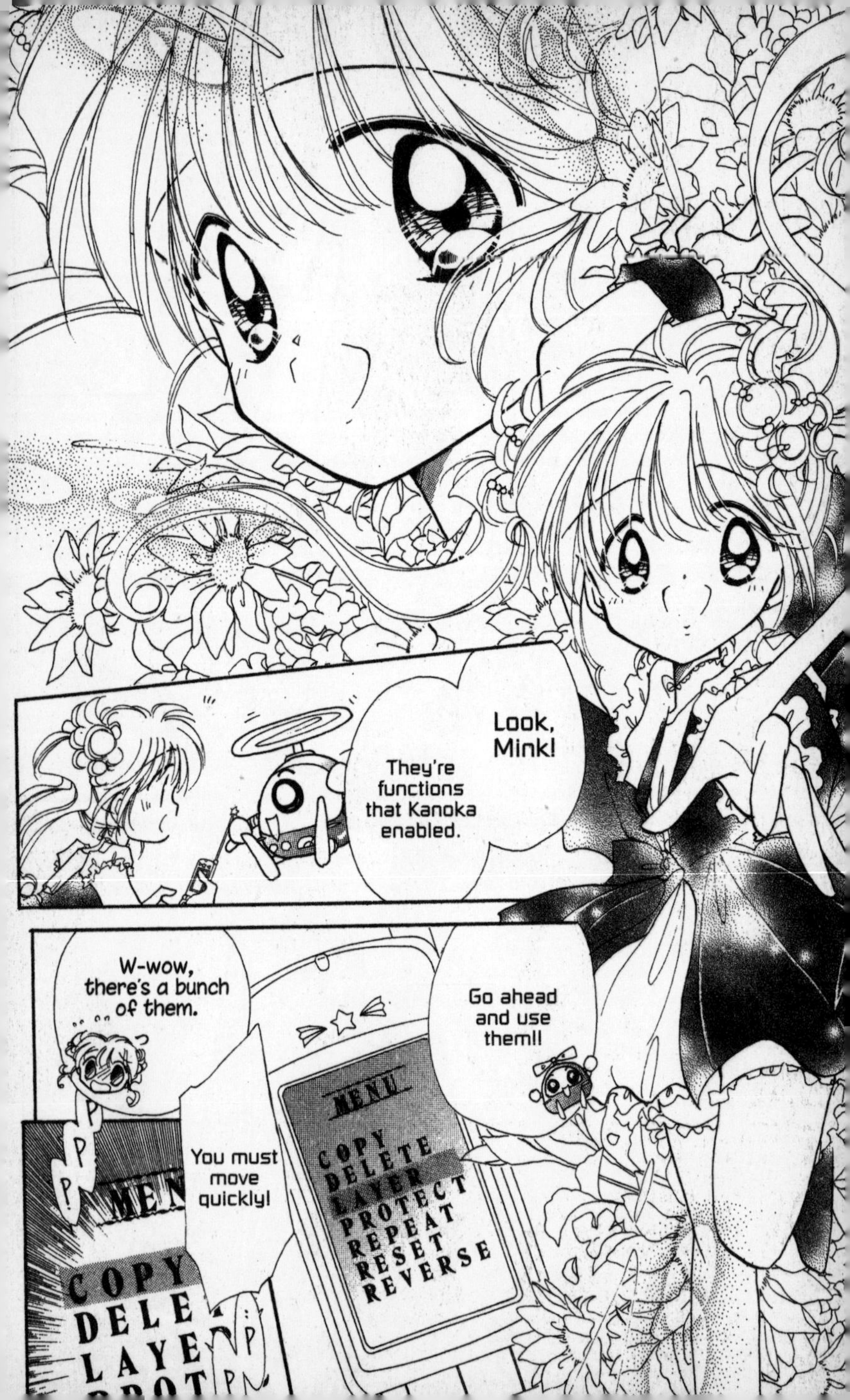

Look, Mink!
They're functions that Kanoka enabled.
Go ahead and use them!!
W-wow, there's a bunch of them.
MENU
COPY
DELETE
LAYER
PROTECT
REPEAT
RESET
REVERSE
You must move quickly!
P P P

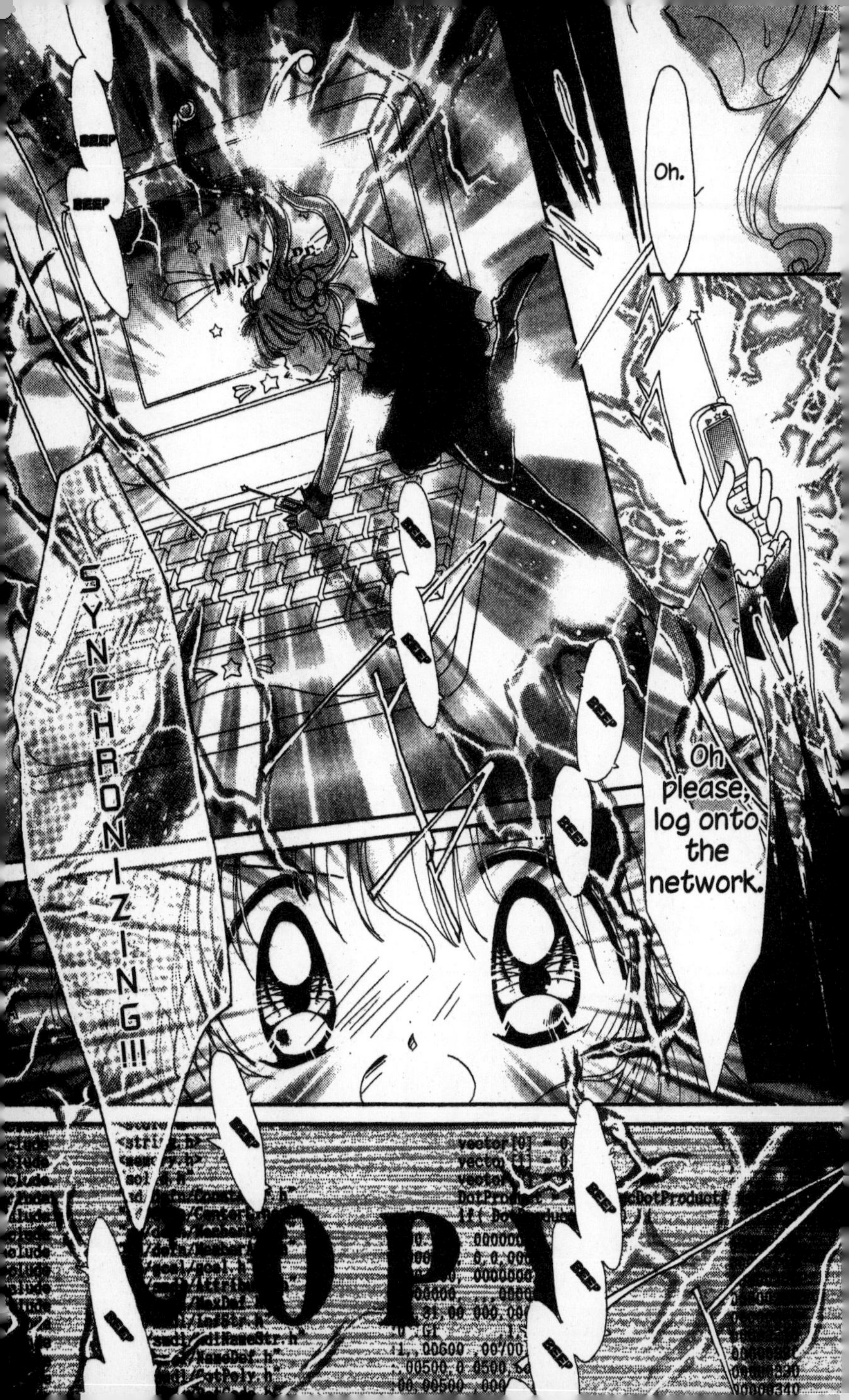
Oh.
WANN
Oh please, log onto the network.
SYNCHRONIZING!!!
COP

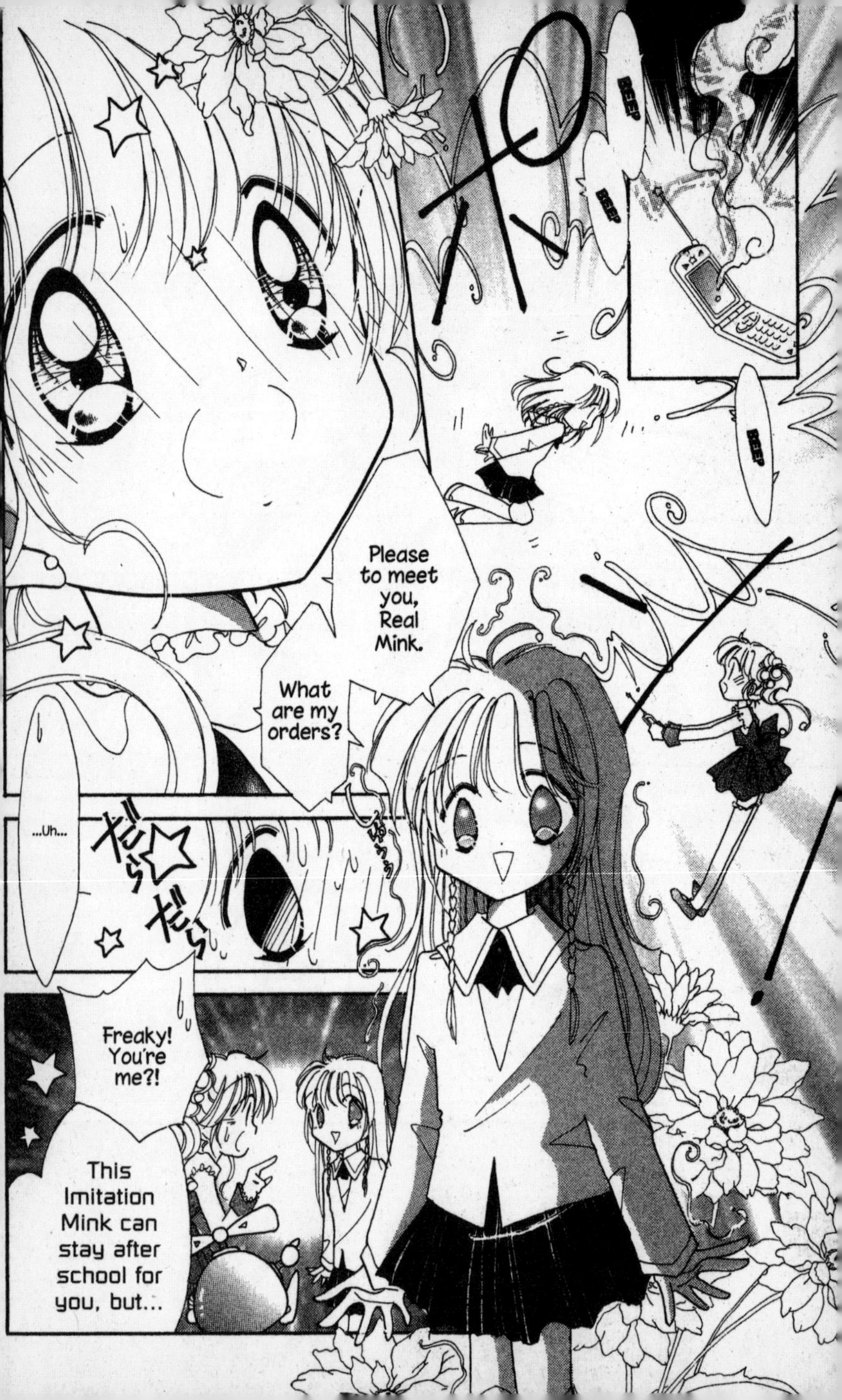
BEEP
BEEP
BEEP
Please to meet you, Real Mink.
What are my orders?
...Uh...
だら だら
Freaky! You're me?!
This Imitation Mink can stay after school for you, but...

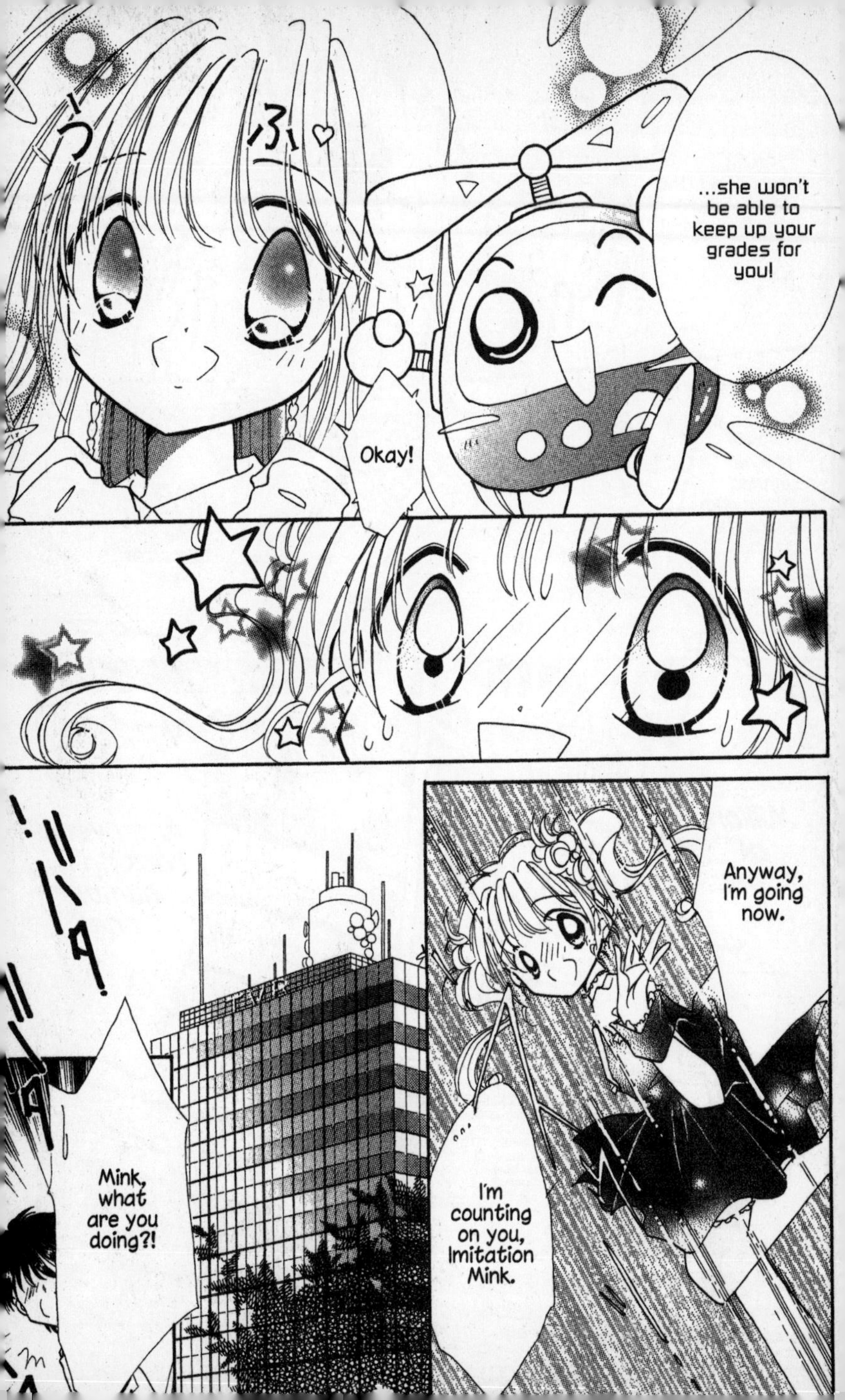
...she won't be able to keep up your grades for you!
Okay!
うふ♡
Anyway, I'm going now.
I'm counting on you, Imitation Mink.
Mink, what are you doing?!

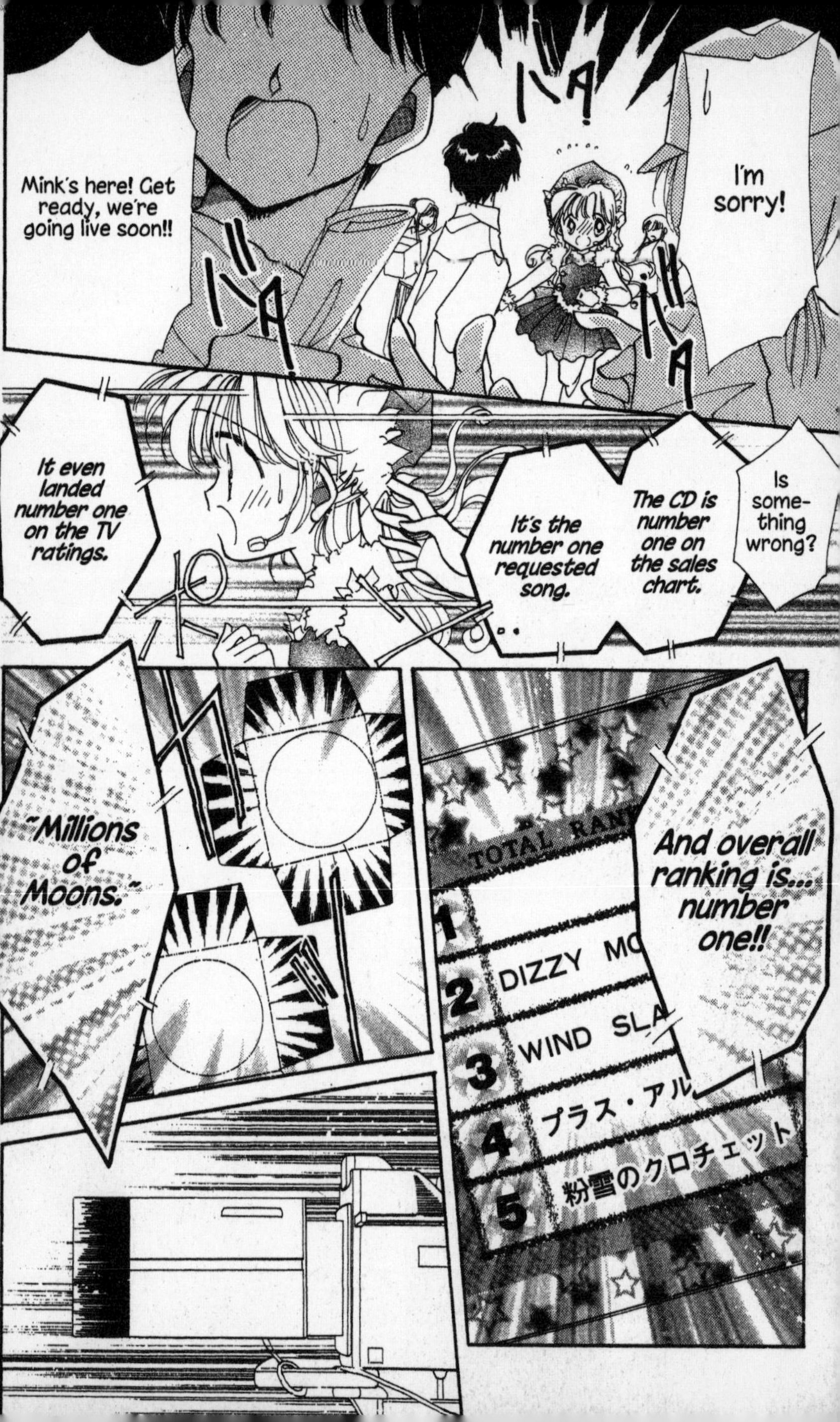
I'm sorry!
バタ!
Mink's here! Get ready, we're going live soon!!
Is something wrong?
The CD is number one on the sales chart.
It's the number one requested song.
It even landed number one on the TV ratings.
And overall ranking is... number one!!
TOTAL RAN
1
2 DIZZY MO
3 WIND SLA
4 プラス・アル
5 粉雪のクロチェット
~Millions of Moons.~

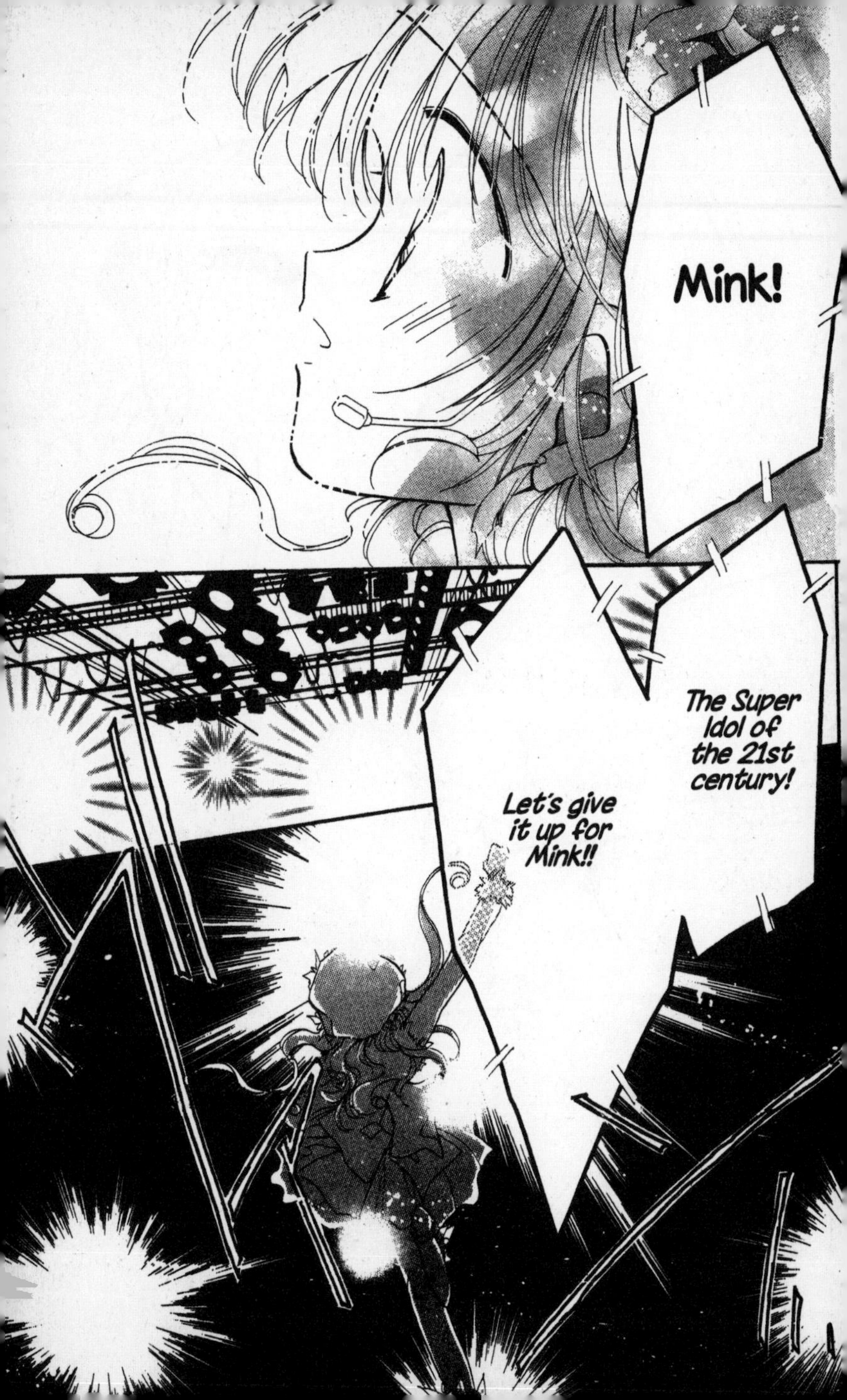
Mink!
The Super Idol of the 21st century!
Let's give it up for Mink!!

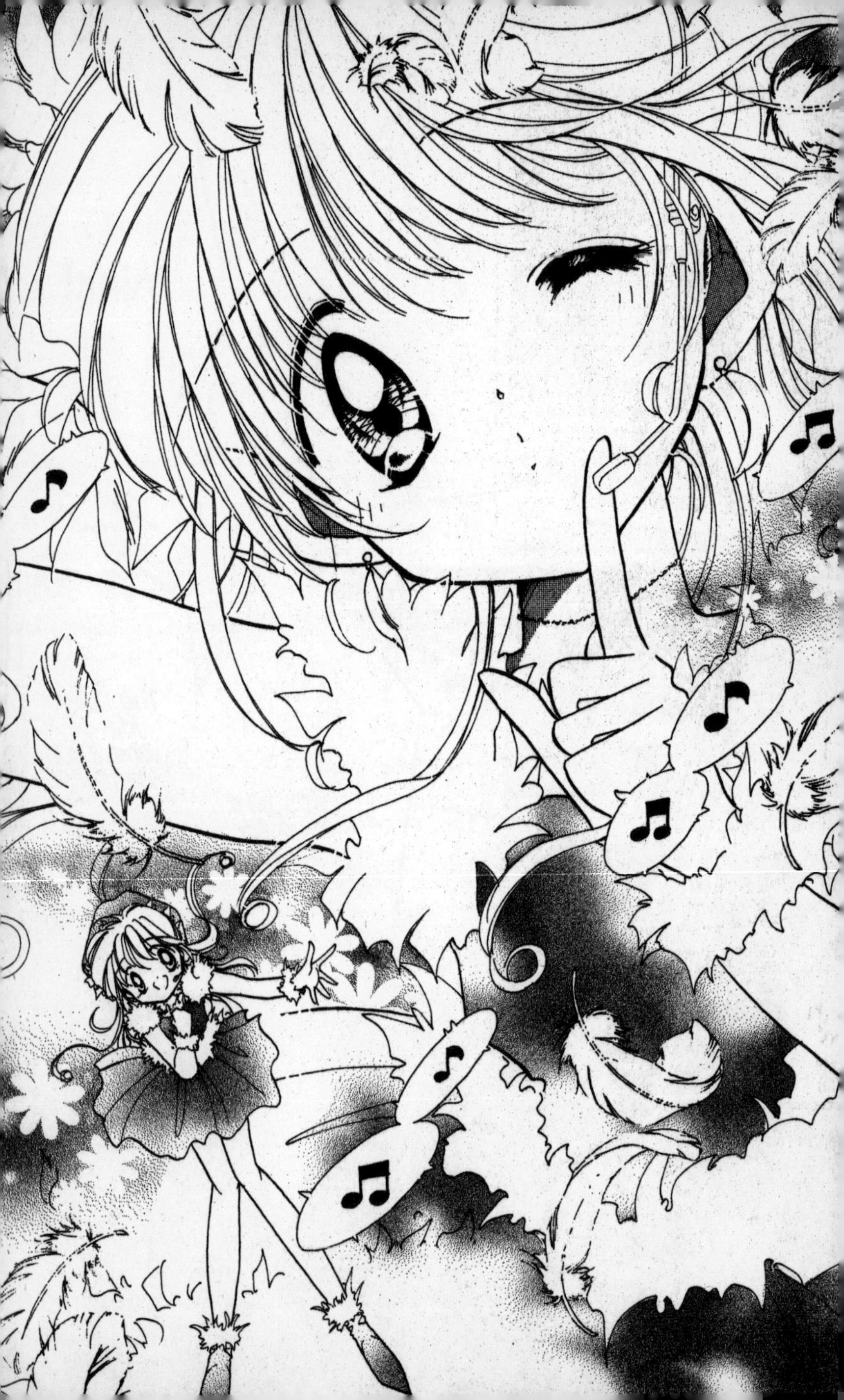

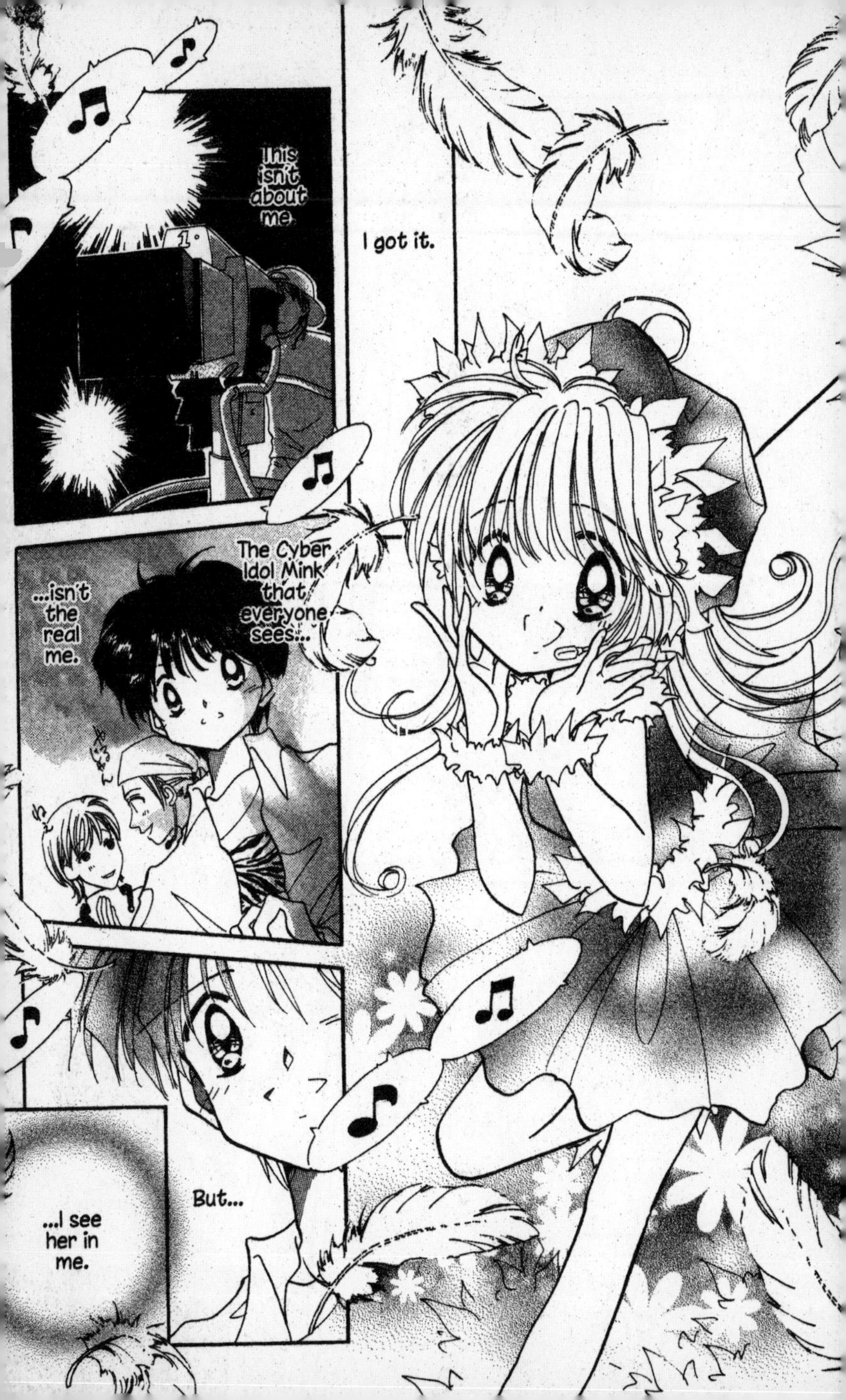

I got it.
This isn't about me.
The Cyber Idol Mink that everyone sees...
...isn't the real me.
But...
...I see her in me.

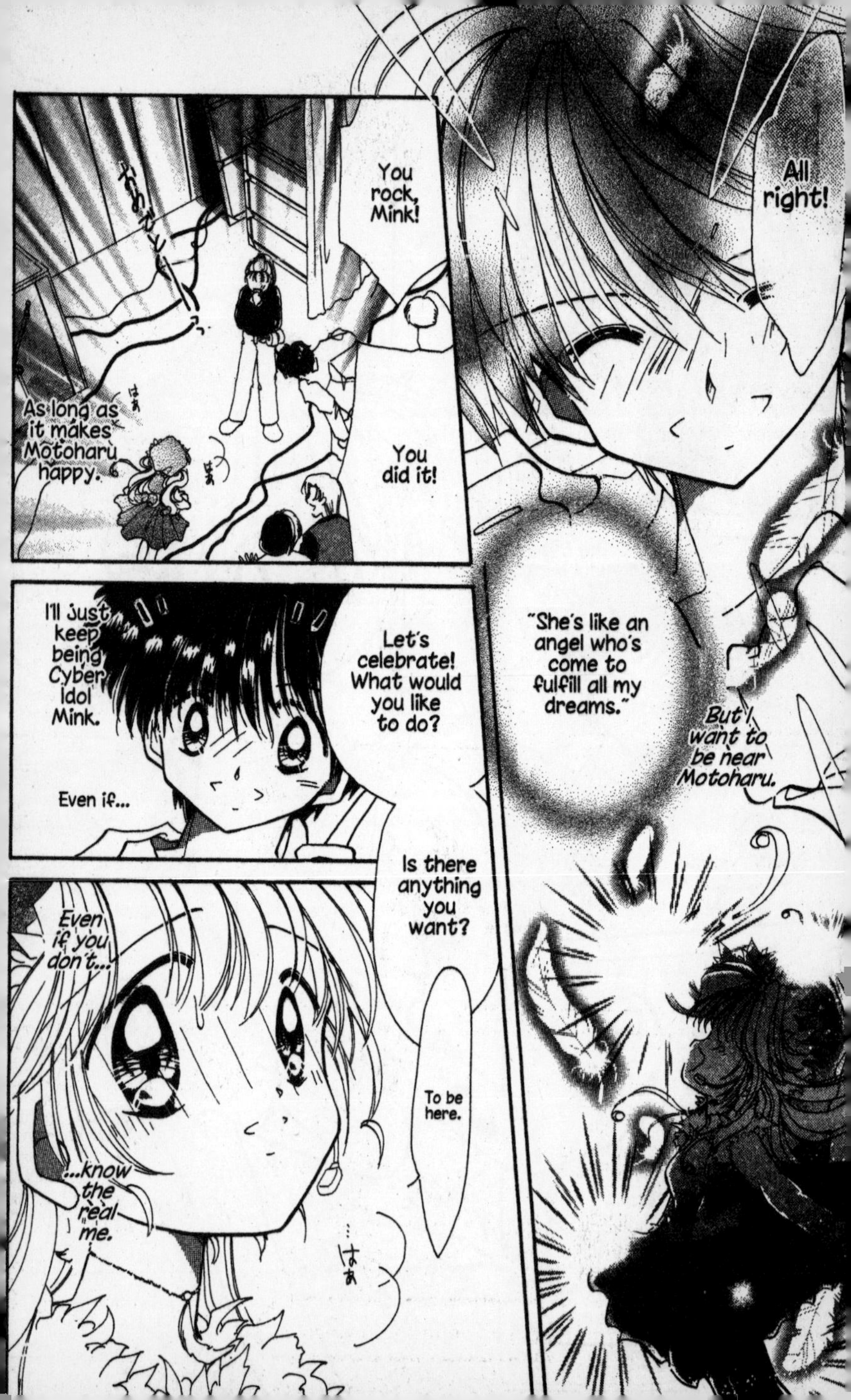
All right!
"She's like an angel who's come to fulfill all my dreams."
But I want to be near Motoharu.
You rock, Mink!
You did it!
はあ
はあ
As long as it makes Motoharu happy.
Let's celebrate! What would you like to do?
I'll just keep being Cyber Idol Mink.
Even if...
Is there anything you want?
Even if you don't...
To be here.
...はあ
...know the real me.

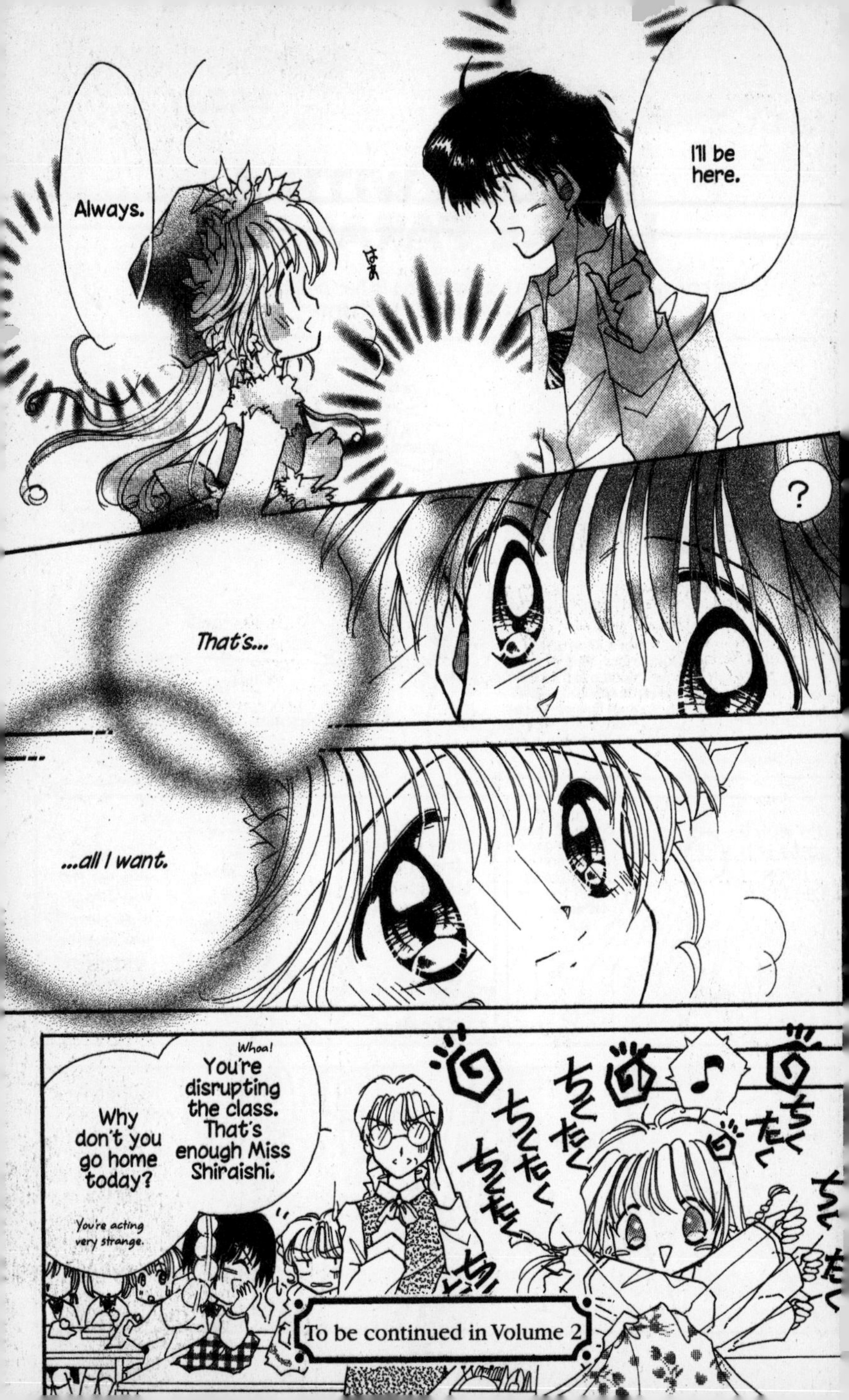
I'll be here.
はぁ
Always.
?
That's...
...all I want.
ちくたく
ちくたく
ちくたく
♪
ちくたく
ちくたく
ちくたく
Whoa!
You're disrupting the class. That's enough Miss Shiraishi.
Why don't you go home today?
You're acting very strange.
To be continued in Volume 2

MANGA ESSAY

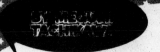

IN LOVE WITH A LITTLE PARAKEET

The one guy Megumi can't stop loving is her pet parakeet, Peach.
Let's talk about his charm.

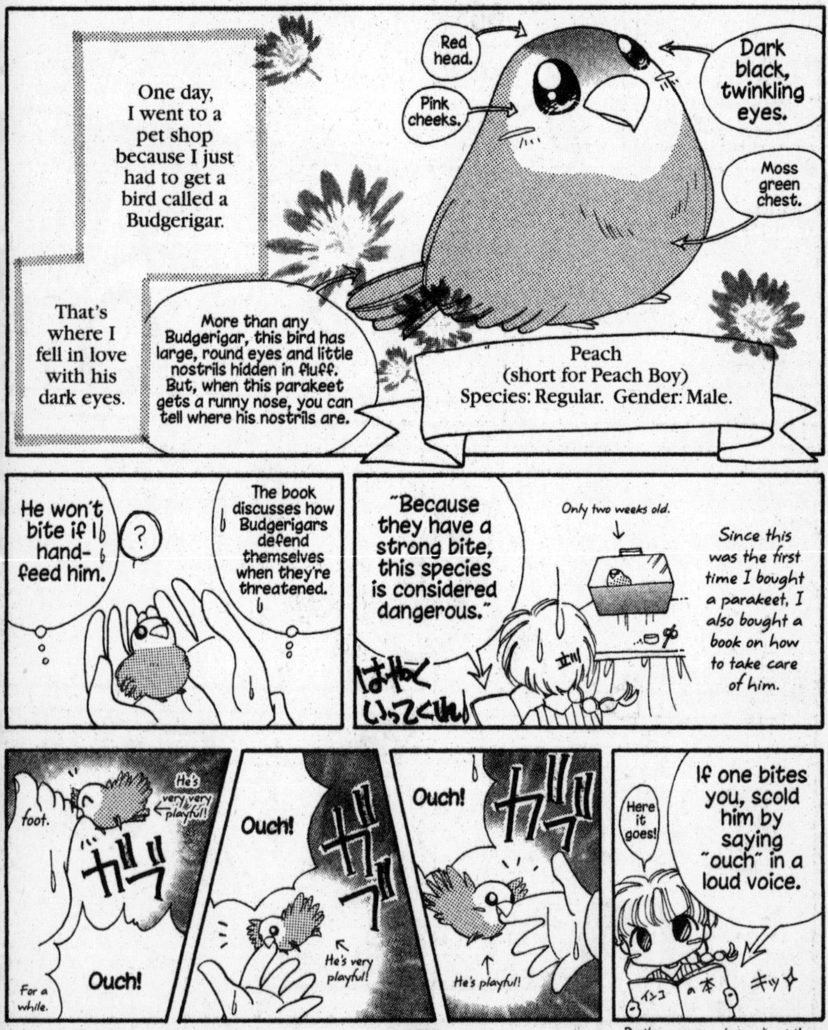

Dark black, twinkling eyes.
Red head.
Pink cheeks.
One day, I went to a pet shop because I just had to get a bird called a Budgerigar.
Moss green chest.
Peach (short for Peach Boy) Species: Regular. Gender: Male.
More than any Budgerigar, this bird has large, round eyes and little nostrils hidden in fluff. But, when this parakeet gets a runny nose, you can tell where his nostrils are.
That's where I fell in love with his dark eyes.
Since this was the first time I bought a parakeet, I also bought a book on how to take care of him.
Only two weeks old.
"Because they have a strong bite, this species is considered dangerous."
はやく いってくれ
The book discusses how Budgerigars defend themselves when they're threatened.
?
He won't bite if I hand-feed him.
If one bites you, scold him by saying "ouch" in a loud voice.
Here it goes!
キッ
インコの本
Ouch!
ガブ
He's playful!
Ouch!
ガブ
He's very playful!
He's very very playful!
foot.
Ouch!
For a while.

By the way, you also can't pet them.

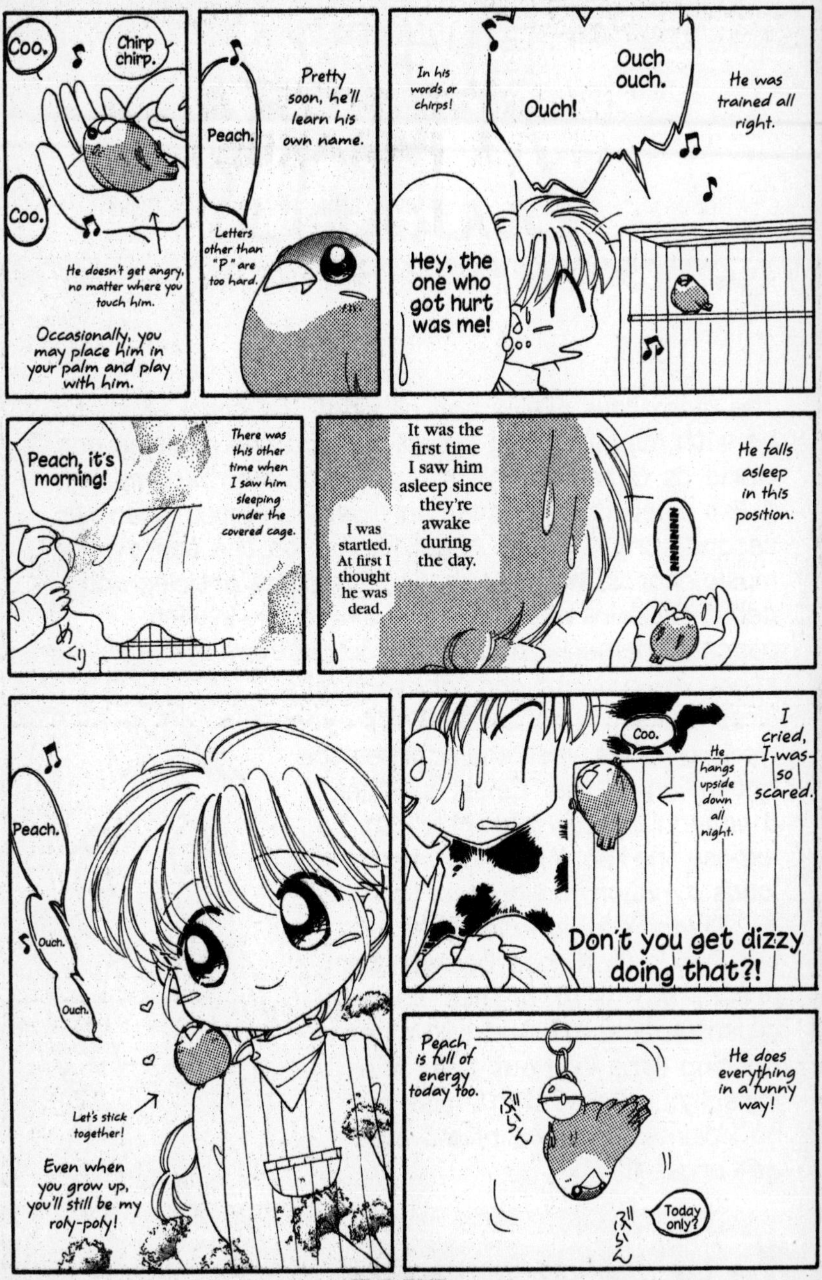
He was trained all right.
Ouch ouch.
Ouch!
In his words or chirps!
Hey, the one who got hurt was me!
Pretty soon, he'll learn his own name.
Peach.
Letters other than "P" are too hard.
Chirp chirp.
Coo.
Coo.
He doesn't get angry, no matter where you touch him.
Occasionally, you may place him in your palm and play with him.
He falls asleep in this position.
NNNNNNN
It was the first time I saw him asleep since they're awake during the day.
I was startled. At first I thought he was dead.
There was this other time when I saw him sleeping under the covered cage.
Peach, it's morning!
めくり
I cried, I was so scared.
Coo.
He hangs upside down all night.
Don't you get dizzy doing that?!
He does everything in a funny way!
Peach is full of energy today too.
ぶらん
ぶらん
Today only?
Peach.
Ouch.
Ouch.
Let's stick together!
Even when you grow up, you'll still be my roly-poly!

THE END

COMING SOON!

電脳少女☆Mink

The glamorous life is not all what it's cracked up to be with Mink juggling school life and the exciting pop world as Cyber Idol Mink. As she quickly becomes an A-list celebrity, her star only gets brighter when her second song, "Velvet Angel," soars to the top of the music charts. With TV shows, magazine articles and a debut CD, Mink has it all--including a run-in with popstar nemesis Azumi, who's out to steal her spotlight and sabotage Mink's first headlining concert! Mink's cyber world crashes when she catches the attention of the "Celebrity Killer," a scandal-hungry reporter out to expose the real Mink! And when she lands a major motion deal to star as Illiya's passionate girlfriend, will Mink's first kiss be with her dream guy Illiya or her secret crush Motoharu? And will Mink's adoring fans find out that Mink is really...a fake? Don't miss out on Volume 2 or you might just get erased!

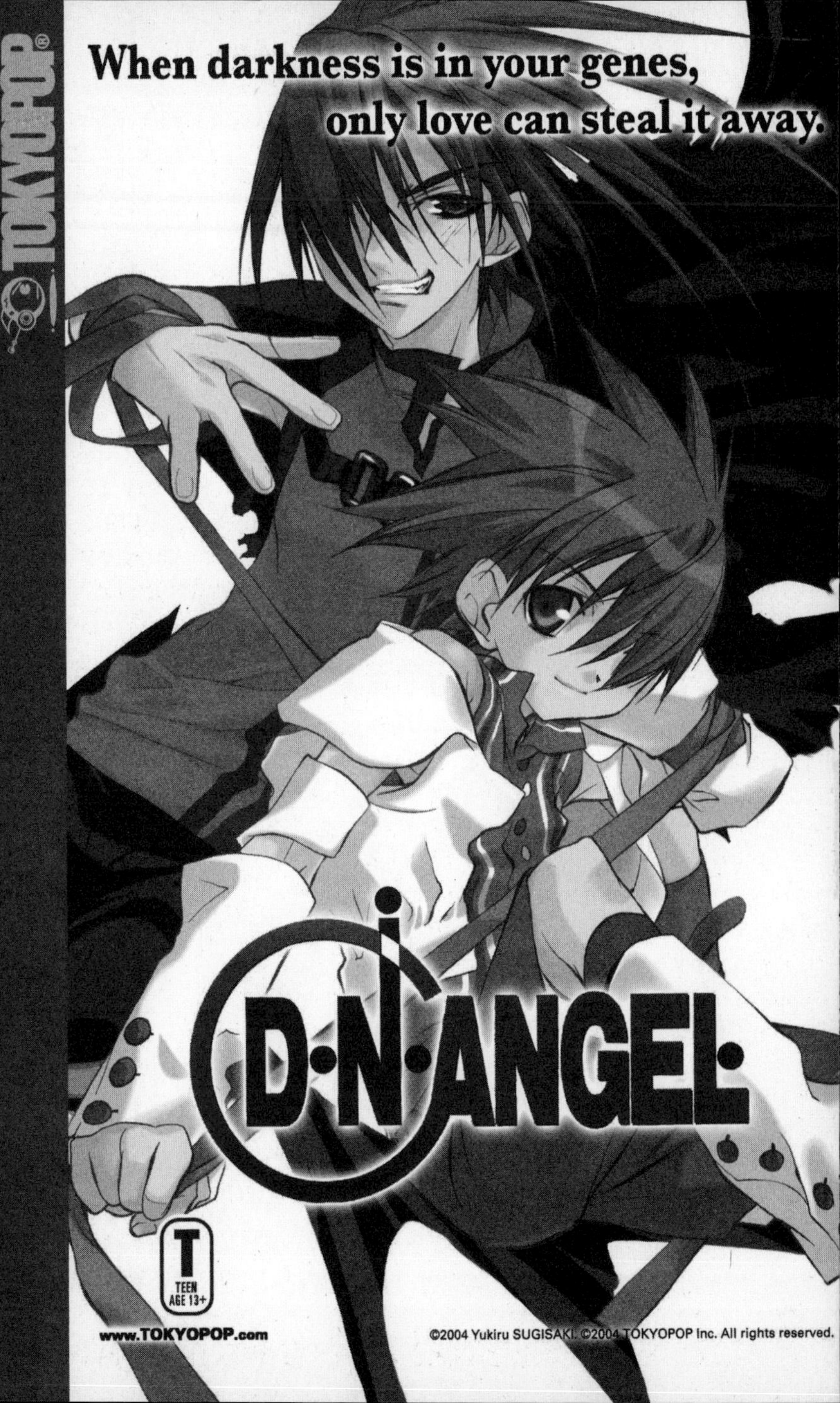
TOKYOPOP
When darkness is in your genes,
only love can steal it away.
D•N•ANGEL
T
TEEN
AGE 13+
www.TOKYOPOP.com
©2004 Yukiru SUGISAKI. ©2004 TOKYOPOP Inc. All rights reserved.

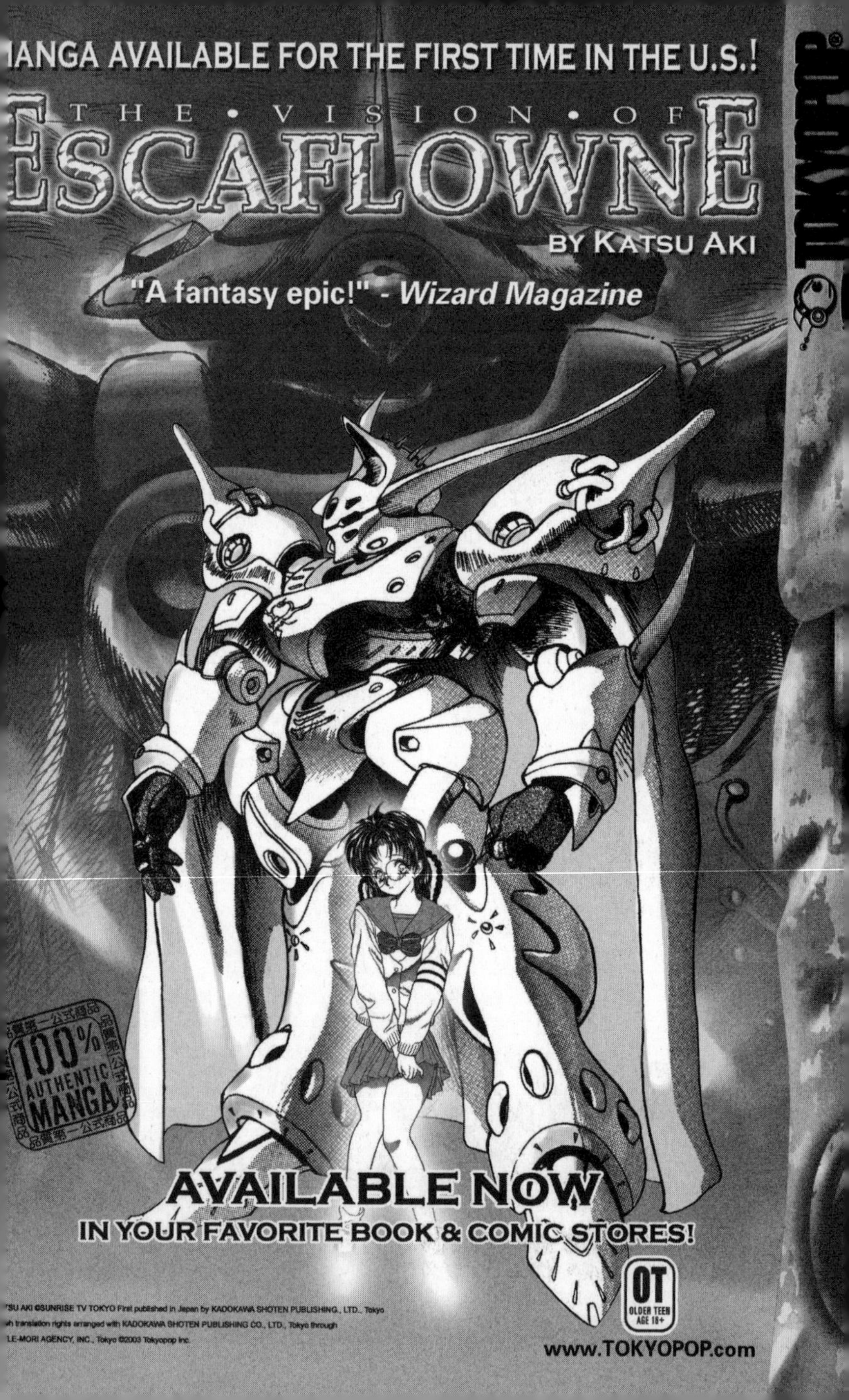

IANGA AVAILABLE FOR THE FIRST TIME IN THE U.S.!
THE • VISION • OF
ESCAFLOWNE
BY KATSU AKI
"A fantasy epic!" - Wizard Magazine
100% AUTHENTIC MANGA
AVAILABLE NOW
IN YOUR FAVORITE BOOK & COMIC STORES!
OT
OLDER TEEN AGE 16+
'SU AKI ©SUNRISE TV TOKYO First published in Japan by KADOKAWA SHOTEN PUBLISHING., LTD., Tokyo
h translation rights arranged with KADOKAWA SHOTEN PUBLISHING CO., LTD., Tokyo through
LE-MORI AGENCY, INC., Tokyo ©2003 Tokyopop Inc.
www.TOKYOPOP.com
TOKYOPOP®

STOP!

This is the back of the book.
You wouldn't want to spoil a great ending!

This book is printed "manga-style," in the authentic Japanese right-to-left format. Since none of the artwork has been flipped or altered, readers get to experience the story just as the creator intended. You've been asking for it, so TOKYOPOP® delivered: authentic, hot-off-the-press, and far more fun!

DIRECTIONS

If this is your first time reading manga-style, here's a quick guide to help you understand how it works.

It's easy... just start in the top right panel and follow the numbers. Have fun, and look for more 100% authentic manga from TOKYOPOP®!